THE HIRED GIRL

Laura Amy Schlitz

WALKER BOOKS

First published in Great Britain 2015 by Walker Books Ltd
87 Vauxhall Walk, London SE11 5HJ

This edition published 2016

2 4 6 8 10 9 7 5 3 1

Text © 2015 Laura Amy Schlitz
Cover illustration © 2016 Martina Flor
Art acknowledgments appear on page 470

The right of Laura Amy Schlitz to be identified as author of this work has been asserted by her in accordance with the Copyright, Designs and Patents Act 1988

This book has been typeset in Kennerly

Printed and bound in Great Britain by Clays Ltd, St Ives plc

British Library Cataloguing in Publication Data:
a catalogue record for this book is available from the British Library

ISBN 978-1-4063-6593-1

www.walker.co.uk

For my mother and father
with gratitude and love

PART ONE

Girl with a Cow

Sunday, June the fourth, 1911

Today Miss Chandler gave me this beautiful book. I vow that I will never forget her kindness to me, and I will use this book as she told me to – I will write in it with *truth* and *refinement*.

"I'm so sorry you won't be coming back to school," Miss Chandler said to me, and at those words, the floodgates opened, and I wept most bitterly. I've been crying off and on ever since Father told me that from now on I have to stay at home and won't get any more education.

Dear Miss Chandler made soft murmurings of pity and offered me her handkerchief, which was perfectly laundered, with three violets embroidered in one corner. I never saw a prettier handkerchief. It seemed terrible to cry all over it, but I did. While I was collecting myself, Miss Chandler spoke to me about the special happiness that comes of doing one's duty at home, but I didn't pay much heed, because when I wiped my eyes, I saw smears on the cloth. I knew my face was dirty, and I was awful mortified.

Then all at once, she said something that rang out like a peal of church bells. "You must remember," she said, "that dear Charlotte Brontë didn't have a superior education. And yet she wrote *Jane Eyre*. I believe you have a talent for composition, dear Joan. Indeed, when I used to mark student essays, I always put yours at the back of the pile, so I could look forward to reading them. You express yourself with vigor and originality, but you must strive for truth and refinement."

I stopped crying then, because I thought of myself writing a book as good as *Jane Eyre*, and being famous, and getting away from Steeple Farm and being so rich I could go to Europe and see castles along the Rhine, or Notre Dame in Paris, France.

So after Miss Chandler left, I vowed that I will always remember her as an inspiration, and that I will write in this book in my best handwriting, with TRUTH and REFINEMENT. Which last I think I lack the worst, because who could be refined living at Steeple Farm?

Today I thought I might go up to the Presbyterian – mercy, what a word to spell! – church and return Miss Chandler's handkerchief. It has been a bad week for writing because of the sheepshearing and having to stitch up summer overalls for the men.

I washed Miss Chandler's handkerchief very carefully and pressed it and wrapped it in brown paper so my hands wouldn't dirty it. I'm always washing my hands, but I can't keep them clean. Sometimes it seems to me that everything in this house is stuffed to the seams with the dirt that the men track in. Even though I clean the surfaces of things, underneath is all that filth, aching to get loose. It sweats out the minute I turn my back. I scrub and sweep the floors, but the men's boots keep bringing in the barnyard, day after day, year after year. Luke is the worst because he never uses the scraper, and when I look at him fierce, he smiles. He knows I hate to sweep up after him. Father and Matthew never think about it one way or the other. Mark is my favorite brother because he wipes his feet sometimes, and when he doesn't, he looks sorry.

But it isn't just the men. They bring in the smells from the cowshed and the pigsty, but I'm the one who has to clean out the chicken house and scrub the privy. My hands are always dirty from blacking the stove and hauling out the ashes. They're as rough as the hands of an old woman.

But this kind of writing is not refined.

I put on my Sunday dress and took the packet with Miss Chandler's handkerchief. I so hoped she would be in church. It seems a hundred years since I saw her last.

We don't go to church at Steeple Farm. When I was little, and Ma was alive, she used to take me to the Catholic church in Lancaster, but that's nine miles off, and Father says the horses need to rest on Sunday. They aren't resting today; they're harrowing the lower field. But the Presbyterian church is less than three miles away, so I can walk.

Ma married outside her Faith, but she told me Father used to be very pious and religious before I was born. That's why he named my brothers Matthew, Mark, and Luke, and if I'd been a boy, I'd have been John, instead of Joan. When I was a baby, we had three bad harvests in a row, and Father made up his mind that religion was hogwash. So when Father wants to work on Sundays, he does, and we never go to church anymore.

I find I'm in two minds about this. I remember how when I was a little thing, the services seemed so long. My legs hurt from sitting still, and I wasn't allowed to swing my feet. If I fidgeted, Ma would put her hands on mine to stop me. But St. Mary's had stained glass in the windows, and the light glowing through the colors was so beautiful it made me feel holy inside.

After the service Ma would light a candle in front of

a statue of the Blessed Mother, and I loved *her*, because she was as slender as a girl, with a smile that looked as if she was teasing someone she loved very dearly. I still pray to her – I carry a picture of the statue in my mind – and sometimes she answers me back, though I'm never sure if the voice is hers or Ma's, or if the whole thing is my imagination.

It was warm this morning. I tried not to walk too fast, because I didn't want to look red faced and hot when I saw Miss Chandler. My Sunday dress this year is heavy cotton. I declare, that dress is a sore spot with me. Father always asks the storekeeper what's cheap, and that's what he buys. This year what was cheap was a chocolate-brown twill with little bunches of purple flowers on it. Something went wrong with the printing, and the flowers are all blotched and don't look like flowers at all. Because the pattern was spoiled, the cloth was so cheap that Father bought the rest of the bolt and says it can be next year's new dress, too. I was so despairing that I went upstairs to cry. One of my books, *Dombey and Son*, is about a girl named Florence and her awful father that she loves even though he never pays any attention to her. But Florence has pretty clothes and she doesn't have to work as hard as I do, so I guess it's easier for her to love her father.

Father says I grow so fast there's no use wasting money on my clothes. He calls me an ox of a girl, and I wish he wouldn't, because when I look in the mirror, that's what

I see. I wish I weren't so tall and coarse-like. Even my hair is ox colored, reddish brown and neither curly nor straight, but each strand kinked and thick and standing away from the others. My braids are almost as thick as my wrists, and my wrists are all thick and muscled from scrubbing.

The Presbyterian church isn't as pretty as St. Mary's, because there is no colored glass. But it's very clean and bright inside, and the morning was fine, and the ladies wore their best hats. I looked for Miss Chandler's hat, which has the wing of an arctic tern on it, but I couldn't see it. I saw two girls from school, Alice Marsh and Lucy Watkins. I sat down in the back and was glad they couldn't see me. Alice isn't so bad; she will speak to me quite pleasantly if Lucy and Hazel Fry aren't with her, and she doesn't tease. But I think Alice is a coward, because she lets Lucy and Hazel decide who her friends should be. I wouldn't let another girl make up my mind for me like that. I can never decide whether to be grateful to Alice because she is kinder than the others, or whether I ought to despise her for being such a poltroon. So I do both.

I *hate* Lucy Watkins and Hazel Fry. After Ma died I didn't do the washing as regular as I might because there was so much else I had to do – all the cooking and putting food by. The men didn't seem to mind so much if I was behind with the laundry, and I guess that first year I looked slatternly, because Ma wasn't there to help me with my clothes. That was when the other girls set their faces against me. I remember we had to read a poem by William Shakespeare, and the part about spring was so beautiful, with flowers called lady's-smocks painting the meadow with delight. But the second part of the poem was about winter, not spring, and it was about someone called Greasy Joan keeling the pot, and that's when Lucy Watkins started giggling, and the other girls joined in. At recess they called me Greasy Joan. I told the teacher. It was Miss Lang then, and I loved her dearly, though not so much as dear Miss Chandler. Miss Lang said that now that I was growing up to be a young lady, I must work hard to keep my hair neat and my clothes pressed. She said – I remember how she lowered her voice when she said it – that my things were not so fresh as they might be. I knew she meant to be kind. But I also knew that what she meant was that I smelled bad. I was dreadfully ashamed, and I never felt the same toward Miss Lang after that. She must have rebuked Lucy and Hazel, and she made them stop calling me Greasy Joan. But sometimes they'd put their heads together and giggle, and I knew they were still thinking it.

It was warm in the church, and I tried to keep my mind on the sermon, though my conscience was not too bad troubled when I couldn't, because I am a Catholic, not a Presbyterian. Then I wondered if the Blessed Mother would be angry with me for being in a Presbyterian church, instead of St. Mary's. So I said a Hail Mary to her inside my head, and told her I was sorry. I explained that I wasn't there because I was going to turn Protestant, but because I wanted to see dear Miss Chandler. The Blessed Mother said she wasn't worried about me turning Protestant, but she thought I might stop working so hard at hating Lucy Watkins and Hazel Fry. I thought about that and I supposed it was true. It's not good to hate people in a holy place, when you're asking God to forgive you the same way you forgive the ones who trespass against you. But it seems to me that if I stop hating Lucy Watkins and Hazel Fry, I might lose something. I decided I would stop hating them during the service and take it up again after I got out. I asked the Blessed Mother if that would be all right, and she said it would be an improvement. So with that settled, I tried to fix my mind on what the minister was trying to say.

The minister was a pink-faced man and he talked slow. He spoke about the Pearl of Great Price, and then he started talking about treasure and how where our treasure was, our hearts should be. I thought about how I didn't go to St. Mary's because it was nine miles off and how if I was a Christian martyr, I'd ask Father for the horses, even though he'd be unkind. Maybe I'd walk, even. I started to repent, but then the minister gave his sermon another twist, and it turned out what he was really after was more money in the collection plate. Then I felt awkward because I hadn't brought any money with me, and

I was worried that people would stare at me when the plate went round. Father never gives me any money because he says what does a girl who is given everything want with money. When Ma was alive the egg money was hers, and I'm the one who cleans the chicken house and gathers the eggs and makes the mash for the hens. But Father won't let me have the egg money.

I fell into a daydream about what I'd do if the egg money was mine. I'd buy cloth for a new dress. A stripe would be best because if you match the stripes and set them right, you can make your waist look smaller. I think I could get it right if I tried. I'd buy books, too. There's a store in Lancaster that has books that only cost a nickel. Miss Chandler says those books are trivial and unwholesome and she hopes I will never read them. I wonder what's in them. I have three books – the ones she gave me – plus Ma's Bible, and I just ache to read more. Miss Chandler used to lend me books. I'd hoped that if I gave back her handkerchief she might say we could go on being friends, even if I can't come to school anymore.

Miss Chandler has a little bookcase full of books in her rooms. At the end of school, she invited all us older girls – Lucy and Hazel and Alice and little Rebecca Green, who has consumption but wasn't too sick to come – to her boardinghouse. We had chicken salad and ice cream and looked at photographs of Europe on the stereopticon. And we passed around a beautiful poem called "The Eve of St.

Agnes" and read it aloud, and I thought it was the most wonderful poem I ever read. Even Lucy and Hazel were civil to me, and I wished the evening would never come to an end.

But of course it did. And now I can't go back to school. And Miss Chandler wasn't in the church, not this week. I waited under the oak tree and watched everyone come out to be sure. Alice waved to me, and I waved back, but I didn't go forward to speak to her. I went home and fixed dinner for the men.

Wednesday, June the fourteenth, 1911

I didn't think it would be so hard to write in this diary every day. Late spring is always busy on the farm. I spend my days rushing from one have-to to the next have-to. When I can snatch a moment between them, I read one of dear Miss Chandler's books. I'd rather read than write.

My books aren't exactly prize books, because our school doesn't hand out prize books. But for the past three years, Miss Chandler has taken me aside, privately, and given me a book at the end of the year. I told her we had none at home, and I think she was sorry for me. The books she gave me are bound in soft, limp leather, with thin paper, gold edged and elegant, like Bible pages. I have *Jane Eyre* – that was the first year – and *Dombey and Son* – that was the second year – and *Ivanhoe* – that was last year. I've read and reread them all, but *Jane Eyre* is the best, because it's the most exciting and Jane is just like me. *Ivanhoe* has dull patches, but it's very thrilling when Brian de Bois-Guilbert carries off the noble Jewess Rebecca because of his unbridled passion. *Dombey and Son* is good, but it makes me feel guilty because I'm not as good as Florence Dombey. I like best the part where her father strikes her and she runs away to Captain Cuttle. He takes such good care of her. Sometimes at night I like to pretend I'm Florence Dombey, lying beautifully asleep in a clean white bed, with Captain Cuttle tiptoeing around, making me a roasted fowl.

But Father never strikes me, thank heavens. He used to whip the boys when they were younger, but Ma wouldn't let him lay a hand on me. She said it wasn't modest for a man to whip a girl. So Father never did, but he said I was too big for my britches even though I didn't wear any. That's his idea of humor – to say something insulting and unrefined. I wish I hadn't written it in this book.

Today I will contemplate the view from the kitchen window and describe the beauties of nature. I guess that's refined enough for anybody. I'm sitting on the kitchen table because I just gave the floor a good scrub, and it's still wet. Father is in town buying a part for one of his machines, and the boys are working in the lower field. I can watch them from the window, so they won't come back to the house and catch me idling.

The panorama from the kitchen window is very striking because the ground falls away from the house and the barnyard on all sides. Our house and barns rest on the top of a steep hill. The hill is so steep that the land wasn't too dear, and my great-grandfather got a bargain when he bought it. He named it Steep Hill Farm, but after a time it became Steeple – there isn't any steeple nearby, so the name would be confusing to strangers, except that strangers seldom come this way. The farm is fourteen acres and has been in the family for nigh on eighty years. The youngest son is always the one to inherit the property. Luke will have Steeple Farm some day, though Father says he's lazy and a disappointment.

The strawberries are close to ripe just now. I half fancy I can smell them, sitting here by the open window, with my diary on my knee. The breeze is very refreshing. The sky is lofty and celestial blue, with gossamer clouds o'erhead, and the wind chasing them all over the sky. The fields are verdant green, and—

Later that evening

Oh, oh, oh! I am in the most miserable *pain*! My whole face is swollen and throbbing and I would cry my eyes out, except that screwing up my face pulls my stitches. And oh, how horrible I look! I am accursed – the unluckiest girl who ever lived! I have often thought so, but this proves it.

How contented I was, writing in my book and contemplating the view of Steeple Farm from the kitchen window! How little I dreamed that this was the beginning of another misfortune! I looked out the window and saw that Cressy, the Jersey cow, had escaped from the cow pasture and was heading up the hill to the farmyard.

It would be Cressy, of course. Luke says Cressy and I are alike – both of us too smart for our own good. Cows were meant to be stupid creatures, Luke says, and so were women, but Cressy and I are the exceptions that prove the rule. I abominate Luke for saying that, but I agree with him about Cressy. She's a bad cow. She never stays where you put her. She'll find the weakest section of fence and lean her fat red rump against it, swaying back and forth until she works the top rail loose. I've seen her do it. Last year she got out and trampled the strawberry bed and there were no strawberries to sell. Father was awful angry.

I leaped off the table and ran out the door to catch her. I didn't think to put my boots on – I was in the slovenly slippers I wear around the house. I seized her by the halter and started to drag her back to the pasture. She balked. She gazed at me as if she couldn't imagine what I wanted.

I wanted to slap her, because she knew perfectly well. Of all the cows in the world, she's not stupid. But I said, "Cush, cush," in my best cow voice, and tugged her halter, and she started forward – only her great, heavy hoof came down on my foot. Heaven knows it's not the first time a horse or a cow has trod on me, and it won't be the last, but I don't recollect the other times hurting so bad. I guess it was partly my slippers and partly the way her hoof came down. I yelled with pain and slapped her shoulder, and she blinked at me with those long cow-y eyelashes, playing stupid. I leaned on her and shouted at her and tried to make her get off, but she was like a stone cow, she was so still – and all the while my foot felt as if every bone was splintering.

What I did next was stupid. I won't say it wasn't. I bent over and tugged at that leg of hers, as if I could pull her off my foot. It was a brainless thing to do, because a cow's strength is ever so much greater than a girl's, and even if it weren't, cows' legs don't move sideways. But I guess I startled Cressy, tugging on her leg like that. So she decided to move forward, and her other front leg came forward, swift as lightning, and kneed me in the eye.

I screamed. There was blood everywhere, and I screamed so loud that Cressy took off. I put my hands to my face and at once they were coated slick with blood, and blood was running down my cheek and inside the collar of my dress. I didn't know if my eyeball had been knocked out of the socket or if I was going to be blind. I *couldn't* know, and I couldn't think. I only knew I hurt and there was too much blood, so I kept screaming. It was Mark who got to me first, thank God, and he hurt me, swiping the blood away with his rough sleeve and shouting at me, demanding to know what happened. Finally I heard him say, "Thank God, Sis, it's not your eye. It's the skin above it. It's not your eye." And then, as if he couldn't quite believe it, he covered my good eye with his hand and asked, "Can you see?"

I could. My eyelashes were sticky with blood, and already my eye was swelling up so that the world looked bizarre. It was too colorful, the green grass and the blue sky and the blood beads on my eyelashes. I gulped, "Yes," and Mark put his arms around me. It was just for the moment, but I loved him for it. The last time he held me like that was the day of Ma's funeral. And he said, "Thank God, thank God."

Then Matthew and Luke were there, and Mark said I ought to have a doctor, and Luke took off like a shot to bridle a horse, and Matthew went to catch Cressy. Mark took me inside and tried to stop the bleeding with a rag dipped in cold water. Even though I was in pain and terribly frightened, I remembered I'd left my diary on the table. I made Mark wash his hands and hide it under the dish towels.

When Dr Fosse came, the wound was still bleeding. He wanted to stitch it – Dr Fosse's a great one for stitching – but I couldn't bear the thought of a needle so close to my eye. Dr Fosse said not to make a fuss, and he told me how earlier this week he put fifteen stitches into the arm of a seven-year-old boy, and the boy never shed a tear. That shamed me, but I still couldn't stand it. Luke held me down with one knee and Mark held my head still, and Dr Fosse stitched me up, and all the while he was going on about that seven-year-old boy and asking why I couldn't be brave like him. With all my heart, I hated that nasty, unnatural, unfeeling little boy. But at last the stitches were all done, and Dr Fosse wiped my face clean and checked to see if my toes were broken. None of them were.

Afterward, I was horribly ashamed that I yelled so loud. Luke said I bawled like a heifer. I have always thought that if something dreadful happened, I would be very brave, but when someone has a needle next to your eye, it's different. I might have been brave if it hadn't been my eye. All the same, I was mortified because Rebecca in *Ivanhoe* wouldn't have carried on like that, and I don't believe Jane Eyre would have, either. But Florence Dombey would've. She cries her way through all eight hundred pages of *Dombey and Son*. Just because she's unloved.

After the doctor left, I went to my room and slept a short while, but then Matthew rapped on my door. He said it was suppertime and they'd all agreed to make do with a cold meal, because of my eye. He seemed to think that was handsome of them, which aggravated me. I thought about not answering, pretending to be asleep, and not coming down. But then I remembered last winter, when I had the grippe and couldn't get out of bed for four days. The men made an awful mess of the kitchen. They left the dirty dishes in the sink, and everything was sticky and greasy and crumby by the time I was well enough to come downstairs. And in four days they never once cleaned the privy. Oh, dear heavens, that is vulgar again! But how am I to be anything but vulgar, living in such a house?

I went downstairs and sliced ham and bread and cheese and made sandwiches. I put out jelly and pickles and cold baked beans. I couldn't chew, because my face was too sore, but I had a glass of milk and some of the beans. Father looked at me and said, "That eye's near swollen shut. Maybe that'll keep you from reading instead of doing your chores." How heartless he is! He was vexed with Mark for sending for the doctor, because the wound might have mended without stitching, and now there'll be a bill to pay.

All through supper, Father reminded Mark of the expenses we've had this spring. Mark didn't answer back. He just shoveled in his food. Every now and then Father would fall silent, and we'd think it was over, but then he'd start up again.

It was an unpleasant meal, even for Steeple Farm. But the men ate just as much as usual. When I stood up to clear away the plates, I felt frail and shaky. I wondered how much blood I'd lost and if it was enough to make me faint. I wished I could faint, right in front of everyone. But I didn't. I cleared up the dishes and slipped my diary out from under the dish towels and brought it upstairs.

I looked at myself in the mirror, and oh, I wanted to cry. My face is all swollen and out of shape, and bright purple, and then there are those four black stitches, each one crusted with dark-red scabs. I thought about praying, but I wasn't sure what to pray *for* because what's done is done. I said, "Dear Mother of God," and for a moment I imagined the Blessed Mother shifting the baby Jesus into the crook of her arm, so that she could reach out and lay her soft hand on my cheek. I imagined her saying, "There, now," the way Ma used to do, and all at once I missed Ma so much I couldn't stand it.

Then I was very pathetic. I went to my chest and took out Belinda, the rag doll Ma made for my sixth birthday. I crawled into bed with Belinda in my lap and rocked her. When I was six, I thought Belinda was the most beautiful doll in the world, better than any wax or china-faced doll. Now that I'm fourteen, I wonder how Ma managed her. Belinda's pigtails are merino wool, and Ma made her wig so beautifully you can't see her scalp through the yarn. And Belinda's dress is silk, which Ma embroidered with flowers. The silk must have been a remnant, but even so, Ma must have spent a lot of her egg money to buy it. All the time that went into making me that doll – her petticoat is trimmed with three rows of ruffles, and there are more ruffles on her apron. Oh, Ma loved me; that much is sure and certain.

One thing about Belinda is a secret. Under the ruffles, her apron is stiff. It's stiff because Ma sewed money inside the hem – dollar bills. I don't know how many; from the stiffness, it might be ten or even fifteen. The summer before she died, Ma told me she was going to stitch the money inside Belinda's apron, and that money was just for me, for a time when I really needed it. "Not for toys," she whispered, and I remember how hot and sharp her whisper felt against my ear. "Not for toys or clothes or candy or pretty things. That money's for something important. If I'm ever not here to help you, remember that money's there for you, right in Belinda's apron."

I was nine years old, and scared. I didn't like her talking about a time when she wouldn't be around to help me. I suppose I knew even then that Ma wasn't strong. She was too delicate to be a farmer's wife. She had terrible headaches, and sometimes she'd stop working because she couldn't get her breath. Even at nine, I was stronger than she was. Sometimes at the end of a day, she'd say, "I've worked you too hard," but then she would smile and touch my cheek and say, "but never mind, you're a strong girl and a good girl and a great help to me. That's the thing you've got to remember." And I did remember it, after she died.

I wish I looked like Ma. She always said she wasn't

pretty, but she was small and thin and quick in her movements – like Jane Eyre, maybe. I'd like to look in the mirror and see Ma's face instead of my own. But the only thing I inherited from Ma was her blue eyes. For the rest of it, I look like Father, with a face as wide as a shovel, and broad shoulders and a big mouth. It's not such a bad look for the men – Luke is even handsome – but it's wrong for a girl. I'd rather look like Ma, more delicate and refined. But oh! just now I caught a glimpse of myself in the mirror – all swollen and purple and goblin-ish! – and I'd give just about anything to look like myself again.

Monday, June the nineteenth, 1911

Today was washday. It was dreadfully hot, and I thanked God when I finished with the boiling water and moved on to the rinsing stage. I was wringing out Father's trousers when I saw someone coming up the hill. It was a lady in a dove-gray suit and a leghorn hat. I raised my hand to shade my eyes, to make sure it wasn't a mirage of some kind. But it was dear Miss Chandler, and there could be no doubt that she was coming to see me.

I dropped Father's trousers and raced down the hill to meet her. Joy gave my feet wings; I felt like the Roman god Mercury. The only thing was, I forgot about my face. My bruised toes were all right, but my face hurt something awful when I lit off like that. Never mind: I clamped one hand over my stitches and bounded like a deer. In an instant I was at her side. "Miss Chandler!" I panted, and I would have clasped her hands, except they were full. "Miss Chandler!"

She gazed at me searchingly. She was out of breath from climbing the hill, and her cheeks were pink. She was carrying a big armful of snowball blossoms, wrapped in wet newspaper, and the satchel she brings to school. The idea flashed through my head – it was bright and quick, like a shooting star – that she might have books for me in her satchel. Then I felt a pang of shame because it was miracle enough that Miss Chandler had come to visit me. I shouldn't have thought beyond that.

"Dear Joan," said Miss Chandler, "are you quite well?"

I'd forgotten how awful I look. The bruises have changed color since Wednesday. They aren't bright purple and shiny anymore; they're a sort of thunder color. The swelling on my forehead makes a puffed-up ridge that looks like a third eyebrow. When Miss Chandler gazed into my face, she winced, and I remembered how frightful I look. Of course, I *would* be wearing my oldest dress – a loose Mother Hubbard that used to be blue; it's a nasty shade of yellow-gray now – and my feet were bare. I looked awful and I knew it, but it's been so hot all week. And who puts on a good dress to do the laundry?

"I had an accident," I began, and together we turned

to climb the hill. I made my steps short to match hers. I walked backward in front of her, so I could feast my eyes on her face.

It's a curious thing, but I always remember Miss Chandler as being taller than she is. She's really a little woman, but I think of her as being bigger than me, so when I see her, it's a surprise. She's beautiful, though, for an older lady. Even though she was warm and out of breath, she looked perfectly lovely. Her snow-white hair was done up just right, and her suit fit so elegant. Ma used to say that if I became a schoolteacher one day, I'd have pretty clothes. They have suits for girls my age – Peter Thompson suits, they're called – but I've never had one. Hazel Fry has two: a dark-blue one for everyday and a pale-blue linen for good.

It turns out Miss Chandler knew about my accident. Dr Fosse told his wife about it, and their hired girl, Betty, is sister to Emily, the girl who works at Miss Chandler's boardinghouse. "Then it's true, Joan?" Miss Chandler stopped to rest under the shade of a maple tree. "You were kicked in the face by a cow?"

"Kneed is more like," I said, and I acted it out for her. She looked so worried that I made fun of myself as I told the tale. I clowned for her, heaving away at the leg of an imaginary cow. Miss Chandler was still flushed from climbing the hill, but she smiled, and something smoothed out in her face.

But even as I was telling my story, making it funny to set her mind at ease, I was worrying. If a lady pays a call on you, you ask her in, of course, but I didn't want Miss Chandler to see inside our house. Everything's so coarse-looking and old-fashioned and falling apart. And I didn't know what to give her to drink. It's too hot for a cup of coffee. The prettiest thing to give her would be a glass of lemonade, but we never buy lemons. There's a tin of tea in the pantry, but it's awfully old. Ma was the one that drank tea; Father likes only coffee and beer.

Then an idea came to me, and I was so excited I interrupted dear Miss Chandler, who was saying how providential it was that my eyesight hadn't been damaged. "We can have a picnic!" I said. "Wait here, and I'll fetch you a chair to sit on. It's cooler in the shade than in the house."

"I mustn't stay," Miss Chandler said, and I saw her eyes pass over the fields. I wondered if she was looking for Father.

"Please," I begged, "just for a little while! I have a surprise for you. And I still have your handkerchief, with the violets on it. Please stay."

I could see in her face that she wasn't sure if she wanted to stay. But she laughed a little and handed me the flowers. "I brought you these," she said. "Mrs Lansing at the boardinghouse said I might pick them. She sends her best wishes and hopes you'll soon be feeling better."

I said, "How very kind" in my best manner, but I wanted to laugh. I could see that Miss Chandler had imagined me like an invalid in a book, lying in bed and having flowers brought to me. Instead I was up and doing the wash. Why, I cleaned the chicken house the day after the accident – I figured if I was going to be miserable, I might as well get the chicken house cleaned at the same time. I hate that job.

I took the snowballs into the house and set them in the sink. I smoothed out the pieces of wet newspaper, to read later on, and dashed out with one of the kitchen chairs. I set it in the shade for Miss Chandler, and I went back in to prepare our picnic. Thank heavens I had the strawberries! Ripe strawberries and real cream are good enough for anybody. If the Queen of England came to Steeple Farm, I shouldn't be ashamed to give her our strawberries and cream.

I charged upstairs to Ma's hope chest. There were linen napkins inside – hemstitched – and little china bowls with roses on them, too fragile for everyday. I found silver spoons and rubbed the tarnish off them as quick as ever I could. The kitchen tray's all scratched and stained looking, but I covered it with a napkin, and I sugared the berries well – brown sugar is tastier, but white is daintier, so I used white. Then I poured on the cream. For a moment it puzzled me what the tray would sit on, because the kitchen table's too heavy to drag outdoors. But I picked up a stool, and set the tray on that, and carried the whole kit and caboodle out to the elm tree.

"Here's the surprise," I said, and set down the stool and the tray. "I picked the strawberries just this morning, and the cream came from the cow that kicked me in the face."

Miss Chandler laughed. She has such a sweet laugh, not loud like mine, and she looked quite happily at the strawberries and cream. They did look lovely.

"I'm afraid I interrupted your work," she said, "and you have no chair."

"I don't need one," I said, and sat down at her feet. I almost forgot and sat cross-legged, which I do when I'm on my bed, but in the nick of time I sank down gracefully and tucked my feet under my skirt. At that moment – with my own bowl of strawberries and cream, knowing that Miss Chandler had come to see me because I was hurt, and knowing but trying not to think about the books she might have brought me – I was perfectly happy.

But I didn't stay happy. Not perfectly happy, anyway. The first trouble was that I couldn't think of what to say to Miss Chandler. Usually I saw her in school, where she was always teaching me something, and I could think of tons of things to say – my opinions about poetry and famous writers and so forth. But she'd never come to call before, and I felt shy. I think she did, too, because there were pauses between everything we said. Then she began to tell me about a new pupil she'd met at an ice-cream social: "One who reminds me of yourself, dear Joan." This new girl is named Ivy Gillespie, and Miss Chandler says she is like me: "A regular bookworm and, I think, quite *clever*." My joy was poisoned by jealousy as I imagined Ivy Gillespie going to school when I can't, and Miss Chandler liking her better than me.

It seems to me that teachers are a little bit heartless. They greet each new wave of pupils and choose which ones they'll like best, and then, when the students grow up and leave school, they forget all about them and turn to the next wave. I thought those thoughts and I was in a kind of panic, because I was sore with envy. I didn't want to be. Miss Chandler was sitting there right in front of me, and she might never come again, and if I couldn't enjoy myself having strawberries and cream with her – well, I didn't know what was the *matter* with me.

Then I noticed Miss Chandler looking over my shoulder, nervous-like. I turned to see what she was looking at, and there was Father, coming up the hill. I forgot all about Ivy Gillespie and worried about Father. I could tell from the set of his shoulders he wasn't in a good humor, and all at once I recollected that I hadn't finished the laundry, and his trousers were lying on the grass. I knew Father wouldn't like seeing Ma's silver spoons or the little china bowls. Or the strawberries, either, because most of those we sell.

But there wasn't anything I could do. I couldn't hide the picnic things or make Miss Chandler vanish into thin air. I stopped listening to Miss Chandler and started to pray. *Holy Mother of God*, I thought, *don't let Father be ugly to Miss Chandler*.

His footfalls came closer. At last I couldn't stand waiting any longer. I got to my feet and turned to face him. I saw him with Miss Chandler's eyes. Father's a powerful man, and big. He was wearing his barn clothes, and you could smell them. His shirt was soaked with sweat and he had his sleeves rolled up, and he didn't smile. "Father," I said, "this is Miss Chandler. She came to call on me." He didn't say anything, the way he does, so I added, "My teacher."

"You don't go to school," Father said curtly. He turned his head and spoke direct to Miss Chandler. "My daughter won't be coming back to school. She's needed at home."

"I understand. Of course," said Miss Chandler. She sounded fluttery. "Joan told me about her duties here. I hope you don't think that I would try to come between a girl and her duty."

It flashed through my mind that I wished someone would try to come between me and my duty. But there wasn't time to mull over that. I was watching Father's face. He looked from the tray and the empty bowls over to where the washtub stood, as if to say Miss Chandler was keeping me from my duty this very minute.

He did it so pointedly that Miss Chandler caught on. Her cheeks turned pink, and she looked flustered. I stiffened my spine and said, "It was very good of Miss Chandler to call on me. She heard I was hurt, and she brought me flowers."

Miss Chandler picked up her satchel. She started to fumble at the latch. "I thought perhaps Joan might be laid up in bed. I brought her some books to help pass the time."

She drew out the books. There were three of them – two small reddish-brown books, one of them right thick, and a bigger book that was green, with gold letters on the spine. I reached for them. I couldn't help myself. I knew that Miss Chandler was in a hurry to leave, and that Father might go into one of his tempers any moment. I wanted those books in my arms, safe.

But Father was too quick for me. His arm lashed out, making a barrier between Miss Chandler's books and my hands. She flinched and stepped back, clutching the books to her breast. Father's arm is as hard as iron, and she was as frightened as if he'd struck her. The way he moved, so fast and strong and angry – it wasn't proper to treat a lady caller like that.

"She don't need books to *pass the time*." His voice was thick with scorn. "She can waste time without you helping her, I guess. She reads too much as it is."

"I don't," I began indignantly. "I only read at night – mostly."

"Joan has a great thirst for knowledge," Miss Chandler said. Her voice was shaky, but she was taking up for me. My heart swelled with love. But at the same time, I wished she would stop. It never does any good to speak against Father. "I've never had a brighter student, or one who works harder. I'm not saying she must return to school, but a girl can better herself if she has books. I'd like to help Joan." She was trembling, but she spoke with such fineness and dignity – I've never seen anyone so brave and so ladylike at the same time. "I know that some people think that a girl becomes less womanly if her intellect is overdeveloped, but it is my belief that a girl is better fitted for marriage and motherhood—"

Father laughed. It wasn't a natural sound, or a happy one. When most people laugh, it's like water splashing over the lip of a pitcher. The thing happens easily, and it wants to go on. Father's laugh was like coughing up something from the back of his throat.

"Marriage and motherhood!" he said. He jerked his head toward me. "Who's going to marry *her*? No one's going to take her off my hands. She don't need books to fit her for marriage and motherhood."

Miss Chandler glanced at me. It was a quick look, but I saw that she was sorry for me, and I was ashamed. Sometimes I'm glad when people are sorry for me, but this was different. Father never said before that no one would want to marry me. I didn't know he'd thought it through.

"If Joan does not marry," Miss Chandler said tremulously, "she will need an education more than ever. I understand that her mother—"

Father's face darkened. "Her ma filled her head with nonsense," he said. "She wanted Joan to be a schoolteacher. Well, she can't be a schoolteacher, because she's needed at home. She's got work to do here, work she's fit for." He fixed his eyes on the trousers, then looked hard at Miss Chandler. "You needn't come back," he said, and went up the path to the house.

I stood dumbstruck. I couldn't believe that he'd spoken to Miss Chandler that way – to *Miss Chandler.* I heard her take in her breath, and the way she did it, I didn't have to look to know she was almost crying. I understood. There's something about Father that weakens you. It's the choked-down anger inside him. It's like stagnant water, heavy and murky and sickening. Whenever I have words with Father, I feel poisoned, even two or three days after.

And of course, Miss Chandler isn't used to being treated like that. Everyone in these parts knows she's a good teacher and a real lady. I put out my hand to touch her sleeve. "Please—" I didn't rightly know what I was saying *please* for. *Please don't cry,* maybe. Or: *Please don't let him keep you from coming again.* But she said under her breath, "I'd better leave," and her hands were shaking as she jammed the books back in her satchel.

I followed her down the hill. I found myself jabbering,

saying that Father hadn't meant what he said, that it was just one of his humors. I told her she *must* come again and told her the times when Father is usually out. But she wasn't listening. She wanted to get away so bad. She hadn't even fastened the satchel properly, and through the open part I saw the gold letters on the green book. *The Mill on the Floss*. Miss Chandler had told me about that one, and I'd *so* wanted to read it. I felt the sting of that loss, and shame swept over me, because I was thinking about myself, instead of Miss Chandler. It isn't that I don't love Miss Chandler. I do – I do – with all my heart! It's just that I couldn't help seeing the title on the book.

I gave up pursuing her when we reached the spot where the hill leveled out. She wasn't answering me, or even listening, because she was too busy pretending she wasn't crying. I ought to have thanked her for all her kindness, but I didn't think of it. *Thank you* goes with *good-bye*, and I wasn't ready to say good-bye. But at last I blurted out that I would never forget her. And then we separated, and both of us were weeping.

Tuesday, June the twentieth, 1911

It's past midnight and I can't sleep. I can't lie still. My face aches and I can't stop hating Father. These past two hours, I've done nothing but toss and turn. I've been plumping and folding my pillow, trying to make it cradle my head, but it won't. My hatred has crawled into the pillow slip and made a lump.

So I've left my bed and lit a candle to write in this book – *dear* Miss Chandler's book. I remember how when she gave it to me, I had a notion that I might one day write something very eloquent and beautiful in it, something I could show her. Now I know I'll never see her again.

I am heartbroken about Miss Chandler. It strikes me that I haven't any other friends – Miss Chandler was the only, only one – and suddenly I'm so hot with rage that I want to pace and stalk the room and beat my fists against the wall. I think of everything that Father's taken away – first my education, and now my last friend. And I want to shriek at him – but I only write in my book. I don't want Father to hear me and come into my room. He'd take my candle – candles cost money, and he'd say I was wasting. He'd take my book. Only he doesn't know about my book. I must be careful to hide it, always.

I *hate* Father, and that makes me feel wicked. I'm sure the Blessed Mother wouldn't hold with me hating him so much. It's unnatural to hate my own father. But why isn't *he* more natural? Why doesn't he care one bit for my happiness? When I think of him telling Miss Chandler not to come again – ! – and I recall the contemptuous sound in his voice when he said no one would marry me – ! – it *chokes* me with hatred.

I wouldn't have thought the not-marrying part would hurt so much. Even when I was a little girl, I never planned on getting married. I never liked any of the boys at school. They're all so *crude*. Alice Marsh has a crush on Cy Watkins, and he carries her books from school, but I never cared for any boy like that. The only man I was ever really interested in was Mr Rochester in *Jane Eyre*. He's depraved but he isn't crude. He speaks so beautifully and asks such interesting questions. And he never minded that Jane was plain, because he was capable of *true love*. If I were ever going to marry, it would only be if I found *true love*. But I don't expect to find it. Nobody around here is the least bit like Mr Rochester. I guess Father's right – if I did want to get married, I'd have to marry someone around here, and the girls outnumber the boys, so it's likely I wouldn't be asked. But the way he said it – as if I'd *have* to be one of the girls that nobody wanted – gnaws at my vitals. I felt so humiliated. And in front of Miss Chandler, too!

I stopped writing just now so that I could look in the mirror and judge how pretty I am. Sometimes I look better by moonlight or candlelight – the darker it is, the prettier I look. But of course, I'd forgotten my face. When I looked into the glass I saw the madwoman in *Jane Eyre* – a countenance fearful and ghastly, savage and discolored. Of course I couldn't see exactly *how* discolored I was, because the light was dim. But I look frightful. I think of Father saying, "Who's going to marry her?" and it seems true.

Not that I want to get married. I'd rather be a school-teacher. That was Ma's plan for me.

But I can't be a schoolteacher, because I haven't enough education. And if I can't get married, there's nothing for me in the future. I'll be stuck here my whole life long. Now I see that's the worst of what happened with Father today. He crushed my last hope. That sounds like something someone in a novel might say, but it's true: I have no future. He won't allow me an education; I haven't any friends; I'm not even allowed to borrow books. My life stretches ahead of me, empty save for drudgery, farm work and housework, day after day, season after season. That's what Father's life is like – mean and narrow, with the whole world wrapped up in *this farm*.

Only he doesn't mind it. He wants me to be like him, yoked to the plow, toiling away, counting every penny, hating every kind of weather that falls from the sky. He never reads, he barely thinks, he has no God but Mammon, and he loves nobody.

I wonder if he ever loved Ma. I don't think he could have – not much, anyway, because if he'd loved her, she wouldn't have been so unhappy. I once asked Ma why she chose to marry Father, and she smiled in a way that was like wincing. She said it wasn't a question of picking and choosing. There was never anyone else. By the time Father came along, she was twenty-six and an old maid.

I believe she wished she'd stayed an old maid. It

wouldn't have been easy for her, because she lived with Great-Aunt Alma, and Great-Aunt Alma is a horrible old woman. But I think life with Father was worse. Ma always warned me against getting married. She wanted something different for me.

I remember when I was seven years old and first went off to school. I wasn't sure whether I wanted to go, because the boys hated school. But Ma made me a new dress out of her old blue calico, and that tipped the scales in the other direction. I headed off to school in my new dress, determined to behave myself, because sometimes Luke was whipped in school and then Father whipped him again when he came home.

My teacher was Miss Lang. She set the oldest girl in charge of the other students and took the whole primary class outside and had us sit under a tree. She sat in a chair and read to us from a book of fairy tales by Hans Christian Andersen. She read "Thumbelina." I'd never heard such a story in my life. I could see it before my eyes, painted in the brightest, most delicate hues – that tiny little fairy child, rowing her flower-petal canoe. Oh, how I longed to be that fairy and row that tiny canoe! And then, how terrible it was that poor Thumbelina was carried off by a toad! Luke used to put toads down my back, and I've always hated them. And then, after Thumbelina got free of the toad, she was carried off by the horrid june bug!

And *then* – when she was shut of *him* – Thumbelina

found the poor dead swallow, resting in its tomb below the ground! I knew it would be shameful to cry in school, and I didn't want the teacher to think I was a baby, so I bent my head to hide my tears. But I couldn't bear the sorrow of the dead swallow. And the joy I felt, when Thumbelina nursed him and he turned out not to be dead after all! The joy and the wonder and the rightness of it!

Only, after that, the stuck-up mole with the black velvet coat wanted to marry Thumbelina. She had nothing but trouble with the men, poor thing! Luckily the swallow rescued her, flying her away to a land of orange trees and butterflies and freedom. Oh, that story! I never, never could have thought of anything so beautiful. When it was over – I couldn't help myself – I forgot to raise my hand, and I cried out, "Oh, please, teacher, read it over, read it over!"

Then I was aghast because I had called out, and I thought Miss Lang would punish me. But she gave me a lovely smile and said, "When you learn to read, you will be able to read that story all by yourself."

I became a scholar that day. I hung on Miss Lang's words and did whatever she told me to do. Miss Lang said that learning the letters was the beginning of reading. So when I lay in bed at night, I stroked my ABCs on my pillowcase and made consonant sounds under my breath. I learned to read – quickly, quickly. So quickly that Miss Lang came to visit Ma.

I was peeling potatoes for supper. Ma told me to take them outside, so that she could talk to Miss Lang alone. I went out, wondering if I'd done something bad and what it might be. Ma told me nothing until later, when she put me to bed.

Ma was different that night. She had a fierce look on her face that frightened me a little because Ma was usually so meek. But I sensed that she was happy in some way I couldn't understand. She stroked my cheek and said in a low, proud voice, "Miss Lang says you have a keen intelligence."

I didn't know what that was. Ma saw the question in my eyes. "She means you're right smart," she whispered, "real smart. She never had a child learn to read so quick. And she says you work hard, and have"— she paused to recollect the phrase —"real intellectual curiosity."

"What does that mean?" I whispered.

"It means you needn't marry a farmer," Ma said, and her eyes were far away. "You needn't marry anyone, unless you've a mind to it." She brought her hand down and squeezed my chin harder than was comfortable. "You could be a schoolteacher, like Miss Lang."

I considered this. I admired Miss Lang, with her crisp white shirtwaists, and her dark hair, and her silver-rimmed glasses. I liked the way she could rap her ruler three times on the desk and make everyone fall silent. I tried to nod my head to say that I was willing to be like Miss Lang, but Ma's hand was still on my chin.

"That's settled, then," she said. She bent down and kissed me. From that day on, she had a vision of my future life, and she made sure I lived up to it. I loved reading and arithmetic, and history gave me no trouble, but I disliked spelling and didn't care about geography. Ma made me spell words, and she pestered me with questions about cities and countries and capitals. She didn't know the answers and I knew she didn't, so sometimes I made them up. But that made me feel bad inside, so the next day in school I'd find the true answers in the big dictionary or Miss Lang's atlas. When I was eight, I won the primary grades' spelling bee. By the time I was nine, I'd come to love geography; it was the igloos and the whale blubber that caught me. I could draw any continent in the world, freehand, and label the countries and the capital cities.

I loved school, and I loved coming first in all my classes, but it wasn't my studies that excited Ma the most. She had a vision of the life I would live. "You'll board somewhere, likely," she would say, and I'd see her eyes narrow as she pictured the boardinghouse where I would live. "You'll be able to choose a respectable house, and you won't have to dirty your hands with the ashes or the privy. You'll send out the laundry." She looked almost dreamy-eyed when she said that. We always hated wash-day. It's fifty buckets of water for every load of laundry. The scrubbing hurts your back, and the lye soap eats the skin right off your hands.

"You'll have pretty clothes and you'll buy them with your own money," Ma went on. "You'll send them out to be washed, and you'll be able to keep them nice."

"And I'll have books," I said, taking up the story. "Lots of them. And a hat with feathers, and I'll go to the circus every time it comes to town." I'd never been to the circus, and it was a sore point with me.

"You'll have your own money," Ma said again. "If you want to spend it on the circus, you won't have to ask permission. Whatever happens, you'll have your own money and you won't have to get married." She always came back to that. "People will look up to you. A schoolmarm is always respected. You'll have money and respect and you won't have to work yourself to death."

I was always frightened when she talked about working herself to death. I might have been young, but I knew she was doing just that. She was so thin her bones stuck out, and often she got short of breath. Sometimes she'd turn a funny color and drop into a chair. But another part of me couldn't imagine that she could ever die and leave me. It happened quite suddenly. There was a dry spell the summer I was ten, and we didn't want to lose the tomato plants. We were carrying water to them. All at once I heard her cry, and I saw her drop both buckets. I ran to her at once. But she was dead before the water soaked into the ground.

I thought the world had come to an end. I didn't know

how I could bear it. I even had an idea that if I couldn't bear it, if I couldn't, *couldn't* bear it, God might relent and give her back to me. But though I suffered as much as any child could, she was gone. And overnight, I'd become the woman of the house. There was so much work to do, and nobody to help me get through it. I think Miss Lang was very good to me that first year, because I often fell asleep in school, and she never punished me for it. But I never forgave her for telling me I had to be cleaner about my person. I ought to have been grateful, I guess. But I never was and still am not, to this day.

And I feel the same way about what Father did today. I'll never forgive the sound in his voice when he said no one would marry me. It sometimes seems to me as if I live in a world where everyone thinks I'm worth nothing – Luke and Father – and there's nobody on my side at all, with Ma dead and Miss Chandler sent away. But I know I'm not nothing. And somehow I'm going to fight my way forward, though I don't know how, and I don't know where I'll end up.

Thursday, June the twenty-second, 1911

How hard it is to write with refinement, when my life is so sordid and melancholy! But today there was a glimmer of light, a rare flash and gleam: the presence of Hope. It was not that the black clouds parted, revealing a sky of celestial blue – no, the stage of my life is shrouded by curtains of Stygian darkness. But lo! For a brief moment, a crooked thread of lightning defied the gloom.

It happened like this. I was shelling peas, and I set the newspaper pages from Miss Chandler's bouquet on the kitchen table so I could read while I was working. We don't often see a newspaper at Steeple Farm. Father says they're a waste of money. I can't say I mind much, because what's going on in the world is confusing and often dismal. But I sat down to read, and the first article I came upon was about the Amalgamated Railroad Employees striking in sympathy with some locomotive workers.

At first my eye just passed over the words, because I don't know what *Amalgamated* means and I have no way to look it up. I don't even know if it's the employees that are amalgamated, or the railroad. When you see a big word like that, it's like finding a cherry pit in your piece of pie – you want to spit it out and get on with what you know. Though that is not an elegant metaphor, and I'm ashamed of it. The metaphor about the lightning and the Stygian darkness is much finer.

But the newspaper article started me thinking about *strikes*. Father says that any man who goes on strike is lazy and not fit to call himself a man. But Miss Chandler – at least sometimes – is in sympathy with the strikers. She especially pities the coal miners, who are so often killed below the ground, and she thinks it's dreadful when their wives are left widows, and their little children have to go down the mines. She doesn't believe it's right to strike, but she prays for the strikers, and she says the mine owners are in the wrong. I wonder if she would pray for the Amalgamated Railroad Employees. Railroad work is dangerous, and it occurs to me that maybe the strikers aren't lazy but only desperate to change their lives, as I am.

I started to think of what would happen if I went on strike. It seems to me the household would fall to pieces. If I just sat and folded my hands, the fire in the stove would go out and we'd have no hot water. There'd be no meals cooked, and no butter churned, and no clean clothes. Nothing would get mended or tidied. The privy would be filthy, and the garden would go to seed, and the birds would get the cherries and the blueberries and – well, I'd *have* to feed the chickens and give them fresh water, but I wouldn't gather the eggs. Everything would be as nasty and untidy and inconvenient as it could be.

I thought about going on strike until Father promised me a better life. That's when the lightning flashed against the Stygian darkness. Father needs my work here; he said so to Miss Chandler.

But then I thought what Father would do if I refused to work.

And I knew I would never dare. It came to me with heavy shame that I'm a coward where Father is concerned.

Even the thought of defying him scares me. I think of his face, dark as thunder, and the rough contempt in his voice, and my stomach feels small and shriveled, like a grape turning into a raisin. I don't know what Father might *not* do. He might do something worse than anything he's ever done.

I turned over the pages of the newspaper. My heart was palpitating and I'd forgotten about the peas. I hoped there might be some pictures of dresses on the other pages, because I needed something to calm me down. But the other pages were advertisements. There was Situations Wanted and then there was Help Wanted Female. I read those, and they didn't calm me at all, because some of the jobs in the newspaper, I didn't even know what they were. I read "Experienced TIPPERS wanted," and I didn't know what that was. And, "YOUNG LADY of Ability for STENOGRAPHIC POSITION." I'm not sure what *stenographic* is, but the ability of the young lady must be perfectly staggering, because that job pays fifteen dollars a week. Then there was "GIRL for GENERAL OFFICE WORK to use REMINGTON MACHINE" – I think that must be one of those typewriting machines Miss Chandler told me about – and "GIRL to run FOLDING BOX GLUING MACHINE." I suppose there must be a machine somewhere that folds cardboard boxes and glues them at the same time. I can't imagine who was clever enough to invent such a thing.

But then there were advertisements that I understood quite well – advertisements for hired girls. "White girl to cook and help with housework, no washing or ironing, $6 a week." Six dollars a week! I thought maybe that was a mistake, but there was another one: "First-class white girl for COOKING AND HOUSEWORK, wages $6." I laid the paper down and went back to shelling peas, but though my hands were busy, my mind was in a daze. Six dollars a week! With no washing or ironing, either!

I wish I was a hired girl. Of course, I'd rather be a schoolteacher. But I bet those hired girls – foreigners, most of them – don't work a lick harder than I do, and they get paid six dollars a week. And here I am, without a penny to call my own.

Then the idea of a strike beckoned again. I imagined myself telling Father that I wouldn't work unless he gave me six dollars a week. I almost laughed aloud, because Father would cut his throat before he separated himself from six dollars a week. Even two dollars a week, he'd cut his throat – or mine. I imagined myself saying, "I won't lift a finger unless you let me have Miss Chandler as my friend and give me a dollar a week" – and then an idea flashed into my head.

I thought about Ma's egg money. Ma always had the egg money for her own. Raising chickens is women's work, and it's the lady of the house that gets the egg money – the butter money, too, often as not, but I wouldn't dare ask for that. I tried to picture myself asking Father for the egg money. The last time I asked him, I was only ten or eleven, a little girl, really. But now I'm almost a woman. And if I went on strike – maybe not a whole strike, but a small strike – he might be persuaded to let me have the egg money.

It's not as if I'd be asking for six dollars a week. Eggs are cheap in the summer, eight or nine cents a dozen. And I wouldn't be asking him to take a whole new idea into his head. It's traditional, the woman pocketing the egg money.

If I had a little money, the first thing I'd do would be improve the stock. Of course I'd rather have books, right off the bat, and a new dress, but I'd start with the stock. We have Leghorns now, and they're spindly, ill-bred things, and there's no meat on their bones. They're not bad layers, but they're scarcely worth the trouble of cleaning and plucking. When Ma was alive, we had Buff Orpingtons and Spotted Sussex. The Buff Orpingtons were big, handsome birds, friendly and good to eat. And the spotties were like pets: they used to make me laugh with their antics. Leghorns are the most boring chickens on earth. So if I had a little money, I'd buy bigger, better-looking chickens, and I'd work up to a flock I could be proud of.

I saw myself with that flock of chickens – Buff Orpingtons and Spotted Sussex and maybe a Rhode

Island Red or two – and I imagined the egg money bringing in new books and a new dress, rose colored with white stripes. I even started to think about going back to school, but there my imagination balked, because Father's set his mind against that so hard he'll never relent. Even if I were to strike, he wouldn't agree to that, because he'd lose too many hours of work from me. It would be a bad bargain.

But if I did strike – if I dared – I might be able to get him to give me the egg money. And maybe I could get permission to be friends with Miss Chandler. I wouldn't ask her to the house, because Father frightened her. But perhaps I could visit her. If I had her to guide me, and I could borrow books, I could better myself.

I'd save money, just as Ma did. I'd add to that stash of bills inside Belinda's apron. The time might come when I could take that money and use it to change my life. If I had books, if I could scrape together an education, I'd have a future, whether any man ever asked me to marry him or not.

But I'd have to strike first.

I think about going on strike, and how to go about it, and what Father will say. And there is hope, but I am cold with fear.

Last night, the heat broke. I felt the change before dawn. I woke because my skin felt cool, and I wanted the sheet to cover me. It was a blessing. This morning, the sky was a clear, strong blue, and the air was fresh. Even Father allowed as he was glad of the change in the weather, though of course he went on to grumble about how we need rain. I believe Father thinks that if he ever approved of the weather, God would take a mean advantage of him and make it worse.

But the men went out to work in good spirits, and I took heart, because of the breeze coming in the window, and the billow and sway of the curtains. It occurred to me that the idea of the strike might be too brazen – at least, to start with. I thought it might be better to reason with Father and ask him politely for the egg money. I don't *think* this was cowardice but only good sense. It seemed, on so fair a morning, that it wouldn't hurt to ask nicely. I told myself that if he said no, I could go on strike later.

It struck me, too, that there would be no harm in trying to put Father in a good humor. So I decided to make a chicken pie for Sunday dinner. I don't know that Father's ever gone so far as to come out and say he likes chicken pie, but he scrapes the plate whenever I make one. And two of the old hens haven't been laying. I hate wringing their necks, and the business of plucking their feathers is irksome. But I killed them and dressed them and into the pot they went. I steamed them and strained the broth and burned my fingers taking the meat off the bones. Then I stirred up a milk sauce, and rolled out the pastry, and added a little salt pork for flavor, because heaven knows those chickens need all the help they can get.

I fairly flew around the kitchen. I shelled peas and added bacon, because Father likes peas with bacon. I made light biscuits – Father prefers bread, but we have rye bread fresh from yesterday, and the boys and I like biscuits. I sliced the bread and put out butter and honey and cherry preserves and pickles. The whole time I was working, I was planning what I'd say to Father when I asked for the egg money. By the time the dinner was cooked, I'd lost my appetite, because no matter how hard I tried, I couldn't imagine Father saying yes to me. Every time he said no – in my imagination, that is – he said it more cruelly. I was afraid that when the time came to ask, I wouldn't dare.

But I did dare. By the time the men came in, the kitchen smelled like heaven. The crust on the pie couldn't have been bettered. It was golden and flaky and tempting looking, and there were one or two places where the gravy oozed through and made rich-looking puddles on the crust. I saw the boys' faces when they looked at it. Father didn't say anything but sat right down to eat. He didn't even take off his hat until he'd had a helping of pie.

I let them eat. As I said, I didn't have much appetite, but I tasted the pie and worried down a biscuit with cherry preserves. It was a good dinner, and the men were silent as they ate. I didn't speak. I was busy rehearsing what I was going to say. I knew it wouldn't be wise to be too brash.

But I wasn't going to be meeching, either. And I was going to ask *today;* I wasn't going to put it off. I waited until almost all the food was gone. Then I sat up straight and used my most ladylike voice. I began, "Father..."

At first he didn't look up. He was buttering the last slice of bread. Father always folds his bread in thirds and crushes it in his fist. Then he eats it like a stalk of celery, in great bites. I think I'd die if Miss Chandler ever saw the way he eats. When he took the second bite, he fixed his eyes on mine, and I felt a thrill pass through me, because it was now or never.

And all at once I wasn't scared anymore. No, that's not true; I *was* scared, but I wasn't scared in the same way. Instead of being scared stiff, I was scared the way I used to feel when I was going downhill on a toboggan, too fast. It was a jittery, active, mettlesome kind of scared.

"Father," I said calmly, "the other day, you said I wasn't a schoolgirl anymore. I've been thinking on that, and I think you're right. And you said I was needed to do the women's work, and I'm thinking that's pretty near to calling me a woman." It didn't sound as forceful as I'd hoped, but I was on that toboggan and I kept going. "So, since my work is needed, and I take care of the chickens, I think I ought to have the egg money. That's what Ma had."

There was silence after I spoke. Father took another mouthful of bread. He looked as if his whole mind was taken up with chewing, but I knew that wasn't so. It came to me – I'd never thought of this before – that Father isn't quick. He knew he wanted to deny me, but he lacked the words. So he chewed slowly, with his eyes gazing straight ahead as if I wasn't there.

I became aware that the boys were staring. Well, not Matthew, because he was dragging his fourth biscuit in circles around the pie dish, dredging up the gravy. But Mark had stopped chewing and stared at me, bemused. Luke leaned forward with his forearms on the table. I don't rightly know how to describe the look on Luke's face. His eyes were alert, as if he was working a sum in mental arithmetic. At the same time, I almost felt as if he admired me.

That's when I recalled that Luke and Mark never have any money, either. They're as penniless as I am. Father keeps the money in a big stone jar on top of the kitchen dresser. He and Matthew can dip into it whenever they like. But Mark and Luke have to ask permission to take money from the jar, and if Father says yes, they have to write on a piece of paper what they want, and how much it costs, and then they have to put the paper in the jar. If they ask too often, Father takes the slips out and shames them by reading aloud all the things they've wanted in the past.

It's different with Matthew. Matthew has to write down what he takes, but he doesn't have to ask Father's permission to open the jar. Matthew's as tightfisted as Father is. He hates spending money. He's always after me to mend his things, and I can't seem to make him understand that there comes a point where the cloth is so worn out it won't hold another patch or darn. Of course, Matthew's twenty-one, so Father has to consider him a man. But Mark is only nineteen and Luke is sixteen and neither of them ever have a cent.

"The egg money," Father said, after a long time of chewing. "What for?"

I didn't know whether he meant *What do you want the money for?* Or: *For what reason should I give you that money?* I didn't want to tell Father what I might do with the money. So I answered the second question. "For doing my share of the work," I said.

"Work!" said Father. "What do you know about work? The rest of us" – he jerked his head at my brothers – "spend our days in the hot sun, or out in the cold, while you sit in the house and keep your hands nice. What do you know about work?"

It was so unjust I couldn't stand it. I threw my hands

down on the table with such force that the plates rattled. I wanted him to see them, so raw and rough from scrubbing. I had it in my mind to recite to him all the work I do, which is unceasing – the carrying of water and ashes and coal, the scrubbing, the laundry, the cooking and mending and putting food by – but instead I said the wrong thing, and what was worse, I said it the wrong way. "My hands ain't nice!" I protested.

The minute the words were out of my mouth, I felt my face burn. I'd said *ain't* like any ignorant farm girl. I haven't said *ain't* for years. Miss Lang broke me of saying *ain't* when I was seven years old. When I heard myself say it, the shame took all the starch out of me. I could have cried.

That's when Mark spoke up. "I guess Joan does her share of the work," he said. He said it mildly, without looking at Father – he said it as if he were talking to himself. But he said it.

Luke nodded. "Joan's right," he said, and I almost fainted, because I was fool enough to think he was taking up for me. "We're none of us children anymore. All three of us – Matt and Mark and me – do a man's work; you said so yourself. We ought to get something like a man's wages."

Well, that's Luke for you. He wasn't taking up for me; he was feathering his own nest. I wasn't surprised, not really.

"A man's wages," said Father. Once again, he was repeating what had just been said, and again I thought, *He's not quick*. But now he was angry. I could see it in the set of his shoulders. He didn't like me asking for the egg money, but Luke asking for wages was worse.

I kept my eye on him. All of us watched Father, waiting to see which way he'd jump. As it happened, he lashed out at Luke – and I was glad it wasn't me.

"A man's wages," he said, and pitched forward so that he was face-to-face with Luke – face-to-face, and too close. I didn't blame Luke for shrinking back. "You think *you* do a man's work? You think I'd hire you, if I had my druthers? Lazy and feckless as you are? If you weren't my son, I wouldn't let you set foot on my land. I wouldn't give you a boy's wages, much less a man's. You can count yourself lucky I don't give you something else – something fit for the *boy* you are."

Father got up fast, and his chair scraped the floor. I thought he might strike Luke – I thought he might overturn the table; he did once, when Ma was alive. I don't recollect why, but I remember cleaning up the spilled food and broken crockery. But he only stood there with his fists clenched, glaring at Luke.

I stole a glance at my unfavorite brother, and felt his humiliation. Luke's skin is like mine, prone to burn and freckle and blush, and he was as red as a piece of calf's liver. Just at that moment, my heart ached for him.

But I didn't stir. We all sat still, waiting to see what Father would do next. He turned his eyes on Matthew and Mark. "You're not as useless as he is," he said, "but I've no notion of paying you. Haven't I fed and clothed you for twenty years? Ain't I entitled to a little work in exchange – and a little *respect*?" He bellowed the last word so that I started. He swung round on me.

"You'd better jump," he snarled. "You'd better jump, and you'd better cower, if you're going to come pestering me for that egg money. Your ma had the egg money, that's right. I let her have the egg money. But I didn't feed and clothe your ma for fourteen years. I didn't have to eat her burned food, before she learned how to cook a decent meal, and I didn't have to put up with airs and graces and sass. Your ma was twenty-six years old when she married me, and she knew better than to sass me." He gave a short laugh; suddenly he was enjoying himself. "When you're twenty-six, you can ask me for the egg money. I don't promise to give it to you, because you ain't worth it now, and likely you won't be worth it then. But you can ask."

He picked up his hat from the table and set it on his head. He'd won, and he knew it. He swung the door wide when he went outdoors, so that it flew back and slammed.

The boys got up and followed him. Not right away, and not all together, but they slid back their chairs and went after him. They knew they had to work with him all afternoon, and they didn't want to make things worse by lagging behind.

I thought they were like a flock of sheep. They didn't like him any more than I did – I know Luke hated him, at that moment – but where Father led, they followed. Not one of them glanced at me as they passed by. Not even Mark.

I sat at the table with the empty plates. Then I got up and put the kettle to boil, so I could wash the dishes.

I read these words, and I think of how hopeful I was when the day began – and how lacking in hope I am now. It seems to me I have two choices: to accept the way things are, or to strike.

I don't know where on earth I'll find the courage.

But I have to do something. It's like that passage in *Jane Eyre: Speak I must; I had been trodden on severely and must turn: but how?* Somehow I must find the courage to do more than speak – I must defy Father: I must act.

Tuesday, June the twenty-seventh, 1911

I have begun my strike! I write this in the apple orchard – Father can't see me from the window. It's evening, and the air is beginning to cool. The western sky is resplendent, painted with brushstrokes of harmonious color. And

I am triumphant: I have begun, I have begun! I am a little frightened, but so far, it's gone well. Oh, I scarcely dare hope—!

All day yesterday I thought long and hard about my strike, and I think Miss Chandler would say that I've shown *great maturity* and *good judgment*. When I thought about my work, I realized something: even if I weren't a coward about Father (and I'm not as cowardly as I thought I was!) I wouldn't choose to go on the sort of strike where I do nothing at all. For example, the raspberries: they're ripe now, and if I were on a full strike, I'd let them go to waste. But I know that next winter I'll be craving raspberry jam, the tartness and sweetness and that ruby-red color. And so will the boys – Mark loves raspberry jam. It's his favorite.

So I thought it would be a mistake not to make the jam. And it would be an even bigger mistake to let the house go to rack and ruin. It would be cutting off my nose to spite my face, because after the strike, I'm the one who'll have to put things to rights.

As for the garden – well, you have to keep after a garden this time of year. If you turn your back, the weeds will take it. And the chickens need me to feed them, and so do the men. When all is said and done, I don't want to be responsible for anyone starving to death.

So there I was, wondering *how* I might strike, and at the back of my mind was the idea that I'd better make that jam soon, before the raspberries go. I found myself feeling aggravated, because Tuesday is ironing day, and it's hard enough making jam without having to heat the irons on top of the stove. Then it came to me that ironing isn't *necessary*. No one will suffer if I stop ironing. That's when I realized that ironing could be the first thing on my strike. *I'm not going to iron* - except my own things.

If the men's clothes are stiff and wrinkled, I don't care.

The idea of not ironing seemed to open up a whole new world to me. I made up my mind that the men can make their own beds. They're the untidiest sleepers on earth, I think. Luke drags the sheets off the bed and throws them on the floor, and Matthew and Mark - why, they just aren't clean in their habits. I hate messing with the boys' beds, because there's a smell; I don't know what it is, but I know my sheets never smell like that. Ma always said that men are dirty creatures, and though it's not a nice thing to say (and not refined), anyone who launders those sheets would say the same. Well, then: that was another thing I could *not do* on my strike. If Father wants to lie in a smooth, tidy bed, he can just hand over the egg money.

And third of all - but this is the most dangerous one, because it's striking a blow against Father - I'm not going to serve a hot dinner every blessed day. The boys won't mind - they'd just as soon eat sandwiches in this hot weather. But Father will mind. Father insists on a hot meal. That part of the strike feels risky – but I told myself it's got to be risky, because, after all, it's a strike.

I got up and made breakfast, same as always. After the men went out to work, I didn't have four beds to make – I had only one. I didn't tidy the men's rooms, and I left their dirty clothes on the floor. The only thing I did was pull the shades down, to keep the rooms cool. Then I went out to pick raspberries.

It was a fair, cool morning, and I filled two pails with raspberries. I felt so free and naughty, knowing I didn't have to iron, even though it was Tuesday. In the middle of picking the fruit off the canes, I got down on my knees and prayed to the Blessed Mother that Father wouldn't be too terrible.

Then I went inside to pick over the berries. Midmorning I prepared dinner for the men. I made a big platter of sandwiches, took out four bottles of beer, and added a plate of molasses cookies. Just as I had for Miss Chandler, I piled everything on a tray, put the tray on the kitchen stool, and set it out under the elm tree. I tucked a towel over the tray to keep the flies off.

Back in the kitchen, I put on my thickest apron. I think praying to the Blessed Mother did me good, because I'd begun to feel steady inside. When you make jam, you have to keep your mind clear, doing everything in just the right order and just the right way. If you're flighty or muddleheaded, you'll burn yourself and spoil the jam.

I set to work. It's hot work, scalding the jars and melting the wax and standing over the stove. It's sticky, too, and I perspired until my hair was damp. But the smell of the raspberries – I don't know how to describe it. It seems like a hundred smells at once – hot sugar and fresh peaches and grapes ripening in the sun – but it's also just one smell: raspberry, raspberry, raspberry. Smelling that smell and watching the red bubbles churn and froth brought me something like happiness.

By dinnertime, I was in the very crisis of jam making. Matthew was the first to come in. I told him his dinner was outside on a tray, under the elm tree.

He looked confused. I waited for him to ask me why I didn't have a hot dinner on the table, but Matthew never does ask questions. He looked at the kettle, which was boiling and foaming, and went out without speaking. A few minutes later, Father came to the door. He stopped in the doorway and stared at the table, which was covered with clean towels and jam jars set upside down. He said, "What's all this?" My heart beat double time.

"I'm making jam," I said briskly, and skimmed raspberry froth off the top. "Your dinner's on the kitchen stool under the elm tree. There's beer and sandwiches and cookies." And then – I don't know how I found the courage – I went on. "I don't see my way to making a hot dinner every day in this heat. I'm on strike."

I couldn't see Father's face very well. He stood with the light behind him, and I could see that Mark and Luke were with him. There was a brief pause before Father took the Lord's name in vain. Then he said the thing he's always saying, about how a working man has a right to a hot meal. And then he demanded to know what in heaven's name – only it wasn't *heaven* he said – I meant by being *on strike*.

"I don't have any money," I said over my shoulder. The jam was bubbling up high, so I wrapped towels around my hands and took the kettle off the heat for a minute. "I'm bound and determined to do what has to be done in this house, but I want a little money. So I won't be doing anything that *doesn't* have to be done. I'm not going to iron. I've made up my mind about that. And until I get a little money, you and the boys'll have to make your own beds. And I don't see why dinner has to be hot, not when it's ninety in the shade, and I have to make jam." I set the jam kettle on the table and fetched a saucer. I spooned a little jam onto the saucer and lifted the saucer to see if the jam would run or stay put.

It was still runny, so I put the kettle back on the stove. I picked up the wooden spoon and stirred.

Father took the name of the Lord in vain again. This time he added a middle initial, which was *H*. I've always wondered if the *H* stood for *Holy*. I braced myself, because

I didn't know what he might do next – he might shake me, or even slap me.

But he didn't. For one thing, Mark had hold of his arm. And for another – but it was only later that I remembered this – Father's wary of being in the kitchen when I'm putting food by. I remember the first year I canned tomatoes, the jars exploded, one after another, and Father almost lost an eye. The funny thing is, the jars never explode when I make jam – I don't know why. It's the tomatoes that are temperamental.

But Father doesn't know that. He gave an unpleasant grunt and turned away. I was busy with the jam, but I knew at once when he went out, and I felt a great rush of relief. When I peeked out the window a little later, Father was sitting under the elm tree with a ham sandwich in his fist. The way he was eating, I could tell I hadn't spoiled his appetite.

I felt limp – and astonished – and triumphant. Oh, I hadn't gotten the egg money yet – but I'd stood up to Father, and he hadn't come after me. I felt so baffled-happy, I could scarcely keep my mind on the jam. All at once, the smell of it seemed as intoxicating as wine – some rare, racy, aromatic wine, like French champagne, though I've never tasted that. I've only heard about it. But I was drunk with relief and triumph and the smell of raspberries, and I reckon that's as good as champagne any day.

I was proud of myself, and the jam turned out beautifully.

I had time to iron my things and wash up before supper. I made an especially good supper – no point in riling up Father twice in one day – pork chops with gravy, and boiled greens and hominy cakes, and dried-apple dumplings with cream. I was especially cheerful as I served it, and I said no more about the strike. Father didn't speak to me. I think he doesn't know what to do, so he's pretending I'm not on strike at all.

After I finished the dishes, I said, "It's such a lovely night. I think I'll take the mending outdoors." And I took up my workbasket, but *I'd hidden a pencil and this book inside*. And I haven't been sewing, but writing. So there!

Later that evening

I think I will never stop crying.

Father has burned my books.

Wednesday, June the twenty-eighth, 1911

I've locked myself in my room. The door has no lock, but I've wedged a straight chair under the knob. I don't even know why I did it – the men are outside harrowing – except that I need to be in a room where Father can't come.

I've been crying all day. Sometimes I stop for a little. Then I think about what happened last night, and I start up again. It feels like I've rubbed off my eyelashes, I've cried so hard. My face hurts, and my mouth is as dry as cornstarch. I'm queasy and thirsty and wretched.

I wish Ma were here. If Ma were here she'd put her arms around me, and – there! – I've started crying again, wailing like a baby because I want Ma so. I'm sure Jane Eyre and Rebecca wouldn't be so childish – but no, that's worse. I think about my friends, my burned friends, and that makes me cry even harder. I *must* stop. I *will* stop.

I'm beginning to be hungry. I suppose I could creep downstairs and bring a little bread up to my room. I fixed breakfast this morning, same as always, but as soon as the men came down, I came back upstairs. Seems like I couldn't face any of them. I'd hoped – how stupid I was! – that one of the boys might say something kind, but of course they didn't. They don't like me. It took Father to teach me that. I've known for some time that Father doesn't love me, but I didn't know about the boys.

My heart is broken.

I look ahead and I don't know how I can bear the life that's laid out for me. Years and years of it: washing and ironing and scrubbing out the privy, cooking and scouring and feeding and mending, everything the same, day after day, season after season, working myself to death, as Ma did. Only Ma wasn't strong. It'll be years before the work kills me. I see all those years ahead of me, and a dreadful bleakness comes over me and I want to die.

Except that I don't. Even if I could go straight to heaven, like the holy saints, and didn't have to bother with Purgatory, I don't want to die. Miserable though I am, I feel the blood alive in my veins and I know my lungs are taking in air, and when I think of all of that stopping, I feel such horror and sadness that I can't bear it. I could *never* kill myself.

But to go on, after last night – friendless, hopeless, imprisoned in this house of hateful men...

I find myself needing to write it all out in this book, which is blotted with tears and full of sentiments that aren't refined. I meant so much better by this book. But then, I meant to have a better life – I meant to better myself, as Miss Chandler said. Only yesterday, I thought it was possible; I was a cocksure little girl who thought she could win the egg money from Father by going on strike. I want to weep for that girl. But at the same time I'm ashamed of her, because she was such a fool.

I came in from writing last night, with this book still hidden in my workbasket. The sun was down and the house was dim. The men had gone to bed. I came in through the kitchen and I ought to have noticed that the stove was lit and there was a smell of burned paper.

I suppose I did notice, but I didn't stop to think why. The kitchen's always full of smells, and my mind was on other things.

I took a candle so I could read when I got upstairs. I thought I'd read a little of *Jane Eyre* before I went to sleep – the scene in the garden when Mr Rochester asks her to marry him. I went up to my room and lit the candle and set it on my dresser. That's when I saw my precious books were missing. The two round stones I use as bookends were there, and the Bible – even Father wouldn't dare to burn Holy Writ. But the books that Miss Chandler gave me – *Dombey and Son*, and *Ivanhoe*, and *Jane Eyre* – were all gone. I stood aghast. I might have misplaced one of them – left it on the bed or even in the kitchen. But for all three to be missing...

Then I knew. I knew what Father had done, and I knew why a fire had been kindled in the stove. A different kind of father – not mine – might have taken my books as a rebuke, to be returned after I promised to be more respectful. But my books were gone for good. I knew it.

I had to make sure. I guess there was one part of me that cherished a hope that maybe *one* of the books mightn't have burned to ashes; that I might be able to save just one. I ran downstairs to the kitchen and opened the stove. There was nothing but a bed of cinders.

I saw the book covers lying in the slop pail, and I shrieked. The slop pail! Leather stinks when it burns, so

Father tore the books out of their bindings – I could see the tattered linen webs, with only a few shreds of paper still attached. It made it worse that my books had been mauled like that. I seemed to see Father wrenching out the pages that contained my dearest friends: Jane and Mr Rochester, Wamba and Rebecca, Florence and Captain Cuttle and Mr Toots. I remembered Miss Chandler's handwriting on the flyleaves: "To Joan." She wrote that in *Jane Eyre* and *Dombey and Son*, but "To dear Joan" is what she wrote inside *Ivanhoe*.

I ran straight to Father's bedroom and yanked open the door. I wasn't afraid, not one bit, not then; not even when I saw that Father was undressing. He'd lowered his braces and taken off his stockings and boots; he was unbuttoning his shirt. "My books!" I cried. "How could you? You burned my books! You cruel, wicked man, you unnatural father!" And then I echoed Jane Eyre's very words: "You are like a Roman emperor – you are like a murderer..."

"That's enough," said Father. "You shut up about those books, you hear me? They're burned up and good riddance."

"I *won't* shut up," I said. At that moment, I was fearless. In one of Miss Chandler's books – I think it was *Oliver Twist* – I read that when a woman is thoroughly roused, no man dare provoke her. I think I must have been in just that state, because Father seemed startled by my defiance.

I screamed at him, "You *are* like a murderer! You've murdered me – taken away everything I care about, and I'll never forgive you! My books, that Miss Chandler gave me, my only source of—" But there I broke down and sobbed, because I couldn't even say what those books meant to me. During bad times, I've turned to them the way a pious girl might turn to her Bible. There was wisdom in them, though they were storybooks. And poetry. They might not have been books of verse, but they were poetry to me. Miss Chandler says that life isn't worth living if you haven't a sense of poetry.

But I think the most important thing those books gave me was a kind of faith. My books promised me that life wasn't just made up of workaday tasks and prosaic things. The world is bigger and more colorful and more important than that. Maybe not here at Steeple Farm, but somewhere. It *has* to be. *It has to be.*

I glared at Father through my tears, and he no longer seemed like my father but like some misshapen fiend. "Why are you so horrible to me?" I demanded. "You don't show me one bit of kindness or affection; you treat me with miserable cruelty! And now you destroy my books! What have I ever done to you?"

"What I've done to *you*?" echoed Father. "What about what you've done to me? What about what you took from me?"

I threw up my hands. I couldn't think of anything

I'd done that could justify him burning my books and throwing the covers in the slop pail. "Took from you! What did I ever take from you?"

Father stepped forward. "I had a wife," he said, and there was so much hatred in his voice that it sent a chill down my spine. "She was a good worker and a helpmeet, till you came along. We had three sons, and the doctor told her not to have another. He said she wasn't strong—"

I couldn't believe he was blaming me for Ma's death. "She wasn't strong because you worked her to death!" I shrieked. "She was too frail to do all that work! I *helped* her – *you* worked her to death—"

He went for me then. I must have known he was going to strike me, because I dodged the blow and shot for the door. Down the stairs I went, and I had it in my mind to dash out the kitchen door and escape into the darkness. But at the bottom of the stairs I turned to face him. I clutched the newel post to my bosom like a shield. "Don't you dare strike me!" I yelled, and I scarcely knew my own voice; it was so low and harsh and fierce.

I stop now, writing this. Because I think – I *think* – that even though I was shouting at Father, I meant the boys to hear me. It all happened so fast, and I was in the grip of passion. But I *think* that at the back of my mind, there was an idea that if the boys knew Father meant to strike me, they might come.

But they didn't. Father stopped halfway down the

stairs, as if there were a barrier between us that he didn't want to cross. I could feel his glare in the darkness. "She wanted a little girl!" he yelled, and I never heard the words *little girl* sound so terrible in all my life. They sounded like profanity. "After you were born, she didn't give two cents about anything but you." His voice rose to a falsetto; he was mimicking Ma. " 'Joan has to have hair ribbons! Joan has to have a doll! Joan has to go to high school! Promise me you won't ever hit Joan!' " He dropped the falsetto and bellowed, "She turned her back on her husband and forgot her sons! All she cared about was her precious Joan."

"That's not true!" I shouted, but it was no use, because now Father was thundering at me, and the things he said came so fast it was as if they were hailstones. He said I was stuck-up and conceited and a sneak, always reading instead of doing my chores. He said he'd promised Ma he wouldn't hit me, but that a good whipping might have been the saving of me, only it was too late now. He said I was idle and clumsy and such a big ugly ox of a girl that nobody'd ever take me off his hands. I can't even remember all the cruel things he said, but listening to them was like having someone hold my nose and tip back my head and pour poison into my mouth. At first I cried out in defiance, saying I wasn't, and none of it was true. But after a while I only cried. I put my head down on the newel post and waited for him to stop. After a long time

I heard him go up the stairs. He shut the bedroom door with a bang.

Then all was quiet, except for my sobs. But the quiet was terrible. I knew the boys must have heard us shouting, but they hadn't come to protect me. The fight was between Father and me, and they were content that it should be so. If even one of my brothers – oh, Mark! – had come downstairs and spoken up for me, or come to console me, I would have knelt down and clasped my arms around his boots. But there was only silence.

And now I think – oh, it makes me miserable to write it – that some of what Father said was true. I don't mean that Ma did anything wrong. I'm sure she loved us all the same, but she did favor me, and I guess the boys were jealous. I think about Luke, especially, because we used to play together when we were little things. Then he turned seven, and Father took him in hand. Luke turned nasty, seems like overnight. I missed him, but Ma told me that Luke was a big boy now and didn't have time to play with little girls.

I never thought about it before, but that time must have been hard on Luke. One day he was a little boy, playing with me and helping Ma in the house. And the next day, he was outside with Father, not as big or as strong or as good at anything as his big brothers. Father wouldn't have made allowances. Father doesn't like Luke – never has.

So writing this, now, I find myself feeling sorry for Luke. But that makes me angry, too, because I'm already sorry for myself, and having to feel sorry for him seems like another cross to bear.

I can't even pity myself in peace.

It's almost dinnertime. I'll have to go down soon if I'm to get a hot dinner on the table and get back up here before the men come back. I can't face them – I know I can't face Father, and I don't want to see the boys.

I don't see how this is all going to end. I can't spend the rest of my life hiding out in my room. I guess what will happen – oh, I can see it! – is that with every day that passes, my anger will grow duller. I won't forgive – I can never forget – but things will go back to the way they were. Except that now I have no books. No books.

I wish I could run away. When Florence Dombey's father struck her, she ran away to Captain Cuttle – but there's the rub; she had somewhere to go. I don't have any-where. I had a sort of daydream this morning, telling myself I might run away to Miss Chandler. I imagined her clasping me in her arms and saying that I could live with her from now on. I pictured myself helping her at school, teaching reading to the primary class, and ironing her pretty clothes back at the boardinghouse. One way or another, I'd make myself useful, and she'd teach me. Then I'd get a teacher's license and pay her back. Once I had money, I'd rent a room in the same boardinghouse. We'd be together always.

It was a beautiful daydream and made me cry buckets. But when I tried to work out the details, I saw that it wouldn't work, because Miss Chandler couldn't take care of a runaway girl. People would criticize her, and she might get in trouble with the school board. A teacher has to be so careful.

And what would I do if I went to Miss Chandler and she sent me away? What if she told me to do my duty and honor my father, because that's what's in the Commandments? I think my heart would break even worse than it's broken now.

I suppose I could run away to Great-Aunt Alma, but she's almost as horrible as Father.

When Jane Eyre was tired of teaching at Lowood, she prayed for a new servitude. I remember that, her saying, "Grant me at least a new servitude!" She didn't think she could attain anything better, like Liberty or Excitement or Enjoyment, but she thought she might stand a chance with a new job. Of course, it all worked out beautifully for her, because when she became a governess, she met Mr Rochester. But I'm unluckier than Jane, because I haven't education enough to be a governess, and besides—

I've been staring into space for five minutes, thinking and thinking. I've been thinking about a new servitude.

I've been thinking about six dollars a week.

Great-Aunt Alma – Philadelphia – Baltimore.
Hairpins – Ma's old brown hat.
Stitch flounce for brown dress.
Cardboard suitcase – still in attic?
Belinda.

PART TWO

The Spirit of Transportation

I am writing this from the ladies' waiting room, Broad Street Station, Philadelphia. I have escaped! I have achieved the first stage of my emancipation! In a little while, I will go on to Baltimore – that's the second stage of my journey – and from thence I will begin my new life.

I have been through so many emotions today – such terrors and sorrows! such mounting hopes, such exquisite sensations of relief! I'm proud of myself because I haven't been a coward, not one bit. My heart is racing even as I write, but I plan to go on as bravely as a heroine in a novel. For the worst is over, and I believe I have circumvented Father.

Once my mind was made up, I planned my escape

with great care and cunning. I knew I'd have to look older, both to elude pursuit and to convince my future employers that I am a mature and responsible female. I unearthed the bolt of chocolate-brown twill that Father bought for next year's dress and added a flounce to this year's dress, so that the hem almost touches the ground. And I've pinned my hair up in a knot on top of my head. I felt a pang when I put up my hair, because Miss Chandler doesn't like it when girls try to look older than they are. When Libby Watkins – who is only sixteen – put her hair on top of her head, *without even a bow*, Miss Chandler thought it was very sad. She says that girls grow up too fast nowadays. Of course when she said that, I agreed heartily, because Libby's awful stuck-up.

But here I am, only fourteen, with my hair skewered on top of my head and held tight with thirteen hairpins. It's uncomfortable because my hair is so heavy that the hairpins don't anchor it, and the knot lurches when I move my head. But I look older in my long dress – goodness, I look almost matronly! Not half an hour ago, I transformed myself in the ladies' room here. Oh, such a ladies' room! It has pale wood, glossy and smooth as satin, and white marble around the sinks! Everything is so beautifully clean and hygienic and modern! When I compare it to what we have back home—

No. I actually was *going* to compare it, but now I'm not, because thinking about things like that is vulgar.

And I've made up my mind: in my new life, I'm not going to be vulgar. Even though I'm going to be a servant, I'm going to cultivate my finer feelings. I will better myself and write with truth and refinement, just as Miss Chandler said.

Where was I? Oh, yes – my escape. It seems to me that God Himself is blessing my endeavor, because last night Father checked the almanac, and it turns out that rain is predicted, starting tomorrow afternoon. So of course Father's afraid of losing the hay crop, and his whole mind is fixed on that.

I was nervous when I got up this morning, because I knew that *this was the day*. As soon as the men went out to work, I slipped upstairs to pack. I'd set everything aside: my brown dress with the new long skirt; my night-gown, toothbrush, and comb; Ma's workbasket; my Bible; and Belinda – oh! Belinda! With what emotion did I snip open her apron on Wednesday, only to discover *twenty-nine dollars* inside! Twenty-nine dollars! My heart ached when I thought of the long years Ma must have saved to amass such a fortune. I could imagine her trying to get the thirtieth dollar – Ma had an orderly mind, and I know she would have preferred to leave me a round sum. But I guess that thirtieth dollar just wasn't forthcoming, and she was afraid she'd run out of time.

I took fourteen of the dollars and sewed the rest back into Belinda's apron. I brought a cardboard suitcase down from the attic – it was kind of beat-up, but the alternative was carrying my things in a pillowcase. I didn't pack the suitcase, because I daren't walk down the hill carrying it. I smashed it and folded it, so I could stuff it in the buckets I use for picking berries.

Then I dressed myself in last year's sage-green dress, which is disgracefully short, and fixed my hair in two long braids. I stood before the mirror a long time – no, not a long time, because I hadn't time to waste, but a few minutes, I'm sure. My heart was pounding, and I dreaded what I had to do next.

I hadn't packed Ma's embroidery scissors. I took them from the dresser and covered my bruised eye with my left hand. My fingers shook, but I brought the blades of the scissors close to the wound and snipped at Dr Fosse's stitches. It was hard to cut them without hurting the scabs around the wound, but I managed it: *snip – snip – snip*. The part that followed was worse – easing the scissor blade under the threads and tugging them out. The scabs held on to the threads, but the pain wasn't as bad as I expected; it was more the idea of the thing, and only one scab broke open. The whole operation lasted only a few minutes, but by the time I was done, I was queasy and perspiring.

I wiped the scissors clean and replaced them in Ma's basket. There was one more thing I wanted. I tiptoed into Father's room and took Ma's crucifix off the wall. Ma brought it with her when she married Father, and it's hung over their bed for twenty-three years. Of course Father was pious when Ma married him, but he was Methodist-pious, not Catholic-pious. Methodists don't set store by crucifixes; they prefer crosses without anyone on them. I know in the days to come I'll be needing Jesus to watch over me, so I took Him and wrapped Him in my red flannel petticoat.

After that, I was ready. I walked barefoot down the lane – my shoes and stockings were in the bucket. That was the strangest part of today – gracious, it was only this morning! – walking down the hill, in plain sight of the men, and knowing that I was leaving forever. I'd announced at breakfast that I meant to spend the day picking blackber-ries. (The berries are ripe, too, which is another sign from God that I'm leaving home at the right time.)

I tried to walk as if it was just an ordinary day, as if my buckets were empty. I daren't pause to look my last on the home of my childhood. A lot of it I didn't mind leaving – the privy that I've cleaned a thousand times, and the chicken house, and that irritating rosebush that's infested with something that gnarls the roses. But I felt a little sad leaving the chickens, even if they are the most boring chickens in the world. And I felt real regret about leaving my tomato plants. It looks like there's going to be a fine crop this year.

The saddest part was walking past the clothesline – isn't that queer? But as I walked past it, I had this sudden picture in my mind of Ma and me taking the clothes off the line. I remember us folding sheets. We'd stand apart, our arms moving like windmills, perfectly in rhythm. Then we'd walk toward each other with our arms over our heads, so that the sheet wouldn't touch the ground. It was almost like a dance, and the sheets smelled good after a day in the sun, and we were always happy, because taking the clothes off the line meant the laundry was done for the week.

When I came to the blackberry thicket, I went straight into it, with the thorns scratching my skin. Once I was hidden from sight, I put on my shoes and stockings and took the suitcase out of the bucket and tried to bash it back into shape. It didn't look very good, but I packed everything inside it and fastened it with a piece of string. I took the letter I'd written for Father and placed it inside the bucket, with a stone to hold it down.

It was a very aggravating letter. I meant it to be, because I don't want Father coming after me. I told him I was going to stay with Great-Aunt Alma in Lancaster. I never thought I should be grateful to have such a disagreeable relation, but I *am* grateful, because Father hates Great-Aunt Alma and won't want to follow me to her house. Great-Aunt Alma always says that Ma married beneath herself. She and Father had words on Ma's wedding day and haven't spoken since.

The way I reckon it, the men will come in around

noon, and there won't be any dinner waiting for them. Father will be furious, but he won't want to waste time looking for me; he'll want to get the hay in. The boys will make a nasty mess in the kitchen, fixing their own dinner, but this time I won't have to clean it up. Nobody will find my letter until suppertime, and they'll be too tired from haying to follow me to Lancaster.

They might not come after me at all. Father knows that Great-Aunt Alma is so horrid that nobody in her right mind could stay with her long. Very likely he'll expect me to come home on my own accord, with my tail between my legs. By the time he finds out I never went to Great-Aunt Alma's, I'll be settled in Baltimore.

So I think I'm safe. But all the same, I mean to leave a crooked trail behind me – I went first to Lancaster, then east to Philadelphia, changed my appearance, and will go from here to Baltimore. I considered going to New York City, which Miss Chandler says is an *imposing metropolis* but full of foreigners and a little bit vulgar. If I wanted vulgar, I could get it homegrown. So I won't go there.

I wasn't too scared when I took the milk train to Lancaster, because I've done that before, but I began to feel frightened when I got on the train to Philadelphia. I couldn't help thinking about all that lies before me – finding a respectable boardinghouse and looking for work. I guess I could work in a factory, but I'm afraid of that. Last spring there was a terrible fire in one of the New

York factories, and all the girls – the workers were almost all girls – were locked inside, and they had to jump out the windows, ten stories down, or be burned to death. Miss Chandler cried when she told me about it. The horror of it haunted me for weeks. Those poor girls! I think I'll be safer in a regular home, working as a hired girl.

Luckily, I have plenty of money – that's the great thing. I won't have to take the first job I see. On the other hand, I'm all alone in the world. Once I was on my way to Philadelphia, I started thinking about that, and the more I thought about it, the more melancholy I felt. I was bound and determined that I would not cry in public, but I kept catching my breath, and my bosom heaved – or is it *hove*? I think *hove* is a real word, but it doesn't sound right. At any rate, one of the porters – they all seem to be Negroes, and awful nice – came to me and told me, in ever such a kind way, that they were having the last sitting for break-fast, and he didn't want me to miss it if I was hungry. He said he'd show me the way to the dining car.

I never meant to eat in the dining car, because I didn't know what it might cost. But the man was so nice, and so sure that I would follow him, that I had to go. I didn't think I could eat a morsel. But the dining car was so splendid that I forgot my melancholy. The table linen was milky white and starched, and the silverware shone like the harvest moon. A waiter saw me and held out my chair as if I was a lady. On the table was a thick glass goblet filled with ice water, and a little bowl full of butter, and a vase with a pink rosebud. And I smelled ham broiling, and my stomach growled with hunger.

So I unfolded the menu – it was beautiful creamy paper, engraved with black. I almost fainted when I saw the prices. Ham and eggs was sixty cents! – with eggs only nine cents a dozen! The train people ought to be ashamed of themselves, asking for that. At first I thought I should just order dry toast (ten cents) because that was the cheapest thing on the menu, and then I thought I'd order buttered toast (fifteen), but then I just threw caution to the wind and ordered everything I wanted. I don't know what Ma would think of me, wasting a whole dollar on breakfast. I don't know what got into me. I was just so hungry and shaky and scared and dazzled that I couldn't think straight.

I guess the truth was that I wanted it – not just the broiled ham, but the thrill of sitting in that big, bright place, with a pink rose on my table. So I ordered. Afterward, I felt terribly guilty and a little scared by the way I was throwing money away, but much more cheerful. While I waited for breakfast, I watched the world dashing by. How beautiful it was! – fields golden with wheat, or green with corn, and overhead the clouds all white and fleecy, like a flock of new-bathed sheep. And the sky – oh, I don't think the almanac can be right; the sky was so gloriously blue that it must have forgotten all about rain.

When breakfast came, it was delicious and I ate every forkful. I had grapefruit, which was cold and sour, but I never tasted it before and I wanted to see what it was like. And I had buckwheat cakes with maple syrup, and a thick slice of broiled ham, and coffee, because Father never lets me have coffee, and I thought a stimulant might be good for my spirits. At first I found it so bitter that I couldn't think why anyone likes it. But I put in milk until it was white, and three spoonfuls of sugar, and after that I found it very palatable. I drank the whole pot. I believe it *is* a stimulant, for I felt much livelier afterward.

When I arrived in Philadelphia, I bought my ticket to Baltimore, and I went to the ladies' room to turn into a lady. I put on my long dress and fastened up my hair. Then I looked for an unobtrusive place to wait – they have a special room just for ladies – but before I reached it, I came across the most striking piece of artwork I've ever seen in my life.

It's a piece of sculpture, the kind of sculpture that's fixed to the wall, but some of the figures stick out. It's called *The Spirit of Transportation*. I don't think it's made of marble because it isn't shiny, but it is magnificent in every way, and I'm sure it can hold its own with the great works of Classical Antiquity – say, the Parthenon, which I've seen through the stereopticon at Miss Chandler's. I can't believe that the artist was able to make such a fine piece of work about something as dull as transportation. The central figure is a beautiful lady in a chariot – I think she's Transportation – and her chariot is drawn by four horses, all with arched necks and muscular, prancing legs. On the far right are some little cupid babies holding models – a steamboat and a train and something else that looks a little like a fish, which I suppose might be an airship. And behind the chariot there is a man who seems to be having trouble with his oxen, and alongside the chariot there is a kind of fairy maiden in a ball gown, who looks admiringly at *The Spirit of Transportation*.

I quite lost myself, gazing at this work of art. I longed for Miss Chandler, that I might discuss it with her. It surprised me that a great many people rushed by this noble sculpture without a second glance. Of course they had to catch their trains, but here was an opportunity to look at a work of art – it was nothing less; it was a *work of art* – and they were missing it.

It thrilled me, that sculpture. For one thing, it reminded me that in my new life, I may have other such experiences. I needn't always be an ignorant girl. The world will offer itself to me like a chalice brimming with immortal wine, and I will quaff from it. Perhaps in Baltimore I will find galleries and libraries and attend concerts, and go to the theater! I think I'd like to see a Russian ballet. And as I thought over these things, and gazed at the sculpture, I began to fancy that *I* was the lady in the chariot – that somehow the sculpture was about me and my life. Of course that sounds conceited, but Miss Chandler says that great works of art are universal, and in them we behold our everyday struggles and homely joys.

I decided it was an omen. I told myself I was the Spirit of Transportation and that Father was the man at the far left of the sculpture, the one who couldn't control his oxen. I saw myself leaving him far behind, processing in triumph and majesty toward the future.

I have decided to give myself a new name. This is only practical, but it will also be a symbol of my new self. (Besides, I have always detested my last name.) I have long felt that the two most beautiful names in the world are Isabella and Damaris. But after consideration, I decided not to use them, because I can't imagine my future mistress calling me Isabella or Damaris. They don't sound like hired girls' names. Isabella might be shortened to Izzy – which is dreadful – and Damaris can't be shortened because that would be profane.

And besides, if I am to have a new name, it ought to be close enough to my old name so that if someone calls me, I'll lift my head and look sharp.

So I decided on *Janet*, which is close to *Joan*, but ever so much prettier, and not too fancy for a hired girl. Mr Rochester often calls Jane Eyre *Janet* when he's feeling especially fond of her. For my last name, I chose *Lovelace* – because I do love lace, or would if I had some, so it isn't even a lie.

Janet Lovelace! Bound for Baltimore, a new servitude, and the wide, wide world!

Monday, July the third, 1911

I have so much to write and so little time! I haven't yet asked permission to take a candle upstairs at night, and my room is growing dark. Amazing circumstance that I should be living in a house with electric lights! Electricity is a beautiful thing, so clean and easy; you don't have the work you have with kerosene lamps, trimming the wicks and cleaning the chimneys. But of course there's no electricity in the servants' rooms.

All that must be told later. For now, I take up the thread of my tale.

When I left Philadelphia and set off for Baltimore, the train was crowded, and it was mostly gentlemen on board. I couldn't find a seat next to a lady, and I didn't want to sit by a man. I pressed forward until I found two empty seats, put my suitcase in the rack, and slid into the window seat. Then a gentleman – no, he was *not* a gentleman, and I will not dignify him with that name – came and sat next to me. He was young, with hair as yellow as sawdust; stout in a puffy, undistinguished sort of way.

He nodded to me and touched the brim of his hat, but I turned and gazed out the window, so that he would understand that I wasn't the sort of girl who talks to strange men. He didn't pursue the matter, for which I was grateful, and by and by I forgot about him. I began to regret having had such a big breakfast and drunk so much coffee. I knew that a three-hour journey lay ahead of me, and I became very uncomfortable. (Oh, forgive me, Miss Chandler, but I must be vulgar one last time!) I wondered if there might be a ladies' washroom on the train. I thought there ought to be – goodness, people spend whole nights on trains! – but I felt bashful about asking where it was. Also, I was afraid that if I left my seat, the yellow-haired man might guess where I was going, and that would be just *too* mortifying.

So I sat and suffered and tried not to think about how uncomfortable I was. After some time, it seemed to me that at least two hours must have gone by – we had passed Wilmington, Delaware – so there was only one more hour to go. But then the train stopped, with squealing brakes and a great jolt, and it didn't start up again. Outside the window was a cornfield. Presently the passengers began to murmur, and the yellow-haired man got to his feet. "I wonder what's up," he said under his breath. He set off down the aisle.

I seized the opportunity to leave my seat. I found one of the porters and whispered my question to him – I'm sure I was as red as a poppy, but he nodded and said, "This way, Miss," and showed me to the ladies' washroom.

He was so calm about it, so gracious and discreet. For my money, *he* was a gentleman, though he wasn't a white man.

Afterward, I hurried back to my seat. The yellow-haired man hadn't come back, so I congratulated myself on that. But then I began to worry, because it seemed to me that we'd been standing still for some time, and I didn't want to arrive too late in Baltimore. I knew I'd have to find a boardinghouse where I could spend the night. And then, first thing the next day, I'd have to buy a newspaper and look for work.

I was just imagining a kindly landlady who would help me find my way when the yellow-haired man came back. He sat down, and I suppose the next part was my fault, because without thinking I raised my eyes to his. He answered my unspoken question. "Another train broke down in front of us," he explained. "They're trying to fix it. Until that train moves, we're stuck."

I ought not to have spoken, but I wasn't thinking. "How long will that be?"

"Another hour, they say. They're fixing it. Maybe two," he said. I choked back an exclamation of dismay. I'd planned to get into Baltimore around five thirty; if we were two hours late, it would be starting to get dark. If we were three hours late, it would be dark entirely.

I was determined not to speak again, lest the man grow familiar. I turned back to my window and stared out at the cornfield. Now that the train had stopped, it was very warm. All the windows were open but there wasn't a breath of air. People around me were talking – even talking to strangers. I wondered if it would be very improper to talk to the man next to me. His clothes were respectable, and he hadn't tried to press his attentions on me. I glanced at him sideways and saw that he was reading a newspaper. It was a Baltimore paper and I wondered if he lived in Baltimore. If he did, he might know a respectable boarding-inghouse. But I held my tongue, because a girl traveling alone mustn't talk to strange men.

It was another three hours before we reached Baltimore. The sky was dark blue, and the air was dim. I thought of trying to find my way through the unfamiliar streets, and my heart quite sank. I was hungry, too. That morning – oh, how long ago the morning seemed! – I'd had the idea that the difficult part of my enterprise would be escaping from Steeple Farm. Now I knew that the hardest part lay ahead.

Around me, people were gathering up their things to go. The yellow-haired man looked up at the luggage rack and said, "That your suitcase?" and swung it down for me. I thanked him, and he smiled. To me it seemed a kind smile. At that moment, he was familiar and everything else was strange.

So I took my courage in my hands and said, "Please, do you know a respectable boardinghouse where I might pass the night?"

"Can't say that I do," he said carelessly, and I guess my face fell, because he added, "Bound to be one not too far from the station."

I said, "Yes, of course," but to my profound and eternal disgust, my eyes filled with tears. I turned away quickly and didn't look back. He said something after me; I'm not sure what, but I pretended not to hear.

I found the ladies' room and tried to repair the damages from the journey. I looked perfectly awful. My dress was creased and my knot of hair was coming undone, and my face was dirty with dust and cinders. I didn't look respectable – not one bit – and of course the bruise on my face made everything worse. I cried a little, though I'm ashamed to admit it. Then I washed my face and hands and tidied my hair. It took me a little while to find the doors that led to the street.

When I stepped outside, the man with the yellow hair was standing under a lamppost. "Look here!" he said. "You've been on my conscience, not knowing where you're going to spend the night and all. Fact is, I've thought of just the place for you. It's four blocks from here. I'll take you there."

I was so relieved that I exclaimed, "Oh, that is so kind!" but then I remembered caution. So I said, "I mustn't trouble you to take me, sir. If you'll just direct me, I can find my way. Is it a clean place, and respectable?" Though at that moment, I really didn't care about the clean part; I'd have settled for respectable, even if there were mice.

"First-rate respectable," said the yellow-haired man, "but you've got to let me put in a word for you. They wouldn't take just anyone, that's the thing. They know me at this boardinghouse. I'm a commercial traveler, you see."

I said, "Thank you," and he started telling me about being a commercial traveler, but I didn't listen very hard. I was worrying about whether the first-rate boardinghouse would be expensive. I walked beside that man all unsuspecting, like a lamb to the slaughter. Now that I write this, I can see how rash I was. But I'm not used to men being depraved, because I never have any nice clothes.

So I let him lead me to a row of houses with steps in front and deep porches. None of them had a sign saying there were vacancies, and that troubled me, but he pointed to one and stood aside so that I could go up the stairs. He followed me. Once we were by the doorway, in the shadows – oh! the horror and shame of it! – he swung me around, seized me in his arms, and kissed me.

Never could I have imagined such an insult. And the thing itself – the kiss – was *disgusting*. His mouth was wet, and I could feel how hot and sweaty he was under his jacket. But I didn't say a word. I froze like a rabbit. I was so taken aback – the whole thing was so disagreeable – that it robbed me of my power of speech. And then – between the first loathsome kiss and the second one – he murmured that if I didn't have that shiner, I'd be a fine-looking girl. And then – oh, God! – he put his nasty hand on the front of my *dress*!

That infamous touch shocked me into action. I remembered that I was as strong as an ox, and I shoved him with all my strength. I kicked him in the shins so hard my boot hurt. He yelped, and tried to grab hold of me again, but I kicked him again, higher up this time, the way I used to kick Luke when I was a little girl and he tried to bully me. And with that kick, I gained my freedom and preserved my virtue.

I fled. It's a queer thing about cities. If you raced through the streets in a small town, everyone would ask why you were running. But Baltimore's a big city, and the people I rushed by paid no heed to my flight. I had but one idea in my head – to get away from that awful, horrid, nasty man. I was sure he was right on my heels. So I ran like a deer, never looking left or right, darting across streets at random. I was convinced that if I didn't run mighty fast, he would renew his horrid attentions.

I ran until I had a stitch in my side. When at last I stopped, I was at the edge of a park: a beautiful park, with a big fountain trickling water, and beds of flowers.

It's now so dark that I can't see the page.

I will write more tomorrow.

I have a candle tonight. I was a little afraid to ask for one – Malka and I have been getting on so well – but I desperately wanted to write this evening. I am so far behind with my diary! New things happen every day, and I can't write them because I haven't caught up yet.

So I asked for the candle, and Malka looked at me. Malka's eyelids come down over her eyes like hoods, but she can work the muscles around them in a way that makes her look more solemn and shocked than anyone I've ever met. The first time she looked at me that way, I thought I should turn to stone. Since then, I've learned that she gives out that look *all the time*. I can't say I blame her, because it's awfully effective.

She said accusingly, "You've been going upstairs in the dark?"

I said, yes, I had.

"Take a candle," she said, and she handed me a china chamberstick. "Matches are in the dresser. There's a brass box near your bed to keep them in. Don't burn the house down."

I promised I wouldn't – but here I must stop, because I haven't yet come to Malka. I left off my story in the park of Eutaw Place, only I didn't yet know it was Eutaw Place.

It was there that I stopped running. I'd imagined that a big city like Baltimore would be row upon row of houses, all squeezed together; I'd never pictured a park. This park was sandwiched between two broad avenues, so that on both sides of the street, the houses overlooked the garden. Even in the dark – and it wasn't altogether dark, because of the streetlamps – I could see how fine the garden was.

I looked at the houses. They were row houses, but they looked more like palaces – tall and spacious, with balconies and porches and great bay windows to let in the light. Some of them had turrets and panes of colored glass over the doors. Wealthy people lived there, I could tell; it was no place for the likes of me. But the great houses and the tended garden made me feel a little safer. It seemed like a place where criminals wouldn't feel at home.

I glimpsed an iron bench under a tree and sank down upon it. I knew I didn't have time to waste: it was near nine o'clock, and the boardinghouses would be shutting up. I promised myself that after I'd rested a minute, I'd find a place to spend the night.

But I didn't keep that promise. I knew I ought to go back to the train station. This neighborhood wasn't the kind of place where I'd find a boardinghouse. But I was afraid that awful man might be lurking by the station. The thought of running into him again – and him thinking, maybe, that I'd come back for more – oh, I just couldn't bear it! I felt like Thumbelina after she'd been carried off by the ugly toad.

The truth is, I didn't have the gumption to carry on.

It makes me feel bad to reflect upon that, because I want to be noble and courageous. On the other hand, it *had* been a long day. Even during the good parts of it – having breakfast in the dining car and seeing *The Spirit of Trans- portation* – I'd been frightened underneath. And that man had scared me right down to the bone.

So I stuck to the bench. After a while I realized that I was going to spend the night there. I felt sheltered by the big tree over my head. The night was warm, and I was in a respectable part of town. I put down my suitcase to serve as a pillow and curled up on the bench.

It was horribly uncomfortable. The bench wasn't as long as I was, and the suitcase mashed my ear. I thought of all the comforting things inside it – Jesus and Belinda and Ma's money and Miss Chandler's handkerchief – and I started to cry. I was frightened because I was sleeping outdoors like a tramp, and I didn't know a single soul in Baltimore, and I didn't know how I was going to find a job. It seemed to me that Baltimore might be full of wicked men who would force their attentions on me, and I was no match for them. I even thought about going back home.

Then I saw – oh, so clearly! – that I couldn't go home, no matter how bad it was in Baltimore. At home, there's no hope. Father will never change, and he'll never let me have anything. I covered my head with my arm and began to pray.

It had been a while since I prayed. I'd been feeling a

little disappointed in God, because I'd asked Him not to let Father be rude to Miss Chandler – but Father *was* – and then I'd prayed that my strike would succeed – but it *didn't*, because Father burned my books. I know God can't answer every prayer exactly the way you want Him to. But I couldn't help thinking that He hadn't been doing very well by me lately.

Even so, I prayed. It wasn't a proper prayer, just a cry for help, but I felt He was listening. I recited Hail Marys. Then I recommenced crying. All of a sudden – I'd sobbed so hard I never heard him approach – a voice said, "Please let me help you."

I sat bolt upright, ready to jump up and run away. But I didn't – I guess because the man who'd spoken wasn't looming over me. He was hunkered down in front of the bench, balanced on the balls of his feet. It was such a precarious position that I could have stuck out one foot and knocked him over. He was holding his hat in his hands – he'd taken off his hat to show respect. I thought that was nice.

He had a beard, and that surprised me because it's usually older men who have beards, and he was young. His beard was dark and curly and so was his hair. He was solidly built and his shoulders were broad, and he had a large head – not too large, but the kind of head that reminded me of Jupiter, the Roman god. His clothes were handsome and he was well-groomed. In short, he didn't look like the sort of man a girl has to run from – I mean, the sort of man from whom a girl has to run.

"Can I be of any use to you?" he said.

If I am to write the truth – and I vowed that I would when Miss Chandler gave me this book – I wanted to say *yes* right away. I wanted him to take care of me. Then I remembered how stupid I'd been with the yellow-haired man, and I saw I was in danger of being stupid again. So I didn't answer. He took a clean handkerchief out of his coat and offered it to me.

That reminded me of Miss Chandler. I started crying again, and while I cried, the man made noises. They were sympathetic noises, and they were also, somehow, foreign. His voice wasn't foreign; he spoke like an American. But his sympathetic noises weren't like anything I'd heard before. And something about them made me cry harder. Oh, I'm like Florence Dombey; I cry too much. After a little, I wiped my eyes and tried to pull myself together. Men don't like it when women cry, and I wanted that man to like me.

"Won't you tell me—" the man began, but I interrupted him.

"I'm lost," I blurted out. "I came to Baltimore to find work as a hired girl, but the train was late, so I didn't get to town until dark, and I couldn't find a respectable boardinghouse, and I asked a man who seemed kind, but he—" Then I stopped. I couldn't tell this stranger what that man did. "He frightened me," I said pitifully, because that was true, though it wasn't the whole truth.

He nodded as if he understood. "Is he the one who hurt you?"

I thought for a minute he was reading my mind, because that awful man *had* hurt me. Then I saw that he was staring at my face, seeing the bruises that Cressy gave me. "Oh, no!" I said quickly, and touched the swollen place. "That's from home. That happened a week ago."

"Did you run away from home?"

I wished he hadn't asked me that. I ought to have said *no*, right away, but I didn't, and that was as good as saying *yes*. "I had to. My father—" I started to say *burned my books*, but my throat closed. It was a moment before I could speak. "I *had* to run away."

He looked very upset. "What about your mother? Won't she worry?"

"My mother's dead," I said, and he looked down-right stricken and made more of those sympathetic noises. I added, "But I'm not that young. I'm eighteen." I don't know why I said *eighteen*. I'd meant to lie about my age, of course, but I'd planned to say I was sixteen, maybe seven-teen. But for some reason, *eighteen* was what came out of my mouth. "Do you know where I might find a respectable boardinghouse?"

He shook his head regretfully. "I'm afraid I don't. I've never needed one, not in Baltimore. Perhaps tomorrow—"

He shook his head again. "That's no use; you need a place to stay tonight." He stood up. "I have an idea."

I waited.

"I live up the street –" he pointed to a place beyond the trees – "in the corner house, with my parents and sister and my brother David, but just now David's in New York with my father. There are servants' rooms at the top of the house that aren't being used. Perhaps my mother would let you stay there. She might be able to help you find a job. There's even a possibility – but we'll talk about that later on. Will you come with me?"

I stared at him with my heart in my mouth.

"My mother's very good," he said. "She may seem a little brusque at first, but—" He fumbled in his pockets and brought out a card. "I ought to have introduced myself. I'm Solomon Rosenbach."

I took the card. It was too dark to read it, but I felt vaguely reassured. It didn't seem like the sort of thing a villain would do – give me his card.

"Will you come with me? You can't spend the night on that bench. You won't get a wink of sleep—" His face broke into a smile, and it changed everything. He was such a serious-looking person, but that wide, sweet smile made him look as if he were no older than I am. "And I won't either."

He was so *kind*, so truly chivalrous. I could say that he spoke to me with tenderness, except that makes it sound as if he had a particular interest in me, and I'm sure he hadn't. I believe he would have spoken the same way to a lost child or a wounded dog. And the child – or the dog – would have trusted him and followed him home at once.

But I wasn't a dog or a child. I'd trusted one man that night, and he'd insulted me *unspeakably*. "I can't."

He looked thoughtful, turning the brim of his hat between his fingers. Then he smiled again.

"You're quite right, you know. It's dangerous to go home with a stranger. Here's what I'm going to do. I'm going to walk to my house and hope that you'll follow me at a safe distance. Then I'll go inside, and afterward – as soon as I can explain – my mother will come out on the porch and invite you in. Will that suit you better? She's very respectable, my mother. In fact, we all are, but you're right not to take my word for it."

I considered his offer. "Thank you," I said. My voice creaked a little but I didn't cry.

"There's a good girl," he said, and I guess that was patronizing but I didn't dislike it. I followed him just as he said. He ran lightly up the porch steps, and when he reached the door, he wiped his feet on the mat.

My opinion of him rose even higher.

At first I waited on the pavement. Then I crept up to the porch. The windows of the house were open. There were no lights on in the front room, but it was dim rather than dark, because the room behind it was lit, and there was a big archway connecting them. I heard voices, and a woman exclaimed, "Oh, Solly! It used to be cats and dogs!" and then I heard *his* voice, hushing her.

That was when I knew I was safe. Because his mother – Mrs Rosenbach – sounded like a *mother*, an exasperated mother. There's something about the way a mother talks to her child. Listening, I felt kind of homesick.

After that, I couldn't hear much. I can't say I didn't listen, but their voices were low and blurred. Then she came through the archway and a light came on. I didn't know electric lights came on so suddenly. It wasn't like gaslight; it was quicker and ten times brighter. I retreated to the top of the porch steps. The door opened, and Mrs Rosenbach came out.

She stood silhouetted, with the light at her back. I was surprised by how small she was. The top of her head just clears my shoulder. But small or not, she was mistress of the situation. If she'd been a teacher and rapped on the desk with her ruler, everyone would have fallen silent.

"Come in," she said briskly, and I went.

Once I was inside, I didn't look around very much; my whole attention was fixed on Mrs Rosenbach. But I was aware that the house was fine. There was wood paneling halfway up the wall, carved and dark and rich looking, and big paintings with gold frames. It was almost like a church, it was so fancy and solemn, and the ceiling was high above my head.

But I was watching *her*, trying to tell if she would be kind to me. What I noticed first was that she was elegant, more elegant even than Miss Chandler (though not more of a lady). She wore a shirtwaist dress, silk taffeta I think it was. The way the cloth was made, it gleamed like polished copper in the lamplight but was jet-black in the folds. There were pleats down the front, and the buttons went down one side, instead of being in the middle. She had a slender waist and dark hair – it was only a little gray – and keen eyes. And though it was a warm night, and she wore a high collar, she didn't look flushed or creased, and she carried herself like a queen.

"What's your name?"

"Janet Lovelace, ma'am."

"My son tells me you ran away from home." Her voice was courteous, but something else, too: maybe disdainful; maybe severe. "Wasn't that a rash thing to do?"

"No, ma'am," I said, as courteous as she. I surprised myself, answering her so readily, but something about her brought out my mettle. It was a queer thing: Mr Solomon Rosenbach made me feel kind of frail and delicate, but *she* made me strong.

"You don't think it was rash, to come to a strange city where you know no one, and have no place to spend the night?"

"If you put it like that, it sounds rash," I admitted, "but I had to leave home. If I have to sleep on a park bench, I will. But I won't go home."

She took a step forward and looked at me, first as if I was a curiosity, and then more closely. She saw my bruises and winced at the sight of them. She said, almost under her breath, "No, you mustn't go home," and all at once, I realized what she was thinking. She'd gotten hold of the idea that someone at home had beaten me, and I tried to remember just what I'd said to her son. Of course I hadn't mentioned Cressy; and I'd told him I couldn't go home because of Father. He must have jumped to the wrong conclusion.

It wasn't my fault. I didn't lie.

But I didn't confess, either. I don't mean confess, exactly: I didn't explain. I *should* have explained, but the Rosenbachs were looking as if they were sorry for me, and I wanted them to feel sorry for me, because I needed a place to spend the night. So I kept my mouth shut.

"I understand you want to be a hired girl."

"Yes, ma'am. If you could help me find work, I'd be much obliged."

"You have a character?"

I said hesitantly, "I think so, ma'am. Miss Chandler – my teacher at home – she thought I had a good character."

"That's not what I meant. I meant references – a written testimonial to the effect that you are honest and clean and obedient. Have you anything of that kind?"

"No, ma'am."

"You may find it difficult to find work without one. However –" she hesitated – "there may be a place here." She took a step toward a small rocking chair and sat down in it. "Sit down. I should warn you that it's unlikely you'll stay here for long. I've dismissed three servants in the two past months."

"I'd like to work here," I said breathlessly. I meant it. I wanted nothing more than to work in this magnificent house. I could tell that the Rosenbachs were people of culture and refinement. At the same time, I wondered what the other servants had done to displease her.

Mrs Rosenbach said unexpectedly, "Are you hungry? Have you dined?"

"No, but I had breakfast on the train, ma'am. It was a very large breakfast. I'm not hungry."

She sighed. "Solly," she said to Mr Rosenbach, "go downstairs and fix the girl a sandwich. And a glass of milk, I think."

Her son got to his feet and left the room. He was going downstairs, this wealthy, grown-up, well-dressed man, to *fix me a sandwich*. Luke would have called him a sissy. I thought he was manly and gallant.

Mrs Rosenbach rocked in her chair. It's funny – sitting in a rocking chair is kind of a homely thing to do, but the way she did it, with her wrists resting so lightly on the arms of the chair, and just the tip of one shoe showing – why, it wasn't homely at all. A queen might rock that way, if she had a throne with rockers on it.

She said, "Malka is in bed. She's tired out after the Sabbath."

I wondered who Malka was. It struck me that Mrs Rosenbach had the day wrong, because it was Saturday, but I didn't say so.

"Malka is our housekeeper. She was my husband's nursemaid when he was a child. Mr Rosenbach is devoted to her, and when I came to this house as a bride, it was Malka who showed me how to run the household." She corrected herself. "Malka and her sister, that is. Malka is twelve years older than her sister, Minna. My husband and I never wanted a large staff. We value our privacy, and we do what we can to make it easy to run the house. We have hot and cold running water, a gas range, and central heating. The laundry is sent out."

"Yes, ma'am," I said, because I felt I ought to say something. I kept a straight face, but inside I was thinking, *Good, no laundry.*

"Malka's over seventy, and she's no longer strong. Until last year, Minna did most of the heavy work. But last year, Minna received an unexpected proposal of marriage – a widower, a man she knew when she was young. We've tried to replace her, but Malka –" she made an irritable clucking noise – "Malka has very strict standards of housekeeping, and none of the young women have been able to please her. She says young women nowadays don't know what it is to work." She raised her eyebrows. "Are you accustomed to work, Miss Lovelace?"

Miss Lovelace. It sounded so pretty, even better than I'd expected. I answered her by throwing out my hands, showing first the palms and then the backs. I never thought I should be glad of my rough, work-scarred, big-knuckled hands. "Oh, I can work," I assured her. "I grew up on a farm."

"What can you do?"

I took a deep breath. "I can cook and scrub and sweep and dust. I can sew, of course, and mend and darn. And I can kill a chicken, and dress it, and plant a garden and put food by, and make sausage, and blacklead the stove and keep the fires going. I don't guess it matters, if you send the laundry out, but I can wash and starch and iron. And I can whitewash, and tend chickens, and churn, and take up the carpets and beat them, and—"

Mrs Rosenbach lifted her hand. I stopped talking.

"Are you tactful?"

I had to think about that one. "I couldn't say, ma'am. I didn't have to be too tactful on the farm." Then I rallied. "But Miss Chandler said I showed signs of a refined nature. I think I could be tactful, if I set my mind to it."

"You'll need to set your mind to it," Mrs Rosenbach said drily. "What we are looking for is someone who can shoulder the heavy work without making Malka feel that she's an old woman. She's touchy," she added, in a way that made me wonder how much she liked Malka.

I heard footsteps, and young Mr Rosenbach came in with my sandwich. He'd cut it in triangles and put it on a plate, instead of carrying it around in his hand, the way Luke does. He'd remembered the glass of milk, and he'd put sugar cookies on the side of the plate where the sandwich wasn't. He even handed me a napkin. I never met such a man in my life.

Once I smelled food, I was hungry. But I didn't gobble. I took a small sip of milk to show my refined nature and daintily nibbled my sandwich, which was cheese.

Mr Rosenbach said, "Is it settled?" and his mother raised her head and gave him a look.

"Nothing is settled. I'm telling her about Malka."

"She needs a place to spend the night," Mr Rosenbach persisted, in such a mild tone of voice that it didn't seem like nagging. "It's getting late."

I glanced at the clock. It was past ten.

"She may stay here tonight," Mrs Rosenbach conceded. "If Malka doesn't make too great a fuss, she may stay a few days." She turned back to me. "If you do your work well, I will provide you with a written character, which will help you in your search for employment."

"Thank you, ma'am," I said, but I felt a little disheartened, because she didn't seem to think I'd be working for her. "I think I can help your housekeeper without hurting her feelings. And you'll find me very willing."

She tilted her head. There was something about the way she did it that reminded me of that word *satirical*. It isn't a word I think about much, but it flashed through my head just then. "Willing to work in a Jewish household?" she said, and when I didn't answer right away, she added, "You, I think, are not Jewish."

"No, ma'am," I said. I was as taken aback as if she'd asked me if I was an Indian. It seemed to me – I mean, it doesn't *now*, but it did then – as though Jewish people were like Indians: people from long ago; people in books. I know there still *are* Indians out West, but they're civilized now, and wear ordinary clothes. In the same way, I guess I knew there were still Jews, but I never expected to meet any.

"It's just as I said, Solly," said Mrs Rosenbach, "she has no idea." She seemed both irritated and amused. "Have you ever met a Jew before, Miss Lovelace?"

"No – no, ma'am," I stammered, "but I've read about them in the Bible. And in *Ivanhoe*, Rebecca was a Jewess, and she's my favorite character in the whole book."

It was her turn to look surprised. "You've read *Ivanhoe*?"

"Yes, ma'am," I said. I saw that she'd been thinking I was an ignorant girl. That piqued me, but I didn't waste time worrying over it, because I was racking my brain, trying to remember everything I knew about Jews. Most of the characters in *Ivanhoe* were horrid to Rebecca and Isaac, because they were Jews. But Ivanhoe was good to them, and Ivanhoe's the hero. And Rebecca – why, Rebecca's the heroine, and a hundred times more interesting than Rowena, who's mostly just beautiful. I added, "*Ivanhoe*'s a really good book, Mrs Rosenbach."

She surprised me by laughing. "Rebecca is my favorite, too." She exchanged glances with her son. "At any rate, she doesn't seem to have learned much in the way of—" Then she used a word I haven't heard before. It began with "aunty" and ended with "ism," and from her tone of voice, I didn't know whether I was supposed to have learned it or not.

I took a stab in the dark. I wasn't going to let this job slip through my fingers. "I could learn," I offered. "If it would make me a better hired girl, I could learn it."

Mrs Rosenbach shook her head. Her smile was rueful. I was pretty sure I'd said the wrong thing, but she didn't like me any the worse for it. "You're right, Solly. She is utterly without guile. And as you say, she's a stranger in a strange land. I wouldn't want Anna or Mimi wandering the streets at night." She stood up. "I'll show you to a room where you can sleep."

When I began this entry, I thought I'd write the whole story of that night. I meant to describe the house and relate how Mrs Rosenbach helped me put clean sheets on the bed, almost as if I was a guest. I wanted to write how my heart swelled with gratitude when I realized I'd found a safe harbor, and how I knelt by my bed and thanked Our Lord for guiding my footsteps.

I meant to write all that. But my candle is burning low and my hand is just about *falling off*. And I'm sleepy. I daren't risk oversleeping, because Malka is fussy about getting up early – though I am learning to like Malka. In fact, I like everyone here, and Mr Rosenbach best of all.

I don't mean that I've fallen in love with Mr Rosenbach, because that would be silly. He's too old for me – though of course Mr Rochester was older than Jane Eyre. But I *revere* Mr Rosenbach, and I've made up my mind to be grateful to him as long as I live, and always to mention him in my prayers.

Thursday, July the sixth, 1911

Malka was tired from shopping for the Sabbath, so she let me do the dishes tonight. Of course she watched me like a hawk, so I couldn't have made a mistake if I'd wanted to. But I was very careful, keeping my mind on *kashrut* all the time. I never went near the wrong sink.

That's how I began here – using the wrong sink – and it was nearly fatal. When I awoke that first morning, I thought how important it would be to please Mrs Rosenbach and her Malka. I vowed I would leave no stone unturned. But I was afraid to go down to the kitchen first thing, because Malka wouldn't know who I was. I got dressed and held myself in readiness. When Mrs Rosenbach knocked on my door, she seemed pleased that I was up and about.

She led me down the front stairs, but she pointed out the back stairs and said I'd be using them most of the time. I said, "Yes, ma'am, thank you," though I couldn't help regretting the main staircase. Floating down those wide, shallow stairs made me feel like a swan, or maybe a sylph. The back stairs are steep and narrow and mean looking. This house seems to have *hundreds* of stairs – I guess because the ceilings are so high. When I come from the basement to my third-floor room, it's four double flights, and by the time I reach the top, I'm out of breath. I'm grateful I don't have to carry bathwater up those stairs. There are two beautiful bathrooms, one on the first floor and one on the second. I'm allowed to use the one on the second floor.

When Mrs Rosenbach introduced me, Malka was at the stove. She had a dish of buttered eggs that she was cooking slowly, holding the pot off the heat. She looked at me without approval and didn't say anything. I tried a little curtsy. Malka is very short, and I felt like a fool, curtsying to such a little black fly of a woman.

I don't mean to be cruel, calling her a little black fly. That's just what came into my head when I saw her. She wore a black dress, and a print apron, mustard colored with red and pink roses on it, and her head was wrapped in an old black shawl. She wore another shawl around her shoulders, an embroidered one with gray silk fringe. I couldn't imagine wearing all those shawls in July, but Malka is always cold.

After Mrs Rosenbach left, I asked Malka if I could help with breakfast, but she pointed to a chair and said the best way to help would be to keep out of her way. I said "Yes, ma'am," and sat down, obedient as a dog. She wasn't mollified, though; she said she didn't want to be called ma'am – plain Malka was good enough for her. She looked very grim when she said it but also as if her humility were satisfying in some way. It's as if she smacks her lips over things that are sullen or sorrowful. Yesterday she told me about a family she knew a long time ago and how they succumbed to scarlet fever, one by one. It seemed to please her that their dying was so hopeless and long-drawn-out. And she evidently felt that it was a rare treat for me to hear about it. Yet I don't believe she's a cruel woman, only cross-grained and old and like a little black fly.

While she fixed the breakfast, I had time to look around. The kitchen isn't wholly underground, but it has windows looking out on the street, so it isn't as dark as it might be. It seemed to me a queer kitchen because it had so much in it – so many cabinets and cupboards, and two gas ranges, and two sinks, and two refrigerators,

North Stars, they are called. Since then I've learned that Jewish people need more dishes than ordinary people. Mrs Rosenbach has two beautiful sets that she uses only on Passover, which is what the Jews celebrate a week before they celebrate Easter.

The kitchen was surprisingly clean, considering how old Malka was. The only dirty places were high up – shelves where Malka can't see. I itched to prove myself by giving them a good scrubbing. At one end of the kitchen was a little cozy corner that I thought must be Malka's. There was a small grate and a flowered carpet, and two wing chairs, one with a footstool. Between the chairs was a pretty worktable with a knitting basket. Another basket on the floor held an immense striped cat. He is not a mere humble Tom but is called Thomashefsky, after a great actor who is Jewish.

Looking around that kitchen only confirmed what I'd thought the night before: that this would be a good place to work. That cozy corner suggested that the Rosenbachs took good care of Malka, and from all the stoves and refrigerators and china, I felt pretty sure they had enough money to pay me six dollars a week (though I forgot to mention wages that first night. Now I don't know how to bring it up).

I watched Malka cook. She fried fish on a gridiron and toasted bread in an electric machine called a toaster. She kept her eye on the eggs, so that they cooked slowly.

Between turning the fish and the toast, and stirring the eggs, she made coffee and sprinkled sugar on three little glass dishes of blackberries. She darted back and forth between the stove and the table and a little closet across the room from me. There was a shelf inside, and she put plates and cups and silverware on the shelf. When the food was done – and she'd timed things so that everything was ready at once – she put the eggs in a china tureen, and the fish in a covered dish, and wrapped the toast in a towel. She laid them all on the closet shelf. Then she pulled on a rope pulley, and the shelf rose into the air – I could see it from where I was sitting. I'd never seen a dumbwaiter before, but I could tell it was a fine invention.

Malka turned back to the table. I hadn't noticed it, but she'd prepared a plate for me, with a tiny scrap of fish and a spoonful of eggs and two thick slices of toast. She thumped the plate against the table, and snapped, "If you're hungry." Then she stripped off her apron and exchanged it for a starched linen one that hung over the back of a chair. She hurried out – I guessed she was going upstairs to wait at table.

Once she was gone, I went to the plate she'd prepared for me. I felt kind of mortified by the way she'd banged that plate at me, but I was too hungry to be proud, especially as no one was there to see.

We seldom had fish at Steeple Farm, and I'm not very good at cooking it. The thought of raw fish makes me shudder, so I tend to cook it dry. Malka's fish was crisp and salty on the outside, and tender inside. The buttered eggs were even better. I'd have liked more of both, but I couldn't blame the old lady for stinting me, because she hadn't known there'd be an extra person for breakfast.

I cleaned my plate and went over to the sink and washed the dishes. It was wonderful, how you could get hot water just by turning on the tap. I sat back down and started worrying what I'd do if I couldn't get Malka to like me. I told myself there would be other places in Baltimore that would need a hired girl. But I'd made up my mind that I wanted to stay with the Rosenbachs. The house was handsome, and I admired Mrs Rosenbach, and Mr Rosenbach's kindness had touched my heart.

I was roused from my thoughts by the sound of the dumbwaiter. The dirty plates were coming down. I took them off the shelf and carried them to the sink. I thought it would be good if Malka came downstairs and found me up to my elbows in dishwater; she'd see I was willing and maybe realize how nice it would be to have an extra pair of hands. I washed the blackberry dishes first, since they were glass. Then I picked up the tureen. It was white with painted flowers and a little cupid sitting on the lid. It looked special to me, so I washed it very carefully, and I was drying it when Malka came into the room.

She saw the water in the sink and the dish in my hand, and her eyes did that shocked-accusing thing they do so well. And she shrieked. That sounds like an exagger-ation but it really was a shriek, and Mrs Rosenbach heard it, because she came running downstairs to see what was the matter. Malka bore down on me and tried to yank the dish away. She cried, "What have you done?" with such ferocity I really thought I'd broken the dish – except there it was in my hands, without so much as a chip, and clean as a pearl.

Then Mrs Rosenbach said, "Oh, Malka! For heaven's sake!" and Malka went into a torrent of what I thought was German, but what I now know is Yiddish, which is Jewish German. While Malka railed at me in Yiddish, Mrs Rosenbach tried to explain to me in English what I'd done wrong. It seems that the Jews – well, some of them – are very serious about how they eat, and meat and milk dishes are supposed to be kept separate. That's why there were two stoves and two sinks. And the dish I was holding was a milk dish, because the eggs had been made with butter, but I was washing it in the meat sink. And Malka was saying that the *kashrut* – which is what they call the food laws – had been broken and that I'd ruined a dish called Meissen, from Germany, which had been a wedding present. I'd ruined it by putting it in the wrong sink, and that meant the sink was spoiled, too.

I was very frightened to think I'd done all that without knowing it. But Mrs Rosenbach wasn't angry with me; she was exasperated with Malka. She lost her temper. She didn't shout or bang on things, the way I do. When I lose my temper, I'm like a bear with a big club. But Mrs Rosenbach was like an archer shooting arrows; it was kind of delicate and deadly at the same time. She told Malka to calm herself at once, and though she didn't raise her voice, it was sharp enough to cut paper. And she said they were a Reform household now, which I've learned means they aren't so strict about *kashrut*. She said Malka could put boiling water in the sink, if that made her feel better, but Malka said the Meissen dish would have to be buried. Mrs Rosenbach said that was out of the question. She said Malka could put the dish outside the next time it rained, which made Malka shriek again. Then Mrs Rosenbach said she wouldn't listen to another word, which made Malka shut up. On her way out, Mrs Rosenbach shot an arrow of a look at me that told me I was being a lot of trouble and that she wished she hadn't taken me in.

After Mrs Rosenbach swept out of the kitchen – she wasn't wearing a train, but she'd have looked good in one – Malka went to the other sink and filled it with water and cried as she washed the dishes. It wasn't the breaking-down kind of crying but the stop-and-start kind; I'd think she was done and then she'd mutter and sniff some more. I heard her moan that she was the only person in the house who ... sniff, sniff, grumble ... and that she wasn't too old ... sniff, sniff ... she could manage perfectly if only she didn't have to ... moan and sniff ... and she knew a fool when she saw one, and probably Irish as well ... she could manage, she'd always managed, if strangers didn't barge in and add to her burdens ... sniff, sniff, gulp ... she might be old, she might be tired, she might be half dead, but she knew how things ought to be done ... sniff, clear throat, little sob. She went on like that for some time, covering all the ground between pitiful and insulting.

At last the dishes were done and everything put away. When she turned around, I said humbly, "I'm ever so sorry about the dish. I didn't know any better."

"No, you don't," she snapped, "and you never will."

I tried again. "I can clean," I said, and held out my hands so she could see them. "I'm used to hard work, heavy work. Isn't there something I can do for you?"

She stared at me, and a witchlike gleam came into her eyes. Then she went and got a big bucket and started filling it with washing soda and hot water. "The floor needs washing," she said. "You know how to scrub a floor?"

"Yes, ma'am," I said eagerly. I was eager. I was downright abject.

She stood back from the sink, so that I could lift the bucket out. Then she handed me a brush.

"I'll need more buckets," I said, "and a sponge and rags. And vinegar."

I saw her eyebrows rise up very high, but she brought me the vinegar and pointed at the closet where the buckets were. I filled a second bucket with plain water and added vinegar water to a third. Then I settled down to scrub the floor.

No one can say that I don't know how to scrub. Ma taught me, and frail though she was, when she did a thing, she did it thoroughly. I worked as she taught me, a square yard at a time, first scouring with the brush, and then sponging off the wet dirt and rinsing the sponge in the second bucket, and then finishing with vinegar water and drying the floor with rags. I reached under the cupboards and the stoves and dragged out wads of dust and cat hair and things that I couldn't say *what* they'd been. Sometimes it's better not to know.

Except for those underneath things, it wasn't a bad room to scrub. The floor was linoleum, and linoleum's a wonderful thing. It keeps the dirt on the surface, where you can get at it. Ma always wanted linoleum, but the cheapest she could find was eighty-six cents a yard, and Father wouldn't let her spend all that. This linoleum was probably the expensive kind. It wasn't exactly a cheerful pattern – olive-green squares with garlands of flowers – but it was dandy for hiding the dirt. When the rinse water turned dark, I raised my hand and asked Malka if I could change the water. She said, "What, you think you're in school?" which I decided to take as a *yes*.

I changed the water and went back to work. Malka settled down in the wing chair. A little while later, I heard a soft thundery sound. When I glanced sideways, I saw that the cat Thomashefsky had climbed into the old lady's lap. He was purring, and she was scratching the top of his head.

It occurred to me that I might try praying, so I mouthed the words to a Hail Mary as I scoured the floor. Without speaking out loud, I explained to the Blessed Mother that I wanted to stay here and I needed that touchy old woman to like me. Clear as a bell I heard her voice – the Blessed Mother's, I mean, not Malka's. She said, "Be kind."

That irritated me, because the Blessed Mother is always telling me to be kind, as if that were the solution to everything. But I've found it often works – only it's like scrubbing the floor; you have to put your back into it. It takes imagination to do the thing thoroughly. So as I scrubbed I tried to imagine being Malka: old and tired and unable to reach under things. And I imagined how I'd feel if a stranger came in and broke my kitchen rules and ruined my Meissen dish and dirtied my sink.

When I finished I emptied the dishwater and rinsed the sponge and washed out the rags. Then I spoke to Malka.

"I'm sorry I made that mistake with the dish," I said. "I didn't mean it, though."

"I never said you did," she said. I guess I looked at her reproachfully, because she blinked and said, "You'd be all right in a Gentile home. Why don't you work for the Gentiles?"

"I don't know any Gentiles," I said.

She snorted. "You're a Gentile yourself. Gentile means *not Jewish* – don't you know that?"

"I guess I don't," I said. I'd read the word, of course; it's in *Ivanhoe* and the Bible, but I'd never looked it up. I had the idea that the Gentiles were like the Philistines or the Ishmaelites: people who lived a long time ago. "I'm Catholic," I explained, "but I'm not Irish." I thought it would be best to get that straight. Father says the Irish are worthless, and it seems that Malka agrees with him.

"What are you, then?"

"I'm American," I answered promptly. Which was more than she was, with her ravings that sounded so German.

"So who isn't?" said Malka. "What was your family before that?"

"We were Scots," I said, "but that was a long time ago."

"The Scots aren't too bad," she said as if she hated to admit it. "You can scrub a floor; I'll say that for you. *I* can't get down on my hands and knees, not the way I used to."

I wasn't sure what to say. I knew better than to say anything pitying. Then the Blessed Mother inspired me, and I thought of the perfect answer. "The way you cook, I'd say scrubbing was a waste of your time."

That pleased her. I could tell because her mouth tight-ened and she bent over the cat to hide her face. "The last girl was Irish. Would she get her hands dirty?" She gave me one of those piercing looks as if she expected an answer. "All she wanted was money to waste on cheap finery."

"I wish I had some finery," I said. I hadn't meant to say it. The words just slipped out.

"Not cheap finery," Malka argued. "You wouldn't want that."

"I can't afford the expensive kind," I pointed out, and I saw her mouth twitch. I pinched my skirt between my thumb and forefinger, inviting her to admire the blurred flowers on my horrible dress. I clowned a little, rising on tiptoe and twirling like a ballet dancer.

She uttered a musty sound, something between a guffaw and a snort. She couldn't fool me. It was a laugh; I'd made her laugh. I pressed my advantage. "Will you teach me how to do *kashrut*?" I coaxed. "Miss Chandler – my old teacher – said I could learn just about anything, if I set my mind to it. I'd work hard to please you. I need a place, and I think this one will suit me just fine."

The idea of teaching me wiped the smile from her face. "I can try to teach you," she said as if it was a threat, "but it'll be up to you to learn." And she glowered at me, but it was that smack-her-lips kind of glower, as if her pes-simism was as tasty as her fried fish.

Part Three

The Maidservant

Friday, July the seventh, 1911

Today was Shabbos – or getting ready for it – and now
I know why Malka was so tired last Saturday night,
because preparing for Shabbos is hard work. No one is supposed to work *on* Shabbos (which isn't on Sunday at all),
but you have to work like a horse to get ready for it. The
food for Shabbos has to be especially good and plentiful.
So all the cooking for Friday supper and Saturday breakfast and Saturday lunch has to be done by Friday before
sundown, with the food stored away in refrigerators or
warming ovens.

And the house has to be spotlessly clean. Malka and I
were on our feet all day, dusting and sweeping and ironing
the table linens, polishing the glasses and the silver, only

Malka won't let me touch the Shabbos candlesticks. They came from Germany, from the days when Mr Rosenbach was poor. Even though they're plainer than the other silver, they're precious, because they've been in the family so long. I asked Malka if she was afraid I'd steal them. She said I was so rough I'd rub the pattern off.

I think that was meant to vex me, but I laughed as if she'd said something very witty, and a pinched little smile came over her face. She gave me the glasses to polish, first with whiting and leather, and then with a silk handkerchief. I rubbed them until they sparkled. Then there was the cooking – grating apples for pudding, and chopping onions, salting the beef, and making noodles for *frimsel* soup. She had me pluck the fowls and dress them, and she showed me how to make fish balls with lemon sauce, which will be eaten cold tomorrow.

She kneaded the bread and made me watch while she braided it. Then she made cucumber salad while I beat the eggs for sponge cake. Sponge cake is a cake without butter or milk, so it's good for *kashrut*. It's all eggs, but you have to beat them a full half hour. I beat them until my arms ached, but then Malka said I'd *overbeaten* them, and I had to go to the market on Whitelock Street to buy more. I hated the thought of those good eggs going to waste, and I set Malka off on a tirade by saying that we ought to keep a pig. It seems that pigs are very bad for *kashrut*.

But visiting the market was the best part of the

day. I've been indoors all week, mostly down in the kitchen. Going to the market by myself felt like having an adventure. Malka told me not to dawdle, and I didn't, but I *looked*.

The worst part of the day was when dinner was almost ready. Malka told me there was just time for me to run upstairs and change my dress. Everyone is supposed to wear their nicest things for Shabbos, but I don't have any nice things. I've worn my chocolate-brown twill ever since I came here. At night I wash out the parts where I've perspired and hang it by the window to dry.

I had to tell Malka that I didn't have another dress. That isn't really true, but I can't wear the dress I left home in, because it's so short and childish looking. I wish I hadn't told everyone I'm eighteen, because if I'd said I was fifteen, maybe even sixteen, I might have been able to get away with it. But no girl of eighteen would show so much leg, and if the Rosenbachs saw me wearing it, they'd know that I lied about my age.

Oh, what a tangled web we weave,
When first we practice to deceive!

Miss Chandler taught me that, and it's true. When I told Malka I had only one dress, her eyebrows rose so high I thought they'd crawl up under her kerchief and vanish. Her eyes got that tragic, shocked look. I said that

I was hoping to buy another dress with my wages, but she frowned at me sharply and said it was wrong to talk about money so close to the Sabbath. So that was that. I don't know what I'm going to do about my wages. I could buy myself a dress with my Belinda money if I had an afternoon off, but I can't ask for an afternoon off, because Mrs Rosenbach hasn't told me I can stay.

At suppertime, I felt kind of lonesome. On Shabbos, Malka dines upstairs with the Rosenbachs: Mrs Rosenbach, Mr Solomon Rosenbach, and Mirele, who is Mr Solomon's little sister. (I've only caught glimpses of her, but she wears perfectly sweet frilly clothes. It takes hours to iron them.) Mrs Rosenbach's husband is in New York with her other son, David. It turns out that Mr Rosenbach owns a department store – Malka was *affronted* when I told her I'd never heard of Rosenbach's Department Store. There is also a married daughter, Anna, who comes to Shabbos supper when her husband is away and brings her two spoiled children – that is, Malka says they're spoiled. She was there, too.

So I ate dinner by myself. Malka filled a generous plate for me, but I wasn't at the feast. I was a kind of Gentile Cinderella. Upstairs there was candlelight, and wine in shining glasses, not to mention my sponge cake, but there I was, alone in the kitchen. If I'd had a book to prop up beside my plate, I wouldn't have felt a bit lonely. But as it was, I kept thinking of how much my feet hurt. I kept glancing at all the dishes on the sideboard. Once Shabbos starts, Malka can't do any dishes, because it's work, but Mrs Rosenbach says it's all right for me to do them, because I'm not Jewish.

After I finished the dishes, I tidied the kitchen and swept the floor, and now I'm upstairs, feeling melancholy. I think I'm homesick. I never thought I would be that, but when I think of Miss Chandler, my o'ercharged heart seems to swell. I miss the country: the fresh air and the birdsong in the morning. I miss the food. Malka's a good cook, but her meals are all spicy and rich, and my stomach longs for something *plain*. I miss ham, but ham is *treif*, which means the Jews aren't allowed to eat it. And I miss starting the day with a glass of real milk. The city milk tastes kind of faded. There's no life in it.

I miss Mark, a little. But not very much, because I'm still mad at him for not taking up for me. I imagine Mark'll get stuck looking after my chickens. I'm glad of that, because he'll take good care of them. I wonder if anyone will think to pick the hornworms off my tomatoes. Malka has a little patch of garden out back, but her tomatoes are spindly and poor-looking – I'd be ashamed of tomatoes like that, but she seems to think they're thriving.

What I miss most of all is my books. Jane Eyre and Florence Dombey – they were like my sisters. And I wish I had *Ivanhoe* again, because there are still many things I don't understand about the Jews.

Today was a downright awful day. I woke up feeling prickly and queasy, with a familiar pain in my stomach. I felt outraged, because I didn't want all *that* again. But of course, there's no way out of it. It seems to me that God was very hard on Eve, punishing her so cruelly just for eating an apple. He wasn't nearly as strict with Adam. I don't think it was fair. But that is probably a wicked thing to write, and not refined.

I put on my chocolate-colored dress, because what else is there for me to put on? That frets me, too, because in spite of my best efforts, that dress is beginning to smell. Last week I thought if I could only please Malka and win my right to work here, I'd be content. Now it seems I'm likely to stay, but I'm as full of worries as a hive is full of bees. Nagging, buzzing, stinging worries they are, too.

On top of that, the weather was perfectly awful. It was very hot and damp with a white sky, which is my least favorite weather in the world.

After I finished the breakfast dishes, Malka told me Mrs Rosenbach said that I could have Sunday mornings off so I could attend church. I ought to have been grateful, but I wasn't. It isn't that I don't want to go to church, but if my only time off is to be Sunday mornings, I'll never go anywhere *but* church. I won't be able to visit a library or a picture gallery, and all the stores will be closed.

However, since I had the morning off, I thought I'd better take it. I put on my hat and gloves and went out. Malka said there was a Catholic church nearby, and she told me where it was but I got lost. The streets were so hot my head ached, and the sight of families in their Sunday clothes made me feel lonesome and sour and envious.

I tried to work out whether I could tell Mrs Rosenbach that I wanted a different day off, and how I could bring up the question of my salary. Thinking about it got me worried, because in *Ivanhoe* the Jews have a lot of money, but they're very close with it, though Rebecca isn't, of course. Sir Walter Scott says that the Jews have a great *love of gain*. I began to worry that Mrs Rosenbach might not give me any money. It would be a sneaking, stingy thing to do, to make a poor girl work all week and then not give her any wages.

I can't think – I don't *want* to think – the Rosenbachs are like that. Mr Solomon was very good to me, and anyone can see that Mrs Rosenbach is a real lady. And Malka's not stingy. There are little money boxes all over the house, charities for the poor Jews and immigrants and orphans. Malka's always putting coins in them. But then, it isn't Malka who'll be paying my salary.

I soon grew tired of walking in the heat, so I came back to Eutaw Place. Malka had passed the morning making a big *kugel* (which is a kind of noodle pudding) for Sunday dinner. I could tell she was proud of it, so I said it looked beautiful, but I secretly hoped I wouldn't have to eat any, because it was full of raisins and I hate raisins, always have. Of course she spooned a big helping onto my plate, and I had to worry it down. She saw that I wasn't eating very fast, and I had to confess that I didn't like raisins. I was careful to say how delicious the *kugel* was; it was only the raisins that I didn't like.

But that wasn't good enough. Touchy old Malka was offended and said that raisins were a treat, and who did I think I was, to turn up my nose at them? Then I had to listen to a long story about when she was a little girl, when her Mama – only, she pronounces it *Mah-meh* – would give her a handful of raisins on Shabbos as a special treat. I had to hear about what a good girl she was, not spoiled, like young people today. Before I'd heard the end of that, Mrs Rosenbach came down to the kitchen to tell Malka that she was going out and to remind her that she's having her bridge ladies for luncheon on Wednesday. She said she wanted Malka to serve oyster patties.

Then Malka just about *threw a fit*, because oysters are *treif*. She said that over her dead body would oyster patties be cooked in her kitchen (which made a very strange picture come into my mind). Then Mrs Rosenbach turned steely and said that it wasn't Malka's kitchen at all, but hers. I suppose that was her way of reminding Malka that she (Malka) is only a servant, and that if she (Mrs Rosenbach) wanted oyster patties, then she (Malka) would have to cook them. Then Mrs Rosenbach swept out of the room and Malka dissolved in tears. The whole time we were cleaning up the kitchen, she was sniffing and muttering. I tried to sympathize, but she was still angry with me about the *kugel*. Somehow, because I hadn't eaten the raisins, I was on the same side as Mrs Rosenbach, wanting to serve *treif* in a good Jewish home.

Presently I gave up trying to mollify her and just mopped the floor. After I finished, Malka said that since the family was going out, I could go upstairs and lie down. (Earlier I'd told her what was the matter with me. I had to tell her because of the laundry.) She added in a tremulous voice that no doubt I was tired of listening to her.

Well, as a matter of fact, I *was*. But of course I didn't say so. I thanked her and went upstairs. I had no notion of going to my room, though – the attic is hot as blazes in the afternoon. I headed straight for the library.

I've been cleaning the library all week, but Malka's always been at my side, so I haven't been able to snatch more than a peek at the books. I declare, I'm starved for the sight of print. Most of the books are in glass cases, but the books I wanted to examine are too big to fit in a case. The covers are brown and maroon leather, stamped with gold, and the title of the volumes is *The Picturesque World*. When Malka's back was turned, I opened the front cover – the inside cover was watered silk – and looked at the title page.

It's a book about all the beautiful places in the world: cathedrals and grottoes and palaces and parks. There are more than a thousand pictures, and the writing has *Authentic and Original Descriptions by the Best Authors.* It says so right on the title page. I knew that reading that book would take me into another world – the *real* world, not the ordinary world of washing the dishes and mopping the floor. It would be like what Keats said about gazing through a magic casement into *faery lands forlorn.*

So of course I was wild to read it. Miss Chandler used to say that beauty could ennoble mankind, and maybe that book would ennoble me. Or edify me: that's another word she used to use. I think I'd rather be ennobled than edified. It sounds loftier.

I thought the Rosenbachs were out, because I'd heard the front door shut. The house was full of a Sunday hush. I opened the library doors without a sound.

My heart leaped. Mr Solomon was in the room. He sat at his desk with his back to me – there are two desks in the library, one for Mr Rosenbach, and one for Mr Solomon. His head was bent over a big book, and he was muttering to himself.

I stood stock-still. The truth is, I've been wanting to talk to Mr Solomon all week, but our paths haven't crossed. That's odd, when you think about it, because we're living under the same roof. I guess it shows how great a gulf stands between a servant girl and her master.

I knew I should withdraw, because that was what a proper servant ought to do. But I didn't. I stood with my hand on the cut-glass doorknob. I think I was hoping that he'd sense my presence and turn his head and smile at me.

But he didn't. And for some reason, I couldn't bring myself to speak. I don't know how long I stayed there and gazed at him across the carpet. I found myself looking at the carpet, and the mantel, and everything. It's a fine carpet; I run the carpet sweeper over it every morning. I dust the mantelpiece, which is marble, and the Chinese vases, which have butterflies on them. I reckon I know the things in that room better than Mr Solomon does, because when you clean things, you see them up close. But at that moment, the room belonged to him: books, vases, carpet, and all. I didn't belong there.

Mr Solomon kept muttering. I think he was reading a prayer book, because the muttering wasn't in English. What I've caught on to is that Jews are like Catholics and pray in a foreign language, which is Hebrew. I knew I shouldn't disturb a man at his prayers. I was afraid Mr Solomon would see me there, and afraid he wouldn't.

There was a flash of movement. The Thomashefsky cat had been asleep in the green chair, but he stood up and jumped off, landing with a thud. He crossed the carpet and went straight to Mr Solomon, making a little friendly chirping noise.

Mr Solomon said softly, "Ah, Thomas! Am I neglecting you? Do you need petting, you poor morsel?" He leaned sideways so he could stroke the cat. I could hear Thomashefsky purring all the way across the room.

I closed the door slowly, so the latch wouldn't click. I felt hot and prickly all over.

Now that I write this, I believe I was jealous. For one thing, I've *never* managed to stroke that cat. He always ducks under my hand. And I'm aggravated, because here I am in a place of culture and refinement, but I'm only allowed to dust the books, not to read them. I'm mad at myself for wanting Mr Solomon to notice me, and I'm mad at him for ignoring me, as if I were invisible.

I shut myself in my room and took off my dress. I tried to take a nap, but there was a fly in the room. Every time I was on the point of falling asleep, the fly would light on me. I tried to swat it, but it buzzed away. At last I got up and found my book.

It's too hot to write any more.

Monday, July the tenth, 1911

I am so *ashamed*. I'm just *boiling* with shame, because of what I wrote about the Jews having a great love of gain. I *am* to be paid, and handsomely. I'm to earn six dollars a week! My days off will be Sunday mornings and Tuesday afternoons, unless Mrs Rosenbach is entertaining.

Mrs Rosenbach sent for me this morning. I felt rather nervous. I wanted to broach the subject of my wages, but I hadn't figured out how. Everything I thought to say seemed so crude.

Mrs Rosenbach began by saying that I had done very well. She had feared that Malka would be prejudiced against a Gentile. But it seems that Malka – oh, dear, kind Malka! (I wish I hadn't insulted her kugel!) – says that I am hardworking and honest and willing. Mrs Rosenbach said she was surprised by how Malka took to me. I was tempted to tell her that Malka isn't so bad; she just wants someone to make her laugh and listen to her stories – and of course do *every single thing* she says, *exactly* the way she says it, which I do.

Then it occurred to me that it might be better if Mrs Rosenbach went on thinking that Malka was almost impossible to work with. So I smiled mysteriously, as if I had some power over Malka that no other hired girl could ever possess.

After that, Mrs Rosenbach talked about her plans for me. I am to be a parlormaid. She asked if I had any objection to wearing a cap. She explained that a lot of girls won't wear a cap because it makes them look like a servant. I said, "Well, ma'am, I *am* a servant." Now that I think it over, it strikes me that I must have seemed right humble and innocent when I said that. Mostly I don't seem either of those things, because I'm too tall. Then Mrs Rosenbach mentioned the six dollars a week, and I breathed a sigh of relief.

Mrs Rosenbach told me that from now on, she wants me to answer the front door. That's to spare Malka's legs. Mrs Rosenbach says the steps that go from the kitchen to the first floor are awfully steep, and last winter Malka was rushing to answer the doorbell and fell. Luckily she fell up the stairs, not down them, but Mrs Rosenbach worries. That's why she comes downstairs to discuss meals. It just goes to show how fine Mrs Rosenbach is, because in the normal course of things, a servant should come upstairs when her mistress summons her. But Mrs Rosenbach puts her respect for age and infirmity above her status.

She suggested that I should take on some of the cooking on Saturdays. I will be a Shabbos goy, which is a Christian who does the work that Jews aren't supposed to do on Shabbos.

Then Mrs Rosenbach indicated a cardboard box on the sofa. It had an emblem on it – two wavy lines like a stream, and a prancing horse, and the words ROSENBACH'S DEPARTMENT STORE in beautiful copperplate. She said that it was customary for servants to pay for their own uniforms, but that seemed unduly harsh "in view of the fact that I had to leave home precipitously." For a moment I didn't understand, but then I saw she meant that I'd had to run away from home because Father was beating me, except that he wasn't. She went on to say that as I would be greeting her guests, she wanted me to be more formally attired.

Now, that shows how refined she is, because look at the things she didn't say! She didn't mention the fact that I've been wearing the same ugly dress for more than a week, or hint that I'm not presentable enough for her friends. And she didn't insinuate that I was too poor to buy my own uniforms. Now that I think it over, I feel a little guilty, because I'm not as penniless as she thinks. I have my Belinda money. But while she was talking to me, so gravely and politely, I honestly forgot about the Belinda money. I *felt* penniless.

All that time, I was aching to see what my new uniforms would look like. At last Mrs Rosenbach waved her hand in a way that gave me permission to open the box, and she added that she had taken the liberty of putting in a packet of long hairpins, because long pins are more effective with thick hair. I guess she's noticed that my hair keeps tumbling down.

I thanked her and opened the box. Tissue paper, thin as rose petals, and two uniforms – well, really they are housedresses, but they are so pretty! They're cotton but they feel satin-smooth and fresh and crisp; they're better quality cotton than any I've ever worn. And they smell so new – that clean cotton smell, which is almost like milk. Both dresses are blue, because blue is economical and doesn't fade quickly. One dress is a cool-morning-sky blue with a pattern of white ferns on it. The other is closer to a robin's-egg blue, with tiny sprays of buttercups and pink rosebuds. Both uniforms have white Dutch collars and cuffs that unbutton, so the sleeves roll up.

Then there were two darling white aprons, with ruffles over the shoulders, so starchy and pure looking, and two funny, frilly little caps – Mrs Rosenbach gambled on the fact that I wouldn't be too proud to wear them. Underneath the dress aprons was a big canvas apron, dark gray, which will be good for scrubbing. And the little packet of hairpins, none of them rusted.

I could scarcely contain my excitement, seeing those dresses. I kept holding them up and exclaiming and pointing out each detail to Mrs Rosenbach. I guess it was too much, because her mouth turned down at the corners the way Ma's did when I was a little thing and carried on about something or other. It was a tenderhearted look, but more superior in Mrs Rosenbach's case. She said I'd need a black uniform for formal wear, but she'd provide that, too. She added that she was sure I'd want to shop for other things, and she hoped I would consider buying them at Rosenbach's Department Store.

That reminded her to tell me that her husband is coming home on Thursday, which I already knew, because Malka told me. Malka worships the ground Mr Rosenbach walks on. His first name is Moritz, and Malka likes to call him her little Moritz. I hope he won't be a domestic tyrant like Father. I don't think anybody ever called Father little Josiah. Perhaps that's what's wrong with him.

When Mrs Rosenbach was explaining how to get to Rosenbach's Department Store – I haven't taken a streetcar yet, and I can't wait – my tongue got the better of me and I blurted out a question. I asked her if there were books in Rosenbach's Department Store.

Mrs Rosenbach said curtly, "You must not interrupt me, Janet." I felt ever so sorry – interrupting when she'd been so kind – and I said so all in a rush. I explained that I was just starving for something to read. Then I realized I'd interrupted her twice in a row. I clapped my hands over my mouth.

She said, "I'm sure you don't mean to be rude, Janet, but I'm afraid you're rather impetuous." I nodded agreement and tried to look penitent – though I like the idea of being impetuous. It sounds like a heroine. I'd rather be impetuous than placid any day.

After a moment she relented. "My husband's store has an excellent selection of books," she said. Then her brows came together. "Though you may find them costly. They're hardcover books, not dime novels."

I saw in a flash what she meant. She thought because I was a servant, I'd want to read trash. It made me hot under the collar – I guess I *am* impetuous. "I'm not in the market for dime novels," I said haughtily. "I don't think

I would find them edifying or ennobling."

I think maybe I shouldn't have said the *ennobling* part. Mrs Rosenbach's mouth twitched as if she wanted to laugh. Only for a minute, though. Then she said, "I beg your pardon, Janet. I had forgotten your fondness for *Ivanhoe*. If you're interested in reading the classics, you might borrow from our library."

"Might I?" I exclaimed. I think Mrs Rosenbach might have regretted her kindness then, because she went on to say that reading mustn't interfere with my duties, and that the books mustn't be taken down to the kitchen, where they might get soiled, and that I should borrow only one at a time.

I assured her that I would treat her books with the greatest possible care. I promised that I'd make sure my hands were extra clean, and that I would never, never stretch the bindings or dog-ear the pages.

She rose and went into the library. When she came back, she had a book in her hand. It was bound in black leather, with the title in gold: DANIEL DERONDA. It was the kind of book that has a silk ribbon inside, to serve as a bookmark. I love those silk ribbons.

"Perhaps this will edify you," she said, and she handed it to me with a smile that was both sphinx-like and motherly kind.

Today I spoke to Mr Solomon. It wasn't one bit the way I'd imagined it would be. In the sacred privacy of these pages, I've written how I hoped to see him again. Ever since he rescued me, he's seemed like a hero to me, and I've been waiting to thank him. Also – oh, accursed vanity, I should blush to write these words, but they are true! – I've wanted *him* to see *me*. The bruise on my forehead has faded, and my new clothes make me look ever so much prettier.

I thought I was looking my best this morning. I had on the blue print with the rosebuds, and my apron was starched and pressed. I was going up the stairs and Mr Solomon was coming down. (I shouldn't have been on the front staircase, but I forgot.)

It reminded me of the night of the party in *Jane Eyre*, when Mr Rochester spoke to Jane on the stairs, except that Mr Solomon scarcely glanced at me. I ventured, "Good morning, sir."

He looked a little startled. Then he smiled. "Good morning –" he paused – "Jane. It is Jane, isn't it?"

"No, sir," I said, "it's Janet." And I guess I seemed crestfallen, because he looked contrite.

"Janet," he corrected himself. "Of course. I understand you're doing well."

"Thank you, sir," I said, and I launched into the

speech I'd planned for him. It was all about how he'd rescued me, like one of King Arthur's knights, and how grateful I was, and how I'd vowed to mention his name in my prayers every night. I tried to express my thanks in elegant phrases, so that he'd understand that even though I'm a hired girl, I'm not just a hired girl.

But I forgot the beginning of my speech. I plunged into the middle, and had to go back and stick the beginning back in. I could feel my face getting red. The awful thing was that I could tell that Mr Solomon wanted me to stop talking. He looked as awkward as I felt. "I'm glad everything's worked out so well," he said when I paused for breath. "For your sake, and for Malka's." And with that, he brushed past me and went down the stairs.

For my sake, and for Malka's. That's when the truth sank in: to Mr Solomon, I'm just a servant like Malka. In fact, I'm much less to him than Malka is, because he's known Malka all his life. He's her pet among the Rosenbach children, and she calls him *Shlomo;* Malka's almost like his grandmother. But I'm just a servant. The dress that made me feel so pretty is a servant's dress.

I felt like thirty cents. I guess I'd had some fool idea in my head that the way we met, with him rescuing me, would forge a link between us. I'd started to think that Mr Solomon was a little bit like Mr Rochester. Well, he isn't, and that's all there is to it. Mr Rochester knew that Jane Eyre was his equal, even though she was a governess.

But when Mr Solomon looks at me, all he sees is a hired girl. He even forgot my name!

I watched him descend the stairs, and I noticed something. The hair on top of Mr Solomon's head is getting a little bit thin. He's going to have a bald spot there. I didn't know that a man so young could be losing his hair. I wonder if he knows. The idea that he might not suspect makes me feel a little bit sorry for him. It seems very melancholy. Of course, a bald spot wouldn't matter if he were more like Mr Rochester, but—

Altogether it was very unsettling.

Thursday, July the thirteenth, 1911

Today was busy with shopping and getting ready for the return of Mr Rosenbach – Mrs Rosenbach's husband, that is, not Mr Solomon. Malka was determined that the master should have all his favorite foods. She sent me to the market three times to get things she'd forgotten – allspice for red cabbage, Jamaica ginger for the beef, and peaches for dessert. In the midst of all this, the child Mirele complained of a sore throat and asked for a tray of cinnamon toast. It seems that cinnamon toast is invalid's fare in the Rosenbach household. Malka was exasperated because she said Mirele was no more sick than she was, but she had me make the toast and carry up the tray.

I wasn't sorry to be sent upstairs, because I'm curious about Mirele, who seems to do nothing but change her clothes and play with her friends in Druid Hill Park. I iron her dresses and tidy her room, and the one thing I know for sure about her is that she's a slob. Of course *slob* isn't a very refined word, but *slatternly* is too harsh. And in fact, the child isn't slatternly; she is dainty in her person, but her room is the room of a slob. It's nothing to find her hairbrush in her unmade bed and orange peels all over the dresser.

I found little Miss Rosenbach in bed. She wore a summer nightdress decorated with pale-green ribbons, and she was playing solitaire.

"Oh, good," said Mirele, reaching for the tray. "I'm famished. You can put the tray on the bed."

I didn't want to. Those sheets were changed on Tuesday, and I didn't want them full of crumbs and sugar grit. I coaxed, "Wouldn't you be more comfortable at your desk, Miss?"

"No," answered Mirele promptly. "I like eating in bed. When you're sick, you get to have cinnamon toast in bed. That's part of the fun."

I sighed and put down the tray, but Mirele had no intention of letting me leave. "Sit down and talk to me," she commanded.

"I can't," said I. "Malka needs me in the kitchen."

"If you leave, you'll have to climb the stairs to take

the tray back," Mirele pointed out. "It's easier if you stay. It won't take me long to eat two slices of toast. Stingy old Malka, I wanted three. I'm glad you're here, because I want someone to talk to. Are you really eighteen? Mama says if you're a day over sixteen, she'll eat her hat. Are you sixteen?"

"No," I said, with perfect truth. "Your mother's mistaken."

"I'm twelve," she said, and took a gulp of milk.

I stared because she didn't look twelve. She might have been ten or even nine, she was so tiny. It was funny to think she was only two years younger. "I guess you're small for your age," I said.

"Yes. It's good in a way," Mirele explained. "People treat me like a baby, but I get away with more. I don't believe you're eighteen years old. You played with my doll-house, didn't you?"

I had, actually. It was more cleaning than playing, but I'll admit it: I've never seen anything like that doll-house. It's four feet tall, with three floors full of perfect miniature furniture: needlepoint carpets, and cunning little chairs upholstered in striped silk, and a kitchen full of tiny willowware plates stuck with cardboard food. I could never have imagined such an elaborate and expensive toy. If it had been mine – when I was little, I mean – I'd have kept it in apple-pie order.

But Mirele is a slob, and her dollhouse is a mess. That's

a problem for me, because the house has only three walls and you can see inside. The first time I cleaned Mirele's room, I stood in the doorway and checked to make sure I hadn't missed anything. My gaze fell on that dollhouse: a pigsty and an eyesore. The dolls were lying on the floor like drunkards, and the chairs were tipped over, and the dolly beds weren't made – the little quilts and pillows were all over the floor.

I couldn't stand it, so I put it to rights. It didn't take five minutes, and that was the fun of it – you could clean a whole mansion in five minutes. I made the little beds and rearranged the furniture and set the dolls in chairs so that they looked comfortable. And the next day – well, I guess it was silly – I cut up a tiny section of Malka's Yiddish newspaper so the papa doll could have something to read. He did look comical, sitting with that newspaper. After that – well, I allow myself one little change every day. Once I put the baby doll in the bathtub, with the mother kneeling next to him – I rolled up her sleeves to the elbows. Another time I made the china cat sleep on top of the piano. The Thomashefsky cat does that, and I think it's cute.

I guess I do play with the dollhouse, just a little. It makes cleaning that sloppy room more interesting.

"It looked awful the way it was," I defended myself. Then I remembered that I was a hired girl and added, "Miss."

"Don't call me *Miss*," said Mirele. "We're not very formal here, in case you haven't noticed. I want you to call me Mimi. That's what my friends call me."

"Malka calls you Mirele."

"That's Yiddish. We all know a little Yiddish, because of Malka bringing up Papa, but Yiddish is vulgar, Mama says. She prefers *Hochdeutsch*. That means High German. My real name is Miriam, but I like Mimi better. I'm like the girl in the opera." She put down her toast, clasped her hands, and sang in a small, true voice. " '*I call myself Mimi!*' Have you ever been to the opera?"

"No, but I'm going to, someday. And a Russian ballet, too."

"I'll call you Janet, because we're almost the same age," she said. She took a wolfish bite of toast. "Mmmm." Then she began to gobble.

While she ate her toast, I took the opportunity to look at her. Nobody looks her best when she's chewing, and I tried to take that into account, but even if you subtracted the chewing, Mirele Rosenbach was no beauty. She was small and nimble and wore her frilly clothes beautifully. But she had freckles, and her features weren't regular. The lower part of her face came forward in a way that reminded me of a monkey. Her mouth was wide, and her little white teeth were crooked. Though her hair was curly, it was a disorganized kind of curly that made her look windblown.

And yet, if she wasn't pretty, *she* didn't know it. She spoke and walked and moved her hands as if she were bewitchingly pretty. And for some reason, it was hard to take your eyes off her. I guess a novel would have said it was the *play* of her features. She was lively; she was animated; her lips curved with mischief, and her small eyes sparkled.

I wonder if my features ever play. I bet they don't.

I waited for her to finish her toast so that I could carry the tray downstairs. She set down her milk glass and said, "You do your hair too tight. It makes your ears stick out."

I agreed with her. The new hairpins are good; my knot of hair no longer lurches or tumbles down. But those little caps aren't becoming, and my ears look funny sticking out below.

"It's not really your ears," Mirele said, with belated tact. "They're all right. It's the way you do your hair. I'll show you." She slid out of bed and went to fetch her brush and comb. "Sit down. I love doing hair. I'm good at it. It won't take a minute, and you'll look ever so much better."

I thought of Malka downstairs, but the temptation was too great. I sat down and let Mirele – Mimi – pluck off my cap. Never for a moment did I doubt that she would be better at arranging hair than I was. Skillfully she brushed and puffed and coiled. In a matter of seconds, my hair was a burnished crown, and my ears looked smaller.

"That's better," Mimi said judiciously. "You need to grab the hair like a rope, and let your hand slide up, down ... twist, puff, and pin. It makes all the difference, having your hair nice. You have good eyes and a pretty complexion and your bruises are fading. I think your father is just terrible. I complain about Papa, but he would never, never strike me. He never even spanked me when I was little."

"Then why do you complain?" I shouldn't have asked, but it was hard for me to remember that I was the hired girl when Mimi didn't seem to.

"Because he wants me to study all the time – and I de-test reading. It makes my head ache. Even during the summer, when I ought to have some peace, he makes me read." She went to her desk and picked up a stack of books. "Papa gave me these before he left. He told me I had to read one of them. *Little Women* and *Black Beauty* and *Huckleberry Finn*. They're all dreadfully long, and *Huckleberry Finn* isn't even written in proper English. He left me arithmetic, too." She held up a much-smeared page of sums. "Geography and spelling, and German and Hebrew – Hebrew's impossible; I'll never be able to learn it. Did your papa make you learn such awful stuff?"

"No," I said regretfully, "my father didn't want me to learn anything."

"How heavenly!" breathed Mimi. "When Papa comes tonight, he'll want me to show him my arithmetic and tell him about one of those books. He'll be so disappointed in me! I can't bear it. That's why I pretended to be sick. He can't be cross if I'm sick, and if I'm left alone, I can do some of these stupid sums."

"Will he believe you're really sick? Malka knew you weren't."

"Malka thinks I'm spoiled," Mimi said, which is just what Malka does think. "She says each of us is more spoiled than the last. I'm the youngest, so I'm the worst. Anna and Solly are good, and me and David are bad. Though Solly might be in trouble with Papa, too."

"Why?" I asked rashly. I shouldn't have gossiped, but it seemed as though the little minx would tell me every-thing, and I did so want to know.

"Because Papa expects him to learn the business at the store, but all Solly wants to do is to study Talmud. Solly hasn't told him. He doesn't want to disappoint Papa. None of us do. That's how Papa is. Papa's very Reform, and it isn't Reform to study Talmud. Papa says there's wisdom in it, but there's also a lot of medieval superstition—"

"What's Talmud?"

"It's writings about the Torah—" She looked at me with her head on one side. "You don't know what the Torah is, do you?"

I admitted that I didn't.

"It's all right," she said kindly. "Maisie Phillips didn't know either, and she's my second-best friend. She's a

Gentile, too. The Torah's the five books of Moses." She counted them on her fingers. "Genesis, Exodus, Leviticus, Deuteronomy, and Numbers. About a thousand rabbis decided to write everything they could think of about the Torah, and that's Talmud. There are forty-two volumes of it. And Solly wants to study it. He *loves* it. And Nora Himmelrich – that's the other thing he loves."

I echoed, "Nora Himmelrich?" My mind was awhirl. I'd never thought of Mr Solomon being in love.

"He's dead stuck on her," said Mimi. "She's very pretty and very rich, but I don't think she'll have him. If he took over the store, that would be one thing. But I don't think she'll marry him if he's nothing but a scholar."

I thought that was sad. I'd never heard the phrase "dead stuck on" before, but I guessed what it meant, even though I didn't think it was a very poetic way of putting things. "Doesn't she love him?"

Mimi shrugged. "With her looks, she could marry anybody. Of course, Solly's nice," she added quickly, "though my other brother – David – has more go in him. I'm never getting married, myself."

"Neither am I," I said. I wasn't thinking; it just came out.

She gazed at me with interest. "Won't you, though? I'm the only girl I know who doesn't want to get married. It's not that I don't like men – well, of course, they're only boys now, because I'm twelve. Mama says I'm too young to think about boys. But if I were really too young, I wouldn't think about them, would I? It's interesting to see if I can make them notice me, and the funny thing is, I *can*. Lotty Lewisohn and Maisie Phillips are heaps better looking than I am, but the boys like me better. I think I'll be a belle when I'm grown up. I'll let the men take me to dances and send flowers and all that. But nothing else. I won't marry them."

"Why not?"

"Because it's dull," she said, very firmly. "Like Anna. She was never very much fun, but now that she's married, she's too dull for words. Half the time, her husband's away on business, and she has these awful babies. Oskar is my nephew – he's *really* awful – and baby Irma does nothing but cry and spit up. I know it's not nice to talk about spitting up, but both of Anna's babies were born with something the matter with their stomachs, and *all they do* is spit up. And all Anna does is worry about them and change her clothes and wipe down the walls. That's not how I want to spend my life." She stopped for breath. "What about you? Why won't you get married?"

I thought about Father and Ma. "Because I don't like being bullied," I answered. "And I want my own money. I want my own home and my own job. I guess I want my whole life for my own."

"But your whole life is being a hired girl," Mimi protested. "Don't you hate being a servant?"

"I won't always be a servant."

"What will you be, then?"

"A teacher," I said, but she wasn't impressed. In fact, she rolled her eyes and moaned. "Or maybe a great writer, like Charlotte Brontë. What are you going to be?"

"A concert pianist," said Mimi. "Maybe. I'd rather sing opera, but my voice isn't very big. But I could be a concert pianist – except I hate practicing – and wear beautiful dresses and be very famous. Or I could be an actress, like Sarah Bernhardt. She's a Jewess, you know. She's Catholic, but her mother was a Jewess, so she's really a Jew. Or I could run Rosenbach's Department Store. I'd like that. Solly won't take over the store, and I don't believe David will, either. Why can't girls run department stores?"

"I don't know," I said, "but if you're going to run a department store, you're going to have to learn arithmetic."

She wrinkled her nose at me. "That was a low-down, grown-up thing to say," she said accusingly. "How would you like it if you had to do this horrible arithmetic? I bet you couldn't." She shoved her paper in my direction.

I took it. The sums weren't difficult; there were long columns of large numbers, but it was simple addition, nothing more. "I could do it with one hand tied behind me. And the first one's wrong. You carried the numbers in the wrong column."

She made a noise like *ffffttttt* and snatched the paper

out of my hands. Her cheeks were pink, and I was sorry I'd been so boastful, because I saw that she was ashamed. Then her face lit up. "I know what! If you'll do my sums for me, I'll give you a quarter."

I shook my head. "That wouldn't be honorable." I've never been offered a bribe before, and I must say it made me feel superior to decline it. Of course, she only offered me a quarter. I might have been tempted to sell my integrity for a great fortune, but I'd certainly never sell it for a quarter.

Then I relented. "I could help you with your arithmetic," I offered. "It isn't difficult. It's just facts. Once you know your numbers—"

"I do know them!" she said irritably. "I can say them; I just can't get them right on the paper. Oh, now, don't get cross and leave—" because I had picked up the tray and was halfway to the door. "We were getting on so well! If you must teach me, I suppose I could put up with a little of it – only you'll have to let me try new things with your hair. I think we should be friends. Neither of us wants to get married, and I'm interested in you. I bet you'd like to have a friend your own age, wouldn't you?"

"You're not my age," I said. But I was taken aback. It was uncanny how easily she seemed to see inside me. I had enjoyed talking to another girl. "I'm eighteen, remember? That's six years older than you."

"All right, so you're eighteen," Mimi said impatiently.

"We'll agree on that. But we're still both girls, and neither of us is going to get married. Will you agree to call me Mimi, and be my friend?"

I smiled at her; I couldn't help it. "Mimi," I answered, like a promise, and I was still smiling as I went downstairs.

Friday, July the fourteenth, 1911

Another long day preparing for Shabbos, and more fancy cooking in honor of Mr Rosenbach. My feet ache. I can't imagine how Malka's feet must hurt – she has a terrible bunion. She's been surprisingly cheerful these past few days – I suppose because her little Moritz is home, and she likes spoiling him with all his favorite foods.

I have seen her little Moritz. He's a Bantam rooster of a man – short and stout and loud. He always seems to be shouting. I can't distinguish the words, but the sound thunders and reverberates. No wonder Mimi is worried about doing badly at school. And no wonder Mr Solomon is afraid to tell his father that he wants to be a scholar.

I wonder if all fathers are tyrants.

I feel for Mr Solomon, because now that I know he's in love, I notice things I hadn't seen before. For example, he is absentminded and leaves books all over the house – some of them in Hebrew and German, but also books of poetry. Malka fussed one night because he forgot to change for dinner and came in his regular clothes. I didn't think anything of it at the time, but now I can see that these are signs of lovesickness. True lovers are careless like that. Either they dandify themselves, like Mr Toots in *Dombey and Son*, or they forget what they have on.

I think Miss Himmelrich is cruel and shallow to despise her true lover because he doesn't want to run a department store. Perhaps she's like Gwendolen in *Daniel Deronda*, who is beautiful and heartless. I think I'd like to be beautiful and heartless for a while, just to see what it's like. It must be very heady to wear lace and pearls and have men admire you but not pay any heed to them. I would be mocking and capricious and *wild*. But that is the kind of behavior a girl can only get away with if she's beautiful.

I'm afraid I'm going to have very dull love affairs when I'm grown up – that is, if I have any. If any man ever falls in love with me, he's going to be one of the dull ones; I just know it. Likely it's indelicate for me to think about love affairs, but pretending to be eighteen is making me grow up very fast. I'm afraid Miss Chandler would think I'm growing up *too* fast and that the Rosenbachs are worldly. I know it would sadden her that Mimi talks slang. She used to say that it's one thing for a young man to talk slang, but it's unwomanly for a young girl. All the same, I can't help liking Mimi. On my next day off, she's going to show me how to catch the streetcar to Rosenbach's

Department Store. She wants me to buy a wire rat for my hair so we can try out a new style. I think it's ever so kind of her, but I don't know what Mrs Rosenbach would say about her daughter going out with the hired girl. Mimi says her mother won't mind, but I think Malka might, so I haven't exactly mentioned it to her.

I am *so* tired tonight. When I first came here, I thought the housework would be easy, because of not having the laundry to do, or sweeping out the ashes from the stove, or cleaning the privy. And it *is* easier, and far less dirty. I'm getting the knack of managing the gas stove and the electric iron, and it's ever so much quicker to clean the carpets with a carpet sweeper instead of a dustpan and broom. When I finish cleaning, things look *nice*, which is so satisfying and so different from the farm.

But in some ways, there's more work to do, because Malka is so particular. The house is bigger – so many stairs – and we sweep and straighten and dust every morning. The city air is dirty, so the extra dusting is necessary. Then, downstairs, the food is fancier and there's *kashrut* to consider. There's tons more ironing, because the Rosenbachs change for dinner every night. And every week there's Shabbos, which is like spring cleaning and Thanksgiving dinner put together.

Tomorrow I'm cooking breakfast – hot muffins, salmon cakes, plus peaches with cream, because Mr Rosenbach likes them. I'm not worried about anything but the fish. I'm afraid of overcooking it. Malka says she can't watch and tell me how long to cook the cakes because that would be working on Shabbos, and anyone who thinks keeping an eye on me isn't work doesn't know from nothing.

Sunday, July the sixteenth, 1911

Today I made my way to Corpus Christi Church, which is very beautiful – the sublime cathedrals in *The Picturesque World* are not more lovely than Corpus Christi. I wore my blue-with-the-ferns uniform and puffed my hair the way Mimi taught me, but I felt very plain when I got to the church and saw all the well-dressed people getting out of their carriages and automobiles. (I often see automobiles here in Baltimore.) I had to remind myself that the church was God's house and He would want me to come to Mass; *He* wouldn't mind that Ma's old hat is a disgrace. But of course, I mind. I shall look at new hats on Tuesday.

Inside, the church is as bright as a jewel box. There are glorious stained-glass windows, saints and angels and crowns and goblets, all worked in cunning patterns. Even the floor is patterned, and there are gold mosaics on the walls, and candles burning, and the smell of incense. I remembered to genuflect when I went in – I didn't have to think about it; my hand went to my forehead and my knees bent. I knew I was in the *real* Church: one, holy, Catholic, and apostolic.

I'd forgotten about the Mass, though. Not how holy and awe-inspiring it is, but how much time you spend looking at the priest's back without knowing what he's saying. I need a missal, and that's one thing I'm afraid a Jewish department store isn't going to carry. Ma's missal was buried with her. She didn't have a Catholic funeral, so the night before she was buried I crept downstairs and slipped the missal into her coffin. I wanted God to know that she was a good Catholic, even if Father wouldn't allow a funeral Mass. That shows how childish I was, as if God has to look in all the coffins to see who's Catholic and who isn't. I guess He knows.

I wish I had that missal, though. I recognized the sound of the Latin words, but I didn't know what they meant. The priest was old and his voice didn't carry. I was wicked enough to be bored. Not the whole time, but every now and then I found myself wondering when the Mass would be over, just as I did when I was a child.

But there was plenty to look at. Above the altar there's a beautiful, sorrowful Crucifixion, and above that is a great stained-glass window: the Blessed Mother wearing a blue, blue dress. It's a blue that's hard to describe, because it's almost blue-black, but with the sun shining through it, it's like blue fire. Staring at that color, I felt mystified and at the same time contented, as if all I wanted on earth was to go on looking. When we see God face-to-face, we will be fascinated in just that way; I'm sure of it.

Only, my attention did wander after a while, even from the celestial beauty of that stained glass. I suppose that's because I'm full of sin. Since I couldn't follow the service, I silently thanked God for sending me to the Rosenbachs and guiding me to Corpus Christi. I prayed for Mr Solomon, and in a surge of noble renunciation I prayed that Nora Himmelrich might come to see his worth and love him. I prayed for Miss Chandler, and for Malka's bunion, and for all the Rosenbachs. I prayed for my brothers. It was a little bit of a wrench, because I'm still mad at them, but I felt better afterward.

I didn't pray for Father, though. I thought about him burning my books and felt such a surge of rage as I'm sure has no place in a Catholic church. I *can't* forgive him. I mean to replace those books as soon as I can, and if I'm lucky, I'll be able to find the same editions. But the new books won't have Miss Chandler's writing inside. They won't be the same.

After I prayed, I looked around at the church and tried not to notice the ladies' hats. There were some exquisite hats there, and my mind kept wandering to what they might have cost. I made myself stare down at my hands. Suddenly I remembered Ma. When I was little and sat beside her in church, she'd check my hands, and sometimes she'd see that my fingernails were dirty. She couldn't stand that. She'd slip off her gloves and seize my hand and dig under my fingernails with her own. It hurt dreadfully, but of course I couldn't cry out because we were in church. I would twist my mouth and glare at her.

I felt a great wave of love and grief when I remembered that. Dear Ma! She wanted everything fine for me: religion and clean fingernails and a good education. I still can't see how she managed to save up all that money and hide it from Father. She must have known that one day I would need to escape from him. Even after her death, she provided for me.

When the service was over, the priest said that anyone who wanted to stay could pray the rosary. I don't have rosary beads, but Ma taught me how to say the rosary on my fingers, so I stayed. I especially love the mystery of the Coronation of the Virgin, because I imagine the saints in colorful robes, and a blue starry sky, and Jesus smiling tenderly as He crowned His Mother's brow with roses.

After the rosary I knelt in the Lady Chapel and lit a candle and said a prayer for Ma, not that she needs it, because I am sure she's in heaven, not Purgatory. But I sent her my love. I imagined her looking down, tickled pink because I was in a real church and have a job that pays six dollars a week.

When I rose from my knees and started to walk out, I saw the priest. He'd changed from his vestments, but he nodded and smiled at me. Such a kind smile! I felt so happy as I left the church – happy and *purified*. I didn't even mind about my awful hat. (But I'm still going to replace it, because it really is too small and beat-up.)

It occurs to me that one of the best things about my new servitude is that people are pleased with me, and say so. Malka says I am a good, hard-working girl, and Mimi wants to be friends, and today the priest smiled at me. In my old life, nobody ever praised me except Miss Chandler. I hope this craving for approval doesn't mean I'm as vain as Gwendolen in *Daniel Deronda*. But even the Thomashefsky cat likes to be told how handsome he is – you can tell by the way he purrs and flexes his paws – and I sometimes wonder if every living thing doesn't need kind words as much as sunshine and water.

Monday, July the seventeenth, 1911

I'm sure I'm the unluckiest girl who ever lived! I'm so frightened and anxious – I'm writing this by moonlight – I won't be able to read a word of it, but I daren't light another candle. I can't sleep – I *must* pour out my feelings in this book. And oh, Malka is furious with me, and tomorrow Mr Rosenbach will shout at me, and after that, what can I expect but to be sent away?

I was reading in bed and *that's* not forbidden. Mrs Rosenbach said I might read after my work was done.

And Malka gives me a candle every night – she never fusses, no matter how quickly I use them up – oh, dear! I will never find another job like this one, where no one is sparing of candles! But it isn't forbidden to read – I was even reading the book Mrs Rosenbach gave me, which of course I ruined. My bad luck overflows even onto the books I read.

It was a good book, too. It turns out that *Daniel Deronda* is about Jews. At the beginning of the book, Daniel thinks he's an ordinary person, but I peeked at the end, and it turns out he's a Jew. But he doesn't mind one bit! Being Jewish means he can marry a beautiful Jewish girl named Mirah, who is noble like Rebecca but also small and delicate and pure like a child. I wish I were small and delicate and pure.

I was very caught up in the story, and I came to a part where the print was smudged. I took the chamberstick off the table by my bed and held it close to the page. Having the light near at hand made the page brighter, and I kept reading – but then my hair caught fire.

I knew I was in *mortal danger*. But I also knew what to do, because it isn't the first time my hair's caught fire. If you've had long braids all your life, well, every now and then your braid swings around and passes too close to the fire from the range. When that happens, you have to keep your wits about you and put out the fire as fast as ever you can.

Which I did. I threw down the book and flung myself off the bed onto the linoleum and slapped at the flames. And I seized the edge of the quilt and pressed it against my hair to extinguish the last sparks. Then I saw the book lying on the floor – I threw it down in such a way that the binding tore, but who can blame me? If your hair's on fire, you don't put in a bookmark and set the book down carefully. All the same, I felt a pang of remorse.

Afterward, I felt my hair, and I'd lost a little on the right side. The burned edges were crisp and harsh feeling, but nobody will know once my hair is up. The palms of my hands smarted, but they weren't blistered. It could have been so much worse. Then – just in the nick of time! – I remembered the candle I'd been reading by and – oh, horrors! – I'd dropped it when I leaped out of bed, and the bedclothes had caught fire!

I yelled and leaped onto the bed, on my hands and knees. I smothered the flames with the quilt – I used the whole quilt and I pounded it with my fists – and I guess I made a lot of noise, yelling and thumping, but I got the fire out. But then Malka came in, carrying her candle.

Well, she took one look at me and shrieked. I guess she could smell the burned hair – it's one of the worst smells in the world, and one of the strongest. I don't know whether you'd call it *pungent* or *acrid*, but it might be both. She shrieked and fled, forgetting her bunion and not limping a bit. When she came back, she had a great jug of water – it turns out she is deathly afraid of fire and keeps a jug of water in her room – and she dashed it at me, soaking me and the bedclothes and what was left of *Daniel Deronda*. All the time, she was talking frantically in Yiddish and saying *barook-ha-shem*, which I think is maybe a phrase to ward off the devil, because she seems to say it whenever a disaster has been averted.

I guess I was too excited to think very clearly because the water was awfully cold. And I couldn't understand her, but I knew she was scolding me, and then she switched to English and I heard her say something about me burning the whole family alive in their beds. I thought that was unfair, and I told her it was an accident, and for heaven's sake, whoever caught her hair on fire on purpose? I held up the hank of hair that was singed, and she came forward to look, but she stopped and gasped and pointed to the crucifix over my bed. (I hung it up after church on Sunday, because I mean to be a real Catholic from now on.)

She carried on as if my crucifix was a ghost. She told me to take it down right away. She said it was bad enough I'd tried to burn the house down, but she wasn't having *that* on the wall. And I said it was my room and that Jesus was my Lord and my God, and I wasn't taking Him down. And she said it wasn't my room, it was a room in a good Jewish house, and did I know how many Jews had been persecuted and tortured and murdered because of that Sign? And she started talking about mobs of Christians massacring Jews and burning synagogues – which I'm sure *can't* be true; it might have been true in Ivanhoe's time, but real Christians, especially Catholics, wouldn't do such things. She darted forward as if she meant to reach up and take Ma's crucifix off the wall, and I stood on the bed to stop her. That's when Mrs Rosenbach came in.

I must say she was wearing the most beautiful dressing gown. It's what they call a kimono, olive green, with pale-pink blossoms on it, hand embroidered, I think, though I didn't get a close look. And I realized that Malka and I must have awakened her, and she wasn't pleased. She said, "Be quiet, both of you!" and I saw her take in the water on the floor and the soaking bed and the charred place on the quilt. The smell of burned hair was very strong. I started trying to tell her what had happened and how it wasn't my fault. But the minute I opened my mouth, Malka started pointing at the wall and saying that if I wouldn't take the crucifix down, she'd send me packing.

Then Mrs Rosenbach lost her temper and said it wasn't for *Malka* to say whether I should stay or go. Malka burst into tears and started off on all the years she'd served that family and how she would have shed her *last drop of blood* for any of them, but now a *shiksa* who set the house on fire was raised above her. And I said I wasn't a *shiksa*. I'm not sure what it is, but it sounds like something awful. And I said I hadn't set the house on fire, either, just my hair and a little bit of the quilt.

Mrs Rosenbach told us to be quiet again. She thrust her hands into her hair, pressing her palms against her temples, as if she had a splitting headache. What I've caught on to is that Malka gets on her nerves something terrible. I shut up when she told me to, but Malka kept carrying on until she ran out of pitiful things to say. When at last she stopped, Mrs Rosenbach told her in an icy voice to go back to bed.

Of course Malka didn't, because she wanted to see what was going to happen to me. "Janet," Mrs Rosenbach said sharply – I jumped because I'd forgotten my name was Janet – "will you be able to sleep on a wet mattress?"

I said I would. By that time, I'd realized how much trouble I was in, and I was abject; I probably sounded like there was nothing in the world I'd like more than to sleep on a wet mattress. I told her I was terribly sorry that the book was ruined, and I promised to buy her another one out of my wages.

"Take the wet things downstairs," said Mrs Rosenbach, "and hang them in the kitchen to dry. You may get dry sheets out of the linen closet."

I said "Yes, ma'am," and got down on my knees so I could clean up the mess. But Malka started off again, complaining about my crucifix. Mrs Rosenbach looked at it and there was a look of distaste on her face, as if my crucifix was *treif*. She said she'd talk to Mr Rosenbach about it tomorrow, but for now we had best go to bed.

Then she left. Malka left, too – but in a more forceful way. I wish I'd thought to tell her I was sorry, because that would have been a good time to say it. But I wasn't sorry.

I mopped up the floor with the ruined quilt and took it downstairs and hung it up. I was shivering, because my nightgown was wet, and I have only the one, so I couldn't change out of it. By and by the wet part took the warmth from my body. It's still wet, though, and feels very disagreeable.

I don't know what I'll do tomorrow, when Mr Rosenbach scolds me. Before, I had Malka on my side. If I can't get along with Malka, I'll be like the other servants who were sent away. And where will I find another job? I don't think Mrs Rosenbach can write me a good character because I set the bedclothes on fire. Only it was an accident – I didn't do it for my health. Though that is a slangy, disrespectful way of putting it, and I must be careful not to say that to Mr Rosenbach.

I don't see why I can't have Ma's crucifix on the wall. I believe I'm being persecuted. Jesus said that people who were persecuted in His Name would be blessed. So maybe I should leave the crucifix up and go on being persecuted. But if I take it down, Malka might forgive me and plead for me with Mr Rosenbach. I'm sure her little Moritz would listen to her.

Maybe that thought is a temptation. Perhaps I ought to pray and ask God what to do.

I just prayed for a long time.

I think God must want me to go to sleep.

Tuesday, July the eighteenth, 1911

I wish Mr Rosenbach was my father. It feels wicked to covet someone else's father, but how can I help it? I never wanted anyone but Ma to be my mother, but Mr Rosenbach is ever so much kinder than Father.

I was nervous this morning. Malka was sulking – *ominously silent* is the phrase they would use in a novel. She told me that Mrs Rosenbach was having her bridge ladies today instead of Wednesday, so I couldn't have the afternoon off. I didn't dare complain, because I was afraid of being sent away.

By the time Mr Rosenbach rang for me, my stomach was all tied up in knots. My heart beat fast as I opened the library door.

Mr Rosenbach was standing over his desk, reading the newspaper, but he whirled around when I came in. He is mostly bald, but he has a dark mustache that is pointy and waxed and turns up at the ends. He shouted, just as I'd feared he would. "So! This is the little girl who loves books so much that she stays up all night and sets the house on fire! Come here!"

I said that he shouted, and he did. But it was kind

of a joyful bellow, and he beckoned in a friendly way. I stumbled forward – I don't mean I tripped or anything, but I felt off balance. He said, "Closer!" but I couldn't think why he should want me to draw near. There was a far-off corner in my mind where I wanted to laugh because he called me a little girl and the top of his head is about level with my ear.

Up close, he is almost handsome. Not his features, which are irregular, but if you subtracted his face, he might be called handsome. He has good shoulders and he smells like cedar, and his shirts are so beautifully starched.

He said, "Which side?"

"Which side?" I echoed.

"You set your hair on fire. Which side of the head?"

I pointed and he stepped nearer and peered at me. I was too embarrassed to look at him. At last he stepped back. "You were not burned? You were not hurt?"

"No, sir," I said. It struck me that neither Mrs Rosenbach nor Malka had asked whether I was hurt. I guess they could see for themselves that I wasn't.

He persisted. "Hands? Show me."

I held up my hands for inspection. There's a nasty blister on the web of my left thumb. He saw it and made sympathetic noises. They were like the noises Mr Solomon made when I was crying in the park. At that time, I thought they were foreign noises, but now I know they're Jewish noises.

"That's a bad burn. Did you put anything on it?"

"I ran cold water on it," I said. "But that's from yesterday. From ironing."

"Ah," he said, in the German way, as if he were clearing his throat. Then he shouted, "Sit down, sit down!" as if he'd just thought of us sitting and couldn't wait a single minute for it to happen. I sat down quickly and he bounced down opposite me. The way he moves is very energetic and rubbery, and he perched on the edge of his seat as if he was ready to jump up again. "So you love to read?"

"Yes, sir."

"Not dime novels, but *Ivanhoe*? The classics?"

"Yes, sir." I took a deep breath. "I want to better myself."

"She wants to better herself," Mr Rosenbach announced, although there was nobody for him to say it to except me. "She wants to be an educated young lady. So after a hard day's work, she sits up late and sets the house on fire."

"It wasn't the house," I said. I was contradicting him, but by then, I wasn't afraid of him one bit. "It was just my hair. I should have been more careful with the candle, and I'm sorry I woke everyone up. I'm especially sorry that Mrs Rosenbach's book was ruined. But I'm going to buy her a new copy as soon as I can. I'm not sure I can fix the quilt, but—".

He interrupted me. "Enough about the quilt. There are hundreds of quilts in this house, hundreds. They're a nuisance – that's how many we have. No. I have thought it all through, and I know what must be done." He gestured energetically. "We will order you a kimono."

"A kimono," I repeated.

"A kimono, a bathrobe, a dressing gown," he said impatiently, as if I didn't know the word. "Something that covers you from head to toe. Then, when the house is quiet, you can creep downstairs and read in the library, where there are electric lights. In this way, you will continue your education without setting your hair on fire."

I stared at him with my mouth open. He began to laugh. "You would rather I scolded you? To accuse you of – what were the words my poor Malka used – setting us ablaze in our beds?"

I blurted out, "I thought you'd send me away."

"You did?" He cocked his head. "You think I am the kind of man who will send away a little girl – an *American* girl! – who loves books so much that after a long day of putting up with my old friend Malka— Do you like her, my Malka? She's an old torment, isn't she? But I love her very much, and she's fond of you, though now she's angry, so you must eat humble pie. Will you do that? If you do, I think she will forgive you, and you will forgive her, and we will get you a bathrobe, so everything will be all right. I love books myself; do you think

I should send away a servant because she wants to read?"

He paused for me to speak, but I was lost in the thicket of his questions. He leaned forward, resting his hands on his knees. "Janet. I can call you that, because I'm old enough to be your father. How old are you?"

Quick as a flash I answered, "Eighteen." And oh, I hated having to lie to him! But what was I to do? Once you start lying, you have to go on. Lying to him seemed worse than lying to the others, because he looked at me so kindly. I wrote before that he wasn't handsome. He is moonfaced and hawk-nosed and middle-aged. But he has fine eyes: dark and piercing.

"Freyda thinks you're younger."

It took me a minute to see that Freyda must be Mrs Rosenbach. "No, sir," I said stoutly. "I'm eighteen, all right. I guess I seem younger because—" I hesitated. "Because I'm so ignorant. I left school when I was fourteen."

"But you want to go on learning."

"Yes, sir. That's what I want more than anything."

"If that's what you want, who am I to stop you?" He swept his hands apart. "Here are books – novels, histories, poetry. You may read them all. But not too late, not past midnight. You have to get up early to help Malka with breakfast. Many nights, we have retired by ten, and after that, my library is open to you. Do you agree?"

Agree? I thought of myself, reading through those

books – Dickens and Scott and *The Picturesque World*. I could scarcely speak. "Of course I agree! I can't thank you enough – oh, I can never thank you—"

He cut me off. "There is no need to thank me. For a Jew, it is a sin not to educate his children. You are not my child. But you live under my roof; you sweep my floors, you overcook my fish, you burn your hand ironing my shirts—"

"No, sir," I corrected him. "Malka irons your shirts. But I iron your sheets." Then I felt myself get red, because I was afraid it was indelicate to talk about sheets.

He didn't notice. "It's the same thing," he said, which shows his masculine ignorance. If you scorch a sheet, you can bleach it with sunshine and vinegar until the scorch marks fade. But shirts have to be perfect. Malka's awful fussy about the master's shirts, and she's right to be.

He went on. "What I am telling you is that so long as you live under my roof, I am responsible for your well-being. I have no intention of standing between you and the books you love. At the same time, I can't allow you to set the house on fire or ruin your health reading all night. Do you understand?"

"Yes, sir," I said. I was so happy I burst out laughing.

"That's good, very good. But now there's something else we must discuss, and that is Malka. She is very much upset. Will you make it up with her?"

I had forgotten about Malka. "Did Malka tell you why she's mad at me? It wasn't just the fire."

"What, then?"

I linked my fingers together. "I'm Catholic." I'm not a complete Catholic yet, because I haven't taken the Sacrament, but I like saying the words. "So I hung my mother's crucifix over my bed. When Malka saw it, she screamed and told me to take it down."

"And you refused. This she told me."

"I wasn't very tactful," I admitted, "and I guess I raised my voice. But that crucifix belonged to my mother, and I've as much right to be Catholic as Malka has to be a Jew. And I don't think I should be persecuted because of my religion."

He nodded rapidly, but he didn't answer at first. He bounced out of his seat, walked a few steps, spun round, and eyed me as if he were taking my measure. "Malka said you called her a liar."

"I didn't," I said indignantly.

"Did you tell her that what she said wasn't true?"

I felt myself turn red. "I might have," I admitted. "She was saying such horrible things. About Christians and even priests slaughtering Jews – things I knew *can't* be true. But I never called her a liar. I wouldn't be so disrespectful to an old lady."

He threw up his hands. "Yes, but to Malka—"

"Yes, sir," I agreed, because I understood what he

meant. To say that someone isn't speaking the truth isn't the same as calling her a liar. But to Malka, touchy old Malka, it might seem like the same thing.

"So you will be a good, kind girl and ask her to forgive you."

I thought of eating humble pie before Malka, and I winced a little, but only a little. I was still so happy about the books. And the truth is, I'm not a very proud girl. Heroines in novels are proud, but for a hired girl, it isn't convenient.

So I nodded and stood up. "I'll go and tell her I'm sorry," I promised. Then an uneasy thought came to me. "But they weren't true, were they? The things she said?"

He answered slowly, "In America, no."

He has a special way of saying those words, *America* and *American*. It's as if each syllable is precious. He lifted one hand in command, so I sat back down. He pulled up a chair and leaned forward. I knew that he was going to entrust me with something important.

"You must understand that Malka is a child of the Old Country. She was born in Germany in the eighteen forties. When she was a child, she knew what it was to have other children call her a dirty Jew, to spit on her, to throw stones. She never knew her grandfather, who was killed in the riots in Frankfurt. He was beaten to death with a shovel. Malka's grandmother saw it happen and told her the story. Such stories take root in a child's mind."

I understood that. I remember how sad stories haunted me when I was a little thing. One of the boys at school lost a finger chopping wood, and at night I couldn't go to sleep for thinking about the pain and the blood.

"So when Malka sees a crucifix, she remembers how Christians have tormented the Jews."

I protested. "But the rioters who killed Malka's grandfather – they weren't Christian, were they? I mean, they were criminals. Weren't they?"

He looked as if he was sorry for me. "They were Christian men. I don't mean to suggest that all Christians are like that. But Christian persecution has gone on for centuries. And those who have burned and tortured and oppressed us have done so in Christ's name."

"But that was long ago!"

"Not so long ago," Mr Rosenbach corrected me. "It's hard for you to understand, because you've grown up in America, and America is truly the Promised Land. Even here, there is bigotry, but there are laws to protect us. Outside America, there are *pogroms* – massacres. Six years ago, in Kishinev, more than a hundred Jews were killed by an angry mob. The police did not interfere, and the murderers were never punished. The streets were piled high with our dead; even Jewish babies were torn to pieces." He closed his eyes. "I don't tell you these things to hurt you. I say them because they are true."

"But those people in Kishinev—" I faltered. The truth

is, I've never even heard of Kishinev. I have no idea where it is. "Were they Christians? Were they *Catholic*?"

"The mob was led by priests," said Mr Rosenbach. "Not Roman Catholic priests this time, but Orthodox priests: men of God, chanting, 'Kill the Jews.' It was the day after Easter. Good Friday and Easter have always been the most dangerous times for us. We Jews are called Christ-killers, though if you read your Bible, you will discover that Jesus was Himself a Jew, and that it was the Romans who put Him to death."

I felt sick. I had such horrible pictures in my mind: the mobs in the street, the corpses, and Christian priests killing little babies. I felt my eyes get hot, and I was filled with shame. I didn't want to cry. I'm supposed to be eighteen. I blurted out, "I don't see why nobody likes the Jews."

"I, too, have wondered about this," said Mr Rosenbach, with a wry grimace that helped me recover myself.

"My teacher, Miss Chandler, took the newspaper. She used to tell us about things that were going on in the world. But she never told us the Jews were being killed."

"May I ask if Miss Chandler was a Jew?"

"Of course not," I said. Miss Chandler a Jew! "Nobody's a Jew where I come from. The only Jews I knew were Isaac and Rebecca, in *Ivanhoe*. And—" I stopped.

"And?" Mr Rosenbach said, so encouragingly that I had to go on.

"And Fagin, in *Oliver Twist*."

"Ah, Fagin." Mr Rosenbach leaped up and went to one of the bookcases. He stared through the glass doors at the scarlet-bound set of Dickens. "Well, Dickens was a master. When a great writer sets out to create a monster, he creates a great monster. I suppose there are people who hate my race all the more because of Fagin. But Fagin is a bad Jew, because he eats sausages, which are *treif*. And in a later book, Dickens repented of his anti-Semitism and wrote about a good Jew..." He sighed. "Though the good Jew, Riah, is not as memorable as Fagin."

I recognized that word, *anti-Semitism*, from my first night at the Rosenbachs'. "What is that?" I inquired. "What is anti—?"

"Anti-Semitism. The hatred of the Jews," said Mr Rosenbach. "The word is modern, but the hatred has a long history. We've been hated for thousands of years."

"I don't understand it," I said.

He shrugged. "Perhaps we are both too innocent to understand it. But we have wandered from the point. What I was trying to explain is that for Malka, your crucifix is not a symbol of the God you love, but of the Christians who have oppressed the Jews. Can you understand that?"

I thought about Malka. For some reason, it wasn't hard to picture her as a little girl. I imagined her: a little black fly of a child, listening with big scared eyes to her grandmother's stories. "I guess I can," I said. "Anyway, I'll tell her I'm sorry. I never meant to call her a liar. But I still don't know what to do about my crucifix. Must I take it down?"

"That is for you to decide. I have no wish to persecute you for your faith," he said, and though he smiled very kindly, I knew our talk had come to an end.

Now I am writing in the library. After my bath, I put on my old brown dress and crept downstairs to write. It will be midnight in another fifteen minutes, and then I must go to bed, because I promised Mr Rosenbach.

But I want to write two more things. One is that I made up with Malka. It wasn't as hard as I thought it would be. She was sitting in the kitchen with the Thomashefsky cat in her lap, so I went and knelt before her. I acted as if I was kneeling to stroke the cat, but I was really kneeling because I wanted to atone for all the bad things that were done to the Jews.

I told her I was sorry and that I hadn't meant to call her a liar. I had a whole speech planned, very penitent and touching, but before I could say much, the cat bit me. I wasn't hurting him – I was rubbing his cheek with one finger. But he bit me. I swear that cat knows I'm a Gentile.

Malka's face brightened. She'd been listening to me stonily, but having the cat bite me cheered her right up.

She said Thomashefsky was a bad boy, though I know she loved him all the more for it.

But pretending to scold the cat was her way of making up. She asked if I wanted a cookie. When I said I did, she put the cat off her lap and went to the icebox to pour me a glass of milk. While I was eating her cookies, I promised I'd take the crucifix off the wall.

So that's the second thing I did. I took down the crucifix. I decided I'd sleep with it under my pillow. That way, it doesn't bother Malka, but Jesus is still close to me. Even though taking Him down is a little bit like being persecuted, it isn't the kind of persecution where babies are torn apart in the street.

I think this is a good compromise, and I feel peaceful and kind of virtuous. But when I think of the things Mr Rosenbach told me, I don't feel virtuous anymore. I feel ashamed and shocked that Christians can be so bad. And it seems to me that Jews like Mr Rosenbach must be very good not to hate all Christians – though it would be unfair of him to hate me, because I've never done any anti-Semitism.

I wonder what my new bathrobe will look like.

I want to read, but I have so much to write! Today I had my day off, and I spent a fortune – a fortune! – in Rosenbach's Department Store. I rode the streetcar, I met Nora Himmelrich, and I have a new HAT!

I am wildly excited about my hat, so I'll write about that first. It's cream-colored straw trimmed with cornflowers and a pale-pink taffeta ribbon. Mimi says it's a Cheyenne-style hat, which means that the brim turns up in front, more on one side than the other. It's awfully becoming. Mimi says my hat has a lot of style for a dollar and seventy cents. A dollar and seventy cents! Ma would be horrified if she knew I spent that on a hat. But Mimi seemed to think it was a bargain, and in a way it was, because I saw one hat that cost *twelve dollars*. Mimi said that was because it had a lot of ostrich feathers, which are becoming very dear. It's a pity girls don't run department stores, because Mimi seems to know a lot about such things.

Mimi was in a bad humor when we met today, almost silent, except when she was explaining to me about the streetcar. She sat next to me with her nose in the air and a grouch on her face. I made up my mind that I wasn't going to let a little girl of twelve be rude to me without saying anything, so at last I asked her what the matter was. Then she burst out talking.

She said her father was mad because she hadn't read any of the books he gave her, and he held *me* up as an example. He said that here I was, a poor hard-working girl, willing to stay up all night in order to read and study, and there was Mimi, with everything made easy for her, refusing to be educated.

Well, I think Mr Rosenbach has a point. But I didn't say so, because I can see how aggravating it would be to have your father say you ought to be more like the hired girl. Mimi says her father is mad for education. Just now, he is trying to found a new school – it seems like I should write *find* instead of *found*, but Mimi said *found* - for Christian and Jewish children. Mr Solomon and Mr David went to a Quaker school, which is willing to accept Jews, but only if there aren't too many. It's a very good school, but when Mr Rosenbach wanted to send Mimi, they said they weren't going to take any more Jews. They offered to make an exception and have one more if Mr Rosenbach would give the school ten thousand dollars. *Ten thousand dollars!* I think those Quakers have a lot of gall, asking for that. But even though Mr Rosenbach *has* ten thousand dollars – imagine having ten thousand dollars to give away! – he didn't give it to the Quakers. He said with that much money, he could found (find) his own school, so he and his friends are pooling their money to start one. Only I think he's going to be very disappointed, because Mimi doesn't want to go to the new school. She says it's going to be an especially excellent school, and she knows what that means: too much work!

I didn't listen to her as closely as I might've, because I was wondering what else Mr Rosenbach might have said about me. I know he likes me, and I think Mr Rosenbach is a *little* bit like Mr Rochester. I even wondered (though I know this is conceited) if he might have been struck by me the way Mr Rochester was struck by Jane. Jane wasn't good-looking, but she was pure and innocent and all that. I started to daydream about Mr Rosenbach being touched by my purity, but the daydream ran into a snag, because I don't feel very pure. I *am* pure, mostly, because to be impure there have to be men, but I don't *feel* pure because of all the things I've had to clean in my life. Things like privies and chicken houses take the bloom off a girl.

By the time Mimi finished telling me her troubles, we had arrived at the department store. I've never been inside a department store before. There was a fine store in Lancaster called Watt & Shand, but Ma said Father would skin us alive if we ever went in. I believe Rosenbach's is larger and more beautiful – I think I'll describe it at length in a future entry. It's like a palace, with high ceilings and electric lights and glass-fronted cases full of dazzling things. Everything is so shiny and sumptuous and new smelling.

We went first to the book department, to Mimi's disgust. I searched for *Daniel Deronda*, but I didn't find it. The sales clerk is going to order a copy. I did find a copy of

Jane Eyre, and it was the same edition Miss Chandler gave me. I had to buy it – I *just* had to – even though it was three dollars. I've missed Jane dreadfully, and I've missed the feeling of owning a book. Not having any books makes me feel empty and strained and pathetic.

So I bought *Jane Eyre*, and after that we went and bought my hat. By then Mimi's good humor was restored, because she loves shopping. She bought new hair ribbons and a bottle of lilac perfume and a little parasol with fringe. She was so cunning in the hat department, trying on all the hats, and standing way back from the mirror to admire each one. She told me she's made up her mind to run the store when she grows up, instead of being a concert pianist. Her father once told her she could be a lady doctor if she liked, and selling things is easier than saving lives, so she supposes it will be all right.

She was the one who found the Cheyenne-style hat for me and made me buy it. Afterward, I wanted to see if there were any nightgowns I could afford, because I only have the one, and Malka says it's a *shmatte*. She says that about my underthings, too. I asked Mimi what it meant, and she says it means a *rag*.

I'd already spent four dollars and seventy cents, so I wasn't in a hurry to separate myself from any more money. But the idea that all my things were *shmatte*s stung. Mimi took me to the nightgown counter and showed me an entire outfit of ladies' underthings – two corset covers, two petticoats, two pairs of drawers, and two nightgowns – all for four dollars and fifty cents. She said I should buy the entire outfit. Then I wouldn't have to wear the *shmattes*.

I was torn in two. Four dollars and fifty cents is an awful price. But when Mimi added up what the things would cost if I bought them separately – she's quick as a bird when she adds in her head – the price was even higher. Of course, the cheapest thing would be for me to buy muslin and make the things myself, but it would take hours, and they wouldn't have any lace or ruffles on them. And the hours would be hours I could spend reading.

The truth is, I felt this wild longing to have nothing but new clothes. I wanted them right away: crisp, clean, fresh things, all the way down to my skin. I lost my head. When I put down my money, my hand was shaking, but I bought the outfit.

While the saleslady was wrapping everything in tissue paper, Mimi jogged my elbow and said, "Look, that's Nora Himmelrich!" and I turned and saw the girl who captured Mr Solomon's heart.

It was almost a shock, because I'd imagined her wrong. I thought she would be tall and slender and haughty. But this girl was like a girl on a Valentine: fresh and soft and sweet as a puppy. She has fawn-colored curls and big brown eyes and pink cheeks. She looks like the kind of girl who would teach Sunday school – the children would all fall in love with her, but she wouldn't be able to get them to behave.

What she *doesn't* look like is the kind of girl who would break Solomon Rosenbach's heart.

Mimi introduced me with her usual aplomb: "This is Janet, our new hired girl. It's her afternoon off. She's eighteen, too."

I could see that Miss Himmelrich was taken aback, being introduced to the hired girl. She looked at me anxiously. Then she put out her hand, and said, "How nice of you to spend your day off giving Mimi a treat!"

She smiled at me. Of course she has dimples. I could tell she meant to be friendly, but she was nervous, and so was I. I've never met an heiress before. I said, "It's nice of Mimi to show me around. I've never been in a department store until today."

"Really?" she said breathlessly. "Do you like it?"

"I certainly do," I said, and I guess that broke the ice, because we laughed.

After that, we were almost like three girls together – I mean, three girls the same age. It was such fun, going through the store and pointing out things we admired, and giggling together. Nora – I mean, Miss Himmelrich – saw my hatbox, and Mimi made me open the box and try on my hat for her. Miss Himmelrich says my eyes are the same color as the cornflowers. That is the prettiest compliment I ever had. I always thought I had *plain* blue eyes, but maybe I was mistaken. At any rate, it's astounding what a difference a good hat makes.

Then Nora said she wanted a new hat, too, so we went back to the hat department to help her choose. She bought a five-dollar hat covered with pink roses, not a bit nicer than mine, I thought. The store was warm, and Mimi announced that she wanted an egg cream, and we went to the soda fountain across the street. There isn't any egg, or any cream, in an egg cream. There's fizzy water, a little bit salty, chocolate syrup, and milk. I don't think I ever tasted anything better. I felt so happy and festive.

Afterward I thought a good deal about Nora Himmelrich and Mr Solomon. I see now that Mr Solomon would never have done for me: he's too old, for one thing, and too tame for my impetuous nature. But he and Nora might be very happy together. And perhaps I could help him to win his true love. Sooner or later, I'm bound to see Nora again, and perhaps I can persuade her to confide in me. I could tell her what a true gentleman Mr Solomon is, and how he rescued me, and how he always wipes his feet before he comes into the house. Or perhaps I could carry messages between them; that would be very romantic.

At any rate, I hereby renounce all claims to Mr Solomon myself. And if there is any way I can help him to prosper in his suit, I vow I will do it.

It's a hundred and two degrees today. Last night the attic was so stifling that I slept on the library sofa, which was probably taking a liberty of some kind. Luckily no one found me out, because I woke before dawn and crept back to my own bed.

I'm in a bad mood because of Mrs Rosenbach. She's still after those oyster patties for her bridge ladies. Last week she made Malka go to the market on Lexington Street and talk to the fish seller, who's a Gentile. He said he didn't get much in the way of oysters this time of year, and frankly, ma'am, he didn't recommend them, not in this heat. Malka was triumphant. This morning, when we went upstairs to discuss the week's meals, Malka told Mrs Rosenbach what the fish seller said, but I don't think Mrs Rosenbach believed her. Mrs Rosenbach thinks Malka won't serve the oysters because they're *treif* – which is true. But Malka wasn't lying about what the fish man said, and I spoke up and said so.

They argued back and forth about what to give the bridge ladies. Malka suggested a nice cold chicken salad, but Mrs R. said she was tired of nice cold chicken salad. So I said if she was tired of Jewish food, I could fry up some pork chops. The *look* she gave me! Malka, too! It was as if I'd proposed to give the bridge ladies a *dead man's hand*, or some kind of cannibal feast – though that is the sort of metaphor that Miss Chandler never favored. She once told me that my metaphors were too forceful and that I should try to quiet them down.

At any rate, it seems that some *treif* – like oyster patties – is less *treif*-y than other *treif*, and pork chops are completely *treif* and repulsive to both Malka and Mrs R. I am calling her Mrs R. because she hurt my feelings and I begrudge her the dignity of her full name. She was very cool and superior. She began by saying that if I wanted to be a good servant, I must learn not to put myself forward so much. And I mustn't interrupt.

I said, "I'm sorry, ma'am," but that wasn't the end of it, because she said she'd been meaning to speak to me. She was pleased by my efforts to improve my personal appearance, and she hoped I would take equal pains with my *deportment*. It seems that my *deportment* does not please her. She says I walk with too much bounce, and my strides are too long, and I shouldn't swing my hands. She wants me to keep my hands hanging limp at my sides when I walk – not *stiff*, you understand, but relaxed. And she wants me to talk in a softer voice, more *subdued*. Especially when there are guests.

I could feel my cheeks burning. It was like the day Miss Lang spoke to me about not being fresh in my person. I felt ashamed, even though I haven't failed in any of my duties. When you've done something wrong, you expect to be scolded, though you dread it, and you feel sore afterward. But if you've done your best, and someone rebukes you, it's worse. I thought Mrs Rosenbach liked me. But now I see she's like the girls at school and thinks of me as a big, clumsy ox.

While I was still reeling from her insults, she said that Mr Rosenbach had invited me to join the family for Shabbos dinner this week. He told her I'd been asking questions about Judaism, so he wanted me to be present. It took some of the blush from my cheek to know that Mr Rosenbach still likes me.

On the way down to the kitchen, I started to cry. I couldn't help it; I think it was partly the heat. Malka caught me at it, and it was no good telling her I had a cold. That's a funny thing: people in books are always saying they have colds when they're really crying, but having a cold and crying are two separate things, and I don't know why people in books haven't noticed this. In real life, no one would fall for such a weak lie.

At any rate, Malka didn't. But she was nice and said she doesn't know what gets into the mistress sometimes. Usually on Mondays I give the kitchen floor a good scrubbing, but today Malka said it would be good enough if I just mopped it. I had a feeling she was more interested in talking about Mrs Rosenbach than in having a clean floor. She poured out two glasses of cold lemonade, and we settled down in the cozy corner and she told me about some of the times when Mrs R. hurt *her* feelings.

Of course I've heard some of those stories before, because Malka likes to tell them and relive how indignant she was.

After a little of that, Malka asked me if there was any particular reason why Mrs R. might have been so chilly with me. At first I couldn't think of one, but then I told her – Malka, I mean – about going with Mimi to Rosenbach's Department Store. Malka exclaimed in Yiddish and said *of course*, that was what was the matter. She said no lady would want her daughter going out in public with the hired girl. She seemed to think I was crazy not to have known this.

I guess I was crazy. But the Rosenbachs seem so nice – at least, Mr Rosenbach is nice and Mimi and Mr Solomon. It didn't occur to me that they'd look down on me for being the hired girl. The truth is, most of the time, I don't think of myself as the hired girl. I think of myself as somebody *disguised* as the hired girl. After all, I'm not going to be a servant all my life. It's temporary. At some point I'm going to get an education and become a schoolteacher, just as Ma planned.

It isn't as if I was born to be a servant. Heaven knows Father's a miserly man, but he owns his own land and has no debts except the mortgage; he's no one's servant but his own. And besides, this is America, and if Mimi doesn't mind going out with me, why shouldn't I go with her?

Thanks to Mr Rosenbach, I have attended Shabbos! It was a *mitzvah* – that means a *good deed* – for him to invite me. Until tonight, I almost felt as if I knew more about Shabbos than Mr Rosenbach; I don't mean the holy parts of Shabbos, but the unreligious parts, like cooking and cleaning the house. There's a lot of work preparing for Shabbos, and most of it is women's work. The men do only the holy parts: the praying and going to temple.

Now I've seen how the holy parts and the women's parts fit together, like two clasped hands. I think that's a good simile. Two other metaphors for Shabbos are the *Bride* and the *Queen*.

I just stopped writing this in order to examine the sole of my foot. The toe of my stocking has a hole in it, and it's been driving me crazy all day. The hole kept lassoing my big toe and strangling it, and there was no time for me to unlace my shoe and fix it. Then the wrinkled part of the stocking crawled under the ball of my foot and made a blister. I really need new stockings, but I haven't recovered from all the money I spent last week. But I shouldn't be writing this, because talking about money on Shabbos is forbidden, and even though I'm not Jewish, I feel a little bit holy.

Just before sundown this evening, I ran upstairs and put on my robin's-egg dress for Shabbos dinner; you're supposed to look nicer than usual on Shabbos. Malka lent me an ugly little brooch made to look like a bunch of grapes, so I could look more dressed up. For once my hair went up perfectly, and I didn't have to cover it with a cap, because I was a guest.

When I went downstairs, I saw that Mrs Rosenbach had on a beautiful dress, black lace over mauve silk, and Mimi was in pink organdy with a green satin sash. I felt plain next to them, but I tried to be very careful with my *deportment*. I took short steps and didn't move my arms.

Mrs Rosenbach covered the table with a white cloth, and she set out two loaves of fresh-baked bread, which have an embroidered cover of their own – Mrs Rosenbach stitched it herself, and her needlework is exquisite. Then she lit the candles. She shut her eyes and made passes through the air. Her face was still and reverent, and she whispered the blessings in Hebrew; I couldn't understand them, but they sounded mysterious and poetical. After she lit two candles, Mimi went about the room lighting more. The candlelight made the whole room seem quieter and somehow expectant.

Malka and I set the table. It wasn't yet sundown, but the candles have to be lit before sundown, because once Shabbos begins, you're not supposed to light any more fires. While we were putting the finishing touches on the table, Mrs R.'s oldest daughter, Anna, arrived, with her little boy, Oskar, and baby Irma. Baby Irma is a beautiful child with curly hair and her grandmother's dark eyes. When Mrs R. saw her, she held out her arms. She took Irma into her lap and dandled her and kissed her. I never saw her so affectionate before. I wouldn't have known her for the same woman who criticized my *deportment*.

But all that fuss over the baby made Oskar jealous. He is a changeling of a child, frail and clever looking, with a shock of coppery hair. He reminds me of Paul Dombey in *Dombey and Son*. I guess he liked the look of me, because he came to me and yanked my skirt. "Come sit down," he commanded. He has a funny, hoarse little voice. "Then I can sit on your lap."

I was flattered. Here I was, a stranger and a Gentile, but he wanted to be close to me. He didn't care if I was only the hired girl. I let him lead me to a chair, and he climbed into my lap. When he nestled against me, he felt soft, and he smelled like Pears soap.

He took his thumb out of his mouth long enough to speak. "Tell me a story."

I began, "Once upon a time—" but he shook his head.

"Not a fairy story," he said. "No princesses, no kings."

I'd planned to tell him "Thumbelina," but I knew my feelings would be hurt if he didn't like it. "What kind of story do you want? What about?"

"Snakes," he answered. "Bad snakes."

The truth is, I don't know much about snakes, but I took a deep breath. "Once upon a time," I began, "there was a very large, very bad, poisonous snake."

He nodded gravely. I could see I was on the right track. "How big?" he prompted me.

"Enormous," I answered. "He was so big he could wrap himself around this whole house. He had pointy teeth, and he was hungry all the time."

"What did he eat?"

I hesitated, but only for a moment. Inspiration came to me in a blinding flash. "He ate little boys."

"Ohhhh," said Oskar rapturously, and snuggled closer. He stuck his thumb in his mouth and gazed at me with his heart in his eyes.

From that moment on, he was mine. I told him all about that terrible snake, and the little boys he ate, and about one special boy named Oskar, who was clever enough to escape from him. It was like seizing a thread and unraveling a piece of knitting; once I had the thread, the story moved right along. By and by, I realized that the others had stopped talking and were paying attention. Mrs Rosenbach looked amused, but approving. Mimi sidled over to a nearby table and pretended to leaf through the photograph album.

I knew she was listening. The funny thing was, I think I was worth listening *to*. Oskar was spellbound. The snake was in its death throes when the men came back from Temple. Oskar slid off my lap and ran to hug his grandfather, who picked him up and spun him upside down.

When we went into the dining room, Mr Rosenbach blessed his children in Hebrew, starting with Anna and ending with baby Irma. He caught his wife's eyes, smiled at her, and began to sing. He has a fine voice – rich and resonant; Malka told me he was singing from the Proverbs of Solomon, all about the worth of a good woman. It's a Jewish custom for a man to praise his wife for all the work she does for Shabbos. I thought it was splendid for a husband to praise his wife *every single week*, but I also thought it would be more to the point to praise Malka and me, because we were the ones who did the shopping and cooking and cleaning.

After the song, we sat around the table. There was a big cup of wine at Mr Rosenbach's place, and he blessed it and drank from it and passed it to the others; even Oskar had a sip. At first I was on edge, because the way he held it reminded me of a priest, and I was afraid the Jews copied the ritual from the Holy Mass, which would be blasphemy. But then I remembered that Mr Rosenbach said that Our Lord was a Jew, so the *kiddush* – that's what the wine blessing is called – probably came *before* the Holy Mass and not the other way around. Now that I'm writing this, I wonder if Jesus was saying *kiddush* at the Last Supper. I shall ask Mr Rosenbach; I think it is quite an intelligent question, and perhaps he will be pleased with me.

After the *kiddush*, we washed our hands, and Mr Rosenbach blessed the bread. But in the middle of the blessing, Irma spat up, just as Mimi says she does. She was like a little volcano; I wouldn't have thought such a tiny creature could make such a mess. Mimi jumped out of her seat with her fingers pinching her nose. Mr Rosenbach made Jewish noises of sympathy, and everyone started passing their napkins to Anna – whom I should really call Mrs Friedhoff because she's married to a Mr Isaac Friedhoff, who travels all the time because he's in railroads.

I seized the opportunity to prove myself. I commanded, "Don't worry, I'll fix everything!" I seized the dirty napkins and plates and silverware and rushed them downstairs to the kitchen. I ran a bowl of soapy water and put the water and towels and clean plates and a clean tablecloth in the dumbwaiter. Then I ran back upstairs and set the table – luckily, none of the food had been served. After the places were set, I took off Irma's dress – she was just fine in her petticoat, it being so hot – and ran the dress downstairs to soak. I felt like kind of a heroine, because the Rosenbachs aren't supposed to work on Shabbos, and if I hadn't been there, they would have had to choose between having that mess and breaking Shabbos.

When I came back into the room, Mrs Rosenbach raised her eyes to the ceiling and said, "What did we *do* before Janet came here?" At first I glowed with pride, but then I saw that it was an unlucky thing for her to say, because it put Malka in a bad humor.

It was a beautiful dinner. The food was delicious –
soup with dumplings, and baked stuffed fish and roast
chicken, and bread (but no butter), and red cabbage and
cucumber salad and apple sauce, and raspberry pudding
and meringues for dessert. There was singing, too – some
of the songs are kind of melancholy, but everyone seems
happy when they sing them. I was happy, too: after I fixed
up Irma, I felt that I belonged, even if I wasn't a Jew.

After dinner I had the cleaning up to do: a five-course
dinner for eight people – nine if you count baby Irma, who
didn't eat much but certainly made her share of the mess!
I took off my shoes and stockings – oh, what a relief to get
rid of that stocking! – and washed the dishes in my bare
feet.

The sight of me dealing with a mountain of dirty
dishes seemed to restore Malka's good humor. Before I
came, she could only rinse the dishes in cold water and set
them aside to be washed after Shabbos. But I'm allowed to
use hot water and a sponge because I'm a Gentile. Malka
sat in the rocking chair and kept me company. She had
the Thomashefsky cat on her lap, though you're not supposed to stroke an animal on Shabbos. Malka swears that
Thomashefsky is more set on being petted on Shabbos
than at any other time, and he butts her hand until she
renders his due portion of caresses.

Once the dishes were washed, Malka let me go
upstairs to read – I'm reading a very thrilling book called

The Moonstone. At one point, the heroine says, "I ache with indignation, and I burn with fatigue" – or maybe it's the other way around.

I love that. I think I will start saying it.

Monday, July the thirty-first, 1911

I want to read tonight – *The Moonstone* is very exciting and funny, too – but first I want to write about two important things. One is that starting tomorrow I'm going to have religious instruction with Father Horst.

I asked him yesterday. It seemed brazen to go right up to a priest and ask to become a Catholic. Father Horst has a worn-out, irritable look to him when he isn't smiling, and I was afraid he'd think I was presuming too much. But I told him how I long to take the Sacrament, and his face broke out in a smile of true benevolence. When I asked him where I might buy a missal, he *gave* me one. He said someone left it in the pew a year ago, and no one's claimed it, and he's been saving it for the right person, which is me.

It's a dainty little book with black-and-white plates and thin pages edged in gold. It always opens to the Seven Penitential Psalms, so I guess whoever owned it before was either very wicked or very good. I don't much like those psalms because they're mournful. I turned to the

Litany of the Virgin, because I'd forgotten parts of it. It's so poetical: *Tower of Ivory, House of Gold, Morning Star, Mystical Rose.* I love that. I told Father Horst I have a great devotion to the Blessed Mother, and that made him smile again.

We agreed that I should see him for an hour on Tuesday afternoons. His face darkened when I explained to him that sometimes I might not be able to come because of Mrs Rosenbach's bridge ladies. He asked me if my employer was the Mr Rosenbach who owned the department store, and I said yes, and he said he hoped that living in a household of worldly Jews wouldn't keep me from holding fast to my faith. I don't *think* that was anti-Semitism, because I guess there are some Jews who wouldn't want me to have a good Catholic faith, but the Rosenbachs aren't like that. I told Father Horst how good they've been to me and how Mr Rosenbach lends me books. Father Horst looked worried and asked *which* books. I didn't want to mention *The Moonstone*, because it's a little sensational, so I said *Ivanhoe*. It wasn't exactly a lie, because Mr Rosenbach has a copy of *Ivanhoe* and I'm sure he would lend it to me if I asked him. Father Horst seemed relieved and said he was especially fond of the works of Sir Walter Scott.

The other important thing happened this morning, and I'm still thinking about it. I was polishing the brass fittings on Mr Solomon's desk, and one of the drawers wouldn't go in all the way, so I took it out. There was an envelope wedged behind it.

I didn't mean to read what was written on it. I don't think I'd have read it if it had been a private letter, but the thing is, it was verse. It began, *Oh, Nora, when I see your radiant face* – and after that, I had to read on.

> *Oh, Nora, when I see your radiant face,*
> *Fresh, and smiling, like the blushing rose,*
> *And I behold your lithe and girlish grace,*
> *Which cascades from you as the river flows—*

Only I guess he didn't like that line, because he crossed it out and wrote instead:

> *It robs me, nightly, of my night's repose.*

But he didn't like that any better, because he crossed that out, too. Then he changed it to:

> *It robs me nightly of my soul's repose.*

Which I thought was better. Then the poem goes on:

> *I look upon your countenance, and feel*
> *Such ardent longing in my lovesick breast,*

Sweet girl, I beg you, comfort me and heal
The heart that throbs in this tumultuous breast!

Then he crossed that out, probably because he already had *breast* in there. He wrote *tumultuous chest*, and he must have hated that, because he crossed it out so hard I could scarcely read it. Then he had a stroke of inspiration, because he wrote:

This heart that throbs and aches and has no rest!
O fragile nymph! Would that you could be mine—

And then I guess he got stuck, because underneath he wrote:

stars shine?
as long as the stars shine?
could this girl I knew -
I would be ever true -

And then, up one side of the page he wrote:

austerities and strife,
the simplicity of a scholar's wife
the scant diversions of a scholar's wife -
- love?
the stars that beam above?

There he ended and the envelope was crumpled up as if he'd crushed it in his fist. I sympathized with him because there's not much that rhymes with *love* except *dove* and *glove* and *the stars above*, and in my opinion, the stars above are a little shopworn.

My heart beat fast when I read that poem, and divers sensations throbbed in my breast. First there was the sensation of invading Mr Solomon's privacy, which was shameful but thrilling. Then I felt envious, because he wrote Nora a love poem, and that's so romantic. I declare, if anyone wrote a poem and called me a fragile nymph, I would swoon dead away. Though it isn't likely that anyone ever will, because I'm an ox of a girl.

Then I felt dreadfully sorry for Mr Solomon. Here he is, head over heels in love with Nora but cruelly separated from her because he wants to study Talmud instead of run his father's department store.

I can't help thinking it's a pity that Mr Solomon never finished his poem. He should have stuck with it and had the courage to send it. If Nora Himmelrich read his poetry, she might come to appreciate him. I bet she'd like being called a fragile nymph and a blushing rose. Why, even the Blessed Mother must like being called Morning Star and Mystical Rose, or it wouldn't be in the prayer book.

Faint heart never won fair lady, after all.

I am writing this in Druid Hill Park. The sky is clear and last night's rain refreshed the grass. I'm always surprised by how tawny and brittle it can be, and then how it can come back in a night.

How far I've come in this diary! How I've traveled since last I sought to capture the beauties of nature in these pages! Nature in Druid Hill Park is vastly superior to nature in the country. At Steeple Farm, there are splintery fences mended with wire, and ugly sheds and manure piles. But here there are great sheets of ornamental water, and majestic oaks, and fountains and promenades.

I meant to begin instruction with Father Horst today, but he left a note at the rectory saying he had been called out by a sick parishioner. So I walked back to Eutaw Place and fetched my journal.

I feel very elegant, sitting in the shade like a lady of leisure. Before I sat down to write, I went for a stroll and admired the splendid panoramas. You'd think I'd be contented, having nothing to do but enjoy myself, but I found myself wishing I had a parasol to carry. I don't *need* one, because my Cheyenne hat has a wide brim, but the other ladies in the park look so elegant with their parasols. I saw nice parasols in Rosenbach's for ninety-five cents. Oh, dear, oh, dear, how worldly and covetous I've become! I remember Ma telling me always to put money by, and

I vow that I will, but I really need new stockings. If I'm
going to take the streetcar to Rosenbach's again, I might
as well look at the parasols, because—

Later that night

I *hate* Mrs Rosenbach! She has no heart! I see now that
I was deceived by her stylish clothes and refined manners.
I thought she was a real lady, but she is only a *simulacrum*.
Mimi – slangy, vain little Mimi – is worth a dozen of her.
Mimi must get her good qualities from her father.

I'm mad at Malka, too. Who would have thought she
could be so unfeeling? Unreasonable, yes; I would expect
Malka to be unreasonable, because she generally is. But
I never dreamed she could be so callous, especially when
I consider how much she loves Thomashefsky.

Here's what happened: while I was writing, who
should come along but Mimi? Her white sailor suit was
all grass stained and mussed, and she was swinging her
hat by the ribbons. When she caught sight of me, her little
monkey face broke out in a smile, and she scampered over
to join me. How *can* that child look so pretty when she
really is not? It's partly the way she moves, I guess. She's
so light on her feet; she's like a bit of bright paper being
blown over the grass. I wish I were like that.

She sat down next to me and asked what I was
writing. I told her it was my diary, and she asked – just

like that! – if she could read it! I said, "Of course not!" Then she tried to nab the book, but I was too quick for her and sat on it.

After she saw I wasn't going to let her read my diary, she asked why I hadn't talked to her much since the day we visited the department store. I told her I didn't think Mrs Rosenbach wanted us to be friends.

"Did she fuss at you?" Mimi asked sympathetically. "She fussed at me. She said going out together would make you forget your station. It was my fault more than yours, she said. So she shouldn't have fussed at *you*."

"She didn't fuss, exactly," I said, "but she criticized my deportment."

"Oh, *deportment*," said Mimi, rolling her eyes. "She doesn't like my deportment either. Anyway –" with a wave of her dainty, dirty little paw she dismissed the subject of deportment – "Mama's not here, so we can talk. What do you write in your diary?"

"Diaries are private," I said. "Besides, you don't like reading."

"I sure don't," agreed Mimi, and sighed. "Papa's making me read aloud a chapter of *Little Women* every night. I can't stand those March girls. They're always trying to be good, the stuck-up prigs. I don't think Louisa May Alcott understood Jews very well, because there's a bit in it about *meek Jews*. As if all Jews were the same." She flashed her dimple at me. "Do I look like a meek Jew to you?"

"Not much," I said, and she looked smug.

"I'm almost a tomboy," she confided. "I say almost, because I love frilly clothes and I'm not very good at boys' games. But I'm very high-spirited. Just now I was trying to play baseball, only when the ball comes at me, I shut my eyes. Did you ever play baseball?"

"Never," I said. The truth is, I think ball games are unfeminine. I believe ladies should vote and be doctors and maybe even be President, but they should stay tidy and not perspire. Most of my life I've had to get dirty and perspire, but I haven't liked it. If you ask me, it's silly to run after a ball, and that kind of silliness ought to be left to the men.

Mimi said, "Nora Himmelrich plays."

"Does she?" I was shocked. Fragile nymphs shouldn't play ball.

"The girls have got up a team, and she's captain," Mimi explained. "Mama says I shouldn't try to be friends with girls who are older than me, but my two best friends are away. Lotty's in Paris, and Maisie's at the seashore. Nora was nice; she tried to teach me how to hit the ball. But then the other girls came by and—" She stopped. "What's that?"

We'd both heard it: a shrill sound, not the cry of a bird. We listened but it didn't come again.

I returned to the subject of Mr Solomon's beloved. "Do you think Nora likes Mr Solomon?"

"Oh, she *likes* him," Mimi assured me. "Everyone likes Solly. But she's not romantic about him." She cocked her head, listening. "It's a kitten! I bet it's caught in a tree."

It didn't take us long to find the tree. Through the broad leaves of a sycamore, we caught a glimpse of a little creature the color of apricot jam. It mewed most pitifully.

"It's stuck," Mimi said. "We'll have to get it down."

I objected. "If it climbed up, it ought to be able to get down."

"Not necessarily," Mimi argued. She curled her fingers like claws and spoke in her know-it-all voice. "The way the claws hook, they climb up easily, but coming down, they slip." She threw her hat on the ground. "I'm good at climbing trees. Boost me up, and I'll see if I can catch it."

I looked up. The lowest branch was high above my head. "Maybe it'll jump down and land on its feet."

"It won't. It's afraid to jump." Mimi's eyes were sparkling; she was enjoying every minute of this. She nipped forward and attempted to shinny up the tree.

I saw I would have to help. The trunk was too wide for her to get much purchase. I set my diary on the grass and laid my hat on top of it. Then I tried to boost her up into the tree.

She was heavier than she looked. I heaved and lifted as best I could, but it was no use.

"Hold on," grunted Mimi. "If I can get up on your shoulders—" She twisted in my arms and scrambled up.

"I still can't reach!" she complained. "Can't you jump?"

"With you on my back?" I snapped. "No, I can't! Get down!"

I let my knees buckle, and we collapsed onto the grass and disentangled. The kitten mewed. "It'll starve to death up there!" Mimi said despairingly. "Can't you think of something?"

I looked around for inspiration. My eyes fell on the bench where we'd been sitting. Mimi gasped, "You can't lift that!" and she was right, because the bench was cast iron and heavy. I couldn't lift it – but I could drag it. There are some advantages to being a big ox.

Hauling that bench was hard work. I was bent double and afraid of stepping on my skirt. I made Mimi hold up my dress and petticoats, and after that we got on better. By the time I got the bench under the tree, the muscles in my arms burned like fire.

"You're so strong," Mimi said, her eyes glowing, "and so smart."

I knew she was buttering me up. I liked it, but I wasn't going to lose my head. "Take off your boots," I commanded. "I don't want any more scuff marks on my dress."

"All right," said Mimi. She took off her stockings, too, and unbuttoned the front of her sailor suit. "Once I catch the kitty, I can put him inside my vest. Then I'll have my hands free to climb down."

"Good," I said. All this time, the kitten had gone on crying. I swear the little thing knew we were his best hope, and he wasn't going to let us forget about him.

I made sure the bench was steady, and then I stood on it. Mimi hopped up on the bench, climbed up piggyback, and from thence wiggled onto my shoulders. She squirmed, braced herself, and leaped for the branch. "Quick, get down!" she directed me. I hopped off the bench and watched her swing back and forth. With a swirl of petticoats and lace-trimmed drawers, she swung herself into the tree.

I saw the sycamore leaves flutter as the kitten fled. "Kittykittykitty," sang Mimi in a sugary voice.

"Can you catch it?" I asked.

"Shhh. I'll wait a little. You can't chase after a cat too much. Cats have to come to you."

Nobody ever told me that before. I wonder if that's why Thomashefsky always ducks away from me. Maybe it has nothing to do with me being a Gentile. I heard a faint rustle, and Mimi crooned, "Kittykittykitty?"

She coaxed and crooned for the next five minutes, creeping farther and farther out on the branch. I wouldn't have thought she could be so patient. I waited below, saying Hail Marys inside my head. I hope it wasn't sacrilegious. It seems to me the Blessed Mother must love all creatures, including pussycats.

I heard a shriek of protest from the kitten. Mimi

crowed, "Got him! Look out, I'm coming down!"

In an instant she was dangling from the branch. I rushed forward to catch her, but I didn't time it right, or she didn't; she dropped down before I expected. The best I could do was break her fall, and I guess I did. Both of us tumbled to the grass.

Once again we untangled. Mimi reached inside her dress and took out the kitten. He was trembling all over, poor little thing. "Here. You take him while I put my shoes back on." She scooped him into my hands.

I clasped him to my breast. He was so frightened, and so small. At that moment ... well, there's a lot in books about love at first sight, but I've never known if I believed in it or not. But I never felt anything so like it as when I cradled that kitten in my hands. He was so tiny and fragile and scared that my heart ached. It felt soft and swollen with tenderness.

He's such a pretty little thing. He has stripes. His background fur is the color of ginger, but his stripes are darker, like dark brown sugar. There's a milky-white patch under his pointy chin, and his paws have sweet little pink pads and sharp, sharp claws. "His eyes are blue!"

"All kittens have blue eyes," said Mimi, tugging at her stocking. "Just like babies. They change later on. Didn't you know that?"

I didn't. Father hates cats. Every now and then, a stray cat will take shelter in the barn, but Father always shoots it. I explained this to Mimi. Her eyes grew wide and solemn. "I think your father must be the meanest man who ever lived," she said. "Thank goodness you ran away."

We brushed off our dresses and put our hats back on, and I picked up my diary. We headed out of the park, taking turns carrying the kitten. I felt jealous when he was in Mimi's hands, but I knew she had the right to hold him. She was the one who climbed the tree.

"I couldn't have rescued him without you," Mimi assured me. I swear that child can read my mind. "He'll be both our cat. What'll we call him? I think Harry's a nice name."

The perfect name came to me at once. "Moonstone. I'm reading a book about a yellow diamond that shines like the harvest moon. We'll call him Moonstone."

"Moonstone," repeated Mimi, tasting it. She flashed her bewitching smile at me. "That's even better than Harry."

We walked home in perfect accord. I was so happy. I was happy because I was in love with Moonstone, but I was also happy because I felt close to Mimi. We really are friends, Mimi and I. I don't believe she cares one bit that I'm only the hired girl.

But when we got back to Eutaw Place, everything went wrong. Mimi and I took the kitten to show Mrs Rosenbach, and she said it was out of the question that we should keep him. She said they already had the

Thomashefsky cat, and one animal was enough. Mimi argued that Thomashefsky really belongs to Malka, and she (Mimi) is tired of Thomashefsky and would rather have the kitten. Mrs Rosenbach said that was a pity, but Malka had enough to do with feeding Thomashefsky and letting him out of the house a dozen times a day. I assured her I would feed Moonstone and look after him; I offered to pay for his food out of my wages.

But Mrs Rosenbach was adamant. She said she didn't allow her servants to keep pets. Mimi pointed out that Malka had Thomashefsky, but Mrs Rosenbach said that Malka wasn't a servant; she was a member of the family. She said we should take the kitten back to the park where we found it, so it would have a chance to find its way home. She said that it probably lived in the park and hadn't been lost at all. *Now* it was lost, because we'd brought it to Eutaw Place.

I couldn't believe the cruelty of that. I was close to tears. Mrs Rosenbach told me, in the most *patronizing way*, to use my handkerchief, which wasn't fair because I wasn't crying. Mimi lost her temper and said her mother was mean, mean, mean. Mrs Rosenbach sent Mimi to her room and ordered me to take the kitten back to the park. She said that cats are good at finding their way home.

My last hope was that Malka might let me keep the kitten in the kitchen. But Malka said the Thomashefsky cat wouldn't like it, and as if to prove her right, the wretched cat hissed and growled at that poor little kitten. Malka told me to put the kitten out. She said it would find its way back to its mother.

I didn't believe that for a minute. I'm sure that kitten has no mother. Somehow I know that Moonstone is like me, all alone in the world. It was *wrong* to put him back outside, where there are big dogs and automobiles and nasty little boys who throw stones. I really could not bear it, and I cried. At last Malka relented and said I could give Moonstone a little milk before I turned him out.

So I poured out a saucer of milk – I forgot to say that by that time Moonstone was tired of being held and was mewing and scratching. I took one of the cold fish balls we made for supper and broke it up for him. Malka said it was a crime to waste her good fish balls like that, but I told her I wouldn't have any; Moonstone was only eating mine. I put the food on the floor, but the Thomashefsky cat came slinking over, the greedy thing. So I had to feed Moonstone outside, in Malka's miserable little plot of a garden.

I was afraid he would run away but he didn't. At first he hid behind the garbage bins, but I was able to coax him out again. When he tried to lap the milk, he sneezed. I squatted down and dipped my hand in the milk and let him lick it off my finger. I know he's too young to face the world by himself. It hurts my heart, what a baby he is.

I could have stayed with him forever, but Malka called

me in and made me shuck corn. All evening she scolded me because I kept looking outside to see if he was still there. The last time I looked – just before nine – he wasn't, and I can't bear thinking of that little, little darling thing out in the dark.

I can't bear it. It's past midnight, but I'm going to go search for him. No one will hear me creep downstairs and go out the cellar door. And if I find Moonstone, I shall bring him upstairs to my room, where he'll be safe – and if I lose my job for saving his life, I don't care, I don't care, I don't care.

Thursday, August the third, 1911

I am so bereft. I miss Moonstone, though my time with him was so fleeting. I wouldn't have thought I could love anything so much in such a short while. Miss Chandler once told me about a great Italian poet named Dante Alighieri, who fell in love with a girl he saw on a bridge. He never got to know her; he just saw her crossing the bridge and fell in love. I thought it strange and wonderful that a poet could fall in love so quickly and stay in love his whole life long. The girl – her name was Beatrice – was little more than a child. But maybe he loved her just because she was so young. Maybe her youth made him feel tenderhearted, the way Moonstone made me feel.

When I went to search for Moonstone, I found him behind the garbage bins. I coaxed him out and smuggled him upstairs. I'm sure he was glad to see me, because he purred when I picked him up. And oh, he was so cunning in my bedroom, so bright-eyed and graceful that I couldn't take my eyes off him.

Even though it was past midnight, he wanted to play. After an hour or so, I was sleepy. I put him in bed with me and blew out the candle, but he didn't sleep. He thought I was a mountain range, and he wanted to explore. I tried to keep still so he'd go to sleep, but I have a way of twitching my toes back and forth when I'm drowsy, and that made him think there was a mouse under the sheet. He pounced on my toes again and again.

But by and by I slept, and he did, too. When I woke the next morning, there was a little circle of golden fur by my side. How can cats make themselves into such perfect rounds? I looked at him and he was so soft and stripy and golden and young; I kissed him again and again.

Only, when I got up, I found he'd been a bad cat in the night. He'd tried to cover it up, but he'd been bad on my stockings. I couldn't blame him because he was a prisoner in my room, but the smell was nasty. I began to see how difficult it was going to be to hide him, with the messes and the meows and having to steal food from the kitchen.

I didn't know what to do, so I prayed. I begged the

Blessed Mother to show me a way to save Moonstone. I know she heard me, because all at once I remembered what Mrs Rosenbach said my first night here. *Oh, Solly! It used to be cats and dogs!* I saw the significance of those words. Before he rescued me, Mr Solomon must have brought home stray cats and dogs.

So then I knew what to do: ask Mr Solomon for help. Perhaps he could talk Mrs Rosenbach into letting me keep Moonstone. After all, he's her firstborn son, and anyone can see how proud she is of him. I don't always like Mrs R., but she's a very devoted mother.

I shut Moonstone in my room and started downstairs. I tried to think how I might catch Mr Solomon alone. It wouldn't be easy because he often goes to Temple in the morning. I was still pondering when I reached the stair landing. Then impulse seized upon me. I tiptoed down the hall to Mr Solomon's door and stood outside, listening.

I heard a drawer open and shut. He was awake and humming one of those sad-happy Jewish tunes. I knocked. Now that I look back, it strikes me that going to his bedroom was a bold thing to do. But at the time, I didn't think about it. Every day I go into Mr Solomon's room and make the bed, and dust the furniture, and pull the shades down so the room won't heat up. I gather his dirty clothes and check to see if his shoes need polishing, and I comb the hairs out of his hairbrush. Mr Solomon is tidy except for his socks. For some reason, he likes to roll them up in little balls and toss them around. I never know where I'll find them. I don't know why I'm writing this. I guess what I'm trying to say is that it would be easier for me to be shy about men's bedrooms if I weren't a hired girl.

All the same, I jumped when the door opened.

He was dressed and shaved, thank goodness. He looked at me quizzically and said, "Janet?" I could see him trying to work out why I was knocking on his door.

I thought I'd better be quick. I said, "Oh, sir, I'm sorry to trouble you, but I don't know what to do and—"

"Is something wrong downstairs?" he asked. "Is Malka ill?"

"No, no," I said. "But I need your help something awful – I don't know who else could help me." My eyes filled up with tears. I thought of how little Moonstone was, and how he didn't have anyone but me, and how I didn't have anyone but Mr Solomon.

Mr Solomon said, "Can't this wait? Surely after breakfast—" But then he switched to making consoling Jewish sounds. I told him how Mimi and I rescued Moonstone together and how Mrs Rosenbach said we couldn't keep him. I told him how Malka made me shoo him outside and how in the night I couldn't bear it and I had to rescue him again.

"The kitten's upstairs?" he said, before I'd quite finished. "In your room?"

"I couldn't leave him out in the dark," I said. "He's just a tiny little kitten."

"Let me see him," said Mr Solomon.

He followed me to my room. When we opened the door, Moonstone was up on the windowsill, watching the sparrows. He leaped onto the chair and down to the floor, and crossed the linoleum with his little tail held high. My heart swelled at the sight of him. He was so bold, so curious, and so pretty.

Mr Solomon hunkered down and tapped his fingers on the floor. Moonstone pricked up his ears. Then Mr Solomon took his handkerchief from his pocket, shook it loose, and tickled the floor with it.

The kitten was delighted. He began to frisk and scamper and pounce. Mr Solomon played with him – oh, so gently! Ma used to say that men were rough because that was their nature. I wish she could have seen Mr Solomon playing with Moonstone.

"He's a pretty little fellow," said Mr Solomon. With one deft hand, he caught hold of the kitten and turned him on his back. "Actually, it's a she. She's friendly, too. No wonder you lost your heart to her."

I knelt down across from him. "That's just it – that's exactly what happened. I've lost my heart. I can't part with him – her. I just can't!"

He made a soft noise with his tongue against his teeth and dangled the handkerchief over Moonstone's head, so she had to leap for it. Then he waved it in a circle, so that she chased her tail. I couldn't help laughing. Most of the time when you laugh, it's because something is amiss – clumsy or wrong or sad – but when you laugh at a kitten, you laugh for pure joy. "Do you think you can persuade your mother to let me keep her?"

He looked me straight in the eye. "No, I don't. I'm sorry, Janet, but I know my mother. When I was a boy, I was always bringing home stray animals. Then it became Malka's job to care for them, and Mother's job to find them new homes. A kitten is more work than you think. They get into everything, and they need to be watched."

"I'll watch her," I vowed, but I felt my eyes fill with tears. Malka keeps me busy all day long.

"You can't," said Mr Solomon gently. "You have work to do. Besides, Mother won't allow it. She'll be even more set against the kitten when she finds out it's a girl. That means kittens later on. And then there's Thomashefsky. Cats don't like sharing their homes."

"But Moonstone's so little, and she hasn't any mother," I wept.

Mr Solomon took the handkerchief away from Moonstone and handed it to me. "Tell me, Janet," he said, "do you love this kitten enough to want a good home for her, even if she has to live somewhere else?"

I didn't want to answer. I knew where the conversation was tending. I sobbed harder *on purpose*. I'm ashamed that I did that, because it wasn't fair. It was feminine wiles; that's what it was, and I don't think much of feminine wiles.

"You have to answer me," he said, not unkindly, but firmly. "Would you be willing to give the kitty up if you could be sure she was happy and safe?"

I looked down at Moonstone. His wide blue eyes were fixed on the handkerchief. He – no, I must learn to write *she* - didn't like it that the game had stopped. I brushed the handkerchief against the floor, and she leaped forward and caught it between her paws. Then she rolled over on her back and bit the cloth, fierce and merry at the same time. Oh, her little tail, her pink-padded paws, the sweet triangle of her face!

"Yes," I said wretchedly.

"Then I'll help you," said Mr Solomon, and he smiled his sweet-for-a-man smile. "Don't worry. I won't give up until I've found her a good home. We'll start with my sister Anna. She's afraid of mice, which is good. And I think Oskar's old enough to be gentle with a kitten."

I wasn't sure whether I liked that idea or not. Mrs Friedhoff seems like such a shadowy person, nice, but dull, and Oskar seems like a snake lover, not a kitten lover. On the other hand, the Friedhoffs live nearby, and I might be able to visit Moonstone if she went to live there. "She isn't trained," I said, remembering the mess in the room.

"I'll tell Anna to keep a box of sand in the house," Mr

Solomon assured me. "It's easy to train them, if you have a box of sand."

A box of sand. I'd never have thought of that. "What if she says no?"

"I think I can talk her into saying yes. If she doesn't, one of Mother's bridge ladies lost her pug dog a little while ago. I might be able to persuade her to try a kitten." He reached for Moonstone and gathered her up. "I'll go see Anna right after breakfast. Can you find me a basket, or a cardboard box with a lid?"

My heart tightened. "Do you have to take her right away?"

He nodded. "When you ask people if they want a kitten, they say no. But if they see the kitten, it's a different matter."

I could see this. But I could also see something else – that my time with Moonstone was at an end. Right after breakfast, Mr Solomon would take her away. I started to cry again, but this time it wasn't feminine wiles.

I'm shedding tears as I write this, but I'm almost finished. Mrs Friedhoff did take Moonstone, and Oskar made her a little house out of a baby quilt and a cardboard box. Mr Solomon says Oskar spends a lot of time dragging little pieces of string across the floor so Moonstone can chase them. And Anna – I mean Mrs Friedhoff – has promised that some night when she and Mr Friedhoff go out, I can look after Oskar and see Moonstone again.

So I am grateful. I have to be grateful. But I'm sure that Moonstone was meant to be my cat, not Oskar's, not Anna's, not even Mimi's. (Mimi isn't half as sorry as I am that Moonstone's gone. I think she's a very fickle sort of girl.)

After Mr Solomon came back, he asked if I would do something for him. I said, "Anything." Because I *would* do anything for him, but I would prefer it to be something heroic, like saving him from a burning building, or helping him win the hand of Nora Himmelrich. It turned out that what he wanted was for me to forgive Mrs Rosenbach – not only forgive her but apologize to her. Apparently she told him I *flounced* when she said I couldn't keep the kitten, and Tuesday night, everyone could hear me banging the plates when I loaded the dumbwaiter. It seems I'm not supposed to flounce or bang plates. I guess hired girls shouldn't have any feelings.

I didn't want to forgive Mrs Rosenbach, but Mr Solomon looked very earnest and pleading. He said Mrs Rosenbach was hurt by my ingratitude. I wouldn't have thought that anything I did could hurt someone like her, but I guess I should be grateful. She pays me well and she bought me two dresses that are a lot nicer than they have to be. All the same, I wish Mr Solomon hadn't asked me to forgive her, because I was kind of enjoying being angry. On the other hand, I'm supposed to forgive people; I'm *trying* to be a good Catholic.

So I humbled myself and agreed to forgive Mrs Rosenbach and say I was sorry for the flouncing. I *wasn't* sorry, but I strained myself to say so. The apologizing wasn't as bad as I thought it would be, because Mrs R. wasn't cold or scornful, only grave. She said she knew I was disappointed but the important thing was that Moonstone had a good home, and I was free to go on with my duties. She even said she valued my apology, because she knew I was an honest person and wouldn't say I was sorry unless I meant it.

Then I felt guilty, because I didn't really mean it. But there was no point in saying so. I said, "Yes, ma'am." And I was careful not to flounce when I left the room.

PART FOUR

The Warrior Goddess
of Wisdom

Monday, August the seventh, 1911

I have had an adventure!

It was late last night and I was in the library trying to read the *Meditations* of Marcus Aurelius. That was Mr Rosenbach's idea. I finished *The Moonstone* and was going to start *The Woman in White*, which is also by Mr Wilkie Collins. It begins in *such* a fascinating way: *This is the story of what a Woman's patience can endure, and what a Man's resolution can achieve.* How can anyone not want to read that? But yesterday Mr Rosenbach asked me what I was reading. When I told him, he looked thoughtful and said that if I wanted to become truly educated, I must read history and philosophy as well as novels.

So I asked for some philosophy because I thought

that sounded elevated, and he gave me the *Meditations*. It isn't long, for which I am grateful because it's slow going. It seems to me that Marcus Aurelius doesn't want anybody to get excited about anything. I don't want to live like that. If anything exciting ever happens to me, I want to get excited about it. Of course, thus far my life has been tedious because of Steeple Farm and being only the hired girl, but there is such a thing as *real life*, and sooner or later it's going to begin. I suppose I might have to suffer a little because real life is like that, but I hope I will suffer nobly. Mr Marcus Aurelius has some ideas about that, too.

So there I was, reading Marcus, and then I decided to refresh myself with *The Picturesque World*. I look through the plates almost every night; they are so fascinating. As I was musing over engravings of the Alhambra, I heard the sound of footsteps on the front porch.

I was in my nightgown. My kimono is perfectly lovely, cream colored with apple blossoms on it, but I don't always wear it once I get inside the library because these summer nights are hot, and my kimono's too nice to perspire in. I tell myself that if I ever heard anyone coming, there'd be time to put it on. But when I heard the front door open, I didn't think about my kimono. It was nearly midnight, and everyone was in bed: Mr and Mrs Rosenbach, and Mr Solomon, and Mimi, and Malka. *No one* ought to be coming into the house.

And whoever was coming in was coming in stealthily. Usually the front door sticks, so that opening it makes a sound like a sneeze, but this time the door opened slowly, so that the sneeze was muffled and prolonged.

I thought of screaming to rouse the house, but I didn't dare. Isn't that queer? My heart beat like a rabbit's, but my mouth was too dry to scream. I couldn't believe what was happening.

But it *was* happening. And even though my mind couldn't believe it, my body knew it was time to be frightened, because the footsteps were coming *toward the library*. So I moved – oh, so swiftly! – to the hearth. I picked up the poker, grasped it with all my strength, and glided forward – my feet were bare and the carpet is thick and I scarcely made a sound. *I saw the doorknob turn.* As the door opened, I leaped forward and brought the poker slashing through the air.

He swerved and ducked. It makes my blood run cold to think how close I came to killing him. He leaped back and held up his hands in surrender. "Jehoshaphat!" he cried. "Great Jakes, don't kill me!"

At that instant – that very instant – I knew who he was. I gasped, "You're David!"

He gaped at me with a queer mixture of amusement and shock – because I really had frightened him. "Yes, I'm David," he said, "but who are you? What are you doing in Papa's library in the middle of the night?"

I was so startled I almost said my real name. I stammered, "I'm Jo— Janet," like that. I don't think he noticed the slip. "The hired girl. Your father gave me permission to read his books."

"You're Papa's little girl?" he said incredulously. "That's what he calls you, you know: the little girl who loves to read." He gave a shout of laughter and looked at me, and that's when I realized that I was *in my nightgown*. I was dreadfully mortified. Thank heavens it wasn't that awful old rag I brought from Steeple Farm but one of the new things I bought with Mimi.

I know I blushed. I flew to the chair where I'd left the kimono and put it on as fast as ever I could. Even when I'd knotted the belt, I felt flustered. Mr David is so – well, he's *not* handsome, now that I think it over. He has an enormous crooked nose. I couldn't help staring because I'd heard something about Jews having big hooked noses, but I'd made up my mind it was all twaddle, because none of the Rosenbachs have noses like that. Mr R.'s nose is hawkish but it isn't large. Mr Solomon has a handsome nose. Mrs R.'s nose is fine and straight, and Mimi told me hers is what they call retroussé.

But David's – I should write *Mr David's* – nose is large and very crooked. He caught me staring at it and said, "A nose like mine is the banner of a great man, Janet. When it blows, it's a typhoon; when it bleeds, the Red Sea. But it's a monument – never doubt that – a monument to a generous heart, a towering spirit, and an expansive soul."

I stood nonplussed. I never heard anybody talk like that before, and between being embarrassed because of my kimono and almost murdering him with the poker – well, I couldn't think of a thing to say. I just stared at him.

"I broke it." He lowered his voice as if he was sharing a secret. "I was ten years old and walking on top of a fence – showing off for a little girl with blue eyes. I waved to her, she smiled at me –" he shrugged, throwing up his hands – "I lost my balance. Fell flat on my face."

I couldn't help laughing. But while I was laughing, a funny idea stole into my mind. It sounds silly now, but for a moment, just a shred of a moment, I wondered if he might be flirting with me. I mean, he was talking about blue eyes, and I *have* blue eyes. Now that I write it down, I see that what I was thinking was awfully far-fetched. But at the time, it confused me.

And as a matter of fact, *he* confused me. Feature for feature, he isn't as good-looking as Mr Solomon. But he's taller than his brother, lean and easy in his movements, and he wore his shirtsleeves rolled up, and I liked looking at his forearms. His hair is curly and nearly black, and he has his mother's heavy-lidded eyes, except his are full of mischief. He has to be at least eighteen, because he graduated from high school, but he doesn't look much older than that. He's young.

I said, "Why are you here in the middle of the night?"

"I took a late train."

"They're not expecting you."

"*I* wasn't expecting me," he said, which was no answer at all. But I guess he doesn't have to explain himself to me, because I'm only the hired girl. "I wasn't expecting anyone to knock me on the head with a poker, either. Would you really have hit me?" He sounded admiring.

"Yes, sir," I said proudly – because if he *had* been a burglar, I would have shown courage and resolution.

"Papa described you as a nice, bright little thing, and Mama said you get along with Malka. Nobody told me you were dangerous. What are you reading? *The Picturesque World*? Are you a lover of the picturesque?"

"Yes, sir." I liked the way he said that. It sounded so cultivated. "I'm choosing all the places I want to see when—" I almost said, *when I grow up*, but I stopped in time.

"I like traveling, too. Especially France and Italy. Are you interested in scenery, or art?"

"Both. Only I don't know too much about art. I'm trying to learn." I set my palm against the cover of *The Picturesque World*. I was pleased to see that my hand was steady. "I study the plates. I just – use my eyes." He nodded emphatically, as if using my eyes was exactly what was called for.

"I'm an artist. Or I'm going to be," David said, and he sounded confidential again. "That's why I've been away all summer, living with the Gratzes. Isabelle Gratz's uncle is a painter, and he's been giving me lessons. Papa thinks it's just a hobby," he added, "but it isn't. Only you mustn't tell him. I have to tell him myself. What kind of art do you like? What places have you chosen?"

He sounded as if he really wanted to know. I began to thumb through the book. "Lots of places. The Taj in India and the labyrinth at Versailles. And Paris, of course. I'm dying to get to Paris. And Holyrood Chapel in Edinburgh, and the Grotto of Doves at Taormina. And in Spain, the Alhambra." I turned to the page I'd been admiring before he came in: a courtyard made up of exquisitely carved columns, and a fountain resting on the backs of lions. "Have you ever been there?"

"I was there on the Eve of St. John."

He spoke as if the last words held something portentous, which surprised me, because the Jews don't usually go in for saints. "What happens on the Eve of St. John?"

"On the Eve of St. John, the Alhambra is haunted," Mr David answered, "and not just by Christian souls." He tapped the engraving with his fingers. "Those lion statues supporting the fountain are Jewish, by the way. That's why there are twelve of them. They represent the twelve tribes of Israel."

I thought that was interesting, but I was more interested in the ghosts. "How do you mean, haunted?"

"The past returns," said Mr David. His eyes were

faraway and perfectly grave. "On the Eve of San Juan –" he made the words sound foreign, and I felt a thrill go down my spine – "the ghosts walk. I could sense it, Janet. Under the plashing of the water in the fountain, I seemed to hear the clanking of armor and the rattle of swords. At midnight, I heard the lute of the Moorish princess who never eloped with her Christian lover. She appears at the fountain, entreating someone to baptize her and grant her peace. Of course she didn't trouble me, poor little soul, because she sensed I was a Jew. But I heard her music, and I caught a glimpse of her out of the corner of my eye – a sweet, vaporous little person, with a red, red rose in her hair."

His eyes questioned mine. He was trying to see if I believed him. Of course I didn't. I knew he was teasing me – well, I was *almost* sure – and I thought maybe I ought to be mad at him. It wasn't the mean kind of teasing, though. There was something about the corners of his mouth that made me think he wanted me to play, too.

I said slowly, "You left out the lions."

"The lions?"

"Yes. They're honest Jewish lions, and they can't abide humbug. On the Eve of St. John, they come alive, and if a liar passes through the courtyard, they lash their tails and roar as loud as thunder." I darted a sideways glance at him. "I'm surprised you didn't hear them, sir."

He caught his breath. There was a fraction of a second

when I wondered if I'd gone too far; he was the master's son, after all, and I'd as good as called him a liar. But then he laughed – oh my, he did laugh! His voice is like his father's: exuberant and strong and so loud I thought he'd wake the whole house. "I like you," he said, and his smile bloomed until it lit his whole face.

That took me aback. It seemed like a bold thing for him to say, and I was in my kimono and it was the middle of the night. I think maybe I ought to have been offended. I mean, maybe he was taking a liberty. But then again, he might not have meant the kind of *like* that would be taking a liberty. And if I acted offended, he might think I was flattering myself, assuming that he meant he *liked* me the way a man likes a girl. He might laugh at me for being presumptuous. I couldn't stand the thought of that.

I felt so abashed I took refuge in being the hired girl. I turned my back on him and tidied up the books. I marked my place in the *Meditations* and shelved it; I closed Volume I of *The Picturesque World* and set it on the stand next to Volume II. I fiddled with Mr Rosenbach's pencils, making sure the points were facing upward—

"Wait a minute!"

I spun around. Mr David wasn't grinning anymore; he was gazing at me with narrowed eyes. "Stay there a minute – don't move a muscle – don't stir! Can you do that?"

I did. I froze, like a ninny or an obedient child, while

he strode to the desk and rummaged in a drawer for a sheet of paper. He grabbed a sharp pencil from Mr Rosenbach's stand. From one of the bookcases, he selected a tall, narrow book, which he used as a drawing board. He made a half circle around me, circled back, stopped, and began to sketch rapidly. "Hold still, hold still," he murmured, and his pencil scratched the page.

I was afraid to breathe. So I stayed right where I was, but the more his pencil moved, the more afraid I was of what might be taking shape on the page. "Don't freeze your face," he commanded, and after a minute, "Would you mind unbraiding your hair?"

My hair was in a single braid. In this weather, having it loose is like wearing a wool blanket over my shoulders. I thought I ought to refuse, but I knew I'd look prettier with my hair down. So I undid the ribbon and scattered my hair over my shoulders.

He said, "Better," in an absentminded tone, and moved more to the side. I didn't like that because I don't look too good from the side. I don't look that good from the front, either, but it's worse from the side. My jaw is heavy and my neck is too thick. "Why are you drawing me?"

"Don't move your lips," he said, and turned over the page. He said, "Aah!" – not like the *ah* in *papa*, but like the *ah* in *cat*: a sharper sound. "That's better. I've been planning a large canvas – a painting of Joan of Arc. It hasn't been going well. Now I see the model I've been using is too refined looking. I want a strong girl, a real peasant. Why, what's the matter?" I had turned on him, and I felt as fierce as when I'd swung the poker through the air.

"How dare you?" I cried. "What a horrible thing to say to me – *peasant*, unrefined." I was almost too angry to get the words out. "You rude, ungentlemanly *pig* of a man!" I rushed for the door. I felt so bruised – so angry – so bewildered, with him liking me one minute and disdaining me the next. And I knew I must get away from him before I cried. But he is the *quickest* man I've ever seen – he got to the door ahead of me and stood with his back to it.

"Don't be mad," he said coaxingly. "Great Jakes! I never wanted to hurt your feelings! I guess I did, though. I'm sorry. Won't you give me a chance to explain myself?"

I didn't answer because I was near tears. He gazed at me intently. I've never had a man look at me like that before. It reminded me of the Thomashefsky cat when I'm fixing fish. In a way I liked it, but I also wanted to hit him. When I thought of him calling me a peasant, I wanted to *fell him to the earth*.

"Come on, don't be mad," he pleaded. "I didn't mean what you thought I meant. All I meant is that you're not like the model I've been using. She's a silly doll of a girl, not like you at all. You don't want to be one of those bitsy little things with a rosebud mouth and a pinched-in waist and a tiny little brain, do you?"

"I do," I said, almost sobbing, because hearing about the pinched-in waist made things worse. I know I should lace my corsets tighter, but I just can't bear it.

"No, you don't," he said, almost crooning. "No, you don't. You're a magnificent creature – you know that, don't you? Tall and robust and wholesome looking. You're like one of Michelangelo's Sibyls – a grand, bareheaded creature. I think Joan of Arc must have been very like you: a strong young girl with honest eyes and a nice fresh complexion. She was sixteen years old when she led an army into battle; did you know that? I can imagine you doing that – galloping along on a splendid horse, and brandishing a sword instead of a poker."

His eyes sparkled on the last word. He was inviting me to laugh again. I didn't want to, but I did.

"There, that's better," he said, and held out the sheet of paper. "See how I've drawn you? You can keep the sketch, if you want to."

I looked at it. I wish I'd taken the sketch, because I might have studied it at length and learned more about what he thought of me. But at the time, I was embarrassed. I didn't want him to see me looking at my picture too long, because then he would think I was vain.

So I only snatched a look. He'd drawn my hair like a river pouring over my shoulders. And my eyes looked large and thoughtful, and my forehead was all right, I guess. But the line of my jaw was just as bad as I'd feared, and

I thought my neck looked fat. I said quickly, "I don't want it."

"That's all right," he said cheerfully. "I can do better. Maybe you'll let me draw you again. I'd like to make several studies of you." He took a step back and cocked his head to one side. "The arms," he said, "and the shoulders. Your ordinary clothes'll be fine, as long as the sleeves aren't puffed. I'll pay you, of course – it's customary to pay a model. Tell me, Janet, may I draw you again?"

I said, "I don't know."

That's when the clock struck.

It struck twelve, that's what it struck, and it was only later that I was reminded of Cinderella. The two of us stood there, facing each other, and listened to the twelve chimes. I think both of us realized that it was queer for us – master's son and servant girl – to be talking together in the middle of the night. It wasn't proper. I don't mean there was any harm in it, but it wasn't proper.

"I have to go upstairs," I said. I think I hoped he would stop me again, but he moved aside. It became possible to leave the room.

So I went upstairs to bed, but I didn't sleep, not for a long while. It was a relief to get away from him, because there were too many feelings. I wanted to be alone so I could sort them out and name them. I wish I hadn't called him a pig, because that wasn't refined.

I want to see him again. Even though there were too

many feelings, it strikes me that having them all at once, all tangled together, is one of the most interesting things that's ever happened to me.

I wonder if any of Michelangelo's Sibyls are in *The Picturesque World*.

Wednesday, August the ninth, 1911

I am *completely* wretched. In fact, I am so unwell that when I finished the lunch dishes, Malka took pity on me. She threw the dish towel at me and said I was of no use to her when I'm like this and I should go upstairs and lie down. Then she fixed me a hot-water bottle.

It must be a hundred degrees in my room today. The shutters are drawn and there isn't a breath of air, but I have the hot-water bottle in my lap, because it helps with the pain. Yesterday I decided I would try lacing my corsets a little bit tighter, because maybe I could learn to stand it. But by nightfall, I thought I would scream if I couldn't take them off. I don't know how I'm ever going to suffer nobly when I can't bear my corsets.

To make matters worse, when I woke up today, I found I had two big pimples on my face – one on my chin, where I'm used to having a pimple, but the other one *at the end of my nose*. Nothing could be more horrid. I tell myself I will bear my trials bravely, but today I just can't. My stomach aches so, and I'm lonely. I wish Mrs Rosenbach hadn't made me get rid of Moonstone. I shall never forgive her for that, no matter what Father Horst says. He thinks forgiveness is a very important Christian virtue.

I saw Father Horst for instruction yesterday, but I wasn't feeling very religious, because I wanted to take the streetcar down to Rosenbach's Department Store and buy a parasol and some new stockings. I thought there might be time to go after instruction, but I didn't know how long Father Horst would talk. I made the mistake of asking how Orthodox Christians are different from real Catholics, and he went on for a long time about how the Orthodox Christians think that the Holy Ghost comes from the Father, instead of proceeding from the Father and the Son. I guess this is important, but I couldn't seem to fix my mind on it. I kept wondering whether I could find a parasol that would go with my hat.

Then Father Horst apologized, saying that church history was a hobby of his, and he gave me the Baltimore Catechism to learn. It's awful long. There are more than four hundred questions, and I have to memorize the answers to all of them, word for word. I'm sure I can do it but it will take time, and I have so little time.

I did get to the department store, but I was so rushed I snatched up a rose-colored parasol and paid for it before I thought about it. I know it will fade, because pink always does. A white parasol would match my dresses and wear better, too. After I bought the parasol, I went to the book department and picked up *Daniel Deronda*. Then I fell into temptation and bought *The Woman in White*. I know Mr Rosenbach would lend me his copy, but I didn't want him to know that I wanted to read Wilkie Collins instead of Marcus Aurelius. The cheapest stockings were three pairs for twenty-nine cents, so I got them. Then I lost all control over myself and bought a bottle of carnation perfume. When I put it on last night, Malka asked me what the stink was, and truthfully, I couldn't blame her because it does stink. I couldn't wait to scrub it off. So I wasted thirty-five cents.

Mr David came down to the kitchen Tuesday morning and hugged Malka – she said she was too old and frail to be bear-hugged like that, but I know she liked it. Of course I *had* to be scrubbing the inside of the oven when he came down. Why couldn't I have been doing something pretty, like creaming together butter and sugar? No, there I was, in my canvas apron, with my sleeves rolled up and my hands smeared with stove grease. He said, "So this is the new girl?" and Malka said I was named Janet. And he said, "How do you do?" as if we'd never met.

Now he's gone back to New York. Not that I care. I think there might have been some kind of scandal about him coming back from New York so unexpectedly, in the middle of the night. There's been a lot of shouting upstairs. I didn't pay much heed to it, because Mr Rosenbach shouts even when he's happy. But when Mr David went back to New York, Mr Rosenbach went with him, and they were both in a very bad humor. I'm not sure when they're coming back.

I was a fool ever to think Mr David was flirting with me. Of course he wasn't. If he had been, that would have been a little bit interesting, but nothing interesting ever happens to me, because that is not my destiny.

I wonder if Mimi knows what happened in New York.

Friday, August the eleventh, 1911

I can't see why I even bother writing in this book. This must be the most boring diary ever written. Nothing ever happens to me. My whole life is spent scrubbing and cooking and doing dishes. It's the same thing over and over, just like on the farm; the work isn't hard, and I'm paid for my trouble, but it's always the *same*. I don't think it's fair that some girls get to go to school and dances and even Europe, when I'm destined to be nothing but a drudge. Life and youth are rushing by as I chop cabbage and push the carpet sweeper back and forth across the rug.

We're having another hot spell this week. Mr Rosenbach and Mr David are still in New York, so it's a quiet Shabbos. The pimple on my chin has gone away, but the one on my nose is still big and shiny. It's frightful.

I found a picture of the Sibyl Mr David compared me to, in *The Picturesque World*. Her name is the Erythraean Sibyl, and she's terribly homely. She has arms like a butcher and wears a nasty little hat. The only good thing about her is that people seem to admire her; somebody named Lady Eastlake called her "a grand, bareheaded creature," just as Mr David did. I don't know why neither of them noticed the hat. The author of *The Picturesque World* said the Sibyl was "dignified and majestic," as befits a warrior goddess of wisdom. Afterward I looked in the mirror and tried to assume a martial air, but all I could see was the pimple on my nose.

Lately I've been reading the prayer book, and it seems to me that I lack the spirit of repentance. It isn't that I haven't any sins – I am *steeped* in sin – I just don't seem to be able to repent. The catechism says that true contrition should be interior, supernatural, universal, and sovereign, and that makes me realize that I'm not contrite *at all*. I'm sure I ought to feel repentant about not loving Father, but I don't. How could I love and honor him when he never spoke a kind word to me? And I guess I should repent of lying about my age, but where would I be if I hadn't? Back home on the farm, working twice as hard as I work here and not being paid a penny, that's where. It's all so unjust. I know I'm sinful, but I don't think it's altogether my *fault*.

Every time I try to repent, I get angry.

Malka has been having trouble with her bunion and hasn't been out of the house all week. It's dreadfully hot and sticky. I wish the weather would change. I wish anything would change.

Tuesday, August the fifteenth, 1911

It's a curious thing about Mrs Rosenbach. The minute I think I don't like her, she changes and then I do. I told her today was the Feast of the Assumption and that's a Holy Day of Obligation. I said I didn't know how long the church service would last and I was afraid I might be late coming home. But Mrs Rosenbach said of course I must go; Malka could manage until I came back.

Then Malka was vexed and wanted to know just how many Holy Days of Obligation there are. She said she couldn't have me running off to church every time she needed me. Mrs Rosenbach said in a very calm voice that Malka wasn't being fair, because I worked hard, and the house has never looked so clean as it has since I came. Of course that made things worse with Malka. I fetched my prayer book and showed her there were only six Holy Days of Obligation all year, plus Sundays. She sniffed.

It was a very inspiring service, though, because everyone brought flowers and fragrant herbs for the Blessed Mother. I went to the flower market and bought pink roses – I meant to buy white ones because blue and white are the Virgin's colors, but the white ones were all wilted. Anyway, she'd probably like a change. Her altar had so many bouquets they were tumbling over one another, and the smell of flowers and incense blended in the air.

When I got back, Mr Rosenbach – he is back from New York but Mr David isn't – showed me Titian's *Assumption of the Virgin* in one of his books. The real painting is in Venice and he's seen it. He says it's so beautiful it makes you stop short in your tracks. The one in the book is just a line drawing, but you can see what a magnificent painting it must be. Mr Rosenbach says the red of the Virgin's dress is the loveliest shade of red there is. He told me to shut my eyes and imagine it. When I opened my eyes he smiled at me and said he could tell from my face that I'd gotten the color exactly right.

Wednesday, August the sixteenth, 1911

Mrs Rosenbach had her bridge ladies today, and Malka asked me to serve the luncheon. She's having an awful bad time with her bunion. I found a cure for Malka's bunion in a magazine, but you're supposed to rub the bunion with lard, and lard is *treif*. Besides, Malka says it would hurt to rub it. She cut out a big patch in her slipper to let the bunion out, and I could see it. It looks horrifying and un-natural. She's been in a bad humor all week, but I can't blame her, now that I've set eyes on her bunion.

I didn't mind waiting on the bridge ladies because I thought it might be interesting to hear them talk. One of them is Miss Himmelrich, who is an old maid but related to Nora Himmelrich. Another is Mrs Schoenberg, whom I like because she dresses so stylish and always greets me at the door. I don't like Mrs Mueller because she's prissy and has a mean little mouth. I don't think Mrs R. likes her much either, because Mrs Mueller is never invited here except for bridge. The ladies need her for bridge. You have to have four people to play bridge, no more, no less. I don't know how to play bridge, but I think it must be very exciting, because the ladies play all day long, from morning till late afternoon. They never get tired of it.

We always serve special food to the bridge ladies: dainty things that don't take long to serve or eat. The china is so thin you can see the shadow of your fingers through the teacups. Everything has to be just so, from the flowers on the sideboard to the little napkins Mrs R. embroidered with hearts and clubs and diamonds and spades. Usually Malka makes chicken salad, but today Mrs R. wanted cucumber sandwiches (I never had them before but they're good) and corn oysters, which aren't really oysters but fritters. For dessert there were cold berries with sugar syrup and almond cookies and little orange tartlets. The only things served hot were the fritters, so I kept everything in the refrigerator until Mrs R. rang for me. Then I fried the corn oysters and brought everything upstairs.

I divided the corn oysters between the four plates and gave each lady two tiny sandwiches and a green glass goblet with berries in it. It all looked so pretty. Then I poured iced tea and set out sugar and lemon slices. The ladies were upset because Mrs Schoenberg is going to the Catskills to get away from the heat, and that means *no bridge for three weeks*. There was a flash of a moment – I can't believe how naive I was – when I thought of opening my mouth and saying that I could learn to play. I know I could. Miss Chandler always said I was quick to learn. But of course they would never play with the hired girl, no matter how much they wanted their *fourth* (that's the term they use).

Then old Miss Himmelrich said her great-niece Nora could play. The other ladies didn't seem too crazy about this idea. I was arranging the dessert things on the sideboard, and I could see Mrs Mueller's petulant look in the mirror. Malka told me Mrs Mueller is the worst gossip in Eutaw Place, and I bet she didn't want a young girl around at bridge, because she'd have to watch what she says.

Then Mrs R. said graciously that it would be delightful to have Nora.

Of course I thought of Mr Solomon. His fragile nymph would be right under his roof. I wondered if there was some way to make sure he knew Nora was coming. If he did, he might seize her in his arms and reveal his faithful passion. Maybe she would yield to him and promise to be his wife. I was so deep in thought that Mrs Rosenbach said, "Thank you, Janet," and I looked down and saw that I'd set the cookies in a little wreath with the tartlets in the middle, and I'd run out of things to do.

I said, "Yes, ma'am," in that bland submissive way that's right for a housemaid, and went outside, taking care not to flounce. I shut the door. Then Mrs R. called, "Leave the door open, please," because in this heat, you have to keep the air moving. There's a little bit of a breeze today.

I propped the door open with Mrs R.'s bronze pug dog, and I started down to the kitchen. I had reached the top of the back staircase when I heard Mrs Schoenberg say, "Your new girl seems to be working out nicely." That's when I made my fatal mistake: *I stopped to listen.*

Mrs Rosenbach said, "Janet's a good girl. A little rough, but very hardworking."

"She certainly looks hale and hearty," said Mrs Mueller. (How I detest that woman!) "Is she honest?"

"I'm sure she's honest," said Mrs R., "though she may have fibbed about her age. She says she's eighteen."

Old Miss Himmelrich said, "With that figure and that height, she might be twenty."

"If she is, she's very backward," retorted Mrs R. "Of course, she was brought up in the country –" she made the country sound like some kind of Home for the Hopelessly Backward – "but even still, she's rather childish. You should have seen her when I told her she couldn't keep a kitten! But she works like a horse – Malka says she's never had a harder worker, and she gets along beautifully with Malka, which none of the others could. Naturally, Malka's taught her to keep kosher. Last week I asked for oysters and Janet looked me straight in the face and said, 'Now, ma'am, you know Malka thinks that *treif* isn't good for you.'"

There was a burst of laughter. I felt my cheeks burn. I couldn't believe she was *mimicking me*. I could have cried with mortification.

"But your Malka is a treasure," protested Mrs Schoenberg. "So loyal! Who can find servants like that these days?"

There was a chorus of agreement. I heard fragments of stories: one lady's housemaid dressed finer than her mistress; another was bold enough, during the dead of winter, to ask for a fire in her bedroom; another had *followers*. I scarcely listened. My soul was too harrowed up. To be called rough and childish and backward – and I'd worked so hard to please Mrs Rosenbach! Then, out of the chorus of voices, I heard Mrs Mueller say she would never trust a *shiksa* in the house – especially with unmarried sons.

"Janet's not like that," Mrs Rosenbach said firmly. "She's not a flirt. I don't mean she doesn't have her little crushes – just now it's Moritz – but she's as innocent as a child. I have no worries on that score."

"Servants always prefer the master to the mistress," said Miss Himmelrich. "They'd rather take their orders from a man."

"Moritz is much interested in Janet," said Mrs Rosenbach. "He has an idea she's unusually bright. He's trying to get her to read the *Meditations* of Marcus Aurelius, poor girl."

There was another ripple of laughter. I clenched my teeth and vowed I would read every page of those awful *Meditations*. Then Mrs Mueller said in her vile and insinuating way, "She's not a bad-looking girl. I wouldn't want her having her little crushes in my house. What if she falls in love with Solly?"

"I never have to worry about Solly." Mrs Rosenbach sounded serene to the point of smugness. "Solly would never look at a girl who wasn't Jewish. His faith is too important to him. And Janet is scarcely Jezebel."

"Be grateful David's not at home," Mrs Mueller said meaningfully, and Mrs Schoenberg trilled, "Oh, David! Such a one for the girls!"

"He's staying with the Gratzes in New York, isn't he?" Mrs Mueller's voice sounded greedy for details. "I heard there might be a match between David and the Gratz girl."

"There will be no match," Mrs Rosenbach said crisply. "David is far too young to settle down. And Isabelle Gratz is a giddy schoolgirl. I can't imagine how these rumors get started. Whose turn is it to deal?"

I heard the sound of the cards shuffling and the smack of them being dealt on the table one by one. Mrs Schoenberg sighed in an exaggerated fashion and said, "Ach, this hand is more like a foot!" and Mrs Mueller snapped out, "One spade."

They had finished talking about David – and me. They were back to playing cards again. I lingered a few minutes more but heard nothing.

I went downstairs with my mind reeling. I seethed with indignation – I hated Mrs Rosenbach for saying I was backward and like a child. And how dare she mistake my gratitude to her husband for a silly crush? Mr Rosenbach is kind to me and gives me books to read. I should be *base*, I should be *infamous*, if I failed in gratitude to a man who gives me books.

And what did she mean by saying I wasn't Jezebel?

Tuesday, August the twenty-second, 1911

Today I saw Father Horst. Right off, I asked him if Jezebel was very good-looking. He seemed a little startled, but he opened his Bible to Kings and ran his finger up and down the pages. Once he'd reviewed the scriptures, he explained to me that the Bible didn't say what Jezebel looked like, except that when she was an old woman, she painted her eyes. He added that she was very wicked, because she encouraged her husband to worship false gods.

I felt a little bit better after that, because I'd thought that what Mrs Rosenbach meant was that I was too homely to attract Mr Solomon. But she hadn't been saying that.

Then I asked Father Horst about a passage in the prayer book that's been bothering me. It says that we can't have any pleasure without giving pain to Jesus: *We cannot find pleasure to our liking without at the same time offending Him.* If that's true, it's horrible, and I said so. It's worried me a good deal.

I think Father Horst was taken aback. At first he was stern. He said if I wanted to be a good Catholic I must learn to be obedient and not ask so many questions. He showed me the IMPRIMATUR in the book, which is a sign that the Church approves of the book and a guarantee that there's nothing in it that's bad for morality.

But then he softened and asked me if I was worried about a sin I might have committed. I told him I'd become very worldly lately, and how I'd bought a parasol I didn't really need for ninety-five cents. He turned this over in his mind. At last he said that he hoped those words in the prayer book wouldn't be a stumbling block to me. He confided to me that sometimes when he prays to God, he seems to feel the mind and heart of God. (I have felt that myself, but I didn't say so, because it seemed like boasting.) Anyway, he said he was convinced that God was not *petty*. He (Father Horst, not God) said he didn't believe God took offense every time a young girl decided to buy something pretty, though it *would* be nice if I put a little money in the poor box every week. He said God is our Father, and a good father (not like mine) likes to see his children made happy.

He added that it would be different if I'd been uncharitable. God always minds that, because God loves all His children alike, and if you are uncharitable, even in a small way, God feels sorry for the person you are uncharitable *to*.

So I tried to think about whether I've been uncharitable lately. I have harbored uncharitable thoughts about Mrs Rosenbach and Mrs Mueller. And then there's Father, whom I still haven't forgiven.

But then I cheered up because I remembered that this morning, I was charitable to Malka. She was mending her black skirt and her mouth was all pursed up and sour, because sewing black on black is hard on the eyes. I knew she would be offended if I offered to help her in the ordinary way, so I was cunning. I said coaxingly that I wished she'd show me one more time how to fry fish the way she does. If she would, I'd finish stitching her dress.

She snorted and said learning to fry fish was a matter of trial and error, even if I had the right knack for it, which she didn't think I had. But she would try to show me. Then she forked over that dress as if she couldn't get rid of it fast enough.

I wanted to laugh. But now I see that I was charitable to Malka. I didn't do it to please God; I did it for kindness, which I think must be good. Only now I'm feeling conceited about it, which is probably bad.

But I'm not going to worry too much. Father Horst says that if I'm in any doubt about what to do, I should ask God for mercy and forgiveness, because He loves to grant us mercy and forgiveness. It makes Him happy when we ask for it. So I do ask for it. And I've decided I'll give one-tenth of my salary to the church – thirty cents for the collection, and thirty for the poor box, which is a lot for the poor. When I was poor, I'd have been thrilled with twenty-five.

After I left Father Horst, I walked in Druid Hill Park and enjoyed my rose-colored parasol. I passed the building that's going to be Mr Rosenbach's school, the one he's planning with his friends. It's a handsome building, and the children will be able to play in the park at recess, the lucky things. I wished I was a child and could go to that school.

But it's also nice to be grown up and earn your own money. I bought a bag of peanuts and ate them in the shade. Then I took out a pencil and paper, and Mr Solomon's half-finished sonnet, which I had hidden in my bosom. I've been thinking about that sonnet all week, ever since I learned Nora Himmelrich was coming to the house.

I've never worked on a sonnet before. Sometimes Miss Chandler had us write poetry, but we only had to rhyme every other line. Even with Mr Solomon having made most of the verses, it took me a long time to get the lines to scan, but when I finished, I was pleased with myself.

O Nora, when I see your radiant face,
So fresh and smiling, like the blushing rose,
And I behold your lithe and girlish grace,
It robs me nightly of my soul's repose.
I look upon your countenance and feel
Such ardent longing in my lovesick breast!
Sweet girl, I beg you, comfort me and heal
This heart that throbs and aches and has no rest!
O fragile nymph! I beg of thee, be mine!
My better angel, second self, and friend,
While earth endures, I swear I will be thine,
I'll love thee dearly, even to the end!
Truly and tenderly, I'll love thee all my life –
Give me thy hand! and vow to be my wife.

Wednesday, August the twenty-third, 1911

I have given the sonnet to Nora! When she came today, she said, "Hello, Janet," very heartily, which was nice of her – she might have snubbed me in front of the others, but she didn't. I tried to give her a meaningful glance, but there was no time to slip her the sonnet. I had to wait until after the bridge game broke up. Then I seized my chance. When old Miss Himmelrich was talking to Mrs R., I drew close to Nora and said in a low voice, "Excuse me, miss, you dropped this. *I found it*." And I put the sonnet in her hand, wrapped up small and folded in a handkerchief.

Nora looked startled and my heart pounded because I thought she might say the handkerchief wasn't hers, which would have given everything away. But I put one finger to my lips – just for a moment. Her eyes widened.

I must say it was very thrilling. I think I have a gift for intrigue.

While I was washing the dishes tonight, I imagined that Nora accepted Mr Solomon and they asked me to be their bridesmaid. It isn't likely they will, because I'm only a hired girl. But I had a good time imagining it – first a winter wedding, with a velvet bridesmaid dress, and then a spring one, with organdy and lace.

I'm in disgrace and it's all my fault. I'm weeping as I write this, but what good are my tears? I can't take back what I've done. Oh, I am nothing *but* tears, tears and stupidity and regret and mortification. I *ought* to feel mortified. I am to blame. How can I ever look him in the face again?

This afternoon the doorbell rang. When I ran to open the door, I saw Nora Himmelrich. She looked so pale and apprehensive I scarcely knew her. She asked to see Mrs Rosenbach, but Mrs Rosenbach – thank the dear God! – was at the Friedhoffs', because baby Irma has a rash.

I told Nora that Mrs Rosenbach wasn't in and asked if anything was wrong. She wouldn't look me in the eye because she was almost in tears and didn't want me to know. Then she steeled herself and said she'd see Solly, if he was at home. I thought maybe there had been a lovers' quarrel, but of course I couldn't ask.

I showed her into the parlor. I found Mr Solomon and told him Nora was downstairs. I thought he would fly to her with the ardor of a true lover, but he didn't. He said he would come, but he looked taken aback.

I was tempted to linger and try to hear what they said, but I was not quite so base as that, thank God. At least I haven't *that* on my conscience. I went downstairs, but my mind was awhirl. I was so hoping they'd settle their quarrel and get engaged. Oh, what folly! When I think of how happy and curious I felt, I *burn* with mortification!

After a half hour or so, I heard the front door shut. I was in the kitchen, ironing one of Mimi's dresses – they're so frilly they take forever, and in this heat it's awful, ironing. Then Mr Solomon came down, his feet striking each step quick and hard. Malka woke from her nap and cried, "What is it?" and the Thomashefsky cat leaped off her lap and took shelter under the table.

Mr Solomon didn't answer. He never even looked at Malka. He looked at me, and I wouldn't have known him; his eyes were hard and despising and his mouth was compressed. He said curtly, "Come upstairs. I want to talk to you." Of course Malka wanted to know what I'd done. But Mr Solomon said, "I need to speak to Janet alone," and he headed up the stairs.

I had to follow him, but I was scared. I knew right away that something had gone wrong. My heart was in my throat when I entered the library. Mr Solomon pointed to a chair, but I was too agitated to sit. I saw he had the sonnet in his hand – not folded up small and tidy, the way it was when I gave it to Nora, but spread out and creased, as if he'd crushed it in his hand.

"What is the meaning of this?" he demanded. "Who do you think you are, sneaking into my private papers? How dare you show this to Miss Himmelrich? She thought you were my messenger! You've upset her and made a fool out of me! Is that what you intended?"

I was so shaken by his accusations that I couldn't find the right words. I stammered out that I'd found the sonnet by accident – I hadn't sneaked. He paid no attention. He said I had no right to interfere; that I had been presumptuous and deceitful. He said he had no use for a servant who couldn't be trusted, and he would see to it that I never worked another day in that house. Then – this was the worst part – he asked how I could repay the kindness his family had shown me with malice and ingratitude.

At those words I cried out. "It wasn't malice," I said. "It was because I was grateful – I wanted you to be happy! Oh, Solly, can she have refused you?"

I knew the minute his name passed my lips that I shouldn't have called him Solly. I don't know how I came to slip like that – I've been so careful to call him Mr Solomon, even in this book. He was red with anger and his color darkened. "Yes, she's refused me," he said furiously, "thank God! Not that you have any right to ask. What business is it of yours, after all?" Then he repeated, "Just who do you think you are?" I don't know why that was so wounding, but it was, and I wept.

"I wanted her to marry you," I sobbed. "I didn't mean any harm; I wanted you to marry her, because you love her, and it was such a beautiful poem, and I thought you should send it." I reached for my handkerchief but it was downstairs, in the pile of things to be ironed. There wasn't anything to cry into and my nose was running. I had to cover it with my hand, which made me feel *low.* "Don't you want to marry her?"

He stepped forward, glaring, and his hands were clenched. There was a flash of a moment when I thought he might hit me, and I scuttled away from him. He must have seen the fear in my eyes because his face changed, and he said, "No, no," gently, as if he were soothing me. Then his rage burst forth afresh. "What business is it of yours who I marry?" he shouted. "What has any of this to do with *you?*"

It was so hurtful, the way he said *you,* as if I were altogether insignificant. I said lamely, "I took a vow."

"A vow? What on earth are you talking about?"

I tried to defend myself. "Because you were kind to me. Because you saved me from the streets. Mimi told me you were in love with Nora, and I vowed I would do anything I could to make you happy—"

"You thought I would be *happy* –" oh, his sarcasm made me flinch! – "if you read my private papers, and passed on a half-finished, badly written sonnet?"

"Yes, because faint heart never won—"

"I don't have a faint heart!" he shouted. "If I wanted to marry Nora Himmelrich – who has been in agonies since you gave her that sonnet, because she doesn't want to *hurt my feelings* – I would go and tell her so! But I haven't, because I don't. I wrote that idiotic scrap of verse a year ago – a whole year! Since then, I've fallen head over heels in love with another girl!" I gasped. "And Nora, who is a ninny if there ever was one, was so upset by my proposal of marriage, my *unwelcome* proposal of marriage, that she went to another girl for advice, and it so happens *that* girl is the girl I love! *And Nora showed her that poem!*" He paused so that I could take this in. "*Now* the girl I planned to make my wife has read the sonnet I wrote to Nora Himmelrich! God knows what she must think of me!" He smacked the crumpled sonnet against the back of the chair. It was just paper against wood, but it made a louder noise than I would have believed possible. I jumped.

"Now do you see what you've done? At the very least, I've been made to look like a fool; at the worst, I will lose the girl I love – all because of your meddling! Who knows how many other girls Nora may have confided in? She swore it was only Ruth, but I don't know if I believe her – and what in *hell* am I going to say to Ruth?"

I wept very copiously. He had every right to be angry with me, even to swear at me, but oh, I felt so awful! I recalled with shame how excited I'd felt, being part of a love affair. I'd thought I'd done it for him, but now that he was shouting at me I realized that I'd done it partly for myself, because I wanted some romance in my life. But I never meant any harm – I wanted to *help*. And if I lost my job, I had nowhere to go, and I knew Mrs Rosenbach would never write me a good reference, not after she heard what I'd done. I was sobbing, "I'm sorry, I'm so sorry," when the door opened and Mr Rosenbach came in.

I reckon it was a shock to us both, him coming in like that. Mr Solomon and I were so het up that it hadn't occurred to us that anyone *could* come in. Mr Rosenbach seemed out of place; he was so cool and collected. Well, not cool, exactly, because he never takes the streetcar and always walks home, so his shirt was wilted. He'd taken off his hat, and also his necktie, which he'd wrapped around his hand like a bandage. But even though he was hot and damp, the room seemed cooler after he came in. He glanced from me to Mr Solomon and said, "Solly? What on earth are you saying to her?"

Mr Solomon was speechless. I couldn't blame him. "What have *I* said to *her*?" he echoed, while I wailed, "No, he's right to shout at me!"

Mr Rosenbach set his hat down on the desk. He freed his hand from the curled-up tie and set the tie down next to his hat. Then he pulled out a chair and told me to sit. He found a clean handkerchief in his breast pocket and gave it to me. He strolled over to the decanter and poured two glasses of whiskey, a little one for him and a larger one for Mr Solomon. "Sit, sit," he urged us, until Mr Solomon and I sat down. "Now, Janet. Tell me what's the matter."

He spoke so kindly that I had to tell him. I wasn't very clear at first, because my words were blurred by sobs. "Go on, go on," Mr Rosenbach encouraged me, and I told him how Mr Solomon had been kind to me, and I'd made a secret vow to help him win Nora Himmelrich. And I hadn't pried, or looked through his private papers; I'd honestly *found* the sonnet, and I thought it was so beautiful that if Nora could only read it, her romantic heart would surely be touched. But after that there wasn't much I could say in my defense, because it was meddling to give that sonnet to Nora, and I'd made trouble. Of course, it had never occurred to me that Mr Solomon might have finished being in love with his fragile nymph, but men are not constant the way women are, and I guess I ought to have thought of that.

Mr Rosenbach turned to his son and said, "Well?" and Mr Solomon began to tell his side of the story. I think drinking the whiskey calmed him because he wasn't raging; he was just resentful and disapproving. At one point, Mr Rosenbach inquired, "Am I to learn the name of this girl you wish to marry?" and Mr Solomon turned red and said, "I'm sorry, Papa," in a way that made him sound years younger. "I know you and Mama won't like it, and I haven't asked her yet. I mean to ask her, or I meant to, until this—"

"Understandable, understandable," murmured Mr Rosenbach, nodding and rocking as if he was praying – he bobs and rocks when he prays, and so does Mr Solomon. "Still, it would be better if there were no secrets between father and son."

These words cut Mr Solomon to the quick. He blurted out, "It's Ruth."

I saw the look on Mr Rosenbach's face: surprise and dismay. By then I'd stopped crying, because watching them was so interesting. It was like being at a play.

Mr Rosenbach said, "Ruth Kleman? The little Polish girl?"

Mr Solomon straightened in his chair. He looked noble and resolute, as a young lover should. "I know she's not German," he said, "so Mama won't like it. And she – her family – is more Orthodox than we are. But I love her. And I don't think being Orthodox is such a bad thing. Grossvater came to America so that his children could be Jews. Who are we if we fail to practice our religion? I like Ruth's synagogue better than Har Sinai; I would like to worship there. And that's not all. I want to study Talmud. I know it's not what you planned for me, Papa, but I don't care about the store. I respect *you*, Papa, and I love you; I admire what you did, creating the business. But I don't think I'm cut out to be a businessman. The store doesn't interest me. I want to be a scholar. Papa, I'm sorry."

His voice broke on the last words.

I stayed very still. I didn't want them to notice me and send me away. There they were: Solly with his hands clasped around his whiskey glass, and Mr Rosenbach perched on the edge of his chair, with his weight resting on the tips of his toes.

He crouched there, motionless. Then he sprang up. He walked to the windows and opened the shutters to let the air come in, though it was hot outside. He looked down at his desk as if he'd never seen it before, and he touched the letter opener and the blotter. He picked up the ormolu desk clock and fiddled with the gears.

At last he returned to his chair and sat down. "Shlomo," he said – that's the Jewish nickname for Solomon, which nobody but Malka uses – "you are my good son, my first born. I had hoped you would have a gift for business, but my greatest wish is for your happiness. If you love Ruth Kleman and believe she can make you happy, you should marry her. And if you want to study Talmud –" he took up his glass of whiskey once more – "why, then, you will be a scholar. It's not too shabby, to have a scholar in the family. I will be proud of you." He raised his head and looked Mr Solomon directly in the eye. "I will always be proud of my son."

I saw Mr Solomon's face working. He was struggling against tears. He said, "Thank you, Papa," and his father nodded matter-of-factly. I watched as they drained the last of the whiskey in their glasses and set the glasses down, almost in unison. "So," Mr Rosenbach said, "you will go to Miss Kleman and ask her to marry you?"

"I meant to. I want to." Mr Solomon shot me an accusing look. "Only I don't know how, after this rotten business. I don't know what she must be thinking of me, or whether I should ask her father—" He shook his head. "Perhaps it ought to be put off."

"By no means," said Mr Rosenbach, "not if you wish to succeed. If there's one thing I know about women it's this: where matters of the heart are concerned, they don't like to wait. They suffer too much."

Mr Solomon winced. "You think I should ask her now."

"If you love her," said Mr Rosenbach. "If you're sure."

"I know I love her," said Mr Solomon. "And I believe she cares for me, or did, before this happened. But it won't be easy to explain, and I don't know if her father will agree to the match, and then Mama—"

"Leave your mother to me," said Mr Rosenbach, and Mr Solomon heaved a short sigh. He got up and started to go out of the room.

He had forgotten all about me. But Mr Rosenbach hadn't. He cleared his throat and nicked his head in my direction. "What about this poor child?"

I felt a thrill of hope, because *poor child* made it sound as if I might not be sent away. I realized at that moment that I was willing to beg, if I could keep my job. Now that it's over, I wish I *hadn't* begged, because it wasn't dignified. A girl in a novel would have been too proud. "Please," I said, "*please*, forgive me. I know I shouldn't have meddled, and I never will again. Everyone here has been so kind to me, and I haven't anywhere else to go." I felt a sob rise in my throat and I let myself cry. I don't think it was feminine wiles. The truth is, I was so wretched that the tears cried themselves.

"Did you tell her she had to leave?" Mr Rosenbach asked Mr Solomon.

"He said I was untrustworthy," I explained, "and I *was*. But I didn't mean to be."

Mr Solomon looked awkward. I mean he looked as if he *felt* awkward. "I was very angry," he told his father. "I think I had a right to be angry."

"You did, you did!" I assured him. "I was *awful*."

Mr Rosenbach went over to the table and took his rolled-up tie, as if he meant to put it on again. He uncoiled it and hung it around his neck so that it fell down on either side, like Father Horst's stole. He said, as if to himself, "She's very young."

That nettled me, a little, because I'm not as young as all that. Mr Solomon is twenty-three, which is only five years older than I am, or would be, if I really was eighteen. But then Mr Solomon sighed, and my heart rose, because there was something forgiving in the sound. He said, "Let no one be punished on my account."

It sounded to me like a quotation. Later on I told Malka what he said – because of course she gave me no peace until I told her everything – well, not everything; I told her about the sonnet, but I didn't mention Nora's name. And I refused to tell her about Ruth Kleman, because that's Mr Solomon's secret. After Malka exclaimed and scolded and enjoyed herself tremendously – because my being in trouble is meat and drink to her – she told me that what Mr Solomon said is part of a famous Jewish prayer. It's a beautiful thought, I think. I must ask Father Horst if the Catholics have any prayers like that.

And now I vow, on this page, that from this point on I will never meddle with Mr Solomon's life. Or anyone's life. I will remember that I'm a hired girl, and work harder at my job, and if I want something to happen, I will only pray about it and not do anything. I won't go gadding about with Mimi, because Mrs Rosenbach doesn't like it, and I won't hanker after being friends with Nora Himmelrich, because she's above me, and I won't allow myself any silly, idle thoughts about Mr David. I will be good and grateful and read Marcus Aurelius and other improving books, and not flounce, and wear my kimono over my nightgown no matter how hot it is, and not spend money on silly things like parasols and bottles of perfume that smell awful.

I pray that in time I will respect myself again.

Tuesday, August the twenty-ninth, 1911

I have quarreled with Father Horst! I hope that isn't a sin, to quarrel with a priest, but I think he was *wrong*. Though maybe thinking that is a sin, too.

He was glad to see me when I came for my weekly instruction. It seems to me that Father Horst likes me, or used to before today. He is very pleased by how quickly I'm learning the catechism. Once he said he never knew what question I'll ask next, and the way he said it was almost admiring. I'd have sworn he liked me. I like him, too. He's a teacher, after all, and I generally get on with teachers.

But after greeting me today, Father Horst announced that he'd found a new place for me to work. He has a parishioner named Mrs Possit who is looking for a virtuous, hardworking Catholic (but not Irish) girl for live-in housework and help with the children – she has six of them, all under the age of nine. She's willing to pay five dollars a week. Father Horst told Mrs Possit he knew the very person for her.

I was puzzled. I reminded him that I already have a job, but he countered by saying that Mrs Possit is a good Catholic woman and I'd be part of a Catholic household. He said that it was his duty to guide my footsteps on the path to a devout life. All the Possits, even the servants and the babies, come to Mass every morning. And he said that Mrs Possit would be like a mother to me, and he repeated the offer of five dollars a week, as if he thought that was a very good sum of money for me to be earning.

I didn't say that the Rosenbachs give me six, because that isn't why I refused. I don't believe I'm a mercenary girl; it's that I like the Rosenbachs. I explained to Father

Horst how Mr Solomon saved me from the streets, but Father Horst interrupted me and said that I shouldn't say Mr Solomon saved me from the streets because that makes it sound as if I was on the streets. But I was on the streets, I said to him, I almost had to sleep in them, and he said, never mind that now. The point was, he was sure the Rosenbachs were very good people of their kind, but he wasn't happy about me working for a family of Hebrews. I said pleadingly that Mr Rosenbach lent me books and Mrs Rosenbach forgave me for setting the attic bedroom on fire, and you wouldn't find many Christians who are that merciful and kind. I told him how they even let me come to Shabbos one night, as if I were a guest instead of a servant.

That made Father Horst look very grim. He said that was just the kind of thing that worried him – that they would seduce me from my Catholic faith. I assured him that Mrs Rosenbach knows I'm a Catholic and it's all right with her. I started to tell him how she let me come to the church on the Feast of the Assumption, even though it wasn't my afternoon off.

But Father Horst wasn't listening. He asked me how I could be so loyal to a family of Jews when the Jews have turned their backs on Jesus. And for a minute, I didn't know what to say, because I don't think of the Rosenbachs in that way.

"They don't *worship* Jesus," I said, "but they worship God, and if Jesus and God are one in the Holy Trinity, doesn't it come to the same thing?" Father Horst said that was *sophistry*, which is a word I never heard before. I looked it up in Mr Rosenbach's dictionary, but I'm still not sure what it means. Father Horst also called me *intransigent*, which was another word I looked up. It means you stick to your opinions. I think I might be a little bit intransigent, but not in a bad way.

I felt dreadful when Father Horst started calling me names. And I searched my conscience, because I love Our Lord and His Blessed Mother. I don't want to do anything to hurt them. But then I remembered what Mr Rosenbach said. "Jesus was a Jew." I spoke the words aloud. "And so was Abraham and Moses and the Blessed Mother."

Father Horst said that the Jews of the Old Testament were different. They were all right because they lived before Jesus shed His blood in the New and Eternal Testament. But Jesus instituted the New Testament, so He was more like a Christian than a Jew. Then Father Horst said that the Jews were responsible for the death of Jesus, but I said I thought it was the Romans who crucified Him. (Because that's what Mr Rosenbach told me.) Father Horst looked vexed, but he said that it *was* the Romans, technically, but that the Jews had denied Him. He flipped open the Bible to find something bad about the Jews and read to me the part from the Acts of the Apostles where some of the Jews bound themselves under a curse, saying they would neither eat nor drink until they killed St. Paul.

Surely, Father Horst said to me, I could see that St. Paul was on the right side of things and that the Jews were on the wrong side.

Well, I know that St. Paul is a very important saint. But I pointed out that the Bible said that only *some* of the Jews wanted to kill St. Paul, so that must mean that there were other Jews who were all right, and I thought the Rosenbachs must be like them. Father Horst shut the Bible in a way that was almost like slamming it. He said I was a disobedient and quarrelsome child.

I felt quelled when he said that, but some demon inside me made me answer back one more time. I said – in a small voice, but I said it – that I would rather be disobedient and quarrelsome than have anti-Semitism.

Then he was really angry. He said he had no doubt who taught me *that* word, and his manner was so forbidding that I said I was sorry and I hadn't meant it. Though actually I had. I think he *has* anti-Semitism, but perhaps he doesn't know it. But I didn't want him to be mad with me. I explained to him that the Rosenbachs *need* me because nobody else can get along with Malka. And Malka needs me because of her age and her bunion. Then he said Mrs Possit needs me because she has all those children. But I like the Rosenbachs, and I told Father Horst that I'd rather stay with them than go live with Mrs Possit. I think (but I didn't say it) that there is something nasty about the name *Possit*.

Father Horst said coldly that he would inform Mrs Possit that I had declined to accept her kindness. Oh, but he was cross! I fear he will never like me again. I felt dreadful as I walked home, because if Father Horst doesn't like me, he won't instruct me, and I'll never be able to take the Sacrament. I do so long to take the Sacrament. I imagine it will feel like receiving the kiss of a lover – only more ineffable – sweet and welcoming and restoring the soul.

When I got home, I didn't know what to do I was so agitated. I hate it when something ruins my afternoon off, because I have only one a week. I set to mending my torn petticoat, but sewing was the wrong thing to do, because the quarrel kept running through my mind.

I wondered if I was doing wrong, staying with the Rosenbachs, and if this house is a house of *fleshpots*. It does seem to me that since I became a hired girl, my mind is very much set on worldly things. Lately I've been thinking of buying a new dress for Sundays. I like the dresses I have, but they're both blue and I'm tired of wearing blue every single day.

When I finished the petticoat, I knelt down and asked the Blessed Mother what I should do. And she answered me in Ma's old voice. She said there was no sin in being loyal to people who have been good to you. It's disloyalty that's a sin. And she reminded me that pink doesn't wear too well, so if I buy a new dress, I should take into account how it will look once it's faded.

I felt better after that. Now that I write this, I am struck by a new idea. I think Father Horst's idea that the Rosenbachs are trying to make a Jew out of me is crazy. But what if God placed me here so that I might lead *them* to the Church? God must love the Rosenbachs, because they're virtuous. And since they're virtuous, He might want them to be Catholic instead of Jewish. It would be a *mitzvah* - that's the Jewish word for a good deed - for me to tell them about the True Faith.

It seems as though it might be presumptuous, though, converting them. They might not like it, and I'm not a very good Catholic. I'm not even a real Catholic, because I haven't been confirmed. But then, the Bible says that God chooses the foolish to confound the wise, and I certainly am foolish. So maybe I was sent to bring light unto the Rosenbachs.

Though perhaps converting them would be meddling, which I promised myself I wouldn't do.

I thought about this so long that I fell into a kind of reverie and was late helping Malka with dinner. She was very sarcastic at my expense, but I apologized very sweetly, because if I *am* to convert the Rosenbachs, I shall have to be very meek and humble of heart.

I forgot to write that I believe Mr Solomon has been successful in his suit. Of course this is none of my business, but the morning after that terrible Thursday, I found a yellow rose on his dresser. The stem was the right length for tucking into a buttonhole, and I wondered if Miss Kleman gave it to Mr Solomon as a lover's token. I didn't clear it away, though it was limp and bruised. I left it on the dresser. The next day, it wasn't on the dresser and it wasn't in the trash bin, either.

I pondered the matter and concluded that the rose must have been a love token, because otherwise, Mr Solomon would have dropped it in the bin. I imagine he's pressing it in a book to keep forever. He's been in very good spirits of late. I haven't seen him face-to-face, but I've heard him humming, and his step is light. Mrs Rosenbach has *not* been in good spirits, and I'm thinking maybe she doesn't like Mr Solomon marrying a Polish girl. I wonder what's wrong with the Poles. But I'm not going to try to find out anything more, because a good hired girl is supposed to be discreet and not stick her nose in her master's business.

David will be home for Shabbos this week, which means nothing to me except that preparations for Shabbos dinner will be more elaborate than usual. He will want ice cream and he likes it homemade, so I'll have to turn the crank.

Malka's bunion seems to be on the mend.

Saturday, September the second, 1911

Oh, I feel so wicked! I know Father Horst would be shocked, and Mrs Rosenbach would disapprove. And yet – oh, and yet! I'm sure I won't sleep a wink tonight – but I must sleep, or tomorrow my eyes will be red. How I wish I'd bought a new dress last Tuesday! There would have been time, if I'd boarded the streetcar right after my quarrel with Father Horst.

I wish I had. But I'll wear my Cheyenne hat. David's never seen me in that.

I was doing the dishes tonight – Saturday night is the tiredest time for me, because Thursday and Friday are a flurry getting ready for Shabbos, and on Saturday I'm the Shabbos goy. This week was especially busy, because we had company Friday night – sixteen people at table – and today the Friedhoffs came for Saturday lunch. Malka came down with a dreadful headache. I could tell it was bad because she didn't grumble. I told her I could clean up the kitchen by myself and that she ought to go to bed. She didn't even argue with me: poor thing, she must have been in agony! She limped upstairs, leaving me with the dishes. I wasn't too unhappy, because Shabbos was over for another week, and there was a sweet breeze coming through the window.

Then I heard footsteps coming down the stairs – not Malka's uneven, bunion-y footsteps, but swift footsteps. And there he was: David.

He leaned over the stair railing and said, "Where's Malka?" and I said, "She went to bed early," and he said, "Good." Just like that. Maybe I'm conceited, but I can think of only one reason for him saying *good* like that. He was glad he'd caught me alone.

His nose is more crooked than I remember. Whenever I've dwelt on his image – not that I have; it's just that once in a while he crosses my mind – I've tidied up his nose. It really is too big and too crooked. All the same, there's something about him – the way he loped down the staircase and sat on the kitchen table instead of one of the chairs. He's like his father; he has a way of bounding and darting and pouncing, as if he expects something exciting to happen and can't wait for it.

He said, "I'll come straight to the point. I haven't been able to get you out of my mind." Oh, for one moment, how my foolish heart raced! But then: "I want you for my Joan of Arc. Will you come with me to the park tomorrow, so I can draw you with the sheep? I want to, awfully."

He smiled when he said "awfully." That smile would have turned the heads of some girls. But I am made of stronger stuff. And I knew he only wanted me for his sketch. So there was nothing to get excited about.

I said, "I can't," though it didn't come out as forceful as I'd meant it to. I turned my back on him and groped through the dishwater for the knives and forks and spoons. "I have to go to Mass."

"Skip it," he suggested, and I looked up, shocked. Skip Mass? I know that's a sin, and the dreadful thing was, right away I began to imagine myself committing it. Just like that! It shows how weak my faith is. In a flash I thought of how I'd quarreled with Father Horst, and how it would serve him right if I didn't come to Mass.

But I haven't skipped Mass all summer. I know it's a privilege to go to Mass, even though I can't take the Sacrament. Every week, the others kneel at the altar rail, and I have to stay in my seat. I feel like that woman in the Bible who had to be content with the crumbs under the table. But I love the Mass. And how am I to bring the Rosenbachs to the True Church if I skip it? What kind of example would that be?

So I said, "I can't skip it. It's *Mass*."

"All right," he said, and I must say I was piqued that he gave up so easily. He jumped down from the table and took a bottle of milk out of the refrigerator. "Would you like some?"

I left the sink. "No, I wouldn't, and you can't have any, either. We need it for breakfast, in case the milkman's late."

He teased me, holding the bottle out of reach, but I got it away from him without too much of a scuffle. I put the milk back in the refrigerator and shut the door with a good slam.

"See?" he pleaded. "That's why you're such a perfect

Joan of Arc! So militant! When's your next morning off? Afternoons won't do. I want the light. I see you kneeling and gazing up at the morning sky, listening to your saints." His voice became coaxing. "It's going to be a religious painting, you know. Wouldn't helping me be just as good as going to Mass? Just think, if the picture's a success, thousands of people may see it and be converted."

I kept a good strong hold on myself. "That doesn't seem very likely."

"Don't you have confidence in me?" he asked, pretending to be hurt. "Come on, now, Janet! You're not really like that – all sensible and stuck-up. You're a real Joan – full of imagination and the spirit of revolt. And I'm not such a bad artist, either. John Singer Sargent praised one of my sketches – I met him when I was in Florence. He said I had a good sense of line. Do you really want to wet-blanket a man with a good sense of line?"

That's when I said – oh, it was daring of me, but I'm not one bit sorry. "I think you have too many lines, Mr David." Because a *line* is what they call it when a man is flirting. After I said it, I was afraid he would think I was presuming too much, but he laughed.

"You're the limit. I knew I liked you." That way he has of saying he likes me, right out! "Why not come out with me tomorrow? We'll have a good time. After I sketch you, we can go on the boat lake, or I'll hire a carriage and take you round the park. Or we'll go to the drugstore and have ice-cream sundaes. Whatever you like. Won't you?"

It did sound so lovely. Floating on the water in one of those rowboats – or riding through the park like a queen, as if he were my sweetheart. I couldn't decide. But I made one more attempt to put him off. "I don't think your mother would like it."

"No, she won't," he agreed, and looked thoughtful. "But that's because she's afraid that I'll marry a *shiksa*. I'm not planning to marry you; I just want to draw you. What's the harm in that?"

I couldn't see any harm in it. But I didn't say so.

"It's better if she doesn't know," David said firmly, "so we'll meet in the park. First I'll sketch you, and then we'll have our lovely time. What about it?"

I opened my mouth to say I couldn't, but what I said was, "I have to be home by half past twelve."

His face lit up, and now that I'm writing this, all I can see is his face at that moment – his dark eyes sparkling with mischief and triumph. And seeing him so, before my mind's eye, I feel ever so fluttery. But it isn't my heart that flutters; it's my stomach. It's full of cramps and butterflies.

I'm glad my petticoats are all starched. And my blue dress with the white ferns on it is as fresh as a daisy.

If I wash my hair now, it'll be dry by morning.

PART FIVE

Joan of Arc

Sunday, September the third, 1911

I woke before dawn this morning so that I could say the rosary. I felt dreadfully guilty about skipping Mass, and I begged God for mercy and forgiveness. I prayed to the Blessed Mother to let things go well with David, though I really don't know what I mean by that. But she will know. And I believe she heard my prayer, and God forgave me, because the day dawned cool and sunny and glorious.

My hair was still damp, but it went up beautifully – I got it to puff the way Mimi taught me. I pinned my hat at its most becoming angle, caught up my parasol, and stole away to the park. It was thrilling to be going to meet David, and I know I looked nicer than usual. But I was so nervous my teeth chattered. While I waited I almost wished David wouldn't come. Then I thought how horrible it would be if he didn't.

He was later than I expected, but he grinned at me and I felt better right away. He carries his art things in a wooden portfolio, which doubles as a drawing board. Once we fell into step, I felt happy and not so scared. After all, it was only Mr David. And my heart soared, because I knew we would have fun.

Only, just at first, we didn't. He is very serious about this picture he wants to make. First he introduced me to the park shepherd, Mr Mac, who is a stately old man with a white beard. David says he fought in the Civil War. I would have liked to question him about that, but David wanted to get right down to work. He gave me chopped-up apples so I could make friends with the sheep, and he told me to kneel and feed them. I didn't want to, because I didn't want to kneel where the sheep had *been*. I was thinking of my clean petticoats. They didn't stay clean, and the sheep lost interest in me once the apples were gone. They sidled away. David said something under his breath that I think might have been swearing. Mr Mac only shook his head and whistled for his dog.

I was afraid David was displeased, because he hadn't had more than a quarter of an hour to draw me with the sheep.Luckily he has a very buoyant nature. He's like Mimi that way: fussing one minute and laughing the next. He said that sheep weren't hard to draw, and he would sketch me now and add the sheep later on. My job was to stay very still while he sketched me with charcoal. He didn't speak more than a few words to me, and I was forbidden to talk. It was hard to kneel and hold still all that time. Then he asked if I would mind taking off my hat and unpinning my hair and unbuttoning my collar a little.

I knew my hair would never go up so well a second time, not without a mirror and a brush. But I could see that Joan of Arc wouldn't have worn a Dutch collar or a Cheyenne hat. So I yielded to his plea. While I untidied myself, he took out his colored chalks – *pastels*, they're called.

I never realized what hard work it is to sit for an artist. I was glad he wasn't making a sculpture of me. It was exciting to think that I was going to be part of a masterpiece. But it was also boring, because I couldn't speak and my knees ached. And I'd been looking forward to David teasing me and maybe saying more about me being a magnificent creature.

But he was lost in a world of his own. After a long, long time he said I might rest. I got up and looked at his sketches. The charcoal ones weren't that interesting because they were just my shape. But the chalk ones were of my face, and I was astonished how many colors he'd used to draw me. My skin was peachy and rosy orange and brown and blue gray – it was even *green*, where the leaf shadows were. And my hair was every shade of brown:

rust and fawn and chestnut and gold. Oh, but those chalks looked tempting! I asked if I could touch them. He not only said yes, he showed them to me and let me make marks on a piece of paper.

They are all different, those chalks. Not just in color, but in texture: some of them hard and scrape-y and others are as soft as butter. The soft ones get put on top of the hard ones. David showed me how I could put colors together and smear them with my fingers. The smeared chalk looked like velvet.

I was *enraptured*. Then he said he would teach me to draw. He went and got a dandelion and made me look at it, and asked me what color it was. Of course I said yellow and green. But then he said to really look. I saw that the under petals – the green ones under the flower – overlap, and where they overlap there is just a hint of lavender. And there are two circles of petals on the dandelion – the inner circle of the flower is pinker and orangier than the outer circle. The outer petals are more like a lemon, that sharp yellow that reminds you of green, only when you look, there's no green in sight. The stem is more than one color, too. Where the light hits the edge, there's a kind of silvery perspiration – and parts near the bottom are pur-plish red and freckled!

I was so excited, I exclaimed. David led me to a bench and set his portfolio on my lap and told me to draw the dandelion. It looked just awful, because I couldn't figure out whether to draw the flower from the side or the top. With a few deft strokes, David sketched it for me, so that I could see the basic shape. He told me to copy his shape and concentrate on the colors. So I began again.

It's funny, because then I was like an artist. I forgot about David. I loved it so much, trying to draw and seeing the dandelion the way I've never seen one before. I glowed when David praised me, but at that moment he was like a teacher, not a man – I mean, I forgot he was a man. I didn't *quite* forget; I was purely happy when he praised me. But when he guided my hand, I didn't think about him touching me. And when he leaned over me, I didn't feel scared, because my mind was on the dandelion.

Oh, but the time rushed by on winged feet! At last David said that if I wanted a drive or a trip on the boat lake, we should move along. (Last night I'd made up my mind to choose the boat trip, because if we went driving, we might run into Mrs Mueller or even Nora Himmelrich – how horrible *that* would be!) So I said I wanted to go on the lake. He put away the chalks while I tried to tidy myself. I buttoned my collar. My hair gave me trouble, just as I knew it would. I gave up trying to make it puff and secured it with a slipknot.

By the time we reached the lake it was almost noon, and there was a line of people ahead of us. It was such a fine September day; everyone wanted to go on the lake. I was disappointed because I'd had this picture in my mind of me floating over the water with my rose-colored parasol, and David looking graceful and manly, with his sleeves rolled up. He has the most beautiful forearms I've ever seen.

He asked if I had time for an ice-cream sundae at the pharmacy, and I said sadly that I didn't think I had. I suppose I must have looked wistful, because he put out one forefinger and touched me on the nose – which was not dignified or romantic. But then he charmed me by saying that he was going to buy me a sketchpad of my own, so I could practice drawing.

I hope it isn't improper to accept a sketchpad from a young man, because if he remembers to buy me one (he might not remember), I mean to accept it.

As we walked home together, I remembered he was a man. I felt proud, walking with a man, but I also felt shy. Then I had a brilliant idea; I asked him if he knew that bridge in Florence where the poet Dante met his beloved. That got him started on all the things he's seen abroad. Oh, how I envy him! He hasn't really seen the Alhambra – he confessed that he made up the ghost stories he told me, because he wanted to impress me. But he's seen the Swiss Alps and Venice and other places where there's real life. Once he lived in Paris for a whole month, just the way the natives do. He told me about his favorite café in Paris – he used to sit in a café and draw. I wish I could draw in a café in Paris.

Outside the park, we ran straight into Mimi. It wasn't as bad as if she'd been Nora Himmelrich, but she grinned at me in the most provoking way and said she'd thought I was at Mass. I was too mortified to answer.

David answered with aplomb. "I persuaded her to help me instead. I need a model for my new painting – Janet's going to be my Joan of Arc."

He showed her the sketches he'd made – he calls them studies. Figure drawings, those are the charcoals; and color studies, that's what he called the pastels. I wish I looked better in profile. There was one sketch where I thought I looked pretty, and I said I liked that one, and he said briskly not to be silly; that was the weakest one of the lot. Then he ruffled Mimi's hair and asked her if *she'd* like an ice-cream sundae. He asked me if I couldn't be a little bit late, just this once.

I said no, because I was already late, and how would I explain to Malka? But Mimi said yes. David asked me if I'd take his portfolio home, so he wouldn't have to carry it to the pharmacy, and the two of them sauntered off together. He said we'd have *our* ice cream another time. Another time, another time! That's the phrase that sang in my heart as I walked home, carrying the sketches and the portfolio – it was heavier than it looked – and my parasol.

I think David must like me pretty well if he's going to buy me a sketchpad *and* see me another time. Perhaps he will teach me more about how to draw.

I was nervous when I went inside, because I didn't know what Malka would say if she saw me with Mr David's things, but she was dozing with the cat in her lap, and I crept past her on tiptoe. I put David's things back in his room and went to tidy my hair. My skirts were grass stained and there were chalk streaks on my dress, but they'll wash out, I'm sure. At any rate, my apron covered them, and Malka didn't notice. Once she woke up, she scolded me dreadfully, because last night I forgot to scald the dishcloths, so this morning they smelled.

I bore her scolding without fretting, because the truth was I wasn't listening. I was thinking about David.

Tuesday, September the fifth, 1911

Today was a very irritating day. But there! I begin too many entries in this book with "today." I'll start over.

I am *not* in a good humor this evening. (I don't think that's any better.) I sinned, to begin with, and I didn't even enjoy it. I suppose that's what it means when they talk about miserable sinners.

The way I sinned was I skipped instruction with Father Horst. I wasn't sure he'd be willing to see me, not after last week's quarrel and my missing Mass. I thought he might rebuke me or even send me away. But the sinful part was I wanted to meet Mimi so I could ask her not to tell Mrs Rosenbach about seeing David and me in the park. And I wanted to buy a new dress, because it's getting cooler and my uniforms are summery, and the stains from the pastels didn't come out of my blue dress. My apron covers them, but the dress isn't perfect anymore. I always want to have my clothes be nice, but then I rip them or stain them and I never feel the same about them after that.

So there was that. The morning began all wrong because I overslept, and Malka was in a bad humor because she tried to put a shoe over her bunion, which was a mistake. Now the bunion is throbbing again, and she's in agony. Also, she's sulking because she wants an electric carpet sweeper. It's the latest thing, and her sister, Minna, has one. It doesn't just brush the carpet; it sucks the dust right out. Mrs Rosenbach doesn't believe in it, so she refused to order one. That meant I had to hear about all the years Malka's worked for this family and the sacrifices she's made on their behalf.

I felt sorry for Malka, but I thought she would never stop talking so I could get out of the house. My conscience irked me because I thought a really nice girl would have sacrificed her afternoon off to spare Malka's bunion. But I'd planned to meet Mimi at the store, and I wanted that new dress. So I left Malka close to tears and making doomed noises in Yiddish.

I caught the streetcar and met Mimi at Rosenbach's.

We went shopping and I spent *nine dollars and twelve cents*, which is *dreadful*. And what's worse, I'm not sure I like what I bought. I bought a brown suit, and I don't really like brown, no matter how well it wears. Mimi can call it fawn-colored all she likes, but it's still brown. I wish I'd bought the blue one, but the skirt was too short and I'm sick of blue.

I wanted to buy a jumper suit, because it seems to me that they're cheaper than shirtwaist suits. But Mimi said I needed a good shirtwaist suit, German linen or serge, and two white waists: one plain with tucks, and another with lace. She says my uniform dresses make me look like a hired girl, but I'll look like a lady in a good shirtwaist suit.

I gave in to her because she really does know about clothes. And the brown suit was a bargain and it fit nicely. If it weren't brown, I'd be pleased with it. The skirt has eleven gores and flares at the hem, and the jacket has little arrow decorations on the sleeves, which are fancy. I found a plain pleated shirtwaist for thirty-nine cents, and a lacy one for ninety-five cents. Then Mimi made me buy a new pair of gloves. Mine are white, and she said I needed tan ones. That was another eighty-three cents.

I was shocked when she added up all the prices for me – she is surprisingly quick when she adds numbers in her head. But then she said I needed a new hat, because my Cheyenne hat is summery. The new hat is trimmed with brown velvet ribbon and three pinky-brown roses, or maybe they're meant to be peonies.

Then Mimi said I ought to have a little bit of jewelry – a brooch or a necklace with a little cross. The little crosses were quite cheap, but I told her I was a Catholic and I didn't want a cross but a crucifix. I thought perhaps that might be a moment when I could tell her a little about the True Faith. I started to, but she saw a case full of bracelets and we went over to look at them. There was a silver bracelet I liked, but Mimi wrinkled her nose and said it was too plain. That surprised me because it was beautifully engraved with curvy scrolls and lilies of the valley.

In the same department, we stopped to examine a tray of watch lockets. They were enameled with tiny flowers and oak leaves and shamrocks. They were so delicate and bright; they reminded me of Thumbelina. The fronts were gold and enamel, but the backs were only silver, so I thought I might be able to afford one. I didn't need it, of course, but I had this image of myself in all my new clothes and David asking me what time it was. I imagined myself bending my head beautifully – in the vision I had a swan-like neck – and lifting the watch so he could see. I think I must be crazy to have ideas like that, but I did, and it made me want one of those enameled watches terribly.

But they were *nine dollars*. I turned away, aghast. I think if it had been five dollars, I would have been wicked and taken the money from my Belinda fund. Ma told me that money isn't for toys, or pretty clothes, or even books, but I think I'd have bought one of those watches if they'd been five dollars, though five dollars is a dreadful, dreadful price to pay for something you don't need. The funny thing is, I think I wanted the watch even more after I found out it was so expensive. I wonder if I'll ever have anything expensive.

But *nine* dollars. Ma would turn over in her grave. I'd already bought a hat and a suit and two waists and gloves, and I had to buy Mimi an egg cream so I could beseech her not to tell Mrs Rosenbach about David and me walking in the park.

We left Rosenbach's and went to the drugstore. Mimi wanted a chocolate ice-cream soda instead of an egg cream, so I ordered two. I was wondering how to get to the subject of David and me, but Mimi got there first. She used the tip of her spoon to shave the tiniest bit of ice cream off the dollop in her glass. "You don't have to buy me a soda, you know. David already told me not to tell."

She is the most provoking child! It took my breath away, the way she could see through me. I couldn't think of a thing to say back.

"I'm not a tattletale," Mimi said. I could tell she was enjoying herself. "But you'd better not fall in love with David."

"I'm not in love with David," I said hotly. "I'm too young to be in love." And at that moment, I would have given anything to tell her that I'm fourteen, because that would have *proved* it. If you're fourteen, you shouldn't even be accused of anything as horrid as being in love with someone's brother. "I don't care one bit about boys; you know that."

"I know, but I thought I should warn you," said Mimi, still playing with her ice cream. It's not manners to play with your food, but she does it daintily, which is how she expects to get away with it, I guess. "David likes girls, and girls always like David. Malka says he used to chase girls when he was in short pants. Even then they liked him. It's funny, because he has that awful nose—"

"Yes, isn't his nose ridiculous?" I said eagerly. "When he sneezes it must be like a tornado. And when it bleeds, the Red Sea—"

Mimi lifted her eyebrows in a way that made her look just like her mother. "Did he say that speech for you? He didn't make it up, you know. It's from a play."

"Oh, I know," I said, but I hadn't. I bent my head over my soda.

"He likes saying clever things, but they aren't original," Mimi pointed out. "And he quotes poetry to girls, and they like that. I wouldn't; I hate poetry. But David likes it and he uses it on the girls. Then they get spoony and fall in love. Like that Isabelle Gratz."

My ears pricked up. I've wondered if Isabelle Gratz was David's first model for Joan of Arc – the girl with the pinched-in waist and the tiny little mind. "Who's Isabelle Gratz?"

"She lives on Long Island," Mimi explained, "and her father is in banking. He does a lot of business with Papa. David stayed with the Gratzes this past summer and studied painting. He partnered Isabelle at dances and played tennis and croquet and flirted with her – I'm sure he did, though he says he didn't. So of course Isabelle fell in love with him. What made it scandalous is that the Gratzes are more Orthodox than we are – well, if you're really Orthodox, a matchmaker chooses your husband, but the Gratzes aren't as Orthodox as that. But Mr Gratz didn't like Isabelle spending so much time with David, and he told her it wasn't maidenly, the spoony way she carried on when David was around. So Isabelle told him they were practically engaged. It wasn't true, because David never had any idea of proposing to her. But Mr Gratz took David aside and asked what were his intentions, and David said he didn't have any. It wasn't as if he'd kissed her or anything. Mr Gratz was furious and said some very sharp things, and David caught the night train and came home in the middle of the night. Papa had to go back to New York to smooth things over. It isn't the first time David's gotten into a scrape. That's why I'm warning you. David flirts with girls and then he's surprised when they like him back. He says Isabelle's silly, and I guess she is. She has a perfectly elegant way of dressing her hair, though."

"Does she?" I said. I played with my ice cream. "How does she do it?"

Mimi at once went into a long description, dramatizing with gestures and tugging her curls. I concentrated on my soda. It tasted good, but it felt fizzy and funny in my stomach. It's almost the time of the month for me to be unwell, and I wondered if I'd already begun. I was trying to work out exactly how many days it had been since the last time, when Mimi said, "I think David's writing letters to a *shiksa*."

I know now what a *shiksa* is. It turns out I really am one, but there's nothing wrong with being a *shiksa* – it's just a girl who isn't Jewish. "He is?"

Mimi nodded. "She's *French*," she breathed as if this made matters worse, "and the name on the envelopes is Madame Jean-Baptiste Marechaux. *Jean-Baptiste*," she repeated, and I felt a pang of envy because she pouted so prettily and sounded so foreign. "That means *John the Baptist*. It's not a name a Jew would give his son. And it's *Madame* Marechaux, so David's exchanging letters with a married woman. I expect there will be another scandal," she concluded placidly, and drew on her straw.

"Don't suck your straw like that," I said sharply. "That's not a polite noise." The truth was, she was getting on my nerves. "And stop talking about scandals and flirtations. You're a little girl."

Mimi put out her tongue. "You're not much older," she

said. "I still don't believe you're eighteen. Just then you sounded like the worst kind of grown-up. I thought you were better than that."

I didn't know how I felt when she said that. I didn't know whether I wanted to be a grown-up, or a child like Mimi, self-possessed and spoiled and happy so long as she had an ice-cream soda to drink. Luckily it was getting late, and I said so. Mimi consulted her little gold watch and said it was only half past three, but I pointed out it was half past four.

We bickered together on the streetcar. By the time we were home, I was thoroughly tired of her.

I found Malka very low. She's decided that all the rugs must be taken up and beaten before the High Holy Days. Everything has to be very clean for Rosh Hashanah. The electric carpet sweeper would have made the carpets clean enough, but since we have only the ordinary kind, the carpets will have to come up. Malka made up a timetable of how many carpets we'll have to do between now and the twenty-second. It's a dreadful list, because this house is full of carpets. I know this is her way of punishing Mrs Rosenbach – she's going to shame her by working her fingers to the bone. But it's really my fingers that are going to be worked to the bone, because I can kneel to get the carpet tacks up, and Malka can't. And I'll be the one beating the carpets and doing the lion's share of dragging them up and down the stairs.

I felt exasperated, but Malka was crying hard. Sometimes the work is too much for her, but she'd rather die than admit it. I tried to make her laugh by flexing my arm muscles and boasting about how strong I was. She did laugh a little. I can't help worrying, though, because some of those carpets will need two people to carry them, and Malka shouldn't be one of those people. The natural thing would be to ask one of the Rosenbach sons for help, but I can't ask Mr Solly for anything, not after I almost ruined his life by sending that sonnet to Nora Himmelrich. I hate the thought of David seeing me in my oldest dress with my hair tied up in a handkerchief. Beating carpets makes you so dirty. Sometimes it seems to me that David's more powerful than I am – not with his muscles but in some way I can't put my finger on – and if he sees me beating carpets, he'll be even more powerful.

I reckon Thomashefsky sensed I was trying to comfort Malka – I was kneeling on the floor next to her chair – because he actually came up to me and put his front paws in my lap. I was so surprised; I scarcely dared breathe. After all these months of not liking me, he walked straight into my lap, lowered himself into a crouching position, and began to purr.

I think that was the only really nice thing that happened today. That and the fact that I'm not unwell *yet*, though all the symptoms are there. I bet tomorrow will be awful.

Altogether it has been a most irksome day.

Wednesday, September the sixth, 1911

I thought today would be horrid, but I'm in a good mood tonight. Just as I expected, I felt poorly when I got up this morning, and after breakfast, Malka wanted to get started on the carpets. When she heard I wasn't well, she took pity on me and said we'd start with the smallest ones, the ones from Mimi's room and the room that used to be Anna's. We tackled them before the bridge ladies came.

Anna's room was easy because she doesn't live here, and it's neat as a pin. But Mimi's room was a mess, as usual, so I had to pick up after her. Neither of the carpets was very heavy, so I was able to carry them downstairs by myself. I hung them over the clothesline and beat them soundly. I got so dirty and damp – I had on my old brown *shmatte* from the farm – oh, such clouds of dust! It was warm and sticky today. Malka says the longer it stays warm, the better it'll be for us, because soon we'll have to feed coal to the octopus. That's what she calls the furnace – it looks like a big black octopus, with arms that send heat to all the different rooms. Malka says the housework is harder in the winter, because of the coal dust.

But I'm not afraid of coal dust. And I believe I can manage the octopus. I don't look forward to shoveling coal all day, but at least I won't have to carry a coal scuttle up and down the stairs.

It's a queer thing, but beating the carpets did me good.

After I finished them, the pains in my stomach were gone. I hauled them upstairs and hammered them down again. By the time I finished, Malka had made lunch for the bridge ladies. She said I was a good girl and allowed me a break to change and wash up.

At quarter to twelve my packages were delivered from Rosenbach's, and because Malka was still in a good humor, I snatched time to try everything on. I *did* look like a lady, with my new hat and fawn-colored suit. I looked downright citified, and so grown-up! My fall hat is a perfect darling.

Tonight I had a surprise. I came down to read in the library, and there was a package on Mr Rosenbach's desk with a note on it: *For Janet.* Inside was a sketchbook – oh, such a handsome one, with a dark-green cover and rough paper! David explained to me that rough patches in the paper hold the chalk the way a waffle holds butter.

Beside the sketchbook were two envelopes, one filled with willow charcoal – David says it's the best kind for drawing – and another with six colored chalks in it: blue and red and purple and green and orange and yellow. They must be from David's personal supply, because the tips weren't sharp but rounded.

He remembered, he remembered! I don't believe David Rosenbach is a suitable person for me to think about, but he did remember, and oh, I am glad, and I'm going to draw a cup!

I have had such a fascinating conversation with Mr Rosenbach! Now that I work here, I understand how Jane Eyre felt about Mr Rochester. I don't mean being in love with him, but finding him more interesting than anybody else at Thornfield Hall. Jane was a servant, with no one to talk to but the housekeeper, Mrs Fairfax. It's the same with me, except Malka is a lot more aggravating than Mrs Fairfax.

What happened was this: Malka took in the post this morning, and there was a letter for me. The minute Malka saw my name on the envelope, she asked me if I had a young man, because if I did, I wasn't allowed one.

I was frying fish at the time, and I felt her question was tyrannical. I said indeed I did *not* have a young man, and I didn't want one, but if I ever *did* want one, I didn't see what business it was of hers – and then, right in front of me, she tore open my letter and read it!

It flashed through my mind that the letter might be from David, and my heart stood still. Then Malka said, "What's that priest been saying to you?" and I realized my letter must be from Father Horst. I snatched it from her and ran my eyes over the lines. Oh, how repentant I felt! He began by saying that he hoped his letter would find me in good health. He'd missed seeing me at Mass and for my weekly instruction. He feared he was to blame for my absences, and that what he'd said about the Jews had been a stumbling block for my faith. He's prayed about it, and he wonders if he was wrong to try to persuade me to leave the Rosenbachs; he even wrote that perhaps I'd been right to rebuke him for his prejudice against the Jews. At the end of the letter, he said he believed my Faith to be genuine and that he hoped nothing would diminish my desire to be received into the bosom of the Church.

I do think that was kind. And I think it was very humble of him to say that he might have been wrong. I felt kind of consecrated, having a priest say that my faith was genuine. But to Malka, of course, his letter was nothing less than a confession of anti-Semitism. She forbade me ever to speak to him again.

I said I had every intention of speaking to Father Horst again. Then Malka said I would have to choose. She said I'd have to choose between a lying priest and the family that took me in off the streets and gave me the clothes on my back.

Well, of course, that's true, but my blood was up. I said it seems to me I work pretty hard for the clothes on my back. That's when we smelled the fish burning. Malka gave a cry as if she'd seen the murder of a child and grabbed the handle of the frying pan. She burned herself on it and ran to the sink to put her hand under the cold-water tap. Both of us were yelling by that time. I don't rightly recollect what I said.

Then Malka seized Father Horst's letter and said she was going to show it to Mrs Rosenbach. I was frightened because I know Mrs R. doesn't like me. I implored her, but to no avail. Like an avenging Fury she charged upstairs – I couldn't believe how quickly she moved with her bunion.

Thank God, it was Mr Rosenbach who stuck his head out the library door and asked what the noise was about. Malka shoved my letter into his hands so that he could read it. Malka lamented that she'd known how it would be once they let a *shiksa* into the house, and that I'd been telling tales about the family to an evil-minded priest.

I wasn't going to let her get away with that. I said Malka had no business reading my letters, and that Father Horst was a good man, and that nobody had a right to persecute me because of my religion.

Mr Rosenbach's head shuttled back and forth, listening. Then he handed the letter to me and nodded toward the library to signify that he would talk to me there. He said, "Malka, *mamele*," in a coaxing and tender voice, and put his arm around her so that he could steer her downstairs. I couldn't tell what he was saying, because it was in Yiddish, but he was trying to soothe her. It wasn't working very well.

I withdrew to the library. I reread Father Horst's letter and felt a great wave of relief when I read the last part. Ever since our quarrel, I've been afraid Father Horst would bar me from taking the Sacrament. I was afraid I'd lost my chance to receive the Body and Blood of Christ.

When Mr Rosenbach came back, he said, "Sit, sit," though I was already sitting. He sat opposite me, perching on the edge of the chair the way he does. He spread his hands and looked sorrowful – he is nearly as good at looking tragic as Malka is. I braced myself.

"Miss Lovelace, I beg your pardon."

"You do?"

"I do," he said. "Malka had no right to read your letter. I shouldn't have read it, either. You are quite correct: no one has a right to persecute you for worshipping God in your own way. This is America."

Am-ehr-ee-kah. He makes it sound so beautiful.

"Malka is a child of the Old Country. When she was young, a servant had no privacy. If she had a letter, the housekeeper could read it. Malka forgets that we are in the New World, where even a servant has rights. I hope you can find it in your heart to forgive her."

He paused so that I could say I would. I want Mr Rosenbach to think I'm sweet-natured and forgiving, even if I'm not. After a moment, I said grudgingly, "She's been having an awful time with her bunion."

He smiled and leaned forward a little. "Miss Lovelace, may I ask —?"

"Yes?"

"It's none of my business." He linked his fingers and looked down at the carpet. "You don't have to say a word.

But I find I am devoured by curiosity. What exactly did you say to the good priest, when you rebuked him?"

Well, I didn't mind answering. "I told him he had anti-Semitism."

His face broke out in a broad grin. He tried to suppress it; he put up his hand to groom his mustache, but there was no hiding it: he was delighted with me. "You accused a priest of anti-Semitism?"

"Yes, I did," I said staunchly. "He wanted me to work for a Catholic family named the Possits. And I said I wanted to stay here, because you've been good to me. Then he said I was obstinate, and I said I'd rather be obstinate than have anti-Semitism."

"Yet he apologized," Mr Rosenbach pointed out. "That surprises me. By worldly standards, he is your superior in age and sex and station. I think perhaps he is a good man, this Father Horst."

"Yes, sir, he is," I said gratefully. "He's taken a lot of trouble with me. He's giving me religious instruction, and he gave me a prayer book. It's a nice letter, don't you think?"

"Very nice," Mr Rosenbach agreed. "Father Horst has a good reputation. I believe he is very active on behalf of the poor in his parish."

I knew that was high praise, because Mr Rosenbach is also very active on behalf of the poor. He's a member of the Hebrew Benevolent Society, and he's on boards and things.

Mr Rosenbach asked, "So he's giving you religious instruction? I thought you were already a Catholic."

"I am, really," I explained, "on the inside. My mother was a Catholic. But I've never been confirmed."

Mr Rosenbach leaned back in his chair. "Interesting, isn't it, how often we inherit our religion from our mothers? In Judaism, you know, the birthright of faith comes from the mother. A Jew is the child of a Jewish woman."

I said, "Yes, sir," but my mind had gone on ahead. I wondered if this might be a good time to broach the subject of the True Faith. I hadn't planned on talking about it so soon, but here we were, talking about religion. I might not get so good an opportunity again. I said hesitantly, "Father Horst says the Jews deny Christ."

"That is true," Mr Rosenbach said serenely. "I believe your Jesus lived, of course. He was a real man, and I'm sure He was a good man. But I don't believe He was God, and I don't think He was the Messiah."

It took me a minute to figure out that word *Messiah*. I always think of it as *Mess-EYE-uh*, but he pronounced it *Mss-SHEE-ock*. My eyes rested on Mr Rosenbach as I worked it out. He'd kicked a footstool into place, and he was regarding me with interest, as if he was enjoying our conversation. And yet – it struck me then, and it struck me cold – hellfire yawned before him. "Mr Rosenbach," I said urgently, "don't you *ever* feel that Jesus Christ was the Son of God?"

"No, I don't," answered Mr Rosenbach. "I believe in one God, only one God. But you raise an interesting question, one I have often pondered." He crossed his legs and gazed up at the ceiling. "Can the truth be divined through intuition? In other words, when we *feel* something is true, does it follow that our feelings are trustworthy? Plato, of course, tried to establish a method of argument based on geometry—"

I was curious about Plato, but I wasn't going to be led off the track. "Mr Rosenbach," I persisted, "have you ever gone off by yourself and *tried* to feel that Jesus Christ is your Savior? Maybe if you were to go somewhere quiet, and sit still and open your heart to Him, you might be saved from damnation. Don't you think it might be a good idea to *try*?"

"Miss Lovelace," said Mr Rosenbach – he spoke kindly but laughter lurked in his eyes —"have you ever gone off to a quiet place, and sat very still, and tried to imagine that Jesus Christ is *not* your Savior?"

"I couldn't do that!" My hands flew up; I found I was clutching my heart. "Not after He died for me! It would be *awful*! It would be treachery."

Mr Rosenbach bowed his head. "Religion has much to do with loyalty." He was quite serious now. "I can never decide if loyalty is a different substance from faith, or the same thing. Please understand, Miss Lovelace: I'm not asking you to betray the God you worship. I'm only asking you to put yourself in my shoes. I am as convinced of the truth of my faith, and as bound to be loyal to it, as you are to yours. I don't think either of us should turn apostate."

I didn't know what an apostate was, but I looked it up this evening. I thought it would be like an apostle, but it's just the opposite. An apostate is someone who turns his back on his faith.

I said, "But what if you – I mean, where will you go when you die?"

"We Jews do not worry about hell. Nor do we talk much about heaven. It's enough for us to know that God keeps faith with those who sleep in the dust."

I thought that was a beautiful phrase. I tried to imagine a life that wouldn't end in heaven or hell or Purgatory. It seems to me that if there were no hell, you wouldn't have to behave yourself too much. The funny thing is that the Jews do behave themselves. They go to a lot of trouble for their God, keeping *kashrut* and putting money into all those little charity boxes. There's something very fine and disinterested in being good when there's nothing to be gotten out of it. I blurted out, "I think Judaism is a noble religion." And I *do*, but I also think it's not very profitable. I'd rather go to heaven when I die.

Mr Rosenbach looked pleased. He left his chair and went to the bookcase. "I wonder if you'd like Plato? His Socratic dialogues are like little plays. I think you would find them stimulating. Tell me, how did you enjoy Marcus Aurelius?"

I was tempted to lie. "Not very much," I admitted. "I couldn't seem to get through it. I thought Marcus Aurelius was awfully stuck on himself. And he never got excited about anything."

"Ah!" said Mr Rosenbach. It was that throat-clearing kind of *ah* that reminds me that he's German. "Of course! You are a romantic, and the temperament of Marcus Aurelius does not accord with that. All the same, you might like Plato." He plucked a volume off the shelf. "Here we are. *Theaetetus*. It seeks to explore the difference between knowledge and wisdom. Would you like to try it?"

Of course I said I would. I can't seem to resist trying to please Mr Rosenbach. I was glad to see that the book was thin, though, because I'm in the middle of *The Dead Secret*, which is thrilling. I opened the book and read a page or two. It seemed puzzling, but not dull. In fact, it piqued my curiosity.

When I looked up, Mr Rosenbach was gazing at me in a most melancholy way. I said, "Mr Rosenbach, what's the matter?"

It wasn't the kind of question a hired girl should ask her employer, but Mr Rosenbach didn't seem to notice. "I was wishing my Mirele were more like you." He grimaced. "Every night I force her to read to me from *Little Women*. My daughter Anna read *Little Women* when she was ten, and she couldn't get enough of it. But Mirele stumbles over every other word. She hates it. I've asked her again and again, 'What would you *like* to read?' Do you know what she says to me? *Nothing, Papa, I don't like to read.* I went to the bookstore and the clerk recommended *The Wonderful Wizard of Oz.* He says it's trash, but all the children are crazy for it. But Mirele doesn't like *The Wonderful Wizard of Oz.* My friends and I are creating a new school, a magnificent school—" He gestured toward his desk, which was covered with papers. "The children will learn because they *want* to learn, not because they're afraid of being punished; they will be encouraged to think and feel and create. We will have classrooms in the open air; the children will study nature in the park—" He threw up his hands. "But Mirele, my Mirele! I'm afraid she will be as great a dunce as she's been in every other school."

He began to pace, talking under his breath. He had forgotten I was there. "And yet she is intelligent. I would swear to it. When she was little, I thought she was the quickest of all my children. So funny, so curious, so clever – and yet, this child of my body *will not read.*" His left hand closed in a fist, and he hammered the air. "Even *The Wizard of Oz* she will not read!"

An idea flashed through my mind. It wasn't a single idea, more like a series of pictures: Mimi standing well back from the mirror so that she could admire herself; Mimi squinting at her watch and getting the wrong time; Mimi frowning over a silver bracelet and saying it was too plain. My mouth fell open. "Mr Rosenbach, what if she can't *see*?"

He stopped in mid-stride. "Can't *see*?"

I nodded. "Up close. What if she can't see? She told me that reading makes her head ache. She can't do sums on paper, but she can add up money in her head. And on Tuesday, when we were in your store, I saw a silver bracelet engraved with flowers – I liked it, but Mimi said it was too plain! What if she can't see little things, close-up things? Reading would strain her eyes—"

He looked at me with such hope. "But if she has trouble seeing, why hasn't she told me?"

That was such an easy question that I almost laughed. "Because she'd have to wear glasses! You know how vain she is." I guess he didn't, because he looked dumbfounded. "Maybe I shouldn't say that about your daughter. But Mimi's as vain as a peacock, and I bet she'd die rather than wear eyeglasses." I realized I was telling tales and was ashamed. "The truth is, Mr Rosenbach, I'm just as bad. I think about clothes all the time. I never had any pretty things till I came here, and, well, I just think about clothes a lot. And Mimi's the same way. I guess it's because we're about the same age –" I saw a vast abyss open at my feet, but I leaped over it – "I mean, we're growing up. Both girls, I mean."

He came to me and grasped my hands. "Miss Lovelace," he said, squeezing so tight that my fingers stung, "if you're right, I will thank you a thousand times."

"Mimi won't," I said. "Even if her eyes are bad, she won't want to wear glasses."

"She'll wear them," said Mr Rosenbach so grimly that I wondered if I'd done Mimi a bad turn. He released my hands. "Miss Lovelace, I am indebted to you. This is the second time you've opened my eyes to the lives of my own children. I thank you from the bottom of my heart."

He spoke so heartily that I began to worry. What if I was wrong about Mimi's eyes? "I've meddled again," I said anxiously. "After what happened with Mr Solomon, I promised I'd never meddle again. Now I've meddled."

"You have my permission to meddle," said Mr Rosenbach. "I give you *carte blanche*."

I didn't know what *carte blanche* was, so he spelled it for me and explained it. I thanked him, and he thanked me back, and I saw that it was time to leave. I was almost in the hall when I remembered Malka. She's a maddening old thing, a little black fly with a bunion, but I turned back.

Mr Rosenbach had seated himself at his desk and was glancing over the plans for his school. "Well, Janet?"

"Sir," I said boldly, "I'm going to meddle again. I think Malka ought to have an electric carpet sweeper."

To my surprise, Mr Rosenbach knows about electric carpet sweepers, because he's thinking of selling them in his store. There's a new model called the Hoover that has a brush inside that spins around and around and sucks up the dirt. It's supposed to be better than all the others, and it costs sixty dollars – what a dreadful price! I don't believe Mr Rosenbach minded about the money, but when I told him that Mrs Rosenbach had already said no, he started to shake his head. It seems that Mrs Rosenbach is in charge of all the household decisions, and he doesn't like to go against her.

"I bet Mrs Rosenbach's never taken up a carpet," I said. And I explained to him, point by point, how you have to move the furniture and pry up the carpet tacks, and roll up the carpet and sweep the floor. Then there's the business of lugging the carpet down those steep back stairs, and hauling it over the clothesline, and beating it until your arms ache. And then you have to roll it up and drag it back up the stairs and hammer it down again. "I'm not lazy," I said earnestly, "but there are fourteen carpets in this house, not counting the runners on the stairs, and most of them can't be carried by a single person. And Malka's old. I don't think Mrs Rosenbach knows what she's asking."

Mr Rosenbach listened attentively. He even made Jewish noises of sympathy. Then he told me I should tell Malka not to worry about taking up any more carpets. He said he'd talk to Mrs Rosenbach.

And now I think I have written quite enough. It's past one thirty in the morning, and I'm tired ... and Malka will kill me if I oversleep again.

Mimi just left. I feel shook-up. Imagine her coming up to my room and lying in wait for me, nursing her anger all the while! The way she lit into me...! Oh, it's awful!

It's close to midnight and I'm tired. The Klemans came for dinner; also the Friedhoffs. Malka was fussy all day, anxious lest something should go wrong when Mr Solomon's Intended was coming for Shabbos. She approves of Mr Solomon's engagement, because the Klemans are more Orthodox and less Reform than the Rosenbachs. She doesn't mind that Miss Kleman is Polish, because Malka's part Polish herself.

I didn't much care for Ruth Kleman. She is one of those willowy, narrow-faced girls that makes me feel like a big ox. The only time I liked her was when I caught her looking at Solly. Then her mouth softened and her eyes glowed. All the same, Nora Himmelrich is ten times prettier than Ruth Kleman, and nicer, too – Miss Kleman scarcely looked at me when I took her things at the door, and she said *thank you* in a chilly undertone. She'd never shake hands the way Nora did. I'm afraid Mr Solomon told her the awful thing I did, and now she hates me.

After dinner, there was an avalanche of dirty dishes. While I was tackling them, little Oskar came downstairs and asked me to tell him a story. I couldn't sit down, but Malka pulled him into her lap and gave him a jawbreaker to suck. Oskar wanted a story about snakes and a choo-choo train, so I invented a circus train full of deadly cobras and man-eating tigers and terrible bears. Of course all the dangerous animals got loose, and only the little boy Oskar kept his head and coaxed them back into their cages. I'm afraid it was a very tangled-up story, but it's hard to keep your mind on snakes and *kashrut* at the same time. Once I almost used the wrong dish towel, but Malka stopped me.

It was past eleven by the time I scalded the dishcloths and trudged up to bed on my aching feet. When I got to my room, I saw that my door was shut. That puzzled me because I always leave it open, so the room will cool off. I went inside and there was Mimi, sitting in the middle of my bed (she didn't bother taking her shoes off, the little slob) and glaring at me like a regular spitfire.

"I came to tell you I'm not going to be your friend anymore," she announced, "and what's more, I wish I never had been. Just because of you, Papa took me to the ophthalmologist –" her voice caught on the hard word – "and from now on, I'm going to have to wear glasses, horrible glasses, *all the time*. And Papa says it isn't my fault I read so badly, but he's going to arrange for me to have extra tutoring, so I can catch up with my school-work. *Extra* tutoring!" she wailed. "And he said I should be grateful to you. But I never, never will be!"

I set my chamberstick by the mirror and went to sit by her. Even by candlelight, I could see how red her eyes were. Malka had told me that Mr Rosenbach has a friend on the school board who's an ophthalmologist. The friend agreed to see Mimi this very morning. Malka said her little Moritz was never one to let the grass grow under his feet.

I searched for the right words. "Oh, Mimi, it won't be so bad." I put my hand on her shoulder, but she dashed it away and scowled through her tears. "Once you learn to read—"

"I already can read," she said petulantly, "and I don't *like* it. I don't even *want* to like it. I don't want to be a goody-goody like you, reading Plato and Louisa May Alcott and all that. And you were a sneak, to go to Papa and tell him my eyes are bad. He says I'll get used to wearing glasses and won't mind. I *will* mind. How could I not mind looking frightful? There's a girl in my class – Ethel Marx – she wears glasses, hideous thick things, and you know what we all call her? Grasshopper. Her eyes bulge like a bug's eyes." She crooked her thumbs and forefingers into circles and framed her eyes with them.

It was downright eerie, because she *did* look like a bug. I believe that child could mimic a crocodile if she set her mind to it. I said soothingly, "*You* won't look like a bug." And I'm sure she won't. Somehow Mimi will manage to look fetching in eyeglasses. Now that I think of it, I ought to have said that, because it might have mollified her.

"How do you know I won't?" demanded Mimi. "I was *so* looking forward to growing up, and having boys fight over who gets to carry my books, and wearing a beautiful dress at the Harmony Debutante Ball. I had everything planned. Now it's spoiled, because I'll look a fright, and none of the boys will dance with me, and the girls will tease me – and Ethel Marx will be the worst of all, the mean thing, because I was the one who started calling her Grasshopper."

I was reminded of Lucy Watkins and Hazel Fry calling me Greasy Joan. The memory smarted. "Then it serves you right," I said. I was on the side of Ethel Marx.

I think those words hurt Mimi's feelings, because she leaped off the bed like a little Fury. She dashed to my dresser, pulled out the top drawer, and dumped the contents onto the floor – then the second drawer – and then the bottom one. All my things flopped out: my nightdresses and my aprons and my petticoats and my stockings – and Belinda, who lay facedown on the floor.

"There!" hissed Mimi. "I learned that from one of your horrid *books*! And that's just the beginning of how I'm going to get back at you – you false friend, you snake in the grass—"

I didn't care what she called me. I rushed forward and caught up Belinda, because Belinda was the one thing that couldn't be replaced. I didn't want Mimi to spoil my beautiful clothes, but if worse came to worse, I could buy new ones. But Belinda, my darling Belinda!

Mimi's lip curled. "You've got a *doll*," she said

scathingly. "I knew you weren't eighteen. You say you're eighteen, but you're a baby!"

"My mother made this doll for me," I said. "It's all I have left of her. You touch this doll, and I'll slap your face – and I'm bigger than you are!"

It was childish of me to say that. And I guess I looked more threatening than I realized, because Mimi burst into fresh tears and ran out of the room.

I stood there, hugging Belinda. Then I set her on the bed and put the drawers back in the bureau. My clothes weren't hurt a bit; I'd swept that morning, and the floor was as clean as could be. I wrapped Belinda in my old nightgown and hid her at the very back of the bottom drawer. You can't see her unless you open the drawer all the way. I would have liked to lock the drawer, but though there's a keyhole, there's no key. Hired girls don't get much privacy.

I've written this by candlelight, which goes against what I promised Mr Rosenbach, but I don't want to leave the room, in case Mimi comes back. I hate it that I've lost a friend. Of course Mimi's younger than me, but she was funny and fun and clever. She wasn't a bit of a snob. She seemed to forget I was the hired girl, and I liked how bold she was. I admired the way she always looked so pretty, even if she isn't really, and I liked talking to her about clothes.

It strikes me how few friends I have in Baltimore.

During the week, I'm busy with the work I have in hand, and Mass takes my Sunday mornings, and instruction takes my Tuesdays. I've been to Druid Hill Park, and Rosenbach's Department Store, and the markets where we buy food, but I haven't seen a library or a picture gallery, and I haven't made friends, unless you count Nora Himmelrich, who probably doesn't like me anymore. Unless you count David.

I feel very lonely tonight.

Sunday, September the tenth, 1911

It's past midnight and I'm in the library, hoping that David might surprise me with a visit. I tried to read *Theaetetus*, but I couldn't keep my mind on it. That's not Socrates' fault. I believe philosophy is very fascinating and lofty, and I know I'm going to like it. But you can't read philosophy if you're listening for the sound of an opening door. After I failed with *Theaetetus*, I tried learning my catechism, but that was no better. In fact, it was worse.

He won't come. Why should he? I'll see him on Tuesday; that's plenty soon enough. I'm busy with my diary. It's just as well he won't come.

This morning I wore my fawn-colored suit to Mass. When I was halfway to church, I heard running footsteps behind me. It was David, and he was calling my name. "I've caught you!" he said, and captured my fingers in his. "Don't go to Mass! Come back with me! I'll fetch my drawing things, and we'll go to the park. There's not a moment to lose! Come on!"

I wanted to go. There's a kind of momentum about David; it's as if he were a strong wind that could sweep me off my feet. But I'm not a feather to be tossed about. I was on my way to Mass. I wanted to see Father Horst.

So I said, "I can't. I have to go to Mass."

"Skip it," he said. I think something in my face told him I wasn't going to be as biddable as that, because he switched his tone from breezy to coaxing. "Can't you miss it just this once? I wouldn't ask, but time is of the essence – I need you; I really do. Walk with me, and I'll tell you all about it."

He swung about and began walking as if he expected me to follow him. But I didn't, and after a moment he turned, ran ahead of me, and walked backward. "You're mad because I asked you too late. I don't blame you. Honest to Mike, I didn't know before this morning! We don't open mail on Shabbos, and I didn't see the letter. I only just opened it. Madame Marechaux likes your face!" He spoke the words as if he expected a trumpet fanfare. "The commission's almost mine, don't you see? Only Madame Marechaux wants you facing out, not seen in profile, so I've got to send her more sketches—"

"I don't know what you're talking about," I complained.

"What commission? Who's Madame Marechaux? Why should I care if she likes my face?"

"Great Jakes, haven't I told you?" All at once he was serious. He fell into step beside me. "Madame Marechaux's name is *Shon*." I must have looked blank, because he repeated it. "*Shon*. That's French for Joan. Joan of Arc is *Shon Daar*. Madame Marechaux grew up near Orléans, and Joan of Arc was her heroine. Two years ago, Joan of Arc was beatified, and Madame is praying that the Church will make her a saint. She's very devout, Madame Marechaux – and very fashionable; her husband's just rented a splendid house on Fifth Avenue. She wants a picture of Joan of Arc to hang at the top of the stairs – a big canvas, almost life-size. Madame has asked all the up-and-coming artists in New York to submit sketches, and she said I might, too. She likes me – the other fellows are more experienced, and two of them are almost famous, but she likes me – and now she likes your face. It's the chance of a lifetime. So you see, I'm not just flirting with you – well, I'm flirting a *little*, can't help myself! – but I really do need you, don't you see? I have to draw you as soon as I can and send the drawings to Madame Marechaux!"

I pondered this. It was interesting to find out who Mimi's mysterious *shiksa* was. She was a wealthy lady who wanted a painting, not a sweetheart. So that was good. But I was piqued, too, because I'd thought that David chose to paint me as Joan of Arc because I was *like* her, not in order to please a lady of fashion. It made the whole thing less romantic.

"Can't you?" pleaded David. "Won't you?"

Oh, but I wanted to skip Mass and go with him! I reckon he saw me weakening, because his face lit up with mischief, and he made a dash at me – feinting, as if we were playing that old school game Steal-the-Bacon. He sprang to one side of me, dodged to the other, and snatched my missal out of my hand. Then he retreated, holding the book high in the air and laughing.

I forgot I was a young lady going to Mass. I went after him. I jumped for the book, and at that moment we were quite close, and I saw his hand, silhouetted against the morning sky, and his face – David, with his untidy curls and masculine throat – how different men's throats are from ladies'! – and his whole frame charged with vitality and something else... I don't know what to call it, but I know that I'm drawn to it. I wonder if that's what it's like to be in love, to be drawn like iron to a magnet, without thinking, almost without consent – oh, I *won't* be in love with David Rosenbach, I won't! He's a flirt, and he's a Jew, and I won't be like that silly fool Isabelle Gratz!

Here's the queer thing: that moment – tussling with David over my prayer book – is lodged in my mind like a framed snapshot. I don't know why. Once when I was a little thing, I watched the sun rise on Easter morning. I had it in my head that it would be holy to watch the sunrise. But I watched too closely, because the image of that tiny orange sun got burned into my eye. I saw it for an hour afterward. I was afraid I'd go blind, but I was too scared to tell Ma. I ought to have known better than to stare at the sun.

Anyway, for some reason, the moment with David was like *that*. Not that time stood still, or anything, because it didn't, and neither did we. He frisked in a circle and I revolved around him, leaping and grabbing. "Give me back my missal!"

"Promise me you'll come," teased David.

Then a gentleman and a lady passed by, ever so beautifully dressed. I recognized their faces from Corpus Christi. I realized that I wasn't acting like a lady or a good Catholic, and that people could see. I remembered the passage in *Jane Eyre* where the moon says, "My daughter, flee temptation!" and Jane says, "I will." It seemed to me that this was a temptation, if there ever was one.

I planted my feet and repeated, "I have to go to Mass."

"You can't," said David, grinning. "I've got your prayer book."

I wasn't going to knuckle under to that. "I don't need my prayer book." And I turned on my heel and walked away.

I thought he would follow me, but he didn't. I went on walking. He didn't follow. At last I turned back. "You could draw me tonight, in the library. I'm always there.

I mean, most nights I'm there, between ten and midnight."

He gazed at me despairingly. He stood with one hand entwined in his curls, as if he was about to tear his hair out. It was kind of theatrical. "I can't draw you in the library. I need the sunlight. Besides, there's a dance at the Phoenix Club tonight, and I promised to go. What about Tuesday? That's your afternoon off, isn't it?"

He found out my day off. "Yes, but—" I thought of my Tuesday instruction. I'd told Father Horst that I might not always be able to meet him, because of Mrs Rosenbach's bridge ladies. If I saw him after Mass, I could tell him that the Rosenbachs need me to work this Tuesday. (As a matter of fact, that's what I did tell him. It wasn't a complete lie, because David's a Rosenbach, and sitting for a portrait is a kind of work, but it's more lie than truth. I'd say it's about ninety-five percent lie. Sweet Mother of God, I've lied to a *priest!*)

I wavered. "I guess I could see you Tuesday."

"You're a peach!" he said, and he let out his breath as if he'd been holding it. "Thank you, Janet – I'm truly grateful." He came straight to me, bowed in the most courtly way, and handed back my missal. "I'll walk you to church."

That rattled me, because I hadn't expected it. "No, don't," I said hastily. "There isn't time. I'm going to be late. I have to run."

Then I did run, or I walked so fast that it wasn't

dignified. I felt like a branch that had been snatched from the burning.

I got to Mass in the nick of time. I wanted to pray *hard*, but I couldn't keep my thoughts away from David. I was afraid God would be furious with me, because I'm going to miss instruction two weeks in a row. And I was plotting to deceive a priest. I don't believe even the Blessed Mother could have any patience with that. Finally I remembered what Father Horst said and just begged God for mercy and forgiveness.

For a few moments after that, I felt at peace. But then thoughts of David filled my mind again. I've spent this whole day in a daze, and now I'm waiting. I told David I'm in the library most nights; he might not have known it before, but he knows it now. He *might* stop by after the dance and look in on me and say hello. It would just be friendliness, but he *is* friendly. There wouldn't be anything improper, because I'm not in my nightgown. I changed into my blue dress, the one that doesn't have the chalk stains.

But he hasn't come. Oh, he *won't* come! It will be Tuesday before I talk to him again. All the same, he *might* come back from the Phoenix Club and see the light under the library door. He hasn't come home yet. I'd have heard him. So he might still come.

I wish I'd let him walk to church with me.

I keep thinking of that moment when he said he wasn't

flirting, but then he said he was, because he couldn't help it. Does that mean he can't help flirting with anybody, or just with me? He remembered to buy me a sketch-book, and he knows my day off... But then I imagine him dancing at the Phoenix Club – there will be society girls there, dressed in silk and lace, pretty girls with tiny waists and soft white hands. And I want to laugh scornfully – imagine thinking that David Rosenbach might be interested in me!

And just how old is that fashionable lady, Madame Marechaux?

It's getting late. My hand aches from writing. Tomorrow the Ladies' Sewing Society is coming: luncheon for ten. Malka says it's one thing to cook for the bridge ladies, because they want to eat quickly and get back to their cards, but the sewing ladies are sewing for charity. They take their time eating, and they like a substantial meal.

I'm sleepy and I ought to go to bed.

I might as well go to bed.

I'll wait another five minutes, and if he still hasn't come, I'll go to bed.

Oh, what a day I've had! I don't believe any girl ever spent a more beautiful afternoon, even with the rain – and indeed, the rain turned out to be one of the best parts! I want nothing more than to wield my pen and relive it all. No. One thing more I want: for the library door to open and for David to come in. But I must not be greedy; my cup of happiness is full.

Everything went well today. To begin with, Malka let me off early. She saw me rushing through the lunch dishes and said she'd rather do them herself and save the china. Dear, good, grumbly Malka! I flew upstairs and changed into my suit. I wish I'd worn my lacy waist instead of the plain one, but how was I to know the delights that lay in store for me?

The day was overcast, which was a disappointment, because David wanted me in dappled sunlight, like a woman in an Impressionist painting. David has told me all about the Impressionists, who are modern. He says they're as good as the Old Masters any day, but they aren't much appreciated because some of them are still alive, and the ones that are dead aren't dead *enough*. I like a man who can make me laugh.

We went to the park and David posed me beneath a tree and told me to look rapt. Then he sat on the grass and sketched furiously. From time to time, he consulted his watch. After a little while, he said I could pin up my hair, because it was time to go.

I was disappointed, because I'd hoped we'd be together all afternoon. Only then, David gave me a great mischievous grin and asked me when was the last time I'd been inside a theater. I had to admit I'd *never* been inside a theater, and he said in that case I'd better hurry, because the opera started at two, and he wouldn't miss taking me for a farm.

An opera! I was so excited that my hands were all thumbs and I couldn't manage my hair. But David said it looked fine. We ran to catch the streetcar. All the while, I was thinking, *An opera, an opera! I'm going to the opera, and David Rosenbach is taking me!*

Actually, it wasn't a whole opera I was going to see but what's called a *cabinet opera*. David explained it to me: there would be only a few singers, in costume, and they would sing the finest airs from *La Traviata*. There would be scenery, but no ballet and no big choruses. David said he'd set his heart on taking me to the theater, but there isn't much playing on Tuesday afternoons. Luckily the Columbia Parnassus Touring Company is at the Academy of Music for a week, and they do Tuesday and Wednesday matinees. David said he had a hunch that I'd like the opera better than an ice-cream soda.

Wasn't that beautiful of him? I do think David Rosenbach is the kindest, most agreeable, most gallant man I ever met. To think of him working out in his head what I'd like best, and guessing right, too! Why, it beats everything I ever heard. I almost feel worshipful when I think of it. I try not to feel too worshipful, though, because I think it's bad when girls think too highly of the men. It's more suitable when the men worship the ladies.

On the streetcar, David started to tell me about the opera. He explained that *traviata* is Italian for *lost*, because Violetta, the heroine, is a lost woman. I asked how she got lost, and he said that Violetta had abandoned herself to a life of giddy pleasures. I said that didn't sound too bad to me, which made David laugh. Just then an elderly lady got onto the streetcar. She wasn't at all well dressed, poor thing, but David got right up and gave her his seat. That shows how chivalrous he is. But it meant we couldn't talk anymore until we got to the Academy of Music.

I was tremendously excited, but a little bit scared, too. I wasn't sure I was dressed fine enough for the theater, and I don't know what Mrs Rosenbach would say about me going to the opera with her son. And though I knew that Grand Opera must be the very summit of culture and refinement, I was just a little bit scared that I wouldn't like it. Miss Chandler once saw a Grand Opera called *Norma*, and it was four hours long and there wasn't a word of English in it. She said it was very edifying.

The Academy of Music is a very imposing building,

red-brick trimmed with sandstone. It has a mansard roof, which is French – David told me there was an architect named François Mansart, which is how the roof got its name. David knows so much about everything. He took me inside, and oh, how I wished I'd worn the fancy waist! It was like fairyland, with marble floors and lofty ceilings and two majestic staircases – two carriages could drive up those staircases side by side, that's how wide they are. There was a crystal chandelier, and velvet draperies, and exquisite paintings of nymphs and muses and little rosy cherubs with wreaths in their hands. David called the cherubs *putti*, which is Italian for *little artistic babies*.

Most of the ladies present were better dressed than I was. But there were a few that were in suits, so I didn't feel too bad. I was so awed by the grandeur around me, I was afraid I was gawking like a country bumpkin. So I lowered my eyes and tried to act nonchalant. I think David read my mind, because he murmured into my ear that the privilege of looking around the theater was included in the price of the ticket. He led me over to the frescoes and started telling me about the Greek gods and Muses and the parts where the flesh tones had been well painted. I blushed a little because some of those nymphs didn't have too much on. It seemed funny to be looking at them with a man. But Miss Chandler says the ancient Greeks thought the unclothed form was beautiful, and there can be nothing vulgar or unchaste in the world of fine art.

Our seats were close to the stage. David bought me a libretto, a little pamphlet that explained the story and translated the Italian. I read it, and what I caught on to was that Violetta's giddy pleasures weren't what I'd thought they were. She wasn't just frivolous. She was wanton and depraved, like Céline Varens in *Jane Eyre*. That was how she made her living. I guess she couldn't be a hired girl because she had consumption.

When the music began, it was soft and mournful, almost as if you were in a sickroom and shouldn't wake the patient. I found it beautiful, but I was worried the whole opera might be slow and soft like that. I think my tastes in music are unrefined, because I like fast music better than slow music. Of course you can't have a tragedy with frisky music. But just as I was thinking that, the music became merry and skittish, and the curtain rose.

There were three gentlemen in black frock coats, and two ladies in hoopskirts with ringlets falling over their bare shoulders, and earrings in their ears and fans in their hands. I guess hoopskirts are nonsensical, but I should dearly like to wear one, because they make your waist look small. And oh, the scenery! On one side of the stage there was a little garden, with roses ambling up trellises, and a fountain that spouted real water. But most of the stage was like a ballroom, with sconces and candles, and mirrors and little fragile gilded chairs. There was a long rose-colored couch, which Violetta used when she had to faint. She fainted very gracefully. Her step would falter, and she'd sidle over to the couch. Then her whole body would droop, and she would tumble onto the rose-colored silk. It was awfully effective. I tried fainting onto Mr Rosenbach's couch, but I was like a load of bricks being dumped from a wheelbarrow.

When the people first sang, I didn't know if I liked it or not. The men's voices were as strong as a team of horses, and the women sang like wrens: shrill and tight and complicated. The acting wasn't like real people, either; the men pumped their arms up and down, and raised their eyebrows, and the ladies rolled their eyes and fluttered their fans. It took some getting used to.

But then the shortest, stoutest man – he played Alfredo – began to sing a song called "One Day a Rapture." That's what it would be in English, but he sang it in Italian, which is better. Violetta was languishing on the sofa after an attack of coughing. He seized her hand and sang about the love that palpitates throughout the whole universe. He sang *misterioso*, which I knew must mean *mysterious*. And he said his love was rapture, rapture and torment. The significance of those words – the way the tune explained them – gave me a thrill like nothing I've ever known. I understood then that it wasn't the libretto that told the story of the opera. It was the music, the way it yearned and swelled – the suspense and depth and mystery of those sounds. At that moment,

I knew I loved Grand Opera. I felt those notes in the very fibers of my soul.

When Violetta sang, I began to see why she was twittering like a wren when you get too near its nest. She was afraid of love, as if it were a wave that could drown her. But she desired it, too: the love that palpitates through the whole universe. How could she resist it? Alfredo's love was *true*, pure love, unlike anything she'd ever known. So of course his love conquered her, and he took her to the side of the stage with the trellises and the fountain. That was the country.

Once the lovers were in the country, it seemed like things were going to work out. Violetta's consumption got better. Her love was as pure and true as Alfredo's. She would never have forsaken him, and he would never have betrayed her. But then Alfredo's father came to visit and he was as cruel as mine, maybe even worse, because Father's no hypocrite. Alfredo's father was the kind who acts pious. He told Violetta she must make a *sacrificio* and give up Alfredo, because the way they were living together, without being married, was a scandal. (I don't know why Alfredo didn't marry Violetta. But he didn't.)

Now, if Alfredo's father had come to me, I'd have sent him away with a flea in his ear. But Violetta had a tender conscience, because of having been depraved so long. Once Alfredo's father convinced her it would be best for Alfredo if she left him, she couldn't stand it: she had to make the *sacrificio*. She left the country and went back to her life of giddy pleasures in the ballroom.

That's when I started crying. I knew it wasn't going to go well after that. It seemed so tragic that this poor sick girl had found true love, only to lose it again. I knew it would kill her, and it did.

After the intermission, Violetta came back onstage in the most glorious black dress. It had jet beads on it and black rosebuds and lace around the shoulders. I wish I had a dress like that. Alfredo came to the ballroom and reviled Violetta in front of all the guests, because he thought she was untrue to him. She swooned and fainted dead away on the sofa. By that time, I'd soaked my handkerchief, and David had to give me his.

There was worse to come. In the last act, Violetta was on her deathbed, which was the rose-colored sofa. She wore her hair loose, like a girl's, and a lacy white nightgown. She looked oh, so pale and pathetic! All I could think of was that Alfredo *must* come back before she died. She was gasping and coughing as she sang: "All of life must end, all of life must end!" I felt terrible sitting there, strong as an ox, enjoying myself while she was dying. Because I *was* enjoying myself, no doubt about that. Even though I was crying my eyes out, it was so *satisfying*: grandeur and tragedy and her doomed, true love.

Just when hope had fled, Alfredo came! And Violetta rallied, and she and Alfredo sang together about how they would go away and be happy together, and she would get well. I believed it. Even though I'd read the libretto, I thought there was still hope. There was one moment, infinitely happy and pathetic, when she rose from her couch and held out her trembling arms and her face was alight! But then she collapsed, and Alfredo flung himself down on her dead body. And the curtain came down.

When I came to myself I realized I was clutching my throat with one hand and squeezing David's handkerchief with the other. My face was soaked with tears. The curtains rose and there were the singers, smiling and bowing, and oh, how I clapped! Some people shouted "*Bravo!*" which is what you shout when a man is a good singer. David taught me that if the singer is a lady, it's more proper to shout "*Brava!*" Of course ladies do not shout at all, but I wanted to. I wanted to shout and stamp my feet and whistle. Girls aren't supposed to know how to whistle, but I know how.

David asked me if I enjoyed the opera. I could scarcely speak. He showed me a drawing he'd done of me during the opera – I never saw him drawing me, but I certainly did look rapt. He gave me his arm so he could guide me through the crowd. I ought to have been afraid someone might see us, but all I could think about was Violetta and Alfredo.

Oh, why can't real life be as glorious as the opera? Of course, in real life people fall in love and get consumption and die, but it isn't the *same*. In the opera, the music makes everything deeper and truer and grander. I don't know how to express it. All I know is that it was a good thing that I had David's arm to hold on to, because I stumbled on the grand staircase, and would have fallen if he hadn't steadied me. The people around me were only shadows. Reality was what I had known when I was watching the opera – rapture and torment and the love that palpitates throughout the universe.

When we reached the doors, we saw it was pouring great sheets of rain, so that you could scarcely see. I came back down to earth and cried, "Oh! My new hat!" and David said, "My sketches!" because he hadn't brought his wooden portfolio, just his sketchpad. He thrust the sketch-pad into my arms and said, "Stay inside and keep dry. Don't stir a step!" And he dashed out into the rain.

I stood by the doorway and stared after him. At first I was glad to be alone, because I wanted to think about the opera, but then I began to worry. I knew I was going to get home late, and I didn't know where David had gone. More people left the theater, and I began to wonder what would happen if I was the last one there. Outside the traffic was dreadful; carriages and umbrellas and a broken-down auto whose driver kept honking the horn.

Then I noticed a red umbrella, bobbing and thrusting its way through a sea of black ones. It was a lady's umbrella, but the lady must have been the forceful kind, because she was cutting through traffic like a hot knife through butter. When the red umbrella came closer, I saw that David was underneath it. He was soaking wet, and there were raindrops in his hair, but he looked quite happy.

I stepped outside, under the overhang. He gave the umbrella to me, and put out his hand for the sketchpad. From under his coat he took a piece of dry canvas and wrapped it around his sketches. "You waited! Good girl! I dashed over to the store and bought you an umbrella."

"It's too much," I protested. "First the opera, and now—"

"*I* can't keep it," said David. "Get a look at that tassel! I felt like Lord Fauntleroy, carrying it through town. Besides, I have an umbrella at home, and I bet you don't."

He was right about that, so I gave in. At first we meant to take the streetcar, but the ones that passed were all full, because of the rain. David and I walked home together, sharing the red umbrella. David asked what I thought about the opera and I told him I had never, never seen anything so fine. He said he was proud – *stuck on himself* was the way he put it – because he'd known it was just what I would like. He says I have an instinct for art. What a beautiful thing for him to say! I asked him about the operas he's seen, and he told me about Caruso and Nellie Melba. And then – I felt shy, but it was easier with the umbrella over us both – I asked him about his painting.

He has very noble aspirations. He feels that every

artist has a gift to give to the ordinary laboring man. The ordinary laboring man – or woman – needs to be inspired and uplifted, the way I was this afternoon. David likes painting portraits. He says that some artists look down on portrait painting because portraits make money, and landscapes are more distinguished. But David says a portrait painter can tell the truth about the human soul just as Rembrandt did. He said he wouldn't mind being a great portrait painter, even a society painter like John Singer Sargent.

It's terribly important that he should get this commission from Madame Marechaux (*who is forty-six!*) because she has a vast amount of influence. If she hires him to paint Joan of Arc, he's going to tell his father that he means to be a great artist, instead of the owner of a department store. When he spoke of breaking the news to his father, he looked wretched, because he knows Mr Rosenbach will be disappointed. He (David) had thought his brother would carry on the family business, but Mr Solomon is going to move to New York so he can attend a Jewish school called yeshiva. That means Mr Rosenbach is counting on David. But David has no head for business, and Mr Rosenbach must see that it would be cruel to force an artist into a life of sordid commerce.

I told David that Mimi could manage the store, and he said, "But she's a girl!" Then I flared up and said a girl could do anything a man could do. David said I was a regular fire-eater but maybe I was right.

I wanted our walk to last forever. My boots aren't watertight, so my feet got wet and cold, but I would have followed David to the ends of the earth. That's how fascinating our conversation was.

At last we got home, and I had to face Malka. When I came through the back door, she flew at me and shook me with all her might, which isn't saying much, as she isn't strong. But her nails are sharp and they dug into my arms like an owl's talons. She said I was a bad, disrespectful girl, and she had imagined me murdered somewhere and my body thrown into a back alley. When she stopped railing, she told me that she'd had to make the whole dinner herself. But she didn't get me in trouble. She never told Mrs Rosenbach that I hadn't come home.

I thanked her profusely. Her eyes narrowed and she asked me where I got that fancy new umbrella. I said hastily that I'd bought it at Rosenbach's, and the price was reduced because one of the ribs was a little bit bent. Oh, what a liar I am! I'm sure I ought to be ashamed.

Then Malka demanded to know where else I'd been. She told me not to say I'd been having religious instruction, because no girl ever looked so happy after an afternoon of religious instruction.

I hedged, saying I'd gone shopping, but Malka caught sight of the libretto under my arm. She jabbed her fore-finger at me and exclaimed that I'd been to the opera.

I admitted it. I thought she would scold because it's above my station to go to an opera. But to my amazement, she didn't seem to mind it. She said I'd get up to less trouble at the opera than I would with that lying priest Father Horst. And at least I hadn't run off with a man. Malka's never seen an opera, but she's seen the Yiddish theater, which is more thrilling than any Gentile theater, she says. She saw the great Thomashefsky play Hamlet, which was tremendous.

So she told me all about Thomashefsky, and I wedged in a few words about *La Traviata*, and I happened to mention that Violetta had consumption, which meant I hit upon one of Malka's favorite things to talk about: disease. She took over the conversation and told me all about the people she'd known who had consumption. Not a single one recovered. Telling me about all the long-drawn-out deaths took us through eating supper and cleaning up after it. By the time Malka went to bed, she'd forgiven me for being late (though it's not to happen again).

Now I sit here and wonder what was the best part of the day. The glory of seeing the Academy of Music, David saying I have an instinct for art, Alfredo's aria, Violetta dying in white lace, the red umbrella and the walk in the rain ... I can't decide. It was all so glorious. But though I'm happy, I'm also aware of a kind of restlessness: a yearning, a suspense that is more agreeable than any satisfaction.

If every day could be like this one, I would die of joy.

I am *oysgematert*. That's Yiddish for *completely worn out*. The bridge ladies are meeting at Mrs Mueller's house this week, so Malka said we should change the summer curtains for the winter draperies.

We scrubbed the windowsills, and we took down the curtains, examining the lace for places that need mending. Then we unearthed the draperies, miles of damask and velvet, and pressed them and hauled them upstairs and hung them. It was hard, heavy work, and Malka was in tears most of the time because Thomashefsky never came home last night. He didn't come caterwauling for his breakfast, either.

Malka says he's too old to survive another cat fight, and he's likely been run over by one of those *farshtinkener* automobiles. She feels in her bones that he's dead. As the afternoon wore on, she began to say she was like Thomashefsky, too old to be of use to anyone, and the sooner she was in her grave, the better. (This last was because I told her that if anyone was going to stand on a tall ladder to hang curtains, it was going to be me.)

I sure hope that cat comes home.

I tried to comfort Malka, but by the end of the day I was ready to scream. This house has so many windows. The draperies are hard to iron and so cumbersome that the ironing board kept falling over. I burned my hand on the iron.

Mimi's new eyeglasses have come, and just as I suspected, she looks quaintly pretty in them. When I passed her on the stairs, I told her how becoming her glasses were. She prissed up her mouth and acted as if she hadn't heard.

She's still mad at me. But I went through my things this evening and nothing's out of place. She hasn't touched Belinda, who is still wedged at the back of the drawer.

Mimi's new tutor comes to the house every day. Her name is Miss Krumm, and she has yellow-brown hair in a knobby bun, and a grim expression. Her clothes are dull and respectable – a dun-brown suit – and she carries an umbrella even when the sun is shining. Catch Miss Krumm being caught in the rain! She looks as if she hasn't a particle of humor, and I've been feeling sorry for Mimi, but today Miss Krumm came downstairs with a bashful expression on her face and her hair done up in coronet braids. She looked a hundred times better. So I guess Mimi is holding her own.

I haven't seen David all day.

Thursday, September the fourteenth, 1911

Thomashefsky is still missing, and Malka is very sad. Today she decided we should scrub the inside of the dish cupboard and wash the Passover dishes. I thought that was a waste of time, because the Passover dishes won't be used until spring, and by that time they'll need washing again. But Malka insisted, so I gritted my teeth and filled the sink with hot water. Of course there are two sets of china for Passover – service for twelve.

I forgot to say that it was raining. It has rained without stopping since my beautiful Tuesday, and the house was dead silent, except for the rain. Mr Rosenbach and David were at the store, and Mr Solomon had taken Mimi to the Klemans'. Mrs Rosenbach was at her literary society.

The rain plashed, and I washed the dishes, and Malka sniffed and dried. It was all very melancholy. When the doorbell rang, I snatched off my canvas apron, put on my cap, and raced upstairs.

Mrs Friedhoff stood on the porch with Irma in her arms and Oskar clinging to her hand. She looked just awful. She has a dumpy figure, but a thin face, and today it was downright haggard. She asked if her mother was in, and I said she wasn't.

Mrs Friedhoff's face fell. Then she began to cry. Not loudly, but she blinked and her mouth wobbled and tears rolled down her cheeks. Oskar gazed at his mother with stricken eyes.

I forgot I was the hired girl. I said, "Mrs Friedhoff, you'd better come on in," which was presumptuous, because it isn't my house.

But in she came. I took Irma from her and led Mrs Friedhoff to the parlor. She sank down in the rocking chair, and Oskar climbed into her lap and buried his face in her neck. I asked Mrs Friedhoff if she wanted a cup of coffee. Then Anna – I know I shouldn't call her that, but it's what Malka and Mimi call her – began to tell me her troubles.

It seems her housemaid and cook, who are sisters, are both leaving. Mr Isaac Friedhoff is in the Arizona Territory – something to do with the railroad – and earlier this week, Oskar was sick. (At this point in the story, Oskar twisted around to face me so he could boast about all the things he'd coughed up.) Mrs Friedhoff was up all night caring for him Monday and Tuesday. But by Wednesday morning, he had the appetite of a wolf and had begun to tear around the house, though the doctor said he should be kept quiet. "He didn't say *how* I should keep him quiet," sobbed poor Mrs Friedhoff, "only that he should rest. But Oskar never rests. The first three years of his life, he never slept through the night, and he *won't* take a nap. But around eight last night, he went off to sleep, and I thought *I* should sleep, only Irma had an attack of croup, a dreadful attack, and I thought I might lose her." She found a handkerchief in her handbag and swiped at her eyes. "It was terrible. I'd have sent Isaac for the doctor, if he'd been home, but when is he ever home? I've *told* him we need to get a telephone, but Isaac doesn't like them. I ran hot water until the bathroom filled with steam so that the poor child could breathe. The walls were dripping. Just before dawn, she stopped coughing and slept. Only then Oskar woke up, and he's been like a little wild animal all day." Oskar wiggled guiltily. "I wanted Mother to watch him. If I don't sleep, I'm going to be ill." And with that, poor Mrs Friedhoff wept afresh. Oskar flung his arms around her neck and choked her with his sympathy.

I know what I did then wasn't like a hired girl, but I'm certainly not ashamed of it. "Mrs Friedhoff," I said, "you're *oysgematert*. You go upstairs to your old bedroom and take off your wet things and have a good long nap. Mrs Rosenbach'll be home before long, and until she is, Malka and I will mind the children."

"Oh, Janet, would you?"

"Of course we will," I said. "You know Oskar likes my stories. And Malka'll take care of Irma all right. Your room's all nice and clean for Rosh Hashanah. The bedding's fresh, and we put up the winter curtains yesterday."

It didn't take much persuading to get her to agree. She handed over Oskar and Irma and stumbled up the stairs, sobbing that I was a treasure and a dear, kind girl.

I took the children down to Malka. I handed over Irma, who was wailing in a listless, maddening kind of way. Malka wrapped her in a shawl, very tightly. It seems Mrs Friedhoff's doctor believes that swaddling is bad for babies, but Malka says there's nothing like it for a baby that won't stop crying, and in fact, five minutes after she was tied up like a parcel, Irma went to sleep and wasn't a bit of trouble.

It was Oskar who was the trouble. Malka thought she'd make cookies with him, so I finished washing the dishes while she showed him how to measure out flour and sugar, and how to break eggs. He was greatly interested, but once the cookies were in the oven, he needed some other amusement. I remembered a Hans Christian Andersen story from Miss Lang's book, about a magic tinderbox and dogs with eyes as big as saucers. I told him that; he liked it so much that I told it twice. By the time I'd finished, the cookies were done, and Oskar ate thirteen of them, with milk.

After that, he wanted to go outside, but it was still raining cats and dogs. The phrase "raining cats and dogs" made Oskar prick up his ears and demand to see Thomashefsky, which made Malka sad. He then announced his intention of exploring the dumbwaiter. It seems that Mr Rosenbach once showed Oskar the dumbwaiter and explained how the pulleys worked. I let him crawl onto the shelf and hoisted him up and down until he was tired of it. When at last he crawled out, he began to race around and around the kitchen, making train noises.

We let him run, as it seemed easier than stopping him. After what seemed like an hour, he stopped. "I want," he panted in his hoarse little voice, "to play with some toys."

We didn't have any toys. Malka asked him coaxingly if he'd like to take a nice little nap. Oskar said he wouldn't.

Malka looked at me with desperation in her eyes, and I rose to the occasion. I remembered how Luke and I used to play on the days when Ma aired her quilts. "I'll take Oskar up to my room. We'll make a blanket tent and play Indians. He'll like that, won't you, Oskar?"

Oskar looked intrigued, so I led him upstairs. I rigged a tent by draping the bedclothes over the foot of my bed and the top of the dresser. We crawled inside the tent, and I told Oskar there was a blizzard outside (we made blizzard noises) with wild wolves howling (we howled). Then I was inspired to say that we were starving to death inside our tent, and that we would die if no Indian was brave enough to go out and hunt buffalo. Oskar took the bait. "I'll go," he said, and squared his shoulders. "I'll go kill the buffalo."

"I'll make you a horse," I offered. To tell the truth, I was starting to enjoy myself. I tore strips from my old sage-green dress to make a bridle, and I tied them to the back of a chair. Oskar rode up and down the prairie, rocking the chair back and forth and flapping the reins.

Then he demanded a buffalo. I produced my cardboard suitcase, which he beat to death with his bare hands. He dragged the slain buffalo back to the tent, and we pre-tended to gnaw on buffalo meat. "You're good at playing," Oskar said earnestly.

I felt terribly pleased. But of course, one buffalo was

not enough; he had to hunt another one. Then we killed a few wolves. After the last wolf was dead, he collapsed in the tent beside me.

That was when he saw Ma's crucifix. It had fallen to the floor when I stripped the bed. "What's that?"

In a flash, I saw my opportunity. I don't think I could ever persuade Mr Rosenbach to turn apostate, and Mr Solomon is going to study Talmud. But Oskar is young, and he looks up to me. I hoped I might be able to plant a seed of the True Faith in his soul.

So I told him about Our Lord. I told him how kind Jesus was to children and poor people, and how gentle He was, but Oskar only fidgeted. I told him how Jesus could walk on the water and feed thousands of people with only a few fishes and a few loaves of bread. "But why's he bleeding?" asked Oskar, and I realized I was going to have to tell him about Our Lord's Passion and Resurrection.

I began. I showed him the picture of the Crucifixion in my missal. I was afraid the cruelty of the story would scare him. It appalled me when I was a child and does to this day. I remember asking Ma why my salvation couldn't have come without Jesus getting hurt. But Oskar didn't feel as I did. He demanded, "How'd they get him to go so high up?"

It took me a moment to grasp what he meant. In the picture in my missal, St. John and the Blessed Mother stood below Christ's feet. "They made Him lie down on the Cross when it was still on the ground," I said. "Once He was on it, they stood the Cross up."

"How'd they stand it up?" persisted Oskar. "Did they use a pulley? And how'd they stick the bottom part in the ground? Did they dig a hole?"

I shook my head, aghast. I couldn't answer his question. It never occurred to me to wonder how the Cross was raised, or how it was anchored in the ground. For me, that's not part of the story. The story is about His courage and His love.

I reminded myself that Oskar is very young. Jesus isn't real to him. I skipped forward and told him about the glorious surprise of the Resurrection. I explained that Jesus had opened the gates of heaven to everyone who believed in Him. All at once, I saw that Oskar was looking past me, over my head.

Mrs Rosenbach stood in the doorway. Mrs Friedhoff stood just behind her, but it was Mrs Rosenbach I saw. Her face frightened me. It wasn't that her eyes flashed or her nostrils flared or any of the things you might read about in a novel. But it was stony still. It reminded me of a picture of Medusa I'd seen in one of Mr Rosenbach's books.

"Oskar," she said crisply, "go downstairs and tell Malka to wash your hands and face."

Oskar looked from her to me. Then he put down the crucifix, scrambled to his feet, and clattered out of the room.

Mrs Rosenbach waited until he had gone. "This must never happen again."

I flinched at the sound of her voice. All at once I felt stupid and childish, kneeling on the floor surrounded by the mess: the tent, the torn dress, the banged-up suitcase. I slid the crucifix under my apron, shielding it from her Greek-monster gaze.

"Do you understand what I'm telling you, Janet?"

"Yes, ma'am," I said, in a low voice. "I was only—"

"You were trying to convert my grandson to Christianity," Mrs Rosenbach said, and her voice was like steel: hard, cold, and polished. "I won't tolerate that. Do you understand?"

"Yes, ma'am," I said. "He saw my crucifix, and he asked—"

"I'm not interested in how it happened," Mrs Rosenbach said. "If you ever say one more word about your religion to my grandson, you will leave this house without a reference. Do you understand?"

"Yes, ma'am."

"I will not consult Mr Rosenbach. The decision will be mine alone, and it will be final. Is that clear?"

"Yes, ma'am," I said. I turned away so she couldn't see my face, and I began to gather up the bedclothes. My hands were trembling.

"Mama," said Anna. I'd forgotten she was there. "Mama, there's no harm done."

"How do you know there isn't?" asked Mrs Rosenbach. "You don't know what kind of impression may have been made."

"Yes, but Oskar isn't impressionable," protested Anna. "If it doesn't have to do with snakes or machinery, Oskar doesn't *care*. And I'm sure Janet meant no harm."

"I don't know what she meant," retorted Mrs Rosenbach. "I had thought better of you, Janet," she said, with a grave detachment that made me hang my head. "Set your cap straight and go help Malka with dinner. We'll be dining early, because of the children."

"Yes, ma'am," said I, and made haste to leave the room. I didn't cry in front of her, but I wept as soon as I reached the servants' staircase. I cried hard. Then I wiped my eyes with my hands. I didn't want Malka to see me in tears and ask what had happened.

What I did wasn't wrong. I'm sure of that. Jesus told His disciples to spread the Gospel, and He promised that we would be blessed if we were persecuted for His sake. Every time I say the Creed I say that I believe in the Holy Catholic Church. If I truly believe, how can I fail to share my faith with others?

I'm sure what I did wasn't wrong.

But I feel so low about it. Somehow, Mrs Rosenbach made me feel so ashamed and scared and even remorseful. The worst part was when she said she'd thought better of me.

I wish it was Tuesday and I were back at the opera. It's queer to think that two days ago I was so happy, and now I'm wretched.

Perhaps if I go to sleep I can dream my way back.

Sunday, September the seventeenth, 1911

I went to Mass today. Father Horst greeted me kindly, which made me feel worse about deceiving him. How long ago the opera seems! It was a glorious day, but I've paid for it. I'm worn out with waiting and wishing and longing: waiting for real life to begin, wishing – oh, why should I bother to deny it? – for a kind word from David Rosenbach. After Tuesday, I thought he might come to the library at night, so we could talk.

But David's busy. Not busy working, like Mr Rosenbach, but with engagements: baseball or tennis in the park, dinner parties, and dances. He swoops in and out of this house like the daring young man on the flying trapeze. Malka and I never know how many places to set at table.

He hasn't spoken to me, not once. Of course, we can't very well talk when the others are around. But I've been here in the library every night, listening for his footsteps. I've stayed up long past midnight, hoping he'll come.

I was glad to go to Mass today and think about something that wasn't David Rosenbach. During the service,

I kept my mind resolutely on God. Afterward, I went to kneel down before the Blessed Virgin and think about my sins. I felt so wistful and low-down it was easy to repent.

I examined my conscience, which is always a melancholy business. I haven't done too badly by Malka this week. She's been working me almost to death, because she misses that cross old cat. But I've been patient, and I haven't answered back. I was feeling proud of myself about that, but then I remembered how I lied to Father Horst, which was just pure badness. So I repented that I lied.

I recalled what happened with Oskar and felt uncomfortable. I explained to God how good my intentions were, and how it was just too bad of Mrs Rosenbach to be so cold and withering. But I felt as if I'd missed something. At last I asked the Blessed Mother what she thought, and she said, "Well, you see, Joan, they trusted you." It was then that I saw I'd been wrong. I knew all along that converting Oskar was going against the Rosenbachs' wishes. I went behind their backs. It was a kind of betrayal.

When I came to see this, I felt meaner than dirt. It was true repentance and a very dismal feeling. I said the Act of Contrition and wept bitterly for my sins. As soon as I got home, I went in search of Mrs Rosenbach.

I found her in the parlor with her needlework. She raised her eyes to me but she didn't smile. "What is it, Janet?"

She was so composed; it made my stomach knot up.

My mouth was dry and my voice faltered, because it isn't easy, humbling yourself. I told her I was sorry about Oskar. I said I'd been to Mass and I'd realized what I did was wrong. (I wanted her to know that it was the Church that made me repent, because it might make her think better of Christianity.)

Mrs Rosenbach didn't help me out. Her face didn't soften and she didn't say she forgave me. She just listened until my words dried up. "Thank you, Janet. You may go," she said, and went back to her needlework.

I didn't feel any better after that. I bet Mr Rosenbach would have forgiven me. I wonder if she told him what I did. If she told David, perhaps that's why he hasn't spoken to me.

I haven't been sleeping. I'm like a lovelorn girl in a novel, but girls in novels generally aren't hired girls, and they don't get in so much trouble when they oversleep.

I've been reading a novel called *Trilby*, which David told me about. It's set in Paris and it's all about artists. How I should like to go to Paris! It sounds so beautiful, with the gray slate roofs and the golden river. The artists there don't seem to mind being poor; they stay up all night and drink coffee and talk about art. Trilby, the heroine, looks like me, because she's tall and well developed, with wavy brown hair. She's good-hearted and brave and sweet and funny, but she's a fallen woman. The author doesn't seem to blame her for being depraved, and neither does the hero, Little Billee. I guess things are different in Paris. I'm surprised that I found the book in Mr Rosenbach's library, because I think there's anti-Semitism in it. The villain is a Jew named Svengali—

Hark! A rapping on the library door!

PART SIX

Mariana in the Moated Grange

Monday, September the eighteenth, 1911

How strange to recall how I felt when I broke off this narrative! How sorrowful I was, and how anxious! Today my heart is singing with joy, though David has gone. He's back in New York, showing the new sketches to Madame Marechaux. All day long, I've been praying and praying that he'll get the commission. I'll be ironing a pillowcase or slicing a tomato, and like a flock of homing pigeons, my thoughts fly to David. Then I close my eyes and pray for him – only I scorched a pillowcase, and Malka was sarcastic at my expense.

I don't care what Malka said. So long as I can go on thinking about David, I don't care about anything.

I will take up my tale where the last entry ended and relive every second.

I knew it was David on the other side of the door – David, rapping very gently, using the tips of his fingers. He has such beautiful hands: real artist's hands, tapered and strong and long fingered. Just thinking about his hands makes my skin feel warm. I'm blushing as I write this, I know.

I rushed to the nearest bookcase and stowed my diary behind a row of volumes – I would *die* of mortification if David read my diary. Then I tiptoed to the door. "Who is it?"

"It's David. I want to show you my latest sketch. Stand aside and I'll slide it under the door."

I stood back. There was a crackling, rustle-y sound, and the paper slid toward my feet. It was a copy of the sketch he'd made at the opera: my face in profile, looking rapt. The way he'd done it was clever, because he used a pinkish-buff paper and three kinds of chalk: black, red, and white. With three colors he was able to suggest the colors of my skin and eyes and hair.

I thought it was beautiful. That sounds conceited, but I don't mean *I* was beautiful. A portrait can be a beautiful portrait even if the sitter isn't good-looking. In the sketch, my eyes looked clear and thoughtful, and my lips were parted. I didn't look stupid at all. And I didn't look like a big ox.

"Do you like it?" whispered David.

I did, and I wished I could keep it. Then it struck me

as strange that we were talking through the door. "Why don't you come in?"

There was a low laugh. "I thought you might be in your nightgown."

I made haste to open the door. I wanted to laugh, but I was exasperated, too. All these past nights, I've waited up for him, fully dressed, with my hair up – why, sometimes I've done up my hair three times, just to get it right. And all the while, he was afraid to come in, because he might catch me in my kimono!

"Tell me how you like the sketch," he begged, and though his eyes sparkled, it really was an entreaty; he cared about what I thought. So I told him how beautifully he drew.

He listened very attentively. Of course I don't know anything about art except what I've learned seeing Miss Chandler's pictures on the stereopticon and what I've been able to glean from Mr Rosenbach's books. But even I can see that he is very, very talented, perhaps a genius. I told him it was like magic, the way he could catch my likeness and make my common face seem noble and eloquent. And I praised his sense of line. I'm not entirely sure what that means, but it's what Mr John Singer Sargent said, so it must be all right.

He went on listening. So I said some more things. I asked why he copied the opera sketch, instead of the sketches he'd done of me in the park. He explained that he thinks the opera sketch best captures my character and was therefore the most beautiful.

I felt almost dizzy when he said that. *Beautiful*. Could he really be saying that about me? I ducked my head; I could feel that I looked downright silly with happiness.

He asked if I'd used the sketchbook he gave me and how I was getting on with my drawing. I showed him my drawing of a cup, and he got very excited, because it was so bad. He said the handle was well observed, but the rest was wrong. "You're using your mind instead of your eyes. You think the cup is round, so you draw a circle at the rim."

"But the cup *is* round," I objected.

"Yes, but not at the rim," he said. "You're drawing what you know instead of what you see." He strode over to his father's whiskey tray and took up a glass. He held it in front of me, level with my chin. "What shape is the rim?"

"Round," I said, baffled. "It's a circle."

"Is it?" he asked. "Trace it with your finger. No, don't touch it. Outline the shape in the air."

I did. I started at the left end of the glass, and my finger dipped and rose to the right, and humped back to the beginning. I saw he was right: the shape I traced was a shallow oval, like a saucer. I exclaimed in surprise, and David nodded energetically. "You *see* now! That's it! You've got to *see* when you draw, and what you see—"

"Shhh!" I hissed, not because he was too loud (though he was; we'd forgotten that the house was asleep). "I heard something! Be quiet!"

I flew to the open window and stuck my head out, looking out and down. A shadow moved in the yard below.

David followed me to the window. "What is it?"

"I think it's Thomashefsky!" I said. "I heard his meow! Oh, David! He's been missing for five days and Malka's heartbroken. Quickly!"

I reached for his hand as if we were children. As soon as I touched him, I remembered we weren't. It means something when a girl lets a man hold her hand, but I didn't have time to think about that. I was (well, mostly) thinking about Thomashefsky.

I dragged David down the back stairs to the kitchen. The front part of the kitchen was well lit because of the streetlamps, but the back was shadowy. I didn't turn on the lights because I had an idea that if I did, Thomashefsky might run off again.

David started for the door, but I held him back. "No, no, not yet! I'll get him something to eat." I went to the refrigerator and filled the cat dish with herring. "Let me go to the door."

David stood back and I stepped out into the night. "Thomashefsky? Good boy, sweet boy, want-a-little-fishy?"

No shadow stirred. My heart sank. Then I heard an

accusing *miaow* - the sound a cat makes when he's impatient for his meal. I saw him crouched amid Malka's sorry tomato plants. "Good boy, sweet boy!" I wheedled. "Are you hungry, Thomashefsky? Do you want a little fishy?"

He meowed urgently. I retreated one step at a time, squatting and holding out the dish so he could smell the herring. Slowly he pursued me, writhing against my skirts.

I lured him inside and David shut the door. Thomashefsky sniffed the dish, his tail lashing and then swinging. He crouched down low, extending his tail straight behind him, with just the tip twitching. That's the sign that his food is acceptable.

I hunkered down and watched the cat gobble his supper. I was so happy. I knew Malka would be overjoyed, and I couldn't wait to surprise her. It seems to me now that I felt the last happiness of my childhood. It was simple and peaceful, nothing like the rapturous tempest that surges in my bosom as I pen these lines.

I got up and filled two more dishes for the cat: one with water and another with milk - Thomashefsky likes his little lap of milk. I glanced at David and saw that he was watching me with an odd smile on his face. I would say it was a tenderhearted smile, except that seems presumptuous.

An idea came to me. "Let's slip upstairs and shut the cat in Malka's room!"

David tilted his head skeptically. "Do you really think

you can carry that beast up all those stairs? He always bites me."

I expect this is true, because Thomashefsky doesn't like David. He likes Solly the best, Malka says. But I liked the idea of surprising Malka, and I wanted to show David how well Thomashefsky and I get along. So I reached down and scooped up the cat, but that was a mistake, because he hadn't finished eating. He said, "*Mrrroww!*" He struggled – writhed in my arms, clawed my neck – and escaped.

David came to me. "Did he bite you?"

I touched my neck and found it sticky. "He scratched me."

David threw up his hands as if to say, *Of course.* "I'll get the peroxide. Cat scratches can be nasty." He went without hesitation to the cabinet where Malka keeps her medicines. I guess Malka must have doctored him when he was a little boy. "Come along! I'll tend to you."

I went to him and stood still. My heart raced. Maybe I should have said, "I can put the peroxide on myself." Maybe that's what a pure and proper young girl would have said. But I guess I'm not very pure or very proper, because I wanted him to touch me. I forgot to write that we hadn't turned the kitchen lights on. Our eyes had grown accustomed to the darkness; I could almost have read a book in the front part of the kitchen. But where we were, next to the medicine cabinet, it was dim.

I waited. He took a clean dish towel out of the dresser and poured peroxide on it. He held my chin while he touched the damp cloth to my neck.

I want to remember everything. His thumb was under my chin, tilting it up. And there were two fingers on my cheek – his two middle fingers, I think. The nerves under my skin quivered, and a thrill coursed through me. He was very gentle. He poured the peroxide and stroked my neck with the wet towel three times – Malka always says you must cleanse the wound three times. The first two times, I didn't dare look up. But the third time, I raised my eyes to him and murmured, "Thank you." I wanted to say, *Thank you, David*, but I couldn't say his name.

That's when he kissed me.

At first I felt nothing but shock. I've always wondered about kissing a man – I mean about what you're supposed to *do* when you kiss a man, because the two of you aren't just standing there with your lips frozen together, I know that much. Something happens during a kiss, and I've always wondered what the something was. I've been worried that if I ever got engaged or anything, I wouldn't be able to do my fair share.

And that's just how it was, at first. I felt nothing and did nothing. And then I felt *everything*: bliss so vast and pure that I've thought of little else since. My head swam and I swayed toward him and I was brazen; I rested the palm of my hand against his chest. And I kissed him, and

I knew how. It was *beyond everything.*

He drew back too soon. He inhaled between his teeth and let out a shaky sigh. "I shouldn't have done that."

I thought, *Why not?*

"I shouldn't have," he said again. "It was a caddish thing to do. But for a moment, I thought..." He didn't say what he'd thought, and I wish I'd asked. "Forgive me. It won't happen again."

"Won't it?" I said, dismayed. "But I liked it! I liked it better than anything!"

He started to laugh. In the half-light, his mischievous face was like the face of a seraph (except for his nose). The hollows under his cheekbones were so striking, and his curls were a dark halo. "You're the limit," he said. "Janet, you really are—"

I didn't let him finish. I stepped nearer to him, and I was trembling, but I touched my fingertips to his shoulder and stood there, just stood there, close to him. After a second of terrible waiting, he drew me closer – his hands were on my waist, the back of my waist, and he kissed me again.

He was shaking with laughter, and I felt happiness vibrate between us. The second kiss was better than the first because I didn't waste time wondering what to do. I kissed him, and after he broke away, I raised my face to his, and he kissed me a third time. Oh, his hands on the back of my waist! I felt a tingle that spread and rushed up my spine, and down to my knees, and down to my finger-tips. My scalp crawled and my toes shivered. Every fiber of my being felt that kiss.

And then it was over. I could have kissed him all night long, but he stepped back, deliberately. He took my hand in his. "We'd better stop," he said. "I shouldn't have kissed you – but I'm glad I did." He raised my hand to his lips and kissed it – like a cavalier in a story; it was so romantic I couldn't breathe. Then he whispered, "Good night, Janet," and went up the stairs, leaving me with the cat.

"Good night," I whispered after him. I didn't follow him. I knew our perfect interlude was over, just as I know when Mrs Rosenbach dismisses me, though of course this was entirely different.

I think I'm glad that I didn't chase after him, because it would have been unmaidenly. But even if we hadn't done any more kissing, I wish we'd had time to talk about what had happened and what I felt and what he felt and how things are going to be from now on. I know there are things we'll have to face together – my position in this household, and my humble rank, and whether he will tell his parents now or wait until later, and of course I am a Catholic and he is a Jew, which is the knottiest problem and will have to be thought *through*.

But I can't think through it now. I'm too happy. I'm blissful, even though David went back to New York on the morning train. He'll be back for the High Holy Days – oh, they will be holy to me, because David will come back and kiss me again! All I can think about are his kisses.

Now I understand why people get married. Once you're married you can kiss as much as you like. I wonder why married people don't spend more time at it. I wonder how married men go off to work every morning, when they could stay home and kiss their wives. I wonder how married women set about cooking meals and supervising the servants when they must be thinking of the hour when their husbands will come home and kiss them.

And I wonder about the whole history of the world. Governments and courtrooms and steam engines and combines – all necessary inventions, but how did men come up with them, when they could have been kissing? I think about the conquistadors and how they left off kissing their wives and went sailing across the ocean to conquer a lot of innocent natives who would probably have preferred to stay in their hammocks and kiss *their* wives. It's hard to fathom.

Of course there are other things that married people do. You can't grow up on a farm without knowing about those things, and I've always thought they seemed clumsy and a little strenuous, but perhaps they might not be so bad if David – oh, David! I am sure David could do nothing ungraceful. Why, when he put peroxide on my neck, it was like being anointed with spices in the Song of Solomon.

All I can think of is David. I wash dishes and knead the bread and scrub the sinks and run the carpet sweeper over the rug, and I am happy, because I am reliving his kisses, and longing – fiercely but dreamily – for the day when he will kiss me again. I am so *happy*.

But my happiness is no longer a child's. Now that David's kissed me, I shall never be a child again. My happiness is not contentment, but longing, incessant, passionate *longing...*

Tuesday, September the nineteenth, 1911

Last night I had a dreadful dream. I think it came because I've been worrying about Belinda. Once or twice I've had a notion that Mimi's been in my room; I've fancied I smelled that lilac perfume of hers. But nothing has ever been touched, and Belinda is safe in the back of the drawer.

In my dream I was back on the farm. I came into my old bedroom and saw the floor littered with scraps of cloth. It was Belinda I saw first; Belinda, torn to shreds: her wig clipped, her stuffing dragged out, her flowered dress cut to ribbons. But it wasn't just Belinda; the floor was covered with relics of cambric and lace, tattered bits of petticoats and nightgowns, all pure white and fine enough for a bride.

And Ma was there. She wore her old dress with the faded blue triangles on it. Her face was haggard and she gazed at me without love, almost without recognition. I didn't know if she was the one who had torn my things to shreds, or if Father had done it; I had a nightmarish sense that I might have done it myself, without knowing it. I cried, "I'm sorry, Ma, I'm sorry!" but her face was implacable.

That's when I woke up.

I'd overslept, and Malka was annoyed. When I made Mr Rosenbach's toast, I cut the bread too thick, and it got stuck in the toaster and filled the kitchen with smoke. I burned my fingers trying to get it out. By midmorning I had an awful headache.

But at last it was time for my afternoon off. As I dressed to go out, I remembered that this time last week I was getting ready to see David. He took me to *La Traviata*, and he bought me my red umbrella. Two nights ago, he kissed me. It seems a hundred years ago. I recall Miss Chandler once read me a poem with the line in it: *Ah, love, let us be true to one another!* I don't recollect the rest of that poem, but I've always remembered that line. As I walked to church, I whispered it over and over, like a prayer.

Then I felt bad, because it was almost as if I didn't trust David. It must be the bad dream I had, because I'm sure I do. Only, the way things were, there was no time for us to swear fidelity to each other. We kissed and I am bound to him forever. But we didn't have time to talk about what might lie ahead.

I went to see Father Horst, and he was kind but I felt too dull-witted to pay much attention to him. While he droned on about the suffering souls in Purgatory, I remembered Ma. I thought of what I wrote in this book about kissing, and it struck me that Ma never kissed Father, not once that I recall. Marriage doesn't always mean kissing and happiness. Ma understood that. She wanted me to be a schoolteacher, not a wife; she saved the Belinda money so I could escape from all that, but here I am, thinking of marrying David Rosenbach, who isn't even a Catholic. No wonder she was angry in my dream.

But Ma never met David, and not *all* marriages go bad, I'm sure. I blurted out, "Father Horst, isn't marriage a sacrament?"

He looked astonished and well he might, because I'd veered away from the poor souls in Purgatory. I tried to explain. "I mean, if marriage is a sacrament, it's holy, isn't it? So if someone tried to warn a girl never to get married – I don't mean warning a girl against any particular man, but saying that marriage was a bad thing for a woman – why, that would be a mistake, wouldn't it?"

Father Horst took off his glasses. The way he did it, I wondered if he had a headache, too. He rubbed his closed eyes with his fingertips. "Miss Lovelace, are you thinking of getting married?"

"No," I said hastily, but that wasn't true, because I'd kissed David, and kissing someone and getting engaged are pretty much the same thing. Even Mimi acknowledged as much, when she said that David wasn't engaged to Isabelle Gratz.

"Has one of your employers told you that there's something wrong with getting married?"

"No, Father," I said. I could see where his thoughts were tending. Father Horst is always sure the Rosenbachs are up to no good. "I was just wondering. That's all."

"In my opinion," Father Horst said, "it would indeed be a mistake. Marriage is a woman's destiny. There can be no higher calling for a woman than to marry a man and bear his children, unless –" a light came into his eyes – "you wish to enter the consecrated life. Is it possible you may have a vocation?"

I was a little slow to see what he meant. "A nun?" I said at last. "Me? Oh, no! I could never be a nun!"

"The calling can be extremely subtle," Father Horst said pleadingly. "It can be a very delicate thing, that still, small voice that speaks from the soul. Have you heard that voice, Miss Lovelace?"

"No," I said hastily. It sounded brusque, and I was sorry, because I could see that it would brighten his day if I wanted to be a nun. "I'm sorry, Father, but I'm pretty sure I'm not going to be a nun. I don't think I have it in me. I just wanted to see what you thought about marriage."

Father Horst looked at me quizzically. Then he sighed. "I have to admit, I find it hard to imagine you as a nun," he said, "but God's ways are often mysterious, and I wouldn't want to discourage you. Is there anything else you want to ask, my daughter?"

"No, Father," I said. It was nice of him to be interested, but by then I wanted to get out of there. My conscience is uneasy because I lied to him, and I know he wouldn't like me kissing a Jew.

After I left him, I went to the church to pray. I lit a candle for David before the statue of St. Joseph, because he is the patron saint of artists. St. Luke would have been better, because he was a painter, but there's no altar for St. Luke in Corpus Christi. Then I went to the statue of the Blessed Mother.

It's a fine statue, but I don't much like the expression on her face. I hope it's not blasphemy to say that. The statue is white marble, or maybe it's glazed china; it's very polished looking, but the face always makes me think of the word *perturbed*. It's easy to imagine that statue disapproving of me.

I began by praying that David would get his commission. After that, I was tongue-tied, because what I want most is for David to come back and kiss me some more, but I didn't know whether the Blessed Mother would understand about that. I'm not sure how she feels about me being in love with a Jew. If David and I are going to be together, one of us will likely have to convert. I can see that David might not want to because of the Christians who persecuted and tortured the Jews. But if I convert, I won't have Jesus and the Blessed Mother any longer. I can't expect the Blessed Mother to be in favor of that.

I prayed that something would happen to David so that he might see the light and want to be a Catholic. But I didn't have much faith as I prayed. The day was overcast and the church was dark and my head hurt. At last I just bowed my head and asked God for mercy and forgiveness. Then I got off my knees and left the church. The sky was white and it had begun to drizzle. I didn't have my red umbrella, which would have raised my spirits. I walked home in the rain and longed for David.

Wednesday, September the twentieth, 1911

We're almost ready for Rosh Hashanah. I'd thought we'd cleaned everything that could be cleaned, but today Malka remembered the chandeliers. We washed the prisms in hot water and vinegar to make them sparkle. Tomorrow we'll begin preparing for Friday night's dinner. There have to be sweet things for Rosh Hashanah, so that the New Year will be sweet.

David will be home on Friday!

Something nice happened this afternoon. While I was

pressing the table linens, Mr Solomon came downstairs. He saw that Malka was dozing with the Prodigal Cat in her lap, and he pointed to the ceiling. I took the hint, unplugged the iron, and followed him up the stairs.

Once we were out of Malka's earshot, I asked him if he wanted anything. He said he hoped I would grant him my forgiveness. It seems that Rosh Hashanah has a lot to do with forgiveness. Before the New Year, the Jews try to atone for any injuries they've done.

I was confused. I said very fast: "I'm sorry I read your poem and sent it to Nora Himmelrich."

"No, no, no," said Mr Solomon, showing the palms of his hands. "I'm not asking you to apologize to me. You said you were sorry. No, I'm asking *your* forgiveness. I shouted at you and made you cry."

It touched my heart when he said that. Most men don't give two pins when they make a girl cry. "It was my fault," I said awkwardly. "Anyway, I forgive you."

"You're a generous girl, Janet," said Mr Solomon, and his sweet-for-a-man smile lit up his face. "Thank you. Now that we've forgiven each other, I'll tell you a secret. Two secrets."

In a flash, I thought of David. I thought maybe he'd written Solly and sent a message for me. "Oh, what is it?"

Mr Solomon lowered his voice in a teasing way. "I've never been so happy in my life."

"Are you?" I said. I was glad he was happy, but

disappointed because his secret had nothing to do with David.

"Yes, because Miss Kleman has agreed to be my wife, and Father is willing to send me to yeshiva. If you hadn't sent that sonnet to Miss Himmelrich, those things might never have come to pass. Or they might not have come to pass so soon."

I think this might be true. I guess Mr Solomon would have asked Miss Kleman to marry him eventually, but he might have needed a little push. Sooner or later, he would have told his father that he wanted to study Talmud, but it might have been later. Mr Solomon isn't a go-ahead like David. "What's the other secret?"

His smile broadened to a grin. "The part of the sonnet you wrote was better than the part I wrote."

I was so surprised that I said, "*Was* it?" and he gave a little nod and turned away, because he'd said everything he had to say.

I looked after him, smiling. I do like Mr Solomon, even though he isn't David. I don't always like Mrs Rosenbach, but she raised good sons. David and Mr Solomon are the two nicest young men I've ever met. Likely they take after their father.

With a peaceful heart, I went back downstairs and finished ironing. Then I took an armful of Mimi's freshly ironed petticoats and made my way up to her room.

I was lucky to find her in. Mimi's almost as much of

a gadabout as David, but she was sitting on her bed, playing a game of bridge with herself – she told me she's a
demon at bridge, though she's too young to play with the
bridge ladies. I put her clothes in the proper drawers and
banged the last one shut. "Rosh Hashanah," I announced,
"is a time of forgiveness."

Mimi scowled. I noticed she was wearing her glasses.
She often "forgets" them when she goes out, but she wears
them at home. "I don't see what that has to do with you,"
she said coolly.

"Well, you haven't forgiven me," I retorted, "which is
mean, because I never meant anything bad by you. I just
wanted you to be able to read properly, so you wouldn't
be a dunce. Anyway, your glasses are becoming. If you
were a proper Jewess, you'd forgive me, because it's Rosh
Hashanah."

Mimi's face was a study. Her mouth looked fierce, but
the eyes behind her glasses were thoughtful. The silence
between us lengthened.

"It's Rosh Hashanah," I repeated, "and I've *missed*
you. And starting on Friday, God's going to be making up
His mind whether to write your name in the Book of Life.
How do you think He's going to feel when He finds out
you haven't forgiven a poor servant girl?"

Mimi's mouth quivered. "I don't believe He'll mind,"
she retorted, "because you're not a Jew. Rosh Hashanah is
a time of forgiveness for *Jews*. You're not Jewish."

"You are," I reminded her.

She frowned again. "You think of yourself as a member of this family," she said slowly, "as if you're almost Jewish. But you're not. You'll never be one of us."

She couldn't have known how those words would hurt my feelings, but they did. I guess it showed in my face, because suddenly she cried, "Oh, poor Janet!" She leaped off the bed, scattering the cards, and hugged me.

I was startled, because I'm not used to people hugging me. There was David, and before that, the awful man on the train, and before that, Mark, when Cressy kneed me in the eye. Mimi must have felt my surprise, because after a few seconds, she stepped back.

"Do you forgive me?" I persisted.

"Yes," said Mimi. "I've missed you, too. It was *abdominable* what you did to me, but it's Rosh Hashanah, so I'll let you off." She flashed me one of her starry-eyed smiles. "It's been awful dull with David back in New York and that Miss Krumm coming every day. Did you ever see anything as hideous as that suit she wears? I want to show you something."

She went to her dresser and opened her jewel box. The child is twelve years old, and she really does have a jewel box. It's ridiculous, but she has a set of real pearls and a necklace of green glass beads that came from Venice. Now she took out a gold filigree chain with a magnifying glass at one end. The glass was enameled with sparkling stones and mother-of-pearl. Mimi looped the chain around her neck and lifted the glass by its stem. "Watch."

She flicked a hidden spring and the magnifying glass sprang apart, making two glasses with a bridge in between. She let the bridge rest lightly on her nose, like a butterfly. "It's a lorgnette," she explained. "I made Papa buy it for me, so that when I go to parties I don't look like a dowd. It's nice, isn't it, the way it springs apart? I've been practicing with it." She tilted it coquettishly.

I applauded.

"I bet I'll be the only girl at school with a lorgnette," Mimi said. "Papa says I should save it for parties, but it's too good to save. I have a new dress for Rosh Hashanah, white with white lace. Do you want to see it?"

Of course I'd seen it, because I'd ironed it. It took a good half hour to iron, because it's so delicate; I had to iron it under a cloth. But I didn't mention that, because I didn't want to take the bloom off our forgiveness. Mimi explained why her dress was better than the one Maisie Phillips wore to the last school exhibition. It seems that where frills are involved, Maisie doesn't know when to *stop*.

After we exhausted that subject, Mimi brought up another. "You got in trouble," she said as if she relished my disgrace. "With Oskar. I heard Mama telling Papa about it."

So Mrs Rosenbach told her husband. "What did he say?"

"He said *oy*," Mimi said succinctly. "But it's all right. He wasn't as mad as Mama was, and Anna likes you because you let her take a nap."

I was glad of this, though I still think of Anna as a dull sort of person. Perhaps she wouldn't be so dull if she had more sleep. I sympathize with her because I can't sleep either. I lie awake at night and think of David and imagine all sorts of things. But I don't get to sleep until nearly dawn, and then I can't get up. I feel so groggy and woolly-headed.

But tomorrow is Thursday, and on Friday, David comes!

Thursday, September the twenty-first, 1911

David's back, and a day early. I was trying to make aspic from Malka's pitiful little tomatoes when I heard the front door open. I heard his footsteps and his voice. There's no voice like David's.

I was wild to see him, but I couldn't show it, because Malka was right at my elbow. Presently Mrs Rosenbach came down and told us there would be five for dinner. I hastened upstairs to lay the fifth place, hoping to catch a glimpse of David, but he'd gone to his room to change. Once the supper dishes were done, I prayed that Malka would nod off with the cat on her lap, but she stayed in the kitchen, planning and replanning the menus for Shabbos. After about a century, she went to bed.

I dashed upstairs to find David. He wasn't in the library or the parlor, but I'd listened all evening, and I hadn't heard him leave the house. I was afraid it might seem indelicate to go to his room, but I couldn't help myself. First I redid my hair. Then I took an armful of clean sheets and pillowcases from the linen closet, in case Mr Rosenbach or Mr Solomon saw me. Malka or Mrs Rosenbach wouldn't be fooled; they'd know David's sheets were clean, but men never know about sheets.

I knocked very softly.

"Come in!"

He was lying down with his clothes on – he hadn't taken off his boots, and the bedspread was sullied. Even though I'm deeply, ardently in love, I felt a flash of pure vexation. The carelessness of men, and the dirt! If Malka sees those boot scuffs, she'll make me get the summer spread out of the cedar chest, and that means more ironing. But the flash didn't last long: David got to his feet and tucked in his shirttail. The way he moves – the easy muscles in his shoulders, the way his face went from sleepy to alert – I felt myself tense and melt at the same time. "What is it?" he asked absently.

I set the bed linens on the dresser. "I had to know. Did you get the commission?"

His face darkened and his eyes kindled with a noble

indignation. "I didn't," he said shortly. Then he burst out: "The wretched woman chose LeClerq! LeClerq, can you imagine? Of course you don't know LeClerq, but he's an *idiot*! He can't draw, his perspective's faulty; he couldn't foreshorten if his life depended on it. All he does is slather on a lot of greasy impasto with a palette knife – it's sickening; the man's a fake, but he's French, which makes him a god to Madame Marechaux, and he's not a Jew—"

"Oh, David!"

"The way he carries on about religion, you'd think he was Beato Angelico. Oily little highlights everywhere; it's enough to make you sick. Madame Marechaux said his sketches were imbued with the deepest piety. Can you imagine saying that – *imbued with the deepest piety*? Did you ever hear anything so pretentious in your life?" He snorted. "If she hadn't chosen LeClerq, I could have borne it. Boscov's not bad, not bad at all, and Findley's up-and-coming. I could have stood it if she'd chosen Findley. But LeClerq!"

"Oh, David," I mourned, but he scarcely seemed to hear me. He was wide-awake now, his eyes burning and his hands sawing the air.

"The *time* I've spent with that woman, confiding in her, flattering her; I'd have painted her portrait if she'd asked me... Do you know what she wants me to do? She wants a miniature of her lapdog! *Zizi!*" he shouted. I guessed that was the name of the dog, but it sounded like swearing. "She wants a little picture of Zizi! That's my consolation: I've been asked to paint the dog! She says that I'm bound to be at a disadvantage with Joan of Arc because I'm not a Roman Catholic. What does she know about it? When I'm painting, my religion is painting! I could paint Mahomet flying into the sky on a peacock, or a jackass, or whatever the hell it was. I could feel it, I swear I'd feel it, I'd be *imbued with the deepest piety—*"

"Oh, David," I said, "it's awful! It's anti-Semitism, that's what it is!"

He looked startled. It was as if he'd only just remembered that I was in the room. "I'm sorry. I shouldn't have said *hell* in front of a girl."

"That's all right," I said. "I guess I'd swear, too."

He went to the window and opened it wide. Then he swung back to face me. "Do you know what else she said? She asked if *you'd* be willing to come to New York so LeClerq can draw your head! I'm supposed to share my model with that charlatan!"

"You don't think I'd do it, do you?" I demanded. His indignation was contagious, and I'd caught it.

David seemed to reconsider. "Well," he said judiciously, "it'd be an opportunity for you. New York's swell, and Madame Marechaux would find you a respectable place to stay. I wouldn't blame you if you wanted to go."

"I wouldn't think of such a thing," I said hotly. (Though if anyone but Madame Marechaux were to offer me a trip to New York, I'd jump at it.) "After sitting for you, to sit for a man like LeClerq? I'd scorn it!"

I spoke those words very loftily. It was thrilling, wanting to fight for David. I was sorry he hadn't gotten the commission, but being angry on his behalf made me feel close to him. I believe I have a fiery disposition. If I were a man, I'd probably fight duels for the girl I loved.

David's face broke out in a grin. "You're a peach," he said. I know *peach* is slang, but a peach is such a lovely thing to be compared to: sweet and fragrant and velvety. "You really are, Janet. I've been thinking about you." Then he spoiled it by sighing. "I've been thinking about what happened the other night. I think I should beg your pardon."

"I don't want you to beg my pardon," I said. What I wanted was for him to kiss me again, but I daren't say so.

David shook his head. "I took advantage of you. It wasn't the act of a gentleman. I've always despised men who do that kind of thing – take advantage of a girl because she's a servant—"

"No!" I protested. "It wasn't like that. I told you then; I didn't mind. I liked it ever so much."

His face softened. "I liked it, too," he admitted, "but it was wrong. I hope you'll forgive me—"

I cut him off. "I don't think it was so wrong. I believe I'd have felt it if it were wrong. But I didn't. It felt pure and sweet and—"

"But you're not Jewish," argued David, and I frowned at him. It was the second time in two days I've been told I'm not Jewish. I don't think people should take such pains to tell me what religion I am. "Besides, you're years younger than I am—"

I challenged him. "How old are you?"

"Nearly twenty-one."

"Well, I'm eighteen," I said firmly, but all the sudden it struck me that I'm not. I've grown so used to being eighteen that I forget. It's worrying to remember, because I'm not sure it's legal to marry at fourteen. Of course, I'll be fifteen in just two months, which is ever so much older. I believe lots of girls get married at fifteen. I added, "And my birthday's in November."

"But you're a servant, living under my father's roof," David persisted. "That's the worst of it. If you don't like my attentions – no, hear me out! – you can't run away; you've nowhere to go. And if anyone found out, you'd be the one who'd suffer."

"I'd suffer for you," I said, and meant it. "I'd do anything for you. I'll even forgive you, if you want me to, but I don't see the point in forgiving someone when – when it was *glorious* - and I'm not one bit sorry it happened—" It sounded so brazen that I felt my cheeks get red. I turned my back on him and busied myself gathering up the linen.

I think it did me good to have something to do with my hands, because suddenly I knew what I wanted to say.

"Listen," I said, "about the commission. It doesn't matter."

He looked tormented, which wrung my heart. "What do you mean, it doesn't matter? I've spent weeks—"

"It doesn't matter," I repeated. "You're going to be a great artist. You don't need Madame Marechaux any more than you need her stupid lapdog. Someday you're going to be famous, and when you are, it won't matter that you never made a picture of Joan of Arc."

"But I wanted to tell Papa—"

"Then *tell* him. You don't need a big commission to tell your father the truth. He loves you. Tell him you want to be an artist. He didn't mind – well, he minded a little, but he got over it – when Mr Solomon wanted to study Talmud. Why should he refuse you? He'll *help* you."

"If only he would!" David said passionately. "I'd go to Paris – that's the place to study painting; there's no point trying to make a start in Baltimore. But Papa wants me to work in the store—"

"Mr Solomon didn't want to work in the store, either. He told your father so, and he told him about Ruth." I wondered if David would take the hint. If he's going to tell his father about wanting to be an artist, he might as well explain about us at the same time.

David raked his fingers through his hair. "It's different for me. Solly's always been the good son; I'm the wastrel. When Papa wanted to send me to college, I said, no, I wanted to see the world, so he let me go abroad. The idea was, after I finished traveling, I'd settle down and work in the store. But I keep putting it off. Papa says I waste everything – time and talent and money. He's always saying how intelligent I am, how I could do anything I put my mind to, but—"

"You *can* do anything," I said firmly. "But you'll never put your mind to working in a department store, because God meant you to be a great painter. Tell your father that, and show him your sketches. Once he sees them, he'll understand everything."

He looked at me, his head on one side. It was a look – I scarcely dare write the words! – of warm admiration and affection, and my heartbeat quickened. He crossed the room and stood before me. I think he might have reached for my hands, except that I was clutching the bed linens to my breast.

He cupped his hands over my elbows. It wasn't an embrace, exactly, but he was close to me, and his hands were warm. I could scarcely breathe. I stood absolutely still. At the same time, I was ready to jump out of my skin. Elbows don't get much affection; I guess that's why it felt so powerful.

I held my breath and willed him to kiss me.

"Janet," he said, "you're a brick. You're magnificent – and darling – and I'll think over what you've said. I can't speak to Papa yet – not right on the eve of the holiday – but I'll think it over. Thank you."

I tilted my head back, raising my face just a little. The warmth of his hands against my elbows was like a fire: two fires. I felt a shiver go up my spine. Our eyes met – we were very close – but the room was brightly lit. I wanted the dim kitchen to give me courage, and so did he. After a moment, he stepped back and stuck his hands in his pockets.

I murmured, "I'd better go," and scuttled away like a mouse – only a thousand times larger, of course.

Now it's past midnight, and once again, I'm waiting in the library. My hair is up, this book is before me, and David hasn't come. I don't think he will. Perhaps it's wrong to kiss a girl the night before Rosh Hashanah. I wouldn't kiss a man on Good Friday. Maybe David's upstairs, trying to think holy thoughts, but thinking about me, just as I'm thinking of him.

Friday, September the twenty-second, 1911

I am so mortified! I think I would rather *die* than look Mrs Rosenbach in the face again. That stern and scornful expression – but I think she was *amused*, too, which makes everything a thousand times worse. It was such an awful, awful moment, and I keep reliving it.

I wish I could stop. I want to think about how David defended me, but my mortification is stronger than my love. How can that be? Love ought to be the stronger.

I was taking up the mail when I heard voices in the library: first Mr Rosenbach's and then David's. I thought perhaps David was telling his father that he wanted to be an artist. I wondered if he might be telling him about *me*. I knew it would be wrong to listen, but the temptation was too great. I drew closer to the library door.

David was shouting. "What do I care if your business friends saw us? I didn't do anything wrong! Why shouldn't I take the girl to the opera? She's never been to the theater, and she loved it. She loved the whole tatty production. Why shouldn't she—"

"Because a young man of good family doesn't take a servant girl to the opera!" bellowed Mr Rosenbach. Then he lowered his voice. I missed the next few words. I heard: "... your mother—"

"Great Jakes, you didn't tell her!"

"I did not," responded Mr Rosenbach. He had his voice under control now. "For the girl's sake, not yours. Why should Janet take the blame for your folly? It's you I hold responsible."

"Art is supposed to be for the people," raged David. "All the people, even the servants. This is America, isn't it? Haven't you always said that? Wasn't I brought up hearing about democracy and equality—"

"Democracy does not mean," interjected Mr Rosenbach, his voice rising, "that society doesn't have laws and won't punish those who break them. These laws are important to your mother, which you know very well; you wouldn't have kept your outing a secret if you didn't. You ought to be thanking God it was one of my friends who saw you, instead of one of the bridge ladies."

There was an interval of silence. I imagined David on the other side of the door, clutching his curls with his hands. When he spoke again, I had to strain to catch the words. "All right, I suppose it was rash. But I'm sick of all these *shibboleths* – rules and rites and taboos. It's a free country; but how is a man supposed to be free *in* it?"

Mr Rosenbach's reply was inaudible. David went on, gaining momentum: "The girl let me do some sketches of her head. I needed a model. Afterward, I wanted to give her a treat. She loved the opera. She *loved* it. She's never been to a theater in her life, but she's hungry for art and music and books. Doesn't it ever strike you as a waste? The girl's got brains and grit and imagination, and we've got her downstairs cleaning the oven!"

"Somebody has to clean the oven!" exploded Mr Rosenbach. I realized David was right: he *does* aggravate his father. "Do you want Malka to get down on her knees and clean it, at her age? Janet's young and strong and she gets a fair wage. About which she does not complain, because young as she is, she has more sense than you—"

"All the same, she's better than that," argued David. "She gets Sunday morning off for church, and one paltry afternoon. Has anyone even thought to tell her where the Pratt Library is? She could have a library card; she loves books—"

"I know she loves books," Mr Rosenbach broke in. "I lend her *my* books; she's welcome to read anything in the house."

"What if she wants to read a book by someone who isn't dead?" demanded David. "The world is changing, Papa."

"Since when has the world not been changing?" retorted Mr Rosenbach. I never heard him sound so testy before. "Am I to assume you are now a Socialist? Because we have a *zaftig* hired girl cleaning the oven, you are unhappy with the rules of society? Last year, when the sales clerks wanted an increase in their wages, you refused to go over the books with me. You said it was tedious, and off you went with your tennis racket! Now you're tearing your hair out because we hire someone to keep Malka out of the oven! Are you offering to clean it yourself? And what, may I ask you, is wrong with a library of classic literature? *Du lieber Gott*, but you try my patience! First you flirt with the Gratz girl, and I have to go to New York and patch things up, and now you are full of half-hatched ideas about culture and the lower classes—"

"Janet," said a voice behind me, "you are eavesdropping."

It was Mrs Rosenbach. I spun round to face her. I'd

been so intent; I hadn't heard the rustle of her petticoats.

My hands flew to my face. I know I was red as a brick, and I couldn't defend myself. I fled. I felt so *common*, so much like an ordinary, vulgar servant girl. And that's just what Mrs Rosenbach thinks of me. How can I blame her? There I was, listening at doors. That's what servants do.

No wonder she despises me. Now it will be worse, and she'll never accept me as a wife for her son.

David defended me. That's what I have to remember. He said I have brains and grit and imagination. He thinks I'm made for finer things than cleaning ovens; that I ought to have a library card, and go to the opera.

But he also said the opera was tatty, and that makes me feel ashamed, because I didn't know it was tatty. I thought it was sublime.

I wish I weren't so low-down and ignorant. I wish I were sophisticated and had poise like Mrs Rosenbach, or even Mimi. I wish I had fine clothes and a slender waist and never lost my dignity. I wish I had some dignity to lose.

David likes me the way I am, I know. He says I'm a peach. But when he spoke to his father, he didn't call me Janet; he never once used my name. He called me "the girl" as if I were any old hired girl, and not *his* girl.

It's quiet now. Everyone is at Temple. Even Malka went, though she doesn't often go to services; she says they're for the men. But she went today. The services for Rosh Hashanah are very long, and it's a family tradition to take a walk around Druid Lake afterward. So I'm alone in the house, and I can write at the kitchen table.

My stomach is growling. I can smell roast chicken and brisket and potato *kugel* (no raisins!). I can smell the vinegar dressing for the cucumber salad and the honey from the cakes. That's one thing the books have wrong about love. I haven't lost my appetite. I'm hungry all the time. Last night Malka fussed at me because I ate all the almond cookies in the green tin. We don't need them; we have honey cakes and pomegranates for dessert, and dough balls called *tayglach*.

The table's set and the kitchen's tidy. When I hear the front door, I'll heat up the soup we made Friday morning, put the rolls in the oven to warm, carve the chicken and the brisket, and slice the apples.

It seems so strange to be sitting here, almost idle. I worked for a while learning my catechism, but it made me want to go to sleep. I wish I could sleep, but I have to baste the chicken from time to time, and I ought to *think;* these past two days have been so busy I haven't had time.

Last night I dreamed about Ma again. I don't remember much – only that she was displeased with me and wouldn't look me in the face. Oh, Ma, I can't help it! I can't help being in love! I never knew that love was so irresistible, so desperate. It's just like that song from *La Traviata* – rapture, rapture and torment. The torment's worse than I expected, but I don't want it to stop.

I think about David all day long. There's nothing more absorbing than thinking about him. I count and recount the proofs that he cares for me. From the beginning he said he liked me. He says I'm a magnificent creature and a peach and the limit. He gave me a sketchbook. He took me to the opera, and bought me a red umbrella, and kissed me. He said I'm darling, and that's a real love word. (I wish he'd said *my darling;* that would be better.)

I run my mind over these things, and I am dizzy with joy, but then I'm afraid. I'm afraid because Ma warned me against men – though she never knew David. I tremble, because I've given away my heart. I've given it to a Jew, which is all right on the one hand, because I no longer believe that Jews are so different from other people, or that they're not as good. But on the other hand, the Rosenbachs won't want David to marry a *shiksa.* If David marries me, our children won't be Jewish, because a Jew is the child of a Jewish *woman.*

I don't know how much David will care about that. He isn't religious like Solly. But Mr Rosenbach will mind. He'll want all his grandchildren to be Jews. That makes me feel terrible, because I love Mr Rosenbach. He's never been anything but good and kind to me.

So then I wonder if I could convert to Judaism. If I converted, would my children be Jewish, or would I have to be born a Jew in order to pass it on? I can't find out about this because there's no one I can ask without exciting suspicion. And I don't want to convert, because I'm a Catholic. Even though I've never taken the Blessed Sacrament, in my very bones I'm a Catholic. I don't want to be an apostate. I pray about it, but even when I'm at my prayers, my mind wanders off to David and I can't pray properly. Father Horst says that God loves to grant mercy and forgiveness, but it seems to me that God must be getting awfully tired of me and my problems.

I don't know what to do. I don't know what will happen. I love David and I believe he loves me. I know I could be a good wife to him, though I don't know if our marriage would be legal because of my only being fourteen. David needs someone to believe in him, and I do, with all my heart. If his father disinherited him, I'd work for him. I'd go on being a hired girl so he could paint. We'd be poor, but I'm not afraid of poverty, not if I had David.

In books, lovers have happy endings. Mr Rochester had to go blind, but Jane came to find him, and they were married. And Walter Gay came back from shipwreck to marry

Florence. In *The Woman in White*, Walter Hartright had to rescue Laura Fairlie from an insane asylum, but then they got married. The only person who didn't get married was Rebecca in *Ivanhoe*. Ivanhoe couldn't marry her, because she was a Jew. But that was long ago, and Daniel Deronda—

There's the front door. The others are back.

Sunday, September the twenty-fourth, 1911

I am writing from the eighth floor of the Marlborough apartment building. I've never been so high up in my life. It's dark as I write, and the windows are open; I can look out and see the streetlamps below. The view makes my stomach feel queer. I know I won't fall out the window, but I'm afraid I might be tempted to jump.

I feel like a princess in a tower. I don't mean the aristocratic part of being a princess, because I'm still a hired girl. What I mean is that I'm high above the earth, and I'm here against my will. The Marlborough apartments are luxurious; even the servants' rooms have electric lights. But I don't want to be here. I want to be back at the Rosenbachs', close to David.

When I came back from Mass this morning, Malka said Mrs Rosenbach wanted to see me in the parlor. I went upstairs in a state of clammy trepidation. I haven't spoken to her since Thursday, unless you count things like "Shall I clear, ma'am?"

Mrs Friedhoff was in the parlor with Mrs Rosenbach, and Mr Rosenbach was there, too, reading his newspaper. He lowered his paper to smile at me. Then he went back to reading.

Mrs Rosenbach addressed me courteously. She said she had a favor to ask. It seems that Mrs Friedhoff's mother-in-law and aunt-by-marriage are coming to stay tomorrow and won't leave until Friday morning. That puts Anna in a fix, because she still has no housemaid. Mrs Rosenbach asked if I would be willing to stay at the Friedhoffs' apartment for a week, partly to tidy up, but mostly to look after Oskar.

"You're so good with him," Mrs Friedhoff said pleadingly, "and he's fond of you. My mother-in-law is very strict, and so is her sister. Oskar is so boisterous, and they think he's spoiled." (I think Oskar is spoiled, too, but I didn't say so.) "If you could take him to the park, and let him run –" she fumbled with her purse strap, as if she was ready to bribe me then and there – "or out for an ice cream, or to the zoo; he loves the zoo. I'm willing to pay you for the extra trouble, of course."

Mrs Rosenbach concurred. She said if I would move to Anna's apartment for the week, they would give me eight dollars instead of six. Mrs Friedhoff said apprehensively that the older two Mrs Friedhoffs are awful fussy – she said *particular*, but I know she meant fussy – and her last housemaid left the house a mess.

I didn't want to go, but I couldn't say so. "What about Malka?" I said, thinking, *What about David?*

"Malka has agreed," said Mrs Rosenbach. "The house is beautifully clean, and she'll be able to manage without you for a few days."

My heart sank. I could see that though they seemed to be asking me, I had no choice. Everything had been decided.

"You'll have your own room," Anna assured me, "and I have an Irish girl to do the cooking, so you won't be bothered with that." She brightened. "And you'll see your little cat."

I did want to see Moonstone. And I pitied Mrs Friedhoff, but I couldn't help worrying whether Mrs Rosenbach found out that David took me to the opera. I wondered if I was being banished. But there was no way I could ask, so I said, "I'll get my things."

Mrs Rosenbach said, "Moritz," urgently, as if she were reminding Mr Rosenbach of something.

Mr Rosenbach folded his newspaper and looked up at me. He indicated the sofa across from his chair. "Sit, sit." He stroked his mustache, darted a mischievous glance at the ceiling, and said unexpectedly: "There is a passage in Boccaccio..."

I didn't know what Boccaccio was, and I guess it

showed in my face. Mr Rosenbach answered my unspoken question. "An Italian writer of the fourteenth century. I have him only in German, so I can't lend you the book." He spread his hands palms up, as if in apology. "It's a very interesting passage. Boccaccio narrates the story of a Jew in the court of Saladin the Great."

I nodded as if I knew about Saladin the Great, but I didn't, and again Mr Rosenbach helped me out. "Saladin was a great sultan and a follower of the prophet Mahomet. He wanted to borrow a large sum of money from the Jew, so he questioned him before a court full of powerful Christians and Mahometans. He asked him which was the true faith: the Jewish faith, the Christian faith, or the faith of Mahomet.

"The Jew was confounded. I'm sure you can imagine why. If he said that the Jewish faith was the true one, the Christians and the Mahometans would join forces against him, and he would lose his worldly goods, if not his life. If he praised the Christian or the Mahometan faith, he denied his God."

I was curious now. "So what did he do?"

"He told them a story." Mr Rosenbach leaned forward. The newspaper slid off his lap and fell to the floor, but he paid it no heed. "There was once a rich man with three virtuous sons. The father owned a beautiful and precious ring. All of his sons longed to possess it; each son came to the father in secret and begged for this inheritance.

The father, loving all his sons alike, could not bear to disappoint any of them. He paid a skillful jeweler to make two perfect replicas of the ring. When at last he died, each son came into his inheritance. Each son believed that *he* was his father's heir and favorite; each son believed that *he* had the true ring and that his brothers' rings were merely imitations."

I began, "But which one—?"

"Ah, you come to the heart of the story! You want to know: *which was the true ring!* But a mystery lies at the heart of the story; not a solution. The Jew explained to his audience that the truth as to which was the real ring was lost in the mists of time. So it is with religion: every Christian, every Jew, and every Mahometan believes he inherits the true faith. That is the major point of the story. The minor point is that the Jew, because of his wisdom, survived."

He beamed at me. Mrs Rosenbach stirred restlessly. "Moritz," she said, "would it not be better to say plainly what you mean? I'm sure the girl has no idea—"

"By no means," answered Mr Rosenbach. "I'm sure Janet understands me perfectly, or will when she has had a little time to think."

I cast down my eyes and tried to look modest and knowing, but the truth was, I was at sea. I sneaked a glance at Mrs Friedhoff; she was as baffled as I was. Mr Rosenbach's gaze was kindly, but he was also wearing

what I think of as a teacher look: that encouraging, expectant look teachers give you when they're counting on you
for the right answer.

Then – quick as the flash of a firefly – I knew. Heaven
only knows how I managed it, but I read Mr Rosenbach's
thoughts; I swear I did. I spoke with absolute certainty.
"The story's a metaphor. All three sons believed they had
the right ring, but there was no proof they were right. But
all three rings were precious and beautiful, because they
came from the father, and the father loved all three sons."
I saw that Mrs Rosenbach looked dissatisfied, so I simpli-
fied it for her. "Mr Rosenbach's asking me to respect his
faith. He's telling me, in a kind way, not to try to turn
Oskar into a Catholic. And I won't. I mean, I know better
now."

"*Brava*, Miss Lovelace," said Mr Rosenbach, and I
remembered David telling me that *Brava* is what you say
when a female singer is good. I felt my cheeks grow warm
with pleasure.

Mrs Rosenbach regarded me with surprise and – dare
I write it? – respect. She hadn't thought I could guess the
riddle, but I had. It made me feel a lot better, and not so
ashamed.

I stood up and excused myself. Then I went upstairs
and packed my things. Being a slain buffalo hasn't done my
suitcase much good.

It wasn't far to the Marlborough apartments – only

about a fifteen-minute walk. The building has a mechanical elevator, with a little page boy to run it. I've never gone up in an elevator before. I'd thought it would be thrilling, but it was jerky and slow.

When Mrs Friedhoff unlocked the apartment door, Oskar ran to her and hugged her. Then he threw his arms around me. Moonstone sidled into the room, her eyes bright with curiosity. I wanted to pick her up, but I didn't – Thomashefsky has taught me discretion. She's not a kitten anymore; she's tall and rangy, and her eyes are gold instead of blue.

Oskar wanted me to play with him, but I said no, I couldn't, not when the apartment was such a mess. His blocks and toys were scattered throughout the apartment. Mrs Friedhoff told him to gather every single block and make the tallest tower he could. That was a good idea, because it kept him out from underfoot, though of course I had to stop work every so often to admire the tower.

I rolled up my sleeves and set to work. It made me mad, how messy those rooms were. If I could afford to live in a beautiful place like that, with everything new and handsome and fashionable, I'd keep things nice. Some of the furniture had been dusted in a no-account sort of way, but the lamp shades and picture frames were furry with dust, and the baseboards were filthy. The bookcases had books all jumbled and slanty-wise. In the bathroom, there was a greasy brown ring around the tub, and the space between the toilet and the wall was nasty. That bathroom wasn't fit for a good Jewish home, especially during the High Holy Days. I have pure contempt for the last girl who worked here.

I dusted and wiped and straightened and scoured. Mrs Friedhoff watched me with something like awe. Supper was good, but the Irish girl, Kitty, is careless about *kashrut*. (She isn't really a girl; she's thirty.) She mixes the dish towels and lets the dishes sit in the wrong dish drainer. Kitty whispered to me that what Mrs Friedhoff doesn't know won't hurt her. But her kitchen was spotless, which surprised me, because I'd always heard the Irish were dirty.

After supper, Mrs Friedhoff put Oskar and Irma to bed. To my surprise, she put on an apron and cleaned with me, side by side. By the time we finished, it was half past ten, and the rooms looked lovely. Mrs Friedhoff thanked me and said I should go to bed, because she was sure I must be tired.

I'm not that tired. I feel jittery, because I don't know when I'll see David again. I wonder if I still have Tuesday afternoon off. I could write to David and ask him to meet me in the park, except Malka takes in the mail, and she might recognize my handwriting, and if she did, she'd open my letter.

And what if David never came?

Today was an awful day. The Friedhoffs came – Anna's in-laws, I mean: two pursy-lipped, patronizing old biddies. Of course they patronized me, because I'm the hired girl, but they were horrid to Anna as well. They said that Irma looked sickly and told Anna she'd never raise her. Mrs Friedhoff (the old biddy, not Anna) asked if the beds had been aired properly, and Miss Plaut (the sister) complained about cat hairs on the sofa. Both of them believe that cats are unhygienic, and that Moonstone will suck Irma's breath.

It rained all day. I couldn't take Oskar out, and keeping him amused took every ounce of patience I possess. I felt sorry for him, because the Friedhoff ladies insist on kissing him, and Oskar doesn't like kissing. But he had promised his mother to be good, so he screwed up his elderly little face in a paroxysm of disgust (I think that is a very well-turned phrase) and let them peck at him.

I've had hardly a moment to think, but when I do think, I think of David, who is an easy walk away from this apartment and might as well be in China. More and more, I think I was sent here because Mr and Mrs Rosenbach want to tear us asunder. I keep thinking about a framed engraving Miss Chandler had on the wall of her little parlor. It was a colored picture of Mariana in the Moated Grange, who is a lovesick lady in Shakespeare.

Lord Tennyson wrote a poem about Mariana, who is always wailing, "I am aweary, aweary! I would that I were dead!" I never had much sympathy for Mariana in the Moated Grange because the Moated Grange looks very luxurious in the engraving, and I thought it compared favorably to Steeple Farm. But now that I am marooned in the Marlborough apartment building, I see how little surroundings matter when one is lovesick. My mind is fixed on one object, drawing all its flavors, both bitter and sweet, from the thought of my beloved.

I can't write any more. I'm exhausted from being Mariana in the Moated Grange. Also, Oskar wore me out setting up bowling pins so that he could knock them down.

Tuesday, September the twenty-sixth, 1911

It's still raining. I don't know how Anna stands those Friedhoff women. She meant to take them shopping today, but they looked at the raindrops on the windowpanes and said they would stay in and knit. Oskar tried to please them by reciting the Hebrew alphabet, but they didn't praise him. They said he was spoiled by indulgence. He wasn't even doing anything wrong – just standing there in a clean sailor suit, with his hands behind his back.

I took Oskar back to his room and told him I would play anything, so long as it wasn't bowling. He wanted to hunt buffalo, but I knew that would be noisy, so I persuaded him to hunt alligators in the swamp. We put pillows on the floor to make boats, and I cautioned him to hunt in silence, so as not to scare away the alligators. He did pretty well, except when the water moccasins (which were stockings) bit him. Then he shrieked and writhed in a fearful death agony. I tried to shush him, because I could hear the in-laws whining and clucking in the parlor.

I thought I would lose my afternoon off, but at lunchtime, Anna told me to run along. She knows I'm having religious instruction, and she said I shouldn't miss it.

Father Horst greeted me kindly. He said I seemed a little tired, which I guess I am. He heard me recite the catechism and talked to me about the Church. I tried to listen, but my thoughts kept turning to David.

All at once I interrupted. I asked Father Horst if I could just go into the church and pray by myself. It was rude of me but I couldn't help myself.

He gazed at me searchingly. Then he said of course. He said if I had anything I wanted to tell him, he would be glad to listen; if I needed help, spiritual or temporal, he would try to assist me. But he said my instinct to take my troubles to Our Lord was a sound one.

I muttered *thank you*, because I was ashamed of having been so rude. Inside the church, the light was dim, because of the rain. I went to one of the side chapels and propped my umbrella against the wall, and knelt before the Blessed Sacrament. The stained-glass windows were almost colorless, it was so dark, but the lamp burned in the sacristy. It was cold.

I squeezed my eyes shut and clasped my hands together and implored God to tell me what to do. Tears began to seep from underneath my eyelids; they felt hot against my cheeks. It was a relief to shed them, and I realized how miserable I was. I haven't spoken to David for nearly a week. And I've begun to wonder if he cares for me at all, and my heart is starving.

I wondered if I was miserable because of my sin. I thought I ought to open up my heart to the possibility that I deserved to be unhappy, because I'm such a sinner. The more I thought about it, the worse it was. I lied to a priest so I could meet David; I lied to Malka and the Rosenbachs; I listened at doors; I spent money on clothes that I might have given to the poor; and speaking of the poor, I don't seem to *care* about the poor, and the poor are very important. Of course I wish there weren't any poor people, but I almost never think about the ones there are, and if I cared about them the way Our Lord told me to, I would worry about them once in a while. But I daydream about clothes more than I think about the poor. And I love a man who's a Jew, so I'm thinking of becoming a Jew, and I let him kiss me, even though we're not married, and I'm considering being an apostate even though Ma raised me to be a member of the True Faith.

So I listed all these things before God, and I opened my mind to His chastisement. I waited. But He said nothing. My knees ached from kneeling, and I was sobbing and shivering. I was filled with shame and remorse. But He said nothing.

I thought about what Father Horst had said. I begged for mercy and forgiveness. I opened my heart to receive God's mercy. My soul felt sore and parched, and I imagined His mercy like dew, falling on my soul.

But I felt nothing. He wasn't *there*. The light was burning in the sacristy, the light of His Real Presence, but I couldn't feel Him. I began to recite Hail Marys without counting them, one after another, gabbling, because I was beginning to panic and I needed to feel the presence of God.

And then I stopped. I stopped praying and I stopped crying. I stopped gazing at the lamp as if the moving flame in the red glass could save my soul. I closed my eyes and searched for God.

And He wasn't there.

And then something happened, and I don't know how to describe it, because when I put it in words it sounds like nonsense. The closest thing that I can say is that the absence of God, at that moment, was the presence of God. I felt it and it was true. It wasn't what I'd prayed for. It didn't answer my questions. It wasn't forgiveness or chastisement or permission. It was just – *He* was just – *God* was just – real to me. There was darkness, and the dark-ness was God. There was absence, and the absence was God. There was my longing, and my longing was God. God wasn't there, and at the same time I was more certain of Him than I've ever been in my life.

I stayed there, kneeling. I don't know how long. I don't think it was long at all. Then I got up very quickly, as if someone had commanded me. I stopped trying to repent, not because I wasn't bad, but because it was beside the point. I started walking as if I'd made up my mind about something, which I hadn't.

I came home through the rain. It was hours later that I realized I'd left David's umbrella in the chapel. I feel terrible about it, because I love it dearly. But I'm pretty sure Father Horst will find it and keep it for me.

Now that that *thing* – which wasn't a thing, but I don't know what else to call it – has happened, I see that I was never meant to be a Jew. I don't mean that in an anti-Semitic kind of way, because the Jews are good and noble-hearted and love God. They go on loving Him even though they're persecuted for it. But I have to be a Catholic. Even though what happened this afternoon doesn't make sense when I put it in words, it was real and it was important and it happened in the chapel of the Blessed Sacrament.

I think there must be hope. Somehow it will be possible; *somehow* I will find a way for David and me to be together. But even as I write this, my eyes are closing. I'm worn out and can't find my way.

Thursday, September the twenty-eighth, 1911

I am sunk in misery. The old ladies have decided to stay *through Yom Kippur*, which doesn't begin until sundown on Sunday. I had thought they'd be gone tomorrow, and I'd see David by Friday night.

I believe Mrs Friedhoff (Anna) is as wretched as I am. She's the one who has to talk to them, and their conversation is nothing but whining. Kitty calls the old ladies *the Pills*. They are like pills, too – the bitter kind that get stuck at the back of your throat and don't dissolve.

Today Mrs Rosenbach came to visit. I was handing around cucumber sandwiches when Miss Plaut started saying how sickly Irma was, and Mrs Rosenbach said that they must all remember how many advances had been made in medicine since they (the older Mrs Friedhoff and Miss Plaut) were young, *which, of course, was many years ago.* Ha! It took the old ladies a few seconds to realize they'd been insulted; she'd slipped under their guard that easily. I don't always like Mrs Rosenbach, but I admire her. She can be as smooth as cream and as sharp as a paper cut.

Yesterday it stopped raining, so I took Oskar to the zoo. It ought to have been inspiring to see animals that I've only read about in the geography book, but I kept looking around the zoo for David. I wanted to see him so badly that I was convinced he'd be there. Oskar spent a long time mooning over the boa constrictor. I lost interest in it before he did. I preferred the sea lions and the bears.

When I came back to the house, Kitty took me aside and told me she had awful news. That was when she told me that the Pills were staying. I wanted to scream with frustration. Now it will be Tuesday before I see David again, because he'll be in services all day Monday.

The only good thing, Kitty said, was that the Pills were going to the Rosenbachs for Shabbos dinner, and Anna had said we would have the evening off. (The Pills are particularly nasty to Kitty because she's Irish.)

I went to Anna and told her I was worried about Malka working too hard without her Shabbos goy to lend a hand. Anna told me it would be all right, because Malka's planning to cook everything before sundown and keep the food in the warming ovens. I offered to go over in the evening and help with the dishes. Anna said I was a kind and thoughtful girl, but that I needn't worry about all that. She said Kitty and I deserved a rest, and that she would order a little chicken for just us two.

I'm *not* a kind and thoughtful girl. I'm a hypocrite. I don't care about poor Malka and the dishes. I'm just desperate to be under the same roof as David Rosenbach.

I wish Anna weren't so considerate.

Saturday, September the thirtieth, 1911

David's going to Paris.

Nobody told me, of course. No one would think to tell me. After Yom Kippur, he's going to New York. He'll stay with Mrs Rosenbach's parents for a few days, and then take the steamer to Paris.

I wouldn't have found out, except I overheard the Friedhoff ladies talking. Anna had taken Oskar for a walk in the park. Once she left, the old ladies started to gossip. They didn't bother to lower their voices, because Kitty and I aren't real people and don't count.

They started with Malka's Shabbos dinner, which they thought was indigestible, and then they went on to say that Malka must be failing. They said that it was a pity, Mr Solomon marrying a Polish girl, and that Mirele was unpleasantly pert and would never find a husband. They said Mr Rosenbach was too *Amerikanisch*, and they wondered what dress allowance he gave Mrs Rosenbach, because they were sure she would bankrupt him. And then they said it was a shame to let that youngest son go off to Paris to play with paints, because he'd only get into debt and lose whatever morals he had.

When I heard about David going away, I felt as if someone had punched me in the stomach. I listened but they changed the subject, and after a while I went to my room and shut the door. I paced and paced. I wanted to cry, but I felt like there was something lodged at the back of my throat.

At first I tried, most piteously, to be happy. David must have told his father the truth, and surely it's good news that Mr Rosenbach has agreed to let him study art. And David wouldn't leave without saying good-bye – he *couldn't*. It would be too cruel. So I would see him again, at least one time more – but the thought of saying good-bye to him made me feel sick.

I was so taken up with pacing that I didn't hear the storm come in, but all at once there was a clap of thunder that made me jump. I looked at the window, and the rain was coming down so thick it dimmed the light. I was glad, because the rain would bring Anna and Oskar back from their walk, and I could ask Anna if it was true.

When Anna returned, Oskar was soaking wet, so we put him in a hot bath and then to bed. Once he was asleep, I asked Anna if Mr David was going to Paris, and she said yes. She said he's leaving early next week.

Early next week. She didn't say which day and I was afraid to ask. *Early next week.* That could be as soon as Tuesday – of course he couldn't go on Monday, because of Yom Kippur. I wonder if he's being sent away from me. Oh, David, if you leave me without saying good-bye, my heart will break!

I can't bear it. I haven't even told him that I love him. I know it's the man who's supposed to say that to the girl, but I don't care. I love David Rosenbach, and I want to tell him so. When I think of never seeing him again – never kissing him – never knowing what he feels for me—

Why am I *sitting* here? Why am I writing at a time like this? Why am I letting Mr Rosenbach – why am I letting *anyone* stand between me and my own true love?

It's raining, raining hard, but I don't care.

Monday, October the second, 1911

It's Yom Kippur and I'm alone. Kitty's visiting her folks, and everybody else is at Temple. Anna even took Oskar and Irma, though I'm told the services are very long. I can write as much as I want to, and no one will disturb me.

I'm crying as I write this. Sometimes I go without crying for a little while, and then I remember and gasp as if I felt a stitch in my side. Then I start up again. There have been times when writing made me feel better, but I don't think this is going to be one of those times.

And yet my diary – dear Miss Chandler's book – is close to finished; almost all the pages are covered with ink. It seems right to end this chapter: to finish the book.

My heart is broken.

How strange to look back at that last page, when I resolved to go to David! I must have been desperate, out of my mind. I remember how my heart hammered; how

I slammed shut this book and went to the glass to put up my hair. When I looked in the mirror, there was something in my face I hadn't seen before – a look of resolution, maybe. I'm not sure what it was, but it made me look oddly prettier.

I didn't think about that, not very much. All I could think about was that I must see David. Without making a sound I let myself out of the apartment. The page wasn't in the elevator, and I was afraid to work the machinery, so I ran down seven flights of stairs. When I left the building, it was raining: a steady spatter, no more.

I ran through the rain. It reminded me of the night I came to Baltimore, when I fled from the train station and nobody noticed me: a lone girl running through the streets. The city is large and nobody cares, and I was grateful for that indifference.

Then, as I was crossing the park, the skies split open. When you live on a farm, you pay attention to the weather; it's all anybody talks about, but I've only seen rain like that three or four times in my life. Luke once emptied a whole bucket of cold water over my head, but this was worse, much worse. In less than a minute, I was drenched to the skin. My petticoats, my camisole, my shoes; they were as wet as if I'd been swimming in them. Raindrops struck my head like acorns, dragging down my hair so that the hairpins hurt. The gutters were running and the water was over the tops of my boots.

But there was no turning back. When I reached the Rosenbachs' house, it was hard to see through the rain, but I spied the light in David's window. Late as it was, he was still awake.

I stumbled up the porch stairs and found the front door locked. Mrs Rosenbach believes in locking doors, but Malka doesn't. I thanked God when the kitchen door yielded, and I stepped onto the linoleum, dripping. My boots were so waterlogged I could hardly get them off, and my stockings clung to my feet. I stood by the meat sink and lifted my skirts and tried to wring the water out of them. The Thomashefsky cat watched me from Malka's armchair. He's not used to me coming home in the middle of the night.

I longed to change into dry clothes, but I had none. I unpinned my sodden hair and let it fall over my shoulders. David likes my hair – at least, he likes it when it's dry. In the back of my mind was a story from Miss Lang's book about a girl who was a princess, arriving at a castle during a thunderstorm. In the frontispiece, she was disheveled and driven looking, but she was a real princess, all the same.

I tiptoed up the stairs. When I reached the landing, David's light still shone. He was awake. With shaking fingers, I rapped on the door. I heard the creak of bedsprings and the sound of footsteps. Then the door opened and David stood before me.

I see him now as I write this. He was – is – so

beautiful to me. I can't believe I ever thought his nose was too large. It is noble in its proportions, and his curls are tumbled and glossy, and his forearms are slender and strong. His cuffs were unbuttoned and his shirttail was hanging out. Even his bare feet were beautiful; they were long toed and supple, like the hind feet of a hare.

"Janet!"

My name on his lips. My mouth opened without a sound and tears began to fall from my lashes. When he saw me crying, he opened his arms, and I fell into them.

If I could have died, right then. He was warm and dry and strong and kind; he looked upon me with tenderness; I swear he did, in spite of what happened after. I lifted my face so that he could kiss me. There were so many things at once: fear and relief and the love that flared up between us like the striking of a match.

"Janet, what is it? You're soaking wet."

"It's raining," I explained. That's when he put me away from him. He didn't give me the kiss I wanted, and he put me away from him quite firmly. I cried harder, from self-pity. He looked around the room – he'd been reading. I saw the book on the bed: *The Painter of Modern Life.*

He closed the bedroom door. Then he went to the bed and snatched up the counterpane. He draped it around me like a cloak. "Janet, you shouldn't be here," he whispered. "What happened? Did Anna send you away? What on earth is this about?"

I felt a chill. "Are you going away to Paris?"

His face lit up. "Yes, on Thursday. Did Anna tell you? I'll go to New York and spend Shabbos with my mother's folks. Then next week I'll take the steamer. It was just as you said, Janet! I talked to Papa, and at first he was angry with me – well, it was a big disappointment for him, me not wanting to take on the store, and I felt like thirty cents. But when I told him how much I want to be an artist, he listened to me, really listened. At first he said I could study here, but when I explained why Paris would be better, he said he'd stake me. He said he'd give me a year – I asked for five, and at last we agreed on three – to find out if I had a future as a painter. If I don't, I'll come back and work at the store; I gave him my word. But if my career seems promising, he won't stand in my way. He was –" he stopped to find the right word – "he was splendid. I have you to thank, Janet. I've wanted to talk to him for ages, but I didn't dare. But you believed in me."

"Of course I believe in you!" I spoke too loudly and both of us froze, listening to see if anyone had heard. I lowered my voice. "But, David—"

"What is it?"

"You kissed me," I said. I looked down, because I hated having to remind him. "You kissed me, and now you're going away."

I saw the dawning consternation in his face. "Great

Jakes. I – Janet, I'm sorry, so sorry. I tried to explain—"

"I can't marry you," I interrupted, and I was surprised, because the words came out strong. All night I was like that: weak and strong by turns. "You're a Jew, and you can't marry a *shiksa*, and I'm a Catholic, and I have to go on being a Catholic. If you married me, it would just about kill your father, and our children wouldn't be Jewish—"

David dug his hands into his hair. He looked utterly lost. "Janet, what are you telling me?"

"I'm telling you that I love you." Those words buoyed me up; I'd wanted to say them for so long. "I love you with all my heart and I want to be with you." All at once it was clear what I'd come to say. My words were like bubbles, rising and swelling and catching the sunlight. "Say the word and I'll come with you. To Paris. I'll meet you there. I can't be your wife, but I'll be your friend. We'll be happy together, and I'll give myself to you."

I rushed the last words. I can't believe, now, that I said them. But at the time, I had a vision of David and me in Paris, with David in an artist's smock and me being a *grisette*, like Trilby, though I'm not quite sure what a grisette *is*. I knew what I was offering was mortal sin, but it didn't feel wicked. Just as Violetta didn't seem depraved in the opera, it didn't feel depraved to promise myself to David. My love for him was so pure that I wanted to give him everything, even if I lost myself.

But I couldn't look at him when I spoke those last words. It wasn't shyness so much as a kind of awe. I was offering him everything.

There was a silence so long and hollow that I was afraid to raise my eyes. When I did, I saw he was shocked. "Janet, I couldn't use you like that. It would be wrong."

"I don't believe it would be wrong if we loved each other," I said, but my voice faltered, because the look on his face was so much the wrong look.

"You're a darling girl," David said, but he didn't say it lovingly; he sounded worried. "You're a darling girl, but I don't – I'm not ready to be married, and when I do marry, I want to marry a girl of my own faith. For now, I want to be free. I want to paint, I want to see the world."

"But so do I!" I exclaimed. "We could see the world together!" And as I spoke those words, I realized how much I wanted just that: David and freedom; love and the world. Being together in love, in Paris. *Paris.* "Oh, David, don't you see? You'd still *be* free, because we wouldn't be married. And nobody would blame you. They'd blame me, because they always blame the girl. I'd be the one taking the risk, and I don't care about being depraved, because it doesn't *feel* depraved, not when we're in love—"

"But you ought to mind! You're giving me permission to ruin you, don't you understand? What about your reputation?"

"I don't have any reputation," I said recklessly. "I'm

a hired girl. I don't have any family to cast me off, and I don't know anyone in Paris. And there's no one in the world I love better than you."

"It's impossible."

"It isn't. Not if we love each other," I persisted. "You wouldn't have to pay for me. I've saved money. I have more than sixty dollars. That might be enough if I go steerage—" My voice was rising. In the heat of the moment, we had forgotten to whisper, and that was our undoing. Because at that moment, the door opened and in came Malka.

She let out a shriek when she saw us together. She struck her hands together and wailed. I never saw anyone look so much like a witch, with her white hair thin and uncovered, and her wild eyes, and her bare bony feet with that terrible bunion. She ran to me and slapped my face. Then she flew at David, cuffing him around the shoulders and screaming in Yiddish. David caught hold of her wrists and tried to hold her still, but there was nothing he could do to keep her from waking the household.

Mimi was the first to arrive. I noticed that she'd put her glasses on; she stood there in her nightgown, her curls tousled, her face alight with interest. Then Mr Solomon in his nightshirt, followed by Mr Rosenbach, knotting his bathrobe around his waist. Mrs Rosenbach was the last to arrive; she had covered her nightgown with her kimono. When she saw me, her face went white. I thought she was going to faint.

Mr Rosenbach turned his back to me and waved his hands to shoo them all away. "Freyda, Mirele, leave the room! I will deal with this – it's not for you to see."

Malka was still shrieking. Mr Solomon put his arms around her and drew her away from his brother. "In the name of heaven, David, what were you thinking? Under our father's roof, just before Yom *Kippur*!"

David stammered, "I haven't done anything!"

"You bring shame upon this house," hissed Malka. "You destroy this family, you break your mother's heart, you spit in the face of God—"

"Malka," snapped Mrs Rosenbach, "be quiet! This is none of your business. Mimi, go to your room!" She whirled to face her husband. "I'm staying right here. If my son is carrying on a –" she glared at me so fiercely that I shrank back – "a vulgar intrigue with a servant girl, it's my business as much as yours."

"I'm not!" protested David. "There's no intrigue! I haven't done anything wrong, and neither has she!" He nodded to me. "Tell them!"

"Tell them what?" I was bewildered. I hadn't counted on everyone coming in at once, and I was slow to figure out what they were thinking. Their eyes kept looking past David and me to the rumpled bed. Then I caught on: they thought David and I *were in the middle of doing* what I'd said I might do *in Paris*. Oh, but I was mortified; I wanted to die of shame! I covered my face with my hands and turned my back on them all.

David yanked the counterpane away from my shoulders. "Look at her! She's fully dressed. I wrapped her in the bedspread because she was soaking wet. That's *all*."

The silence that followed was oddly blank – I think because Malka had stopped screaming. Mrs Rosenbach commanded, "Miriam, leave the room."

Mimi darted a look from her mother to her father. They frowned at her like two gargoyles, so she had to obey. After she went out, Mr Solomon seemed to recall that he was in his nightshirt. He turned beet red. "I'm sorry, David," he said formally. "I guess you'd like some privacy." With that, he left the room.

Mrs Rosenbach said, "David, what is she doing here?"

I shivered. I thought of what she would say if David told her I'd come to offer myself to him, body and soul.

David said lamely, "She wanted to say good-bye. Anna told her I was going to Paris."

Mr Rosenbach spluttered, "Pah! Through the pouring rain she comes to say good-bye? Tell the truth! Has she come to your room before? Did you ask her to come here tonight?"

"He takes a *shiksa* to his bed!" wailed Malka. "A poor ignorant girl, he seduces her and lies about it! Now he's ruined her! She was a decent girl when she came—"

"I haven't seduced anyone!" David cast a frustrated look in my direction. "The *last* thing I expected was for her to come here tonight! I don't mean it's her fault," he added hastily. "She's quite innocent. All she wanted was to say good-bye."

Mrs Rosenbach's voice was harsh. "An innocent girl doesn't go to a man's bedroom."

I wanted to defend myself, but my mouth was too dry. A sound from the hall distracted Mrs Rosenbach. "Mirele! I told you to go to your room!"

Mimi peered around her mother. "I guess I won't. Seems to me I'm the only one who knows what's going on here." She pushed her glasses higher on the bridge of her nose and jerked her head at David. "*He's* been kissing her, so she fell in love with him—"

Mr Rosenbach confronted his son. "Is that true? Have you been making advances to this girl?"

David reddened. "No! I mean, yes! I mean, they weren't advances, but I did kiss her. It was an accident. Afterward I told her it didn't mean anything—"

"That's not true!" Indignation restored my power of speech. "You said you were sorry, but you never said it didn't mean anything!"

David winced. "I don't mean it meant *nothing*. What I meant was—" All at once his face softened with a dreadful pity. I braced myself. "You're a peach of a girl, Janet. I like you an awful lot. But I wasn't serious when I kissed you. I kissed you because I like kissing girls. I *always* want to kiss a pretty girl. Some more than others..." He appealed to his father. "The cat scratched her. I was putting peroxide on her face, and I lost my head. It was stupid, I admit it, but I kissed her. Then for some reason she thought—"

He stopped. I felt my cheeks get red, because I knew he was going to say, *She thought I was in love with her*. I waited for this final humiliation, but he didn't say the words. He looked anguished, but I didn't pity him. His agony was nothing compared to mine. "Janet," he said wretchedly, "I've done you an injury. I beg your pardon."

I didn't want him begging my pardon. I stared down at the carpet. There was a loose thread that the electric carpet sweeper had left behind. I bent down and picked it up.

Mrs Rosenbach cleared her throat. "You will leave this house tomorrow, Janet."

"Mama—" protested David.

"Freyda—" Mr Rosenbach began.

"It's impossible that she should stay here," said Mrs Rosenbach. "I won't have this kind of thing going on under my roof." She silenced her son's objection with a sharp movement of her hand. "Enough. I'm sorry, Janet. You've been a good worker, and I don't doubt David is to blame, but you're old enough to know you shouldn't kiss young men, or go to their rooms at night."

The words stung. I did know. Ma always told me that it was the girl's job to guard her virtue. And Father Horst always said the same: he called it purity, but he meant the same thing.

"She's not as old as you think," Mimi interjected. "She's fourteen."

It was as if the whole room caught its breath. Mr Rosenbach's mouth dropped open, and Mrs Rosenbach's hand flew to her throat. Malka's eyes widened to such an extent her face looked like a skull. I gasped. "You read my diary!"

"Yes," said Mimi, "and it's a good thing I did, because you need someone to take up for you." She raised her hands as if to ward off a blow, which was smart of her, because at that moment she was very close to being slapped. "I started reading it because you told Papa I needed glasses. I wanted to get back at you. But then I got interested, because you wrote about me. You said some mean things about me, but you said nice things, too, so I got *more* interested, and I read the whole thing. It's the only book I ever liked, because it's about real people, and I think," she added, backing up hastily, "that you ought to be an authoress." She glowered at David. "Then *you* kissed her and gave her presents and things—"

"You gave her presents?" echoed Mrs Rosenbach, and Mr Rosenbach yelled, "David!"

David looked baffled, as if he honestly couldn't remember. Then he threw out his hands. "She wanted to draw! I gave her a stick of charcoal and a pad of paper! For the love of Mike, it wasn't a diamond necklace!"

"Yes, but you flirted." With a flourish, Mimi removed

her glasses and pointed one earpiece at him. I was wild with mortification and grief, but I knew she'd perfected the flick of her wrist before a mirror. "You always flirt, and you don't see that girls have *feelings*. You treated Janet to the opera, and you bought her a red umbrella –" there was a restless movement from Mrs Rosenbach – "and you said *things* to her. Of course she liked it. And of course she fell for it, because Janet – only her real name's Joan – is very romantic. It all comes of reading books. She used to have three books, and she read them over and over, but her father wouldn't let her have any education and he burned them. So then poor Janet had to run away from home, and she never meant to lie about her age, but the lie slipped out, because she was afraid of sleeping in the streets. And David believed she was eighteen and started flirting and kissing her, and Janet thought she was as good as engaged. Maybe she ought to have known better – *I'd* have known better – but she's only fourteen, and if you ask me, if anybody ought to be sent away, it's David."

Mr Rosenbach lunged forward. I thought he was going to seize David by the shoulders and shake him. "Fourteen!" he bellowed. "First the Gratz girl, and now this poor little *shiksa* of fourteen! Why should I send you to Paris when I can't trust you for one minute in Baltimore! Give me one good reason! You don't *think*, you make a mess wherever you go, you are a disgrace to me in New York, in Baltimore, why should I send you—"

"No, no," I cried, "he has to go to Paris!" I flew to Mr Rosenbach and caught the sleeve of his dressing gown. "He has to! He's an artist, maybe a genius! And you promised, Mr Rosenbach. It wasn't all his fault what happened, and it was good and kind of him to take me to the opera: I loved the opera, just because I'm a hired girl doesn't mean I shouldn't see the opera! And it was my idea to come here tonight, he didn't know I was coming, and he *did* say that if he ever married, he wanted to marry a Jewess." I ransacked my mind for some other plea and found it: the Jewish prayer that I first heard from Mr Solomon's lips. "Let no one be punished on my behalf!"

My voice rang in the silence. That moment, when I was taking up for David, was one of the moments when I was strong. When I look back on that terrible night, there is much that shames me, but it was true love that impelled me to plead for David, and I'm not ashamed of that. It's a strange and piteous thing, because when I dreamed of true love, I dreamed of David loving *me*. But I was the one who loved truly. Knowing that, I can hold up my head, even though I made a fool of myself and my heart is broken.

Mr Rosenbach opened his hands and said, "Freyda." That was all he said: just his wife's name, but he said it urgently, and I knew he was pleading for me.

David came forward and took my hands. As soon as he touched me, I went still. It was always like that between us. The lightest touch of his hand bewitched me, exciting every nerve in my body. "Janet, I'm sorry. I never once suspected you were so young."

"I suspected." It was Mrs Rosenbach who spoke, breaking the spell. "I sensed she was a child; I felt her wanting a mother." She raked her hands through her hair. I recognized the gesture; David had inherited it from her. "I ought to have—" Her voice hardened. "No. Why should I blame myself? The girl looks eighteen and she lied. I wanted to believe her. I wanted a hired girl, not another child to raise."

She reached behind her neck and gathered up her loose hair, twisting it pointlessly into a knot. The knot wasn't becoming to her; it made her look respectable, but haggard and ruthless. "David must go to Paris. It's all arranged, and he needs something to do. As for you, Janet – what's your real name?"

"Joan," I said. She went on waiting until I finished it. "Skraggs."

Mimi breathed, "No wonder!"

Mrs Rosenbach ignored her. "Miss Skraggs, if my son has been kissing you, and buying you gifts, you had every reason to believe you were engaged. But there will be no engagement. If there is any tie between you and my son, it must be broken off. Do you understand me, David? Your father will not send you to Paris if you consider yourself attached to this girl."

David released my hands. He mumbled, "I understand."

His cheeks were red with embarrassment.

"Miss Skraggs, you will catch cold, standing in that wet dress. Go upstairs and take a hot bath. You may sleep here tonight. After Yom Kippur, we'll decide what must be done with you. If you're fourteen years old, you ought to be with your family. I can't believe your father isn't worried about you."

Your family. There was a second when I couldn't think what she meant. Then Father's face swam before my eyes, and I remembered the life I left: the isolation of the farm, the drudgery, the empty future. "No! I won't go back!"

Mimi added her voice to mine. "She can't go back to the farm, Mama! It's too cruel! Her father's mean to her. He burned her books and he *shoots cats!*"

"We'll discuss this after Yom Kippur." Mr Rosenbach came and patted my shoulder. "Don't worry, Janet. We'll find a new place for you, a good home; never fear."

That's when I began to cry in earnest. I realized I'd lost everything: David, my heart, my pride, even my job. I covered my face with my hands and wept. Malka took me by the elbow and led me from the room.

I did what Malka told me. When she ran me a hot bath, I got into it. She brought me one of her nightgowns and a pair of heavy wool socks. The socks were too big and the nightgown pulled across my chest. But the things were warm and dry, so I put them on and crawled into bed. I dragged the bedclothes over my wet head.

I wanted to sleep, to be out of pain.

But I lay awake a long time, sobbing. I hated myself and I hated David. I thought of how I'd offered myself to him, and I writhed with shame. How shocked Miss Chandler would be! And Father Horst; he would think me the most wretched and depraved of sinners. And Ma, oh, poor Ma! She tried to warn me about men, but I didn't pay attention. She saved all that Belinda money, so I could escape from the farm, but here I was, about to be sent back, all because of my own folly.

Then I cried because I wanted Ma. I cried until my nose was stuffed up and I couldn't breathe. But I guess I cried myself out, because unconsciousness claimed me, and at last I slept.

It was still dark when I woke up. The skin on my face felt raw, and my mouth was dry. I was chilled with that queasy kind of cold that you only get very early in the morning, when you're not supposed to be awake. I thought it might be four, maybe four thirty.

I tried to think what to do. I remembered Mrs Rosenbach saying that they would send me back to the farm, and Mr Rosenbach saying patronizingly that they'd find me a good home. A good home, as if I were a stray cat! I wasn't fit to marry his son, but he'd find me a good place – somewhere else where I could keel the pots and dust the books I'd rather read. All at once my temper rose.

I slid out of bed and put on my dress. It was

nasty-sodden, but I'd made up my mind what to do. I'd go to Corpus Christi and wait until Father Horst came to unlock the church for early Mass. Father Horst would help me escape from the Rosenbachs. With luck, I'd get away before they had a chance to send me back to the farm.

My mind was clear and hard, ticking off what I had to do. I'd go down to the kitchen to get my boots and stockings. Then I'd slip out the back door. The biggest snag in my plan was that all my things were back at the Marlborough apartment building. I'd left Anna's easily enough, but it wouldn't be so easy to get back in. I checked the pockets of my dress, but I didn't have a cent.

While my mind was working out the best way to escape, my heart was telling me another story. The story was that somehow David would know I meant to leave and stop me. It was crazy, I know that now, but I wanted it so much that I believed it. It seemed impossible that David didn't love me.

I descended the stairs slowly, pausing to listen every few steps. I imagined David coming out of his room. His eyes would look wild and tormented, because he wouldn't have slept, either. He would grasp my hand and lead me back to his room, where we could shut the door and talk in whispers. He would confess to me that he *did* love me, but that he'd been afraid to say so before his family, because I was a *shiksa*. I would forgive him; he would kiss me, and we would run away to Paris.

I imagined it all. I strained to hear his footfalls on the stairs. I'd reached the first floor. My hand was on the newel post – and I heard the stairs creak.

"Janet!"

My heart leaped. And then it plummeted, because the voice wasn't David's. It was Malka's voice, and Malka was hobbling down the stairs; Malka in her flannel wrapper and embroidered shawl. "I knew it," she croaked. "I said to myself: She'll run away. She's a headstrong girl; she'll run out during the night, and we'll never set eyes on her again. I kept watch," she added gruffly and proudly. "I've been sitting up in bed, listening. There's a crick in my neck that won't go away in a hurry."

I started to say, "I'm leaving—" but she clamped her bony arm around me.

"No, you're not. You're going to come downstairs and let me make you a cup of coffee. And then you're going to listen to me, because you're a good girl."

I'd cried all night. I'd thought I had no more tears to shed. But there was something about her calling me a good girl that started me howling again. She dragged me down to the kitchen, and I couldn't shake her off, because she was clinging to me, smelling of camphor and onions and old age. My eyes were blind with tears, and I was afraid of treading on her bunion.

She sat me down at the kitchen table. She lifted Thomashefsky and plunked him down on my lap. Of course he wouldn't stay. She made coffee – I watched dully – and she put in cream and sugar with a lavish hand: too much cream and sugar, which is what I like. I didn't know she'd noticed how I take my coffee. She made me toast, sopping with butter and gritty with cinnamon and sugar: cinnamon toast, the Rosenbachs' cure-all. "Now, you eat that," she commanded.

I didn't think I could. Heroines in books don't eat when their hearts are broken. They pine away. But my stomach gave an agonized rumble, and I realized I was ravenous. I ate, and it was good. I drank two cups of coffee, one after another. Crying always makes me thirsty.

"Now what?" Malka said, after I'd finished a third slice of toast. "Have you given up on running away?"

That nettled me, because I hadn't. "I won't be sent back home, and I can't stay here. Mrs Rosenbach doesn't like me. And David—"

"That good-for-nothing!" spat Malka, and she said a Yiddish word I've never heard before. I don't know what it was, but you could tell from the sound that it was really bad. My anger leaped up. "Don't you dare say that about David!"

Malka leaned across the table and poured herself a cup of coffee. "He's a young fool, that's what he is. And you're another. Even if you weren't a *shiksa*, it wouldn't be right. He won't be ready for marriage for another ten years, not that one. Fifteen, even. What do you want with him?"

"I love him."

Malka rolled her eyes. "Love! You think it lasts, but it doesn't. You forget about him, you hear me? You've got to think of the future."

"I *am* thinking of the future. I tell you, I won't be sent home—"

Malka made an impatient gesture with her hands. "Nobody's going to send you home. There was talk about it, yes, but my little Moritz has another idea." She leaned across the table, her witchlike eyes gleaming. "I talked to him while you were having your bath. He wants to send you to that fancy school he's opening next year. He says if you're only fourteen, you're even smarter than he thought you were. You're smart enough to do well, and they need Gentiles. The school's meant to be half and half, but they're short of Gentiles."

She tapped her spoon against the table, punctuating her speech. "You'll work for Anna another year. You're good with Oskar. Once David's out of the country, you'll come back here every week; you'll be our Shabbos goy. When the school opens, Moritz will see that you receive a scholarship. You'll get your education, just as your mother wanted. You can grow up to be anything you want – not that there's any shame in being a hired girl." She glanced around the kitchen as if reviewing all the things we've cleaned together. "You've done a good job here. You talk back, and you oversleep, and you shouldn't kiss the master's son. But still. You're a fine girl, and you've earned your way."

I stared down at my empty plate. I couldn't think. I'd offered myself to David and he didn't love me; I'd been mortified before the entire family; Mimi had read my diary. I was fourteen again, and in danger of being sent home. Now there was something new: I was to go to school. I ought to have been glad, but I felt numb. I wanted to climb the stairs and go back to bed.

"You'll go to school and get an education," persisted Malka, "and then we'll see. Who knows what you'll become? The world's changing – not for the better, if you ask me – but in these crazy modern times, a girl can be anything. A doctor, even."

"I don't want to be a doctor." I knew I sounded sullen and ungrateful, but I didn't care. "I hate sick people. And I can't take a scholarship from Mr Rosenbach. He *patron-ized* me. I won't accept charity."

"Yes, you will," Malka said threateningly. She got up and came around the table and locked her arms around me. "You take that education," she said against the top of my head. "When life offers you something good, you take it, you hear me? You go to a good school, learn everything you can, and grow up to be a woman. That's what you'll do," she finished, and she held me so close I felt her old heart beating.

So I gave in. I even took a crumb of comfort, because she loves me. It wasn't what I would have chosen.

I wanted David to love me, not Malka. But I guess I'm a beggar and can't be a chooser. Being proud belongs in novels. In real life, you eat the cinnamon toast, even if your heart is burning.

And my heart is burning. It isn't just a figure of speech. When I think of David going away, the pain is like a fist against my breastbone, hot and sore. A mist rises before my eyes as I write this, and teardrops splash onto my inky words. He's going away. He'll see Paris and forget me; I know he will. I've lost him, my only love: the artist who was going to show me Paris; the man who was going to teach me to draw. I weep for the conversations we never had and the kisses I wanted to take from his lips. We never even said good-bye.

But in a year's time, I will go to school. I don't seem to care about it, but it's what Ma would have wanted. It's what I wanted, once. I wanted it more than anything.

In a year's time, I will go to school.

PART SEVEN

Girl Reading

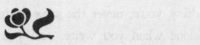

Sunday, September the twenty-ninth, 1912

This morning Mimi bought me a present, a blank book from Rosenbach's Department Store. She plunked it down on the ironing board and said, "Here. Now you can write another diary."

I retorted, "Why? So you can read it behind my back?" which I thought was very cutting. But Mimi only flicked open her lorgnette and answered, "So you can be an authoress."

I've never been able to get Mimi to feel any remorse over reading my diary. Whenever I try, she flashes me one of her starry-eyed, admiring looks (she's practicing that look so she can use it on boys) and says my diary was the best book she's ever read. That's where I lose ground. I'm unmanned by flattery.

I thanked her for the blank book, which is handsome: crimson leather with stiff creamy pages. I didn't promise to write another diary, though. Once someone reads your diary, you're never the same again. You realize you're not alone when you write, and you start to write for the person who will read your words. I *think* that's a bad thing, but I'm not sure, because I do think of being an author someday, and authors have to commune with their readers.

After Mimi left and I finished the ironing, I went to my room and took Anna's old dressing case from under the bed. Anna gave me the dressing case after she found out that Mimi read my diary. It has a lock and key, so I can be private.

It's been almost a year since I opened this diary. So much has changed since I locked it away! There are nine blank pages left at the end: I'm going to fill them up with everything that's happened, lock up the book, and begin the new year. I've become very Jewish, because it seems to me that the real New Year begins in the fall, with house-cleaning and Rosh Hashanah.

And school! I'm starting school tomorrow, and I'm very excited. I'll be studying Algebra and Latin, Ancient History, Art, English Literature, and Creative Expression. Mr Rosenbach took us to see the school building, and it's sumptuous. The house on Auchentoroly Terrace used to be a mansion. There are high windows everywhere, so the rooms are full of light, and at the foot of the grand staircase, there's a statue of the Roman god Mercury. I expect to feel very aristocratic, going up and down those stairs.

It's strange and wonderful to be a student again. On Thursday, Anna and Mrs Rosenbach took Mimi and me to buy clothes – schoolgirl clothes, not maid uniforms. We began at Slesinger & Son's, because the school letter says all pupils must wear comfortable shoes with a flexible sole, so we can exercise in the gymnasium. We are also required to have thick wool sweaters made to a particular pattern, because the fresh-air classrooms will be cold. Mine lacks half a sleeve. Malka's helping me with it. Dear Malka! I am still her Shabbos goy, but a Russian girl comes in twice a week to help her with the heavy work. Malka says the Russian girl is a *klotz*, and she only loves me.

After Mimi and I bought our shoes, we went to Rosenbach's Department Store. I bought a holly-green sailor suit, a waist with Gibson pleats, and half a dozen hair ribbons – I haven't worn hair ribbons for a year and a half. Anna bought me a rose-plaid jumper suit and a primrose silk that will be good for school dances, if anyone asks me. She insisted on paying for them because she says looking after Oskar has been hard on my clothes. That's true, but I've come to *love* Oskar. We have splendid games together. He'll start kindergarten tomorrow, and I expect he'll do well, because he's very clever. Every

Monday we visit the Pratt Library and read the snake books in the children's section. I taught him to sound out the letters, and one day – it was astonishing, how fast it happened – he began to read! I was never so proud of anyone in my life.

I did a wicked thing on Saturday. While the Rosenbachs were at Temple, I went to the store and bought one of those watch lockets I've been hankering after. It's dark-green enamel, with pansies on it. My heart beat fast when I put down the nine dollars, but I told myself I'll be needing a watch, with work and school and Oskar to look after. I *know* I won't look like a scholarship pupil with that locket around my neck.

After I came home, I put on my first-day-of-school clothes and peered at myself in the mirror. A schoolgirl smiled back at me: a wide-awake-looking girl, with a pink hair ribbon and a locket round her neck. She looked happy and prosperous, as if she'd never known passion (only I have) or worked like a drudge at Steeple Farm.

Father has written. Mr Rosenbach made me write and tell him I was safe. At first I was terrified that Father would make me go back to the farm. But when Father wrote back – and it took him three months! – he wrote that Mark is married to Carrie Marsh, and she does the woman's work now. He added that if I wanted to live with a pack of dirty Jews, it was all right with him, only I'd better not think I could come sashaying home when it suited me. Well, I have no notion of sashaying home. When I left Steeple Farm, I left forever. And I don't think a man who never washes his neck has any right to cast aspersions on the Jews.

I didn't want to show Father's letter to Mr Rosenbach, because of the anti-Semitism, but Mr R. asked to see it. I think he was surprised that Father is so horrid. I wasn't surprised. At first the nastiness hurt my feelings, but then I felt relieved. I'm glad Father doesn't love me, because I don't love him. Father Horst says I must find it in my heart to forgive him. I'm going to someday, but I haven't gotten around to it yet.

The good thing about writing Father was that afterward I was free to write Miss Chandler. She was overjoyed to hear from me, but I think she is a little bit prejudiced, because she's worried that the Rosenbachs are educating me so they can convert me to Judaism. I sent her a copy of *Daniel Deronda*. Dear Miss Chandler taught me so much! Maybe she'll let me teach her about the goodness of the Jews.

Mr Solomon married Ruth Kleman last April and moved to New York so he can attend yeshiva. I still think he'd be better off with Nora Himmelrich (except they don't love each other), but he and Ruth seem to be happy so far. David is in Paris, studying at the Académie Colarossi.

Moonstone has become my cat. She wakes me every

morning, purring and tickling my face with her whiskers. I think I would rather have a cat than a sweetheart, after all. They are less trouble, and even the handsomest sweetheart is sadly lacking in fur.

I still think about David. When I flipped through this diary, I came across the passage where I wrote that his kiss changed me from a girl into a woman. That seems like the sort of thing that should turn a girl into a woman, but now that I look back, it seems to me that I was awfully young at the time. I'm almost sixteen now, but I don't feel grown up. All the same, it was passion that I felt for David, not a childish crush. It was thrilling and painful and beautiful. Being in love was one of the most interesting things that ever happened to me.

But it wasn't the only interesting thing. Last Easter I was confirmed, and that was not only interesting, but important. It's an awe-inspiring thing to take the Sacrament. Each time I approach the altar rail, I feel reverent and buoyant, as if my body were recalled to life, as well as my soul. But the sad thing is now that I'm a true Catholic, I sometimes lack religious fervor and am apt to oversleep on Sunday mornings. Kitty and I say the rosary together (she is Catholic, too), and when we hear the church bells, we stop work and pray the Angelus. I'm glad to be religious, because religion is tremendous. Sometimes it doesn't feel tremendous; sometimes it feels like being inside a fence. But God is spacious and mysterious.

I have seen the Ocean! This past summer, after Oskar and Irma had chicken pox, we went to Atlantic City, and I beheld the majesty of the *unplumm'd, salt, estranging sea.* Often I got up early so that I could watch the sunrise. I would walk barefoot at the edge of the water and think about David – not just David, but myself and love and art and death. When I behold the ocean, I *know* that the world isn't just the grind of small tasks and small thoughts. The world is wide and wild and grand. Someday I will sail my little bark into the great ocean of life, braving the winds and the tide. And while the waves may dwarf me, they will not belittle me, because I will be the *master of my fate* and the *captain of my soul.*

Mr Rosenbach is determined that I shall learn philosophy. I read several of the Socratic dialogues and I liked them, but eventually I got tired of Socrates winning all the arguments. So I wrote a dialogue where I taught Socrates some important things about the nature of true love. The dialogue ended with Socrates saying submissively, "Yes, that is so." When Mr Rosenbach read it, he laughed so hard he nearly died. Just now we are reading Shakespeare together. First we read *Macbeth,* which is thrilling, and then we read *As You Like It.* I like it when Rosalind says, "Men have died from time to time, and worms have eaten them, but not for love." That's exactly how I feel about David Rosenbach.

I thought I would love David forever, but now I'm

not so sure. I think of him often, but not as much as I did. He sends me postcards from Paris, but they are identical to the ones he sends Mimi. There isn't a particle of sentiment in them, and I know why. He's afraid of inflaming my propensities. Mimi says her friend Maisie Phillips's brother, Sam, would be sweet on me if I gave him a little encouragement, but I'm not going to do it, because he's a Methodist and not interesting. Also, I'm busy: I'm planning to write an epic poem about the life of a Vestal Virgin. I was hoping to start it tonight but decided to finish this diary instead. I'll begin it tomorrow, in Mimi's new book.

Tomorrow, oh, tomorrow! What will my destiny be? Maybe I'll be a teacher, as Ma encouraged me to be. Or a great novelist, like Charlotte Brontë. Or perhaps I'll be a famous journalist like Nellie Bly and investigate insane asylums and fascinating places like that. One thing is sure: after I've paid Mr Rosenbach for my schooling, I mean to go to Europe. I'll see the bridge where Dante met Beatrice, and the Alhambra, and the slate-gray roofs of Paris. Maybe in Paris I'll pay David to paint my portrait – because by then I'll be ever so stylish and self-possessed, and maybe he'll fall in love with me, and I'll *spurn* him.

Or maybe I won't.

Fortunately, I don't have to decide just now, because my immediate tomorrow dictates only that I start school. School! As Shakespeare would say, *O wonderful,*

wonderful, and most wonderful wonderful! and yet again wonderful, and after that, out of all whooping!

I think about Ma, telling me to get educated, and dear Malka, who told me to grow up and become a woman.

And so I will.

ART ACKNOWLEDGEMENTS

PART ONE:

GIRL WITH A COW

Theodore Robinson (American, 1852–1896)

La Vachère, 1888

Oil on canvas, 86 3/8 x 59 5/8 in

(219.4 x 151.4 cm)

The Baltimore Museum of Art:

Given in memory of Joseph Katz

by his children, BMA 1966.46

Photography by Mitro Hood

PART TWO:

THE SPIRIT OF TRANSPORTATION

Karl Bitter (1867–1915)

The Spirit of Transportation, 1895

Terra-cotta bas-relief

30th Street Station, Philadelphia

Photography by Paul Burkhart, *The Daily Philly*

PART THREE:

THE MAIDSERVANT

William Arthur Breakspeare (1855–1914)

The Maidservant, 1881

Oil on canvas, 15.53 x 11.2 in (39 x 28.5 cm)

Tameside Museums and Galleries Service:

The Astley Cheetham Collection

PART FOUR:
THE WARRIOR GODDESS OF WISDOM
After Michelangelo (1475–1564)
The Erythraean Sibyl, Sistine Chapel, 1508–1512
Engraving
From *The Picturesque World* by Leo de Colange, 1878
Photography by Laura Amy Schlitz

PART FIVE:

JOAN OF ARC

Jules Bastien-Lepage (1848–1884)

Joan of Arc, 1879

Oil on canvas, 100 x 110 in (254 x 279.4 cm)

The Metropolitan Museum of Art:

Gift of Erwin Davis, 1889 (89.21.1)

Image copyright © The Metropolitan Museum of Art.

Image source: Art Resource, NY

PART SIX:

MARIANA IN THE MOATED GRANGE

Sir John Everett Millais (1829–1896)

Mariana, 1851

Oil on mahogany, 23 ½ x 19 ½ in

(59.7 x 49.5 cm)

© Tate, London 2015

PART SEVEN:

GIRL READING

Winslow Homer (1836–1910)

Girl Reading on a Stone Porch, 1872

Oil on panel, 6 x 8 ½ in (15.2 x 21.6 cm)

Image: Sotheby's

AUTHOR'S NOTE

In *The Hired Girl*, I have tried to be historically accurate about language. This has led me to use terms that are considered pejorative today, such as *Hebrew*, *Mahomet*, and *Mahometans*.

I used *Mahomet* and *Mahometan* for two reasons. The word *Muslim*, which is now preferred, was not in use until much later in the twentieth century. And, as a reader of *Jane Eyre*, *Ivanhoe*, and *The Picturesque World*, Joan would have encountered the words *Mahomet* and *Mahometan*. These are the words that were used at that time.

Similarly, many Jewish people today find the term *Hebrew* offensive, but the fact that many Jewish organizations in Baltimore used it (the Hebrew Sheltering and Immigrant Aid Society, the Hebrew Literary Society, the Hebrew Orphan Asylum, etc.) suggests that at the turn of the century, the word *Hebrew* was used with pride.